ACCLAIM FOR *SPLIT*

"I loved this book! Once I started reading, I was hooked! It was a sexy, edgy, and refreshingly unique romance! Definitely a new favorite!"

—AestasBookBlog.com

"Wow! My head is spinning and my heart is rejoicing. Sweet, tender, unexpected, heartbreaking, and so beautifully healing. It's like nothing I've ever read before."

—Mia Sheridan, *New York Times* bestselling author

"Heartwarming, raw, and sexy. JB Salsbury did an amazing job on this one! With pacing so intense, it knocked me off my feet."

—Tijan, *New York Times* bestselling author

"This book had my heart *racing*. Emotional, intense, and highly addictive. I couldn't turn the pages fast enough."

—J. Daniels, *New York Times* bestselling author

"Visceral. Addictive. Out of this world intense. A roller-coaster ride from start to end, *Split* will take your breath away."

—Katy Evans, *New York Times* bestselling author

"5 stars! Highly recommend! I went into *Split* completely blind and at first had no idea what to expect. But then the book swept me away."

—Pepper Winters, *New York Times* bestselling author

"This is a page-turner read so give yourself plenty of time to finish this book in one sitting." —HeroesandHeartbreakers.com

"Salsbury's fast-paced romance contains characters who are capable of taking one's breath away. The book is sexy, dark and its hero Lucas is the epitome of the perfect alpha male. There are also a few surprises in this thrilling tale, so don't complain that you haven't been warned. Plenty of secrets, jaw-dropping moments and raw emotion makes this one unforgettable read." —*RT Book Reviews*

"JB Salsbury crafts a masterful romance with *Split*. It grabbed me by the throat and punched me in the heart."
—Claudia Connor, *New York Times* bestselling author

"An addicting, wild ride of epic proportions that will stay with you long after you've reached the end."
—Harper Sloan, *New York Times* bestselling author

"Riveting and heartbreaking, *Split* is a must-read and one of my favorites of 2016."
—Rebecca Shea, *New York Times* bestselling author

"A powerful punch of deep emotion, sexy characters, and ingenious writing—this is the book you've been waiting for."
—Pam Godwin, *New York Times* bestselling author

"A brilliantly constructed romantic thriller you'll devour in one sitting! The *perfect* amount of sexual tension and sweetness rolled up with my favorite of all: a *dangerously* hot alpha male, makes this one addictive read!"
—Elizabeth Reyes, *USA Today* bestselling author

WRECKED

ALSO BY JB SALSBURY

Split

WRECKED

JB SALSBURY

FOREVER

New York Boston

Forever
Hachette Book Group
1290 Avenue of the Americas, New York, NY 10104
forever-romance.com
twitter.com/foreverromance

First Edition: July 2017

Forever is an imprint of Grand Central Publishing. The Forever name and logo are trademarks of Hachette Book Group, Inc.

The publisher is not responsible for websites (or their content) that are not owned by the publisher.

The Hachette Speakers Bureau provides a wide range of authors for speaking events. To find out more, go to www.hachettespeakersbureau.com or call (866) 376-6591.

Library of Congress Cataloging-in-Publication Data has been applied for.

ISBNs: 978-1-4555-9636-2 (paperback), 978-1-4555-9638-6 (ebook)

Printed in the United States of America

LSC-C

10 9 8 7 6 5 4 3 2 1

To my brother Bo.
Your contagious love of the ocean and unwavering
love for me inspired this story.

ACKNOWLEDGMENTS

I want to start with a heartfelt thank-you to God for giving me the ability to tell stories.

Thank you to my husband and two beautiful daughters for their support during the long writing days, the weekends away, and the nights I'm promoting. It is your love that inspires me.

To my parents, thank you for your constant support. And Dad, thank you for reading every single book I publish. It means so much to me.

A huge thank-you to my big brother Bo for answering all my questions about deep-sea fishing. This book wouldn't be what it is without your wisdom, experience, and guidance. You were also the inspiration behind Celia and Sawyer's undying love for each other, having taught me from a young age what it means to love your sibling unconditionally, support them through life's trials, and always be available. Love you, bro. PS: Skim the dirty parts, m'kay?

I'd like to thank Amanda, her husband, Ryan, and her brother Cody for helping me with the military research. The firsthand knowledge you provided was invaluable.

Thank you to the amazingly talented Claudia Connor for reading for me and for always pushing me to write better. More importantly, thank you for your friendship. Love you, D.

To my editors Megha Parekh and Amy Pierpont, as well as everyone at Forever Romance and Eternal, and my agent MacKenzie Fraser-Bub, thank you for believing in me and my stories.

All my love goes out to the members of JB's Fun Cage, the bloggers, and all the readers who have supported me through the years. I wouldn't be here if it weren't for you.

I want to give a special heartfelt thank-you to all the men, women, and families of the United States Armed Forces who have sacrificed and continue to sacrifice more than we will ever understand. Words would never be enough to show my gratitude for your service and your sacrifice. From the depths of my soul...I thank you.

WRECKED

PROLOGUE

ADEN

Three months ago…

"Hey, Sarge, can I have a word?"

With my ass on a cot and doubled over lacing up my boots, I avoid looking at LaRoy. If I make eye contact he'll only take that as an invitation to air his concerns. The same bullshit concerns he's been airing for the last few weeks. "Not now, Private."

His boot steps close in, signaling he's not going to let this shit go. "Colt."

With a final tug on my shoestrings, I push up to stand and face my brother-in-arms head-on. "As long as we've been fighting side by side, how many times have I let you down?"

The trained Special Forces soldier in him stiffens his spine and snaps back a quick "Not once, sir," but his wary expression betrays his strength, showing the worry of a friend.

"Grant, I said this before and I'll say it again." I strap on my gear while I continue. "You have nothing to worry about. The United States government gave us a job, to train Iraqi forces so that they can defend themselves against ISIL. We've done that, and we have a formidable team to show for it."

"I don't disagree with you, Aden, but…" He turns back toward the sound of our men chanting as they prep for our op—the last op of our deployment before we get to go home back to the States.

The air is electrified with a palpable energy reminding me of the days before playoff games in high school when the locker room felt alive with the excitement of a team about to annihilate the competition.

To keep from being overheard, Grant steps closer. "It's not the men I'm worried about, it's their leader."

I resist the urge to pinch the bridge of my nose. "Al-Bishi is intense, but he's harmless—"

"How do you know that, Aden?" There's anger in his voice and a flash of something wild in his dark eyes.

"Because he's a twenty-six-year-old husband and father of two little girls who live in a city that is controlled by evil. He is invested in our mission."

He scoffs. "Invested. Is that what he told you?"

"No, that's what my gut tells me and my gut hasn't failed us yet."

He steps back with a humorless bark of laughter. "Fine. But I too am invested in our mission, Colt. I'm twenty-eight hours away from a flight home to my wife and baby who I haven't seen in over a year."

"This isn't a meat-eating op, our only job is to provide backup if needed. Al-Bishi and his men are ready to handle this alone, there's no reason why you won't make it home to Kim and Eva."

He shrugs. "I'm keeping my eye on that asshole and if I see so much as a muscle twitch in the wrong way I'm puttin' a fucking bullet in his skull."

Now it's me who steps close. "Grant, I get it. You're feeling the effects of a fifteen-month deployment. The paranoia, trust me, I fucking get that—"

"You don't get shit." He turns to stomp out of the room, but turns back one last time, his eyes blazing with the angst I heard in his voice. "Strap up, Sarge. As much as you can carry. We're gonna need it."

* * *

"*Hadhih laysat munawara.*" This is not a drill. I address both the Iraqi team as well as my own in Arabic. "*We have intel that there are two ISIL leaders currently hiding in this village.*" I turn toward Al-Bishi, who is standing at my left. "*You'll take orders from Al-Bishi. My team has been instructed to provide backup only. Any questions?*"

When the group of eighteen stay silent, I nod for Al-Bishi to command his men.

"*Shukraan laky a sadiq.*" Thank you, friend.

It's never sat well with me that he refers to me as "friend," as it implies we're on equal ground when I'm his commanding officer, but I've let it slide for the sake of peace. Feeling eyes on me, I find LaRoy glaring a hole right through me. *Twenty-four more hours, Grant. Hang in there, brother.*

Al-Bishi runs through the plan to hike the four kilometers to the outskirts of the small village, then to surround the house and when they're all in position to infiltrate.

With adrenaline coursing through our veins, we make quick work of the hike down into the valley, making sure to say alert and low to avoid being spotted. The only noise we're putting off is the steady crunch of our boots to the dirt.

The scent of livestock alerts me that we're close, so I motion for my guys to get down and be on the lookout. Pride fills my chest when I see Al-Bishi give a similar command to his men and they follow his order with ease.

Schmitt pulls up to my side, flashing me an eager smile. I've never met anyone as excited for battle as Camden Schmitt. It's as if he came out of the womb a soldier, and although I dig his enthusiasm, his thirst for combat can make him unpredictable.

"Don't."

He chuckles quietly. "Oh come on, Sarge. One last time before I go back to Britney and I'm stuck in civilian life."

"My job is to get you to your wedding in one piece or Brit will have my balls."

I know I don't need to remind him of our team's role in this op, but I do anyway. "Backup only, Private."

"Party pooper." He drops behind me as we edge along the wall that runs the length of the small village.

We spread out behind the Iraqi soldiers and wait for them to enter through the gate. Al-Bishi gives the command and his men pour in like water to surround the house.

I motion with one arm for my team to follow and as we do, I feel LaRoy has my six. Whatever makes him feel better. I make a note to myself to talk to him about getting some help for his delusions as soon as we hit US soil.

Seamlessly my team of eight works like appendages of one well-oiled military machine. Having fought side by side for the past seven years, we're able to read each other's body language as we file in behind the Iraqi team. My senses are on hyper-drive as I identify the smell of smoke from a dwindling fire, my vision picking up the tidy kitchen and the sounds of—where is everyone?

My feet freeze. Breathing stills.

The only sound is the rapid beating of my pulse in my ears.

This is a surprise ambush on a residential location. Where are the women and kids?

My mind draws the conclusion just as the sound of rapid fire explodes all around us.

I point my weapon but don't see the enemy we're firing at.

The plaster walls burst and shatter.

I drop to the ground. Roll to the kitchen to take cover and that's when I see them.

Terrorist militia dressed in all black flood in through the doors and windows. Bodies of men dressed in US fatigues drop all around me with the spray of pink mist.

We were set up.

Grant.

Fuck!

"It's a setup!" I fire my weapon, clearing the way to crawl out in search of my men. "Get out!"

My ears pound as gunfire erupts from every direction. We're completely surrounded. I grab O'Connor as he's firing with one hand and dragging a bleeding and unconscious Iraqi soldier with him.

"Take cover!"

"No!" He fires and a body drops. "I won't hide!" A bullet sings past me and buries itself into O'Connor's neck.

Blood splatters my face.

He falls, clutching his throat.

"Fuck!" I whirl around and send a bullet through the enemy's cranium.

Rage overtakes me.

Al-Bishi is a dead man.

Storming through the house I fire at the black-clothed militants, dropping them one by one as I hunt down the Iraqi commander.

The one I trained myself.

The one I fucking trusted with not only my life but the life of my men!

"Al-Bishi!" My throat burns and with the buzz of gunfire in my ears, my voice sounds more like a whisper. "You coward!"

Then he appears almost as if out of nowhere, or maybe he was searching for me too. Those black eyes shine with the joy of death that I've only ever seen in the face of pure evil.

"*Sadiq!*" His blood-covered face lights up with the joy that comes from a successful op. "American pig!"

My death is only seconds away, and as I raise my gun I welcome the burn of the bullet that'll soon take my life. It's what I deserve for not listening to Grant.

Oh God, Grant.

I say a silent prayer that he'll forgive me for what I've done.

The pop of gunfire sounds.

A force slams into me.

I fall to my back and groan.

A heavy weight on my lungs makes it impossible to take a full breath.

Thankfully, there is no pain.

Only the warm slick blood that flows around my throat.

I close my eyes, grateful that it's over, when something smacks my cheek.

"Sarge! Get up!" Schmitt's over me and for the first time since I've known him, he looks scared. "Dustoff inbound!"

Dustoff. Medivac?

The ground shakes.

A bomb dropped.

"Our backup is here!"

He heaves the weight off my chest.

A flash of brown hair coated in blood and gray matter hits my vision.

With renewed strength I push myself up and—oh God…"No!" I grip Grant's vest and shake him, knowing it's pointless. One side of his head is gone. "No!"

It was Grant who fell on top of me.

He took that bullet for me.

After I ignored his concerns, he sacrificed his life…for me.

"Sarge, we gotta go!" Schmitt pulls my arms off LaRoy and I scramble to my feet. Bombs continue to shake the walls and small-round fire is still popping off randomly.

Crouched low, we maneuver over bodies. More fire. We duck behind a flipped-over table.

"You go!" I fire off a round. Feeling numb and sick I push back all thoughts and allow my training to take over. "Al-Bishi is mine!"

"I'm not leaving you!" He lifts his head up and takes a few shots, then falls hard to my side.

I shove him away with my elbow. "Go! That's an order!"

He continues to press against me.

"Schmitt, dammit! I gave you an or—" He stares up at me with lifeless eyes. Blood forming rivers from his nose and mouth. Smoke curling up from the small bullet hole in his forehead.

Red coats my vision.

I stand to my full height.

The sound of gunfire stopped.

The room is silent.

Dead bodies litter the floor.

Shock overtakes me. My hands shake but I feel nothing.

Only one thought pumps furiously through my mind.

It should've been me.

ONE

Present day…

SAWYER

"I think we should break up." I sip from a tangy margarita, wishing it would cool more than my mouth as the sweat that lies between my skin and my pantyhose is beginning to chafe.

Having just shoveled a heaping forkful of meat dripping in red sauce into his mouth, Mark freezes. He glares at me from behind his fork and strings of cheese dangle from his chin. The four-piece mariachi band starts up a few tables down and even the upbeat rhythm doesn't cut the tension between us.

I probably should've eased into it a little rather than dropping it right on the table between us, but I figure it's like a Band-Aid. The faster the better.

He wipes his chin, chews, and swallows hard before leaning forward to prop his forearms on the table. "You're kidding, right?"

"Mark…" I point to the dollop of red sauce under his pristine white sleeve. "Your shirt."

He doesn't take his eyes off mine, as if he didn't hear me or maybe he's refusing to. "Things have been so good between us."

I sigh internally because he only *thinks* things have been good between us. I've been entertaining ending what little we've started for weeks now. "I'm sure this seems out of left field but..."

He adjusts his position, further rubbing his crisp dress shirt through the offending sauce.

My fingers itch to dig out my Tide stain stick and go to town on what is sure to end up being an ugly and permanent reminder of tonight. "I just don't think we're compatible."

He shoves his plate aside almost violently and I add his emotional outbursts to the list of reasons why I can't stay with him. "You've been living with me for two months, Sawyer. How long have you been thinking about our compatibility?"

"About a month."

"Fuck." He leans back and runs two hands through his usually perfect chestnut hair, flashing that red stain that taunts me. "I knew it was too soon to ask you to move in."

He's probably right about that. At the time it made logical sense—I should know, I made the list. I checked off all the reasons *to* against all the reasons *against* and determined living together solved a lot of our problems. It was more affordable, his place was closer to the office, I was able to make bigger payments on my student loans. The only downside was I wasn't in love with him. And despite the way he's looking at me now—the turned-down lips and puppy dog eyes—he doesn't love me either.

He continues to tug at his hair and the chaos of it has me run my hands over mine in response. "I'm sorry to do this now. I wanted to wait until we got home."

"Wait until we got home." He repeats my own words, then laughs, but I fail to see what's funny so I jut my chin out and wait for him to explain. "Like that would've been easier? We've been to-gether for six months. We have a great time together. Why are you doing this?" His eyes narrow and I catch a hint of the Mark Abbot, CPA to the filthy stinkin' rich I see at the office every day. "Is this be-cause I closed on McMillan?"

My fingers dig into the sleek material of my pencil skirt. "Please, Mark. I'm not that petty." Although his swooping in on my client when I was reeling him in was a Grade-A dickhead move, it's only one of many reasons I'm ending our relationship.

He throws his hands up in defeat. "Then what is it? Why—"

"Can I get you another margarita?" Our waiter clears the empty basket of chips as he eyes my uneaten food. "Would you like a box?"

"We're fine, José!" Mark snaps at the man.

I flash the guy a warm and what I hope is an apologetic smile. "I'm sorry, but no. Just the check, thank you."

He gives Mark a warning look that my soon-to-be-ex doesn't seem to notice or care about, then retreats.

"First of all, his name is Juan. Not José. Second, it's not his fault we're breaking up, so don't take it out on him."

"*We* aren't breaking up, Sawyer. *You're* breaking up with me. I get no say in this, do I?"

"My mind is made up."

"Can you at least tell me what I did wrong? It scares the shit out of me that I've somehow been pushing you away and not even known it. Or that I've been so delusional to think things between us have been great when the whole time you've been miserable."

If that isn't the unanswerable question I don't know what is.

Do I run down the list of things he does that annoy me? That I hate it when he throws his arm over my shoulder in front of peo-ple at work as if he owns me and wants everyone to know? How I hate the way he breathes through his mouth, like his perfect nose is only for decoration rather than functional use? I hate that he chews ice. Takes me to dinner at sports bars when a game is on and never takes his eyes off the screen. I hate that he answers his phone while we're eating. I hate that I have to hold my breath around him every morning because of how much cologne he puts on, that he wears tennis shoes without socks, uses my tweezers to pluck hair out of his nose, doesn't hang up his wet towels the right way, and eats cereal in the middle of the night but doesn't rinse out his bowl so it stinks like sour milk in the morning. He'll think my reasons are ridiculous, but I can't change the things that drive me crazy, they're engrained in me.

"Wait a minute." His voice is softer now. "I know what this is. This is about your sister."

My mind blanks and fury blooms in my chest and heats my cheeks. "Don't bring her into this."

"You've been under so much stress." He rubs his forehead. "I feel like a dick for not seeing this coming."

Every word he says seems to grate along my skin and zap at my nerves. "If you're implying my breaking up with you is some kind of relapse—"

"That's exactly what I'm implying." The expression on his face softens, but it's not communicating understanding as much as pity. "It makes sense that with your sister being so sick you'd start to question everything. Anything emotional could send you back…inside. I'm just saying I totally get it."

I clench my jaw trying to hold back an outburst. "Don't compartmentalize how I feel."

The waiter returns, dropping the check on the table, and then scurries away probably because of the fire shooting through my eyes aimed directly at the man across from me.

Mark leans to the side to fish his wallet from the back pocket of his slacks. "My mom told me this might happen. She said once Celia took a turn for the worse your compulsions would come back."

"You told your mom?"

His *mom*. I'd mentally add his codependent relationship with his mother to my list of reasons why I'm breaking up with him, but I'm too mad to think straight.

"Of course. Good thing too or I might have actually thought you were breaking up with me because of something I did."

"Mark—"

"Have you considered going back to counseling, ya know, once Celia passes—"

"Seriously, Mark, I'll say it one more time. Leave my sister out of this."

He tosses a card into the black folder and peers at me with cold eyes. "Your anger only confirms it. Face it, Sawyer. Celia's dying. The quicker you accept that, the sooner you can move on with your life and that includes us."

And just like that all the anger and frustration drains from my body because in this moment I know without a single doubt that I could never stay with a man who doesn't give a shit about my boundaries.

I warned him.

He ignored me.

I'm done.

I snag my purse from its hanging position on my chair and dig out my phone. With a calmness I didn't think I was capable of, I hit the Uber app and pinch a twenty from my wallet.

I toss it on the table and stand with all the confidence of a woman who is about to walk away without a single regret. "I'll arrange to have my stuff out this weekend."

His cheeks redden and he braces to stand but I stop him with a firm look.

"Don't. This has been over for awhile, but what you pulled tonight confirms my decision." I hook my purse over my shoulder. "Bye, Mark."

"Wait, Sawyer!"

"Señor, you can't leave until I run your card."

"Give me one second, I—"

The heavy, carved wooden door of the restaurant closes behind me and I weave through the parking lot to the main road. I check my phone and thankfully the Uber pulls up seconds later.

The driver, an older man with white hair and who has Bing Crosby playing on the radio turns back to me. "Everything okay, miss." His eyes move over my shoulder to the back window and I don't have to look to know it's probably Mark charging the car.

"Yes. Orangewood and Twenty-Second Street, please."

He steps on the gas harder than I'd expect for a man his age. He's probably figured out I'm trying to get away from a bad date, and I appreciate him for that.

"Bottled water?" He hands me a four-ounce bottle of cold water that I gratefully accept.

"Thank you."

I pull out my phone and hit my sister's phone number. After two rings it goes to voicemail.

"Hey, it's Celia! I'm hanging off a rock face in Utah and can't reach my phone. Leave me a message!"

"Cece, it's me. I'm on my way to Mom and Dad's and was hoping you'd be awake. If not, I'll just talk to you tomorrow."

I slide my phone into my purse and Nat King Cole and Billie Holiday later we're pulling into my old neighborhood. With a few directions, we end up at my parents' house, idling in the driveway.

"I'll wait." He throws the car into park. "Make sure you get in all right."

Smiling to myself, I head to the front door, not at all surprised to see the lights in the front of the house on. It's early on a Friday night. That means movie night. Warmth washes over me at the thought of putting on my PJs and flopping on the couch with my parents and my sister just like we'd do when we were kids. Back when life was easier. Stable.

I knock on the door and soon my dad answers. "Sawyer, what are you doing here?" He wraps me in a hug, but when I pull back I see his excitement bleed from his face and leave worry in its place. "Everything okay?" He looks over my head. "Where's Mark?"

"I broke up with Mark—"

"Sawyer, we didn't know you were coming over." The joy in my mom's voice makes me think she misses those old days when we were all under one roof too. "Where's Mark?"

I open my mouth to answer, but my dad beats me too it.

"They broke up, Darlene."

My mom's overexaggerated shock almost makes me laugh. "You did? Why? Wait, come in and sit down. Where will you stay? You know your bedroom here is always available." She guides me to the kitchen while firing off questions. "When did this happen? Are you okay? We'd love to have you stay here, your sister would be so happy to have you home."

"I was hoping you'd say that." I drop to a stool at the breakfast bar. "I don't have anywhere to go and I can't stand to even look at Mark let alone sleep under the same roof with him."

My mom and dad stand on the opposite side of the bar, both staring at me with concern. "What did he do?"

I kick off my heels and flex my cramped toes. "He just doesn't get me and frankly...I don't get him either. It just wasn't meant to be. I've been wanting—"

A song blares from my mom's pocket, making all of us jump. One, because it's loud and two because it's Dr. Dre rapping "Bitches ain't shit but hoes and tricks." My mom frantically scrambles to get it before the song clip repeats, but in her fluster drops the thing on the floor. My dad shakes his head and I hide my laughter behind my fist.

She finally gets a handle on it. "Celia, what did you do to my phone? I can't have that, it's inappropriate." Her eyes come to me. "He's not with her." She sighs. "I guess they broke up. Okay, hold on." She pulls the phone from her ear and presses speaker. "Go on, she can hear you."

"Sawyer." Her voice is soft, but still carries that take-no-shit commanding tone.

"Hey, Cece. Did I wake you up?"

"Wake me up? Bitch, I have a brain tumor, I'm not ninety."

My parents roll their eyes, but I don't miss the way my dad flinches slightly.

"Come to my room and tell me why you're here without that uptight suit of yours."

"Okay, I'll be up."

"Bring some vodka."

"Celia, no," my mom chimes in. "You know you can't mix alcohol with your meds."

"It's for Sawyer, Mom. Jeez."

I mouth to my mom, "I got it."

"Hurry up." The phone goes dead.

"Is she okay?" I slide my gaze between my parents, noticing the odd nonverbal exchange they're having with each other. "Mom?"

"She's fine, honey."

My dad scrubs his face with one hand. "She's been a little cranky lately."

"Well, then, I better hurry and get up there." I grab a cold bottle of vodka from the freezer and kiss my parents good night.

"Help yourself to whatever you need." My mom hugs me a second time.

"I will. Night."

Dropping my shoes off at the bottom of the stairs, I take the steps two at a time until I'm at the door to the bedroom my sister grew up in. It still has a Foo Fighters sticker on it as well as a biohazard sign that I think she stole from a processing plant the summer of our junior year.

The flickering blue light of the television spills through the crack in the doorway. I push it open and find my sister in the same spot she was in the last time I saw her just a few days ago. Pillows propped behind her back, remote in hand, oxygen tube resting on her upper lip and a bored expression on her face. Her eyes come to mine and she smiles. "Get in here and tell me what happened."

"I called you from the Uber but you were on a rock face in Utah."

She sniffs like it's no biggie.

"Last week you were exploring caves in Phong Nha-Ke Bang National Park."

"Yeah, I just like saying Phong Nha-Ke Bang." She scoots over and pats the mattress. "Sit."

I close the door, just like I did when we were kids and we wanted to talk about boys without our parents hearing. As I settle in next to her, she mutes the TV and tosses the remote to the foot of the bed.

"You and Mark broke up, huh? Not surprised. The guy has the personality of a sheet of paper."

Picking at the label on the cold vodka bottle in my lap, I shrug. "He wasn't right for me, that's all. I'm not in love with him."

She sits up and turns her body to face me. "Let me guess…he wore socks with his Birkenstocks."

I stare dumbly back into her face and even though hers is rounder because of the medication and her hair longer it's still like staring in the mirror.

Celia's my identical twin sister.

"Real funny."

Her lips curve into a grin and she shoves my shoulder. "I'm right, aren't I? You broke up with him because he wore Birkenstocks."

"No."

"Crocs?"

"No!"

"Liar."

"I swear!" Laughter bubbles up in my chest.

"I don't believe you." She crosses her arms over her chest. Waiting.

"It wasn't any of that, it's just..." I stare at my sister's lifted brow and sigh. "He wore tennis shoes without socks. You could make penicillin off the bacteria living in those shoes." I shudder.

"I knew it!" She throws her head back, laughing. "You're sick, Sawyer Forrester."

"That's not the *only* reason."

"Oh, I've gotta hear this." She grabs the vodka bottle out of my hand, unscrews the top, and moves to take a sip.

I smack the bottle away from her lips. "Celia, no! You can't drink."

"*Pfft!* Of course I can." She takes a full mouthful of clear liquid and I rip it from her hand.

"Stop it!"

She cringes as she swallows the straight booze, one eye pinched closed and her lips pursed like she just sucked on a lemon. "Your turn," she grunts out.

I pull a tissue from the box on the nightstand and wipe the mouth of the bottle, earning an eye roll from my sister, then take a healthy swig and cringe as I force the fire down my throat. "Ugh...I hate this."

"I know, it's awesome, right? Go on." She settles back in next to me and pats my thigh. "Nice hose, Sawyer. Those are your Friday night hose, yeah? What shade is that? San Tropez tan?"

As if the liquor went straight to my head instantly, I giggle and hold up one stocking-covered foot. "No, it's called medium buff."

"Huh…it's about five times darker than your natural marshmallow skin tone."

"Shut up."

"Don't get me wrong, it looks good, but if you want to pull it off you'll need an extra pair for your arms." She motions to my neck. "And your face."

I dissolve into a fit of giggles and she follows.

"All right, either you drink or I do." She motions to the bottle.

I take a sip and she glares so I take another until she's satisfied.

"So…? What else?"

"We work together and live together. It's just a lot of *together*, ya know?"

"Hmm…"

"He clips his toenails in bed. Oh, and I've caught him scrolling through my text messages, did I ever tell you that? He said he was looking for a message from someone at work, but really…who does that?"

She looks thoughtfully at the television, then turns back to me. "I think I know what this is about."

"It's not *about* anything. I'm just not in love—"

"You're scared."

I gasp and find myself sitting up a little taller. "I am not."

"Yeah, you are. This is the first serious relationship you've been in since you were 'cured.'" She uses air quotes. "First sign of trouble and you're running."

I laugh, loud, because that's absurd and strangely it makes me feel defensive. "He's mean to waiters, and he breathes through his mouth, not when he sleeps, but like *always*. That has nothing to do with fear."

"I'll give you that, Mark is kind of a douche, but don't you see what you're doing? You're secluding yourself again."

"I am not—"

"How many friends do you have? And don't just throw out a number, I want names."

"You can't be serious."

"Name 'em."

Taking another sip of vodka gives me a few extra seconds to think. "There's Dana—"

"Your assistant doesn't count. She's paid to like you."

My jaw drops, but my sister looks unapologetic as she asks me to continue.

"Maggie is my—"

"Your hairdresser?"

"Oh, so I can't be friends with her either?"

"Fine. Maggie. Go on."

I chew my bottom lip, thinking. "I still talk to Anna from high school."

"Commenting and liking on social media does not count as *talking to*, Sawyer."

"What, you want me to admit I have no friends? I admit it. I have no friends." Tears burn my eyes, stupid booze.

Her expression softens and she frowns. "Life is too short to live being afraid of everything, trust me, I know."

"You're not afraid of anything."

"That's not true." She seems to sink deeper into the bed. "I'm afraid of what'll happen to you once I'm gone."

"Cece, don't talk like that. You're not going anywhere anytime soon. And when the time comes...I'll be fine." It's not really true. Once this brain tumor takes Celia away from me forever I'll become completely lost. She's only four and a half minutes older than me, but she's always been my big sister in every way. She was the one to go first, to lead, to move ahead and take risks while I hung back, always calculating the consequences.

"You're a liar. Grandma dying totally messed you up. You haven't been the same since."

"*Or*...this is just who I am. Just because we're identical twins doesn't mean I don't have my own personality."

"You didn't kill her. She got sick, Sawyer. Old people do that!"

"Yeah, I remember. *I'm* the one who gave her the flu."

"You don't know that."

"Neither do you." She huffs out a breath, clearly exhausted by the age-old argument neither of us has ever managed to win. "Remember when we were in school and we'd go to each other's classes?"

"Yeah, it was always fun to see which teachers we could pull one over on."

"Mrs. Fleming was the only one who could tell the difference between us."

"I swear she was clairvoyant."

She sighs and leans into me, her eyes staring just beyond the bed. "Those were some good times. How many boyfriends did you break up with for me?"

I laugh. "A lot. Remember that James kid who was in love with you kissed me senior year. I almost barfed."

She shivers. "Ick, yeah, he was a horrible kisser. But he had a sweet Corvette."

A few seconds of silence pass between us when she turns to me. "Sawyer, I need you to do me a favor."

At the serious tone in her voice, I set the vodka bottle down and turn to face her. "Anything."

"I need you to go to San Diego and pack up my place for me."

"No, Cece..." I swallow the lump in my throat.

My sister left home four days after she turned eighteen, never even finishing high school. My parents were furious, but they also knew they couldn't hold her back. She moved from city to city and never settled in one place for longer than a year. San Diego became her home a few months before she showed up back in Phoenix with the devastating news of her tumor. She refused to let my parents go pack up her beach house because she said if she did, that meant she'd given up hope that she'd ever get better.

All the doctors said there was only one prognosis for the tumor that's wrapped itself around her brainstem. The pressure would become too much and she'd lose the ability to breathe. That was a death sentence. No one with this type of cancer has ever survived. But we all refuse to believe it, with Celia leading the cavalry.

"Listen..." she whispers. "There's something I need to tell you."

"What is it?"

"I quit treatment a few weeks ago."

"What?" My stomach turns to lead. "Why?"

"The tumor isn't responding to it anymore. It hasn't for awhile."

"What does that mean?" My sinuses burn with the tears I refuse to let fall in front of my sister.

"I'm tired of fighting."

How do I even respond to that? Make a list of all her reasons for living and weigh them against her reasons for giving up? Prove to her that her life is too valuable to just let go?

I sniff and she curls in closer to me.

"Nothing has changed. Don't waste a single second being upset."

I can't dignify that with a response because it's utterly ridiculous so I just sit and hold on to her.

"I didn't tell any of my friends back in San Diego about my head. They ah...they don't know I'm sick."

"Why wouldn't you tell them?"

"Because I don't want to be remembered as the sick girl who everyone felt sorry for because she was dying—"

"You're not going to die."

"Sawyer." She stares at me with green eyes that match my own.

"Miracles happen every day. There's still a chance. I won't give up hope."

"Maybe you're right, but even if I do hang on for another few months or a year I'll never make it back to San Diego, so I need you to go, pretend you're me, and pack up my place."

I sit straight up and glare at her. "Pretend I'm you? Are you kidding? No one will ever buy that."

"Of course they will!" She smiles big and the sight of her excitement is so intense that I feel it in my chest. "I have a closet full of clothes you can wear, your hair is different, but they'll just think I cut it."

"This is stupid."

"It's not! Think about it. You go for a short time, a couple of weeks, tops. Enjoy the sun, sand, and *my gosh*, enjoy the company. It's about time you had a few friends." She shrugs. "Even if they're mine."

"Why can't I just go as myself? I can explain I'm your sister and you're, I don't know, on an archeological dig in Pompeii or something."

"Because if you're you, you can't be me. You'll hole up in my beach house and methodically pack my things while pushing everyone away. If you're me you'll be forced to interact. I wasn't even there for six months, they'll never know you're not me."

"I can't do this, I mean…so many things could go wrong."

"Like what? You'll have to let loose a little, smile more, stop making those fucking lists you carry around, take some risks, basically…pretend you're me."

"And then what?"

"And then you come home and anyone who knew me will never have to know what happened to me. They'll think I've moved on, traveling the world, and sucking the life out of living."

"They deserve to know—"

"Why?" Her brows pinch together. "So they can come visit and cry at my bedside? Send depressing cards accompanied by those fucking white flowers you always see at funerals? You think that's how I want to go out?"

"No, but—"

"No. I've managed to keep my condition a secret from them, and everyone else outside of Phoenix. I need you to help me keep it."

"I don't know, Celia. It was funny when we were kids, but we're twenty-four years old now. We have a responsibility to…to…" *To what?*

"It's all I ask, Sawyer. My dying wish."

"Don't say that!"

Her lips hitch in a crooked grin. "So you'll do it."

This is absurd. I feel sick to my stomach. Responsibility and loyalty pull me in opposite directions. But…she's my sister, and if she doesn't beat this life-robbing growth in her body and I lose her, if I don't do this I'll never forgive myself. "I guess."

"Yes!" She throws her arms around me. "Thank you!"

I hug her back, burying my nose in her shoulder with a groan. This is never going to work. "How am I going to pull this off? What if I'm forced to make decisions?"

"Easy." She reaches over to her bedside table and fishes in the top drawer. "Take this." She plops a coin into my hand.

"A quarter? How will this help me?"

"Every time you're forced to make a decision, whatever it is, no matter how simple or complicated, don't think, just flip the coin."

"You're kidding."

"I'm not. I do it all the time."

"Celia, that's…it's…immature."

"No, it's not. It's living by chance. Let the fates decide."

Chance. Fate. These are things I know nothing about. In my experience, all choices, no matter how seemingly simple, have significance. Choose wrong, pay the price.

In a world where I live in black-and-white and absolutes, my sister lives in tie-dye and liberation. All answers are right answers and even negative consequences serve a bigger purpose. It's insane. Anarchy. Chaos. Everything that makes my pulse race and my palms sweat.

"Life is beautiful and terrifying," she whispers. "And you deserve to feel that down to your bones."

"Okay, Cece." I look her in the eyes and find them glossy with emotion. "I'll do it. For you."

"Thank you." She nuzzles back into my shoulder. "Ya know, my only regret in this life was not taking you with me when I left. I've seen the world, Sawyer. You should've been there too."

"I would've hated it, you know that."

"Maybe, but…if you were with me you wouldn't have locked yourself up like you did. Life's too short to let fear keep you from living."

"Now you sound like my therapist."

"You should listen to her. If I would've known how it was all going to end, how soon it was all going to end, I'd have wanted less time traveling and more time with you."

Her words manage to coil around my lungs and they constrict so I'm unable to take a full breath. "Don't talk like that. We have time, a lot more time."

"Hmm." She smiles sadly and drops to her pillow, pulling the down comforter over her body. "Stay with me?"

"Yeah."

She yawns. "Okay, but go put on some pajamas. I'm not sleeping in the same bed as those pantyhose."

Her eyes drift closed and a look of peace softens her face. I wonder if it's my agreeing to tie up her loose ends in San Diego that's put it there.

I roll the quarter between my fingers.

This should be easy enough. I'll keep to myself as much as possible, bring Celia's stuff back, and she'll be able to live on in the eyes of her friends.

TWO

SAWYER

"What time will you land in San Carlos?" My mom hands me my toiletry bag.

Between what was left in my old bathroom and after raiding Celia's closet, I was able to scratch up enough for a few days out of town. That plus whatever is already there should be plenty to get me through what I hope will be a short trip. Cutoff shorts and baggy tank tops aren't what I'm most comfortable in, but nothing about this trip will be enjoyable, let alone healthy.

My hands shake as I shove a pair of Celia's sandals into my suitcase and zip it up. "Five-thirty, and it's San Diego, Mom."

She rubs her temples. "Oh, that's right." We never could keep up with my sister's living situations. At one point her address was a semi-truck working its way across the country driven by a guy named Panda.

"You sure you're okay with this? I know how much you hate flying. Your dad can go."

"It's fine. I want to go." It'll do my mom no good to tell her the truth, that I really am scared shitless. There's a good chance my plane will go down in some remote area and no one will know where we are so we'll all have to start eating our dead to survive. Or if I'm lucky I'll get stuck in that germ tube next to a guy who was bitten by a monkey and I'll die in a hazmat suit three days later. If it would happen to anyone, it would happen to me. Too late now. I made a promise to my sister and shit-scared or not, I intend to keep it.

"Are you sure? It's not too late to change your mind." My mom stills my hands that aren't yet satisfied with the arrangement of clothes.

Turn off disturbing thoughts. Take a breath. Get a handle on my emotions.

The open door across the hallway where Celia is sleeping catches my eye. I have to do this for her. "I'm sure. Besides, I won't be gone long." I zip up my suitcase and pull it off the bed to the floor. "A couple weeks at the most. I'll pack up, tie up any loose ends, and I'll be back."

She worries her lip. "What about work?"

"I'm using my vacation time and sick days. Dana will call me if something needs my attention." I pat my shoulder bag. "I've got my computer."

"And Mark? What about your things?"

"Dana said she'd throw all my stuff in boxes. It's mainly clothes and small pieces of furniture. Movers are going to pick it all up and put it in storage until I get back."

She hands me my neck pillow. "Do you have a sweater? It gets cold on the coast at night."

"Yeah, Mom." I hug her. "I better get to the airport or I'm going to miss my flight. I'm going to go say bye to Celia."

She nods and grabs my bag to take down to my dad who is most likely waiting by the door with his keys in hand.

I tiptoe into Celia's room and sit on the bed next to her. It seems she's sleeping more and more. Mom said it's the medication she takes for the headaches, and I want to cry every time I see my usually energetic sister sapped of all her strength.

I run my fingers through the mass of strawberry-blond hair that's fanned out around her face. "Celia, I'm leaving."

She whines and her eyes pinch together as if my voice is sending shockwaves of pain through her temple. I lean down and kiss her forehead. "I'll call you when I get there." Her face relaxes and she hums. "I love you."

I take a couple more seconds to watch her sleep and then head downstairs to find my dad exactly where I expected him.

"All set?"

"Yeah." I turn to get my bags and end up in another hug from my mom. "It's okay, Mom." No one's saying what we're all thinking, that Celia's giving up. She's been our strength and if she loses hope in getting better . . . well, I can't even go there, not even hypothetically.

She squeezes me tight. "Don't throw anything out, okay? You know Celia's going to want to sort through her things once they're here."

"I won't."

She pulls away and kisses my cheek.

"I'll be in touch." And with that, I leave to sort through my sister's life.

With the coin nestled safely in my pocket.

* * *

The coastal city of Ocean Beach is nothing like I imaged it would be.

I've seen the movies filmed on southern California beaches, the rail-thin women in string bikinis, tattooed hard-body guys walking around with a surfboard under their arm. So I knew exactly what to expect when I deplaned and hailed a cab to take me to Celia's house. But with my face pressed to the window as we drive through town I wonder if this green Prius is the modern-day version of a Delorean and I've been blasted back to 1972.

This is nothing like The O.C.

The main street that runs through town is lined with palm trees and old storefronts on both sides. Antiques stores, bead shops, tattoo parlors, and those shops that always smell like patchouli and sell pipes for smoking marijuana. There's even a movie theater that has an old-timey marquee sign boasting the three movies currently playing, none of them new releases.

It's quirky. Colorful. Perfect for Celia.

I'm so busy staring out the window I hardly notice when the driver throws the cab into park.

"This is it." He hits the fare meter and eyes me through the rearview mirror. "Eight oh four Sunset Cliffs?"

I blink at the row of cottages that look like playhouses for kids lined up at the cliff's edge. They're all identical—small, white slat boards with hunter-green trim—except one. I don't have to see the number on the door to know that one has to be hers. My sister's place stands out like a pink flamingo in a sea of pigeons.

"Yeah, this is the place." I gather my purse to my chest and push open the car door. The briny breeze slaps me in the face and tosses my hair—already frizzing in the humidity—around my face. The driver follows, retrieving my black roller bag from the trunk and placing it at my side. I shove a few extra dollars at him and rub on hand sanitizer while I stare at my sister's tiny house.

When she left here to come back to Phoenix, she had no idea she'd never be healthy enough to return. My chest grows heavy.

I square my shoulders and the wheels of my suitcase snag on

large cracks of jagged asphalt the entire walk to her place. What causes those? Earthquakes? Or maybe the cliff falling slowly into the ocean? My pulse pounds at the thought.

Sure, the view here is gorgeous, just steps away from a small private beach hidden by cliffs on each side, and it's a balmy seventy-five degrees, but the threat of a natural disaster like a rogue tsunami would make it all impossible to enjoy.

The tiny front porch is decorated in DIY wind chimes made from bottles—and not the cool vintage kind, just regular beer and soda bottles with the occasional string of seashells.

She has a row of colorful rain boots hanging from her porch, each one filled with dirt and the crispy curled-up remains of flowers. I can't take my eyes off the flower graves, thinking the lack of life growing from them carries a sick irony of her leaving and taking the life of this place with her.

I pull my eyes away and notice my sister has an affinity for repurposing. *Lots* of seashells, random-sized driftwood, and an old ship's steering wheel pepper the small beach hut porch.

Thumping up the steps I look around for the red pot the key was supposed to be hidden under. She never did carry a key, even when we were young. She said they held her down. I don't see a red pot, or any pot. Huh...I squat to flip the doormat. It reads *No Shoes. No Shirt. No Problem.* Typical Celia. I flip it over to see if maybe the key is hidden under there, but there's nothing. Blowing out a frustrated breath I pull my bag up close to the door where it'll be safe while I go hunt for help.

My sister had mentioned something about a Mr. Hurtado, the man who rents these cottages and lives onsite. She warned me not to let his gray hair fool me, that he's as fit as the guys half his age and could build a sailboat out of toothpicks and a paper napkin.

The sun is still high over the ocean, thank goodness for long summer days, but if I don't get into my sister's place fast I'll have to find a hotel and I didn't see a single one on the drive through town. Granted, I did see the OB Hostel, but judging by the crowd gathered out front and the cloud of marijuana smoke that filtered into the street, I'd rather take my chances sleeping on the beach.

I find unit one easily enough, and thankfully the sign on the door says SUPERINTENDENT with a doorbell and a handwritten note taped above it that reads *Ring for assistance*.

Here we go. Let the charade begin.

I'm Celia. Be Celia.

I pretend my body is made of jelly and smile like I've had two glasses of wine.

That should do it.

With a firm press of the bell there's a slight buzz from inside as if the contraption is as old as the cottage itself. I contemplate ringing again, but first squint to peek through the windows only to find no movement. I chew my lip and wait some more, then ring again. Still nothing. Exhausted, I'm thinking a hotel for one night might not be a bad idea. I can tackle this in the morn—

"Holy shit!"

I whirl around at the sound of a deep voice to find a tall man wearing shorts, a T-shirt, and flip-flops barreling toward me with a big smile.

"You're back!"

I open my mouth to reply but he knocks the wind out of me when he wraps me in a bear hug. My cheek is pressed to his pec and I'm assaulted by his scent—an exotic mix of coconut and cinnamon—strange man, strange germs. My fists ball at my sides to keep from shoving him away.

His arms close tighter around me. "Hasn't been the same here without you."

"Um…" I pat his back with my fist and step away with the hope of extracting myself and thankfully he gets the hint and releases me.

His eyes narrow and he drops his arms when I step back. "Is everything okay?"

This guy is tan, his eyes a light shade of brown that match the color of his skin, and his shaggy hair is almost exactly the same color. He's practically monochromatic and if the color had a name it would be medium buff. He's as handsome as Ryan Gosling, and as my germophobic reaction fades my body belatedly responds to having been pressed against his well-built chest.

I clear my throat and when I try to smooth my hair it feels ten times bigger than it did just minutes ago. Great, my first encounter with a real California hot guy and I look like Roseanne Roseannadanna. "Yes." I shake my head. "I mean, no, not really." *Come on, Sawyer, words!*

"You're different." He doesn't say it like it's a compliment and even though I expect it I can't avoid the pinch of embarrassment.

"Nah, not really." I force myself to relax, hoping to seem more like Cece, but afraid I'm coming off as a ragdoll. "Dude, eight weeks in Bangladesh'll do that to a girl, and…" I point to the mop on my head, an awkward giggle bubbling up from my chest. "I just cut my hair so that's—"

He hooks me behind the neck and his mouth crashes down on mine.

I part my lips to gasp and when I do his tongue slides inside. With one hand on my lower back, he presses me to him. Stranger's tongue in my mouth! The flash of panic dissolves as his kiss turns demanding and coaxes a soft purr from my throat. My knees wobble. I grip his arms to stay steady and it's clear this guy is no stranger to exercise.

Now, I have an average amount of experience with men, dated here and there, Mark for six months, but I have never been kissed like this. Is this a hot California guy thing? Or…is this the kiss of a man who's desperately trying to get a woman to remember who he is. Or maybe, trying to get her to remember who they are together.

Guilt washes over me and I pull back, catching my breath and staring into the hopeful eyes of a man too attractive for a girl like me. For any girl, really, too tempting to be safe. "I'm so sorry."

He cups my jaw, and God, the way he's taking me in, the way his thumbs rub along my cheeks, is it too much to not want it to end? "Don't be sorry. I knew when you left you'd be back when you were ready." His lips tilt into a smoldering grin. "So…Bangladesh for eight weeks, huh? Where were you for the other four?"

She didn't tell him. She just took off, leaving this guy who clearly has feelings for her to wait with no communication for her to return? I should pull his hands off my face, confess everything, but I made my sister a promise. And I don't want to be the one to make this guy's handsome face turn sour with my sister's dismissal.

"Phoenix." My voice is a high-pitched squeak, not that he seems to care.

"What's in Phoenix?"

I blink and it takes me a second to register his question. What's in Phoenix? Only Celia's entire family! She knows this guy well enough for him to kiss her 'til her toes curl but he knows nothing about her.

"My family." I bite out the two words and he drops his hands from my face. It's possible this is how casual relationships work, they kiss and screw and never really dig too far into who the other person is. I suddenly feel naïve and desperate for a change of subject.

"Do you know where I can find Mr. Hurtado?"

He smiles, and oh my gosh, I feel it in my belly. Dimples, straight teeth, confidence. "*Mr. Hurtado*. Look at you, did you become a…" He looks at me from top to bottom. "Like a lawyer or something since you left?"

I look down at my black Ann Taylor dress. I pulled it from Celia's closet, but now remember she bought it for our grandfather's funeral. It's probably a bit formal for the beach. "I just came from a…a funeral."

He sucks in air through his teeth. "Bummer. After you left, Cal moved back to Ventura to be with his grandkids or something. His nephew watches the place now."

"I need to talk to him, do you know where he is?"

"He lives down at the marina, only stops by here every few days."

Shit.

A car horn honks and he waves over my head. "I'm headed out, but…" He steps in close and drops a light kiss on my lips, leaving me standing there like a gaping fish. "We'll catch up later, okay? If you get bored come by the bar, I'll buy you a welcome home drink."

It takes everything I have to shake off the effect of his kiss. "Wait, you said 'the marina.' Where is that?"

"Intrepid Marina off Scott Street. He's on Cal's old boat."

"Brice, hurry up!" A guy calls from the street behind me.

"I gotta go." He winks and jogs toward the street where he hops into a mid-sized pickup truck and waves as they pull away.

I snag my phone, hit a button, and press it to my ear.

"Hey, you've reached Celia! I'm in astronaut school and currently studying a book on anti-gravity that I just can't put down, so…leave a message!"

"You never mentioned Brice, Cece!" I whisper-yell into the phone. "He kissed me! And wow, but…" Instantly my cheeks flame. "It was nothing like James, let's say that." I huff out a breath and stare blindly at the horizon. "There wasn't a key under the red pot and Mr. Hurtado isn't here anymore so I'm headed to the docks to get a key from his nephew. I can't believe I agreed to this. I love you…*jerk*."

I hit END and punch my Uber app and enter the only information I have. Intrepid Marina off Scott Street.

I shove the phone in my purse, then grab my suitcase and make my way to the street to go hunt down Mr. Hurtado's nephew.

I haven't even been Celia for a full hour yet and already I've been kissed by a strange man. If I'm not careful, I'll end up married and pregnant by mid-week.

THREE

ADEN

"Ya snag that dorado off the kelp beds?"

I peer up from fileting my catch at the dock's fish table to see Jenkins staring at me through his one good eye, the other fogged over with cataracts.

"If you think I'm sharing my secret spot with you, old man, you've lost your fuckin' mind."

He grunts with a gargled chuckle. "My mind's been gone for longer than you've been alive."

"I believe it."

It's true, Jenkins is old enough to be my grandfather, but living on a boat docked in a small marina I don't have a lot of options as far as company goes, which is for the best. I have a hard enough time being around people in general. Jenkins is just as annoyed with the population as I am and prefers being alone by his craggy ole self. We're a match made in antisocial hell.

"Mahi-mahi for dinner." It's not a question. Presumptuous old fart. "I'll bring libations."

It's the deal we've had since he first limped up to my boat bitching about my music being too loud. He loves fishing, but arthritis has attacked his hands and his lack of physical movement has made him weak so I do the catching and he brings over cheap booze that I try not to drink too much of because getting drunk on cheap liquor turns me into an asshole.

I dangle the fish scraps off the dock to our resident sea lion Morpheus who snags it, swallows it, and barks for more. "Greedy little shit." I toss him more.

"You keep feeding 'em he'll never leave you alone." Jenkins drops a handful of entrails into the water to be devoured by a school of surf perch.

"I like Morpheus. He's mellow, only bitches when he's hungry." I tilt my head and glare at the pirate-looking old man. "Kinda like someone else I know."

He waves me off and hobbles down the dock toward his boat. "Taught him everything he knows and shows me no respect."

"Don't bring your homemade rum. Last time I drank that shit I hallucinated for a week!"

"Pussy." He grumbles and disappears into the cabin of his sailboat named *Amelia Lynn* after his wife who passed away a couple years before he moved into the vessel permanently. Running away from old memories, he always says.

That I understand.

I wipe my filet knife on my jeans and sheath it, then grab the two thick slabs of meat and head to my boat. The old Rampage, forty-one footer gives me just enough space to sleep and eat. It's nothing fancy, belonged to my uncle Cal before he signed it over to me as a thank-you for taking on the management of his property over at Sunset Cliffs.

Free place to stay, slip fees are affordable, I make decent money selling my catch to the fish market, plus the small percentage I get for running the cottages, it's the perfect life for a guy like me.

Quiet.

Secluded.

And the boat provides an easy escape when I need to.

I pull out a small charcoal grill and light the coals, then head inside to see what I have in the fridge. Great thing about selling my catch to the fish market is I can also do a trade. Fresh coleslaw, potato salad, pasta salad, pretty much anything. I grab a cold beer and pop the top, then flip on the radio and head out back to watch the sunset.

Jenkins is wobbling down the dock toward me, a bottle of cheap gin in his hands and a sway like he's been living on water so long he's got perpetual sea legs.

I open the back latch door to let him on board but he swats me out of the way, pushing past and mumbling a string of profanity.

He heads right inside to pour himself a drink and I flop down into a padded vinyl seat that's worn and ripped on the edges.

When he comes back he takes the seat at the stern and we both stare at what's left of the sun. A flicker of anxiety ticks behind my ribs. Sunset is the calm before the storm, or at least it used to be. That's where the booze helps. Dulls the race in my pulse and tames my thoughts.

I pinch my eyes closed, hoping to push back the incoming assault, and down the rest of my beer in wide-mouth gulps.

"You thinkin' 'bout 'em?" Jenkins is the only person who knows the shit that runs through my head on an endless reel.

The poisonous thoughts build up over time and if I don't spit them out they'll eventually kill me. They almost have before.

"Can't do nothin' 'bout those boys. They made their choice."

It should've been me.

I grunt to let him know I hear him, even if I don't totally agree.

"I'm gonna grab another beer." I push to stand. "Need anything?"

He sips his gin by way of answer.

Once inside I brace my hands on the countertop, breathing through the annoyance I'm feeling at my weakness. I never know what triggers the thoughts to morph into panic, how I can go from staring at the sunset to seeing the mutilated bodies of my brothers and the rising anxiety that makes my hands shake and chest ache.

Three months I've been out. It seems impossible, but the terror and paranoia are happening more frequently.

I snag another cold beer, pop the top, and throw back half of it when Jenkins's cackle filters in through the open door.

"Colt, getchur ass out here, you gotta see this."

I cross the room to the back deck fully expecting to see Morpheus sneaking fish out of the bait tank. Jenkins points down the dock and I freeze at the sight.

A woman.

Hey, I've seen my fair share, most in various stages of undress even, but this particular woman has my lips pulling up on either side.

"What is she doing?"

He laughs and the sound turns into a cough. "She's trying to reach through the gate to get it open."

There's a locked gate at the top of the dock so only residents and boat owners can get in with a code. But on the inside there's a button that releases the lock when leaving, and even though the thing is a good three feet from the gate, it isn't stopping this woman from reaching her arm through the metal poles all the way to her shoulder.

"Ten bucks says she gets in."

"Stupid bet, old man, there's no way she's getting it." I shake his hand and we watch with amusement as she refuses to give up. "She's gonna dislocate her shoulder if she's not careful." He wheeze-laughs. "Oh boy, she's got a stick now."

"What the hell is she doing with that?"

This is the most entertained I've been since Jenkins tried to turn seagulls into messenger birds using live sardines as treats.

Who is this lady and what does she want so badly on this dock that she's willing to make an ass out of herself to get it?

Maybe she's a rep from one of the big yacht companies. They always hire young, beautiful women who don't know their ass from their tits when it comes to boats, but the rich suits don't give a shit. They'll buy anything from a pretty face and a hot body who'll bootlick 'em. But this girl lacks the confidence of a yacht broker. And now that I look harder…Nah, she might be in a dress, but the high neckline doesn't show an ounce of cleavage and the skirt nearly touches her shins. Maybe she works for the bank? My smile falls. Fuck, this could be about Cal's property.

Now I'm really hoping she doesn't get it.

"Here comes Macky." Jenkins holds out his wrinkly old hand and opens his gnarled fingers as much as they'll allow, which isn't much. "You owe me ten."

I sneer as Macky, the pervert, opens the gate for the woman like he's a damn doorman to the Playboy mansion. She says something and I don't miss how he checks out her ass as she passes him through the gate. At the bottom of the slant plank she says something that gets his attention.

With my hip propped on the edge of the boat I watch in horror as he nods and points directly at me. Fuck.

Her lips move and he smiles, then she makes her way toward us.

"She's comin' over here, Colt." There's humor in the old man's voice. "Whoa, she's not too steady on them shoes, though." He laughs again and coughs and cracks up some more.

I'd laugh at her lumbering down the dock because he's right, she's far from steady and looks completely out of place, but the blood in my veins is heating with the incoming threat.

Her eyes narrow on the back of my boat and disgust wrinkles her nose. Then she raises her gaze to the tattered American flag flying just over my head.

"There something I can help you with, sweetheart?"

She glares up at me at my calling her a pet name, which makes me grin.

"*Nauti Nancy?*"

"You don't like the name of my boat?"

"Why are boats always named after women?"

"Because they're run by men."

She gasps and Jenkins coughs into his gin.

"Are you Mr. Hurtado's nephew?"

I jerk at the mention of my uncle, knowing she must be from the bank. "Depends. Who the hell are you?"

She licks a set of perfectly fat lips and stares at my neck, dark, full lashes sprawling out against pale skin that's peppered with freckles. "I'm…" Throat clearing and she juts out her chin. "I'm Celia Forrester."

Celia Forrester.

I know that name.

All my muscles release their tension. "You live in number four."

I wouldn't have thought it possible but her eyes get even wider. "Yes, number four."

"You're back in town."

"Yes." She clears her throat and her eyes drop to my chest. "The key was supposed to be under a pot—"

"Had the locks changed after the break-in."

Those big orbs dart back to my face. "Break-in?"

"Yeah, I left you a message about it, but your voicemail said you were paragliding in New Zealand."

She chews on her thick lower lip, then nods. "Can I get the—wait, you left me a message?"

"That's what I said. Shit, woman, this isn't rocket science." I laugh and take a swig off my beer. "You're Celia Forrester."

"I'm Celia."

Is she fucking for real? "You got a drug problem, freckles?"

She cringes. "No! I do not have a drug problem. What did you call me?"

"Jesus, you two," Jenkins mumbles and slurps on his gin. "Even I know who you are, honey. Cal has a picture of the two of you inside."

I want to kick Jenkins for sharing that tidbit. I should've sent the photo to Cal along with his old watch and his lucky hat that he left behind, but I didn't want to get rid of it. It's not just because the image is of my uncle smiling bigger than I've ever seen with my own two eyes, but it's the woman in the photo too. The wind tossing all her long hair, sun-kissed skin that highlights the freckles on her nose and shoulders, and the kind of smile that reminds me why I fought hard for this country. To protect the kind of carefree beauty in that photo.

But looking at her now, I never would've recognized her as the woman in the picture. Gone is that relaxed and lighthearted smile. Sure she's still good-looking, but in more of an uptight kind of way. Her hair is much shorter, just touching her shoulders, but just as wild, and her body language seems…constipated.

"All I need is a key and I'll be out of your hair."

"Well, come on." I jerk my head for her to come aboard.

She steps closer to the boat and as if she forgot she's over water her body locks up and she sways backward.

"Uh…" She studies the space between the dock and the platform off the back. "How do—"

"Here." I hold out my hand and she stares at it like it's a dead fish. There's still some blood and scales under my nails from cleaning the dorado. "I ain't gonna bite."

She gives me a dull look.

"Take those fuckin' shoes off." Jenkins points to her feet with his drink in hand. "If anything will get you wet out here it's them high heels."

She kicks off her shoes and her toenails are painted a shade so light it matches the color of her pale feet. She reaches for my hand and it feels so small in my palm. I pull her on board with more force than she was expecting and she crashes into my chest. She tilts her head back to look at me and blasts me with the full force of her green eyes. Wide, a little scared, and fuckin' gorgeous. Her full lips part and the wind tosses her hair across her face.

I make no attempt to step back but look down at her and wait for her reaction, because unnerving this girl is highly entertaining.

As if she can read my mind her eyes narrow and she wiggles out of my arms and wrinkles her nose. "What is that smell?"

"That, freckles, is the smell of fish guts and a hard day's work."

She pinches her nose between her fingers.

I nod to the grill, trying not to smile. "You hungry? We've got plenty."

"Oh God, no." She seems to catch herself for being so blunt and drops her hand from her face. "I mean, thanks, but I'm good."

"You sure?" Jenkins grins wide showing off all six of his teeth. "Colt here grills a good filet."

She frowns and the palm of her hand goes to her stomach. "Oh… yeah, no I really, I can't."

"Why not?" I don't really care, but I'm still smiling because I like watching her scramble for an excuse.

"I, a…" She juts out her chin. "I'm a vegetarian."

"Is that right?"

"Can't no one live off plants." Jenkins runs his clear eye up and down Celia's body. "A woman needs protein to grow dem babies."

"He's right." Leaning back against the outrigger I shrug. "Can't make babies without takin' in some meat." I wink.

Her eyes pop wide and a blush overtakes her fair skin. "If I could just get the key I'll let you two get back to…whatever it is you do."

"Suit yourself." I head into the cabin and the soft sound of her feet padding along the floor follows behind me.

So this is my uncle Cal's favorite tenant, Celia Forrester.

Funny…I don't know what I expected when and if I finally met the woman, but I know this hoity-toity girl is not it.

SAWYER

What is it about California that grows the most attractive men?

I was expecting *Cal's nephew* to be, I don't know, less consuming. This guy takes up space and that has very little to do with his size. His cocky smile and confident demeanor seems to absorb all the air in the atmosphere.

Thankfully he's kind of a dick so it's not hard to pull my eyes away from the way his pale-blue shirt hugs his wide chest. Like Brice, Aden is tan but in a more unpolished way that screams of long days spent outdoors. My goal is to keep my gaze to the floor, but like a magnet my eyes are pulled down his abdomen to a narrow waist and thick muscular thighs encased in faded jeans, worn out in parts and spattered with what looks like blood. I shake off a fantasy involving me, those jeans, a bottle of hydrogen peroxide, and my stain-stick. I dip my gaze to avoid staring only to discover he's wearing brown leather flip-flops and even his feet are attractive. My stomach is antsy, flipping and tripping all over itself. Rather than a quarter to assist me in faking Celia I think a bottle of Pepto would've been more helpful.

A framed photo gets shoved into my face and because I'm staring at the floor the movement startles me. The frame is nothing fancy, like one you'd get from a drugstore, and the photo is of two people—*it's Celia*. She's grinning, her hair blowing all around that contagious smile, the happiness of a woman sucking the marrow out of life. She's sitting cross-legged on the beach next to a man with a wide-brimmed hat and longish gray hair. That must be Calvin Hurtado. There's a bucket between them and they both have something in their hands. Rocks or...

"Oysters." Aden nods to the photo.

"I know that." Ugh, I'm a horrible liar. I internally cuss out my sister for asking me to do this.

He grins, sexy and lopsided, and framed in a day's-plus worth of beard growth. It's then I notice now standing this close that one of his front teeth is a little crooked, which adds something boyish to his already handsome face. "Guess that vegetarian thing is more a *selective* preference, huh?"

"Yeah, well...shellfish doesn't count." Dammit, I sound like an idiot. Why did I say I was a vegetarian? Stupid, Sawyer. Celia has always been adventurous and that includes what she ate.

This guy is unnerving.

"If you say so." He shakes his head and turns away. I set the photo down and follow him to the back of the tiny cabin.

The living space inside the boat is small, cramped like a studio apartment where the full-sized bed, living room, and kitchen all share the same space. There's nothing by way of decoration, except for an American flag that spans one wall and is pinned up by thumbtacks. An unmade bed and basic generic plaid love seat round out the décor. Clearly Cal's nephew doesn't have a live-in girlfriend or wife as the place reeks of bachelorhood. There's very little that would point to personal touches, a few dirty ball caps, clothes on the floor, and the kitchen table is covered in what looks like mail—both opened and still sealed. How can he stand living in this disorganization?

"See something you don't like?"

My cheeks flame and I push up close to the table as he sorts through a single drawer. "I don't mean to stare; it's just I've never been inside a boat before...I'm sorry, I don't know your name."

"Aden." He looks up at me with those arresting chocolate-brown eyes. "Most people call me Colt."

"Colt, like...a baby horse?"

He goes back to searching the drawer. "Yeah, or Colt like my last name."

"Oh."

Thick dark eyebrows drop over those eyes as he digs through the drawer that's filled with a bunch of random things—pens, paperclips, small tools. Just watching him makes my palms itch to organize. They make dividers he could slide into that drawer and have a designated space for everything. This way when he needed a paperclip or a rubber band it would be there with its friends in its own little compartment.

"Cal said you're paid up through December." He pulls out a set of keys, looks them over, then tosses them back in.

December? That means Celia paid a year's rent in advance. I make a mental note to ask her about that later. "I won't be staying through December. Actually, I guess now is as good a time as any. I'll be mov—"

"What're you doing?" His gaze is zeroed in on my hands.

I look down and realize I've started to organize the mail into three separate stacks—one for unopened envelopes, one for opened, and one for garbage. "I'm..." *Organizing.* "Nothing." I messy up the stacks and whisper, "Sorry."

He glares at me for a few seconds longer, then returns to his search. "Here they are." He tosses the keys to me only to have them hit me in the chest and fall to the tabletop at my belly.

His eyes settle on my chest. "Sorry about that. I thought you'd catch—"

"It's okay." I snag them off the table and cross my arms over my boobs to get his eyes back on my face.

It works and his gaze slides to mine but not before lingering a second too long on my lips. I hold back a shiver.

"What's this big key for?"

"Your car."

"I have a car?"

He squints.

"I mean, of course. My car. I just…it's been so long since I've driven in my car, so…" God, is this room getting even smaller? I search desperately for a subject change. "You mentioned a break-in?"

"Yeah, I left you a message."

"Right, but um…" I chew my lip, then clear my throat. "Was a police report filed?"

My question seems to irritate him judging by the firm set of his jaw. "Of course."

"Does that happen there often?"

He slams back the rest of his beer and burps, seeming to love the way I recoil when he does. "Well, freckles, if you're asking if people get their shit stolen around here the answer would be yes, but only dumbfucks who don't remember to lock up their bikes or leave their wallets on the front seat of their car."

I blanch at his condescending tone. "Are you implying that I'm a…*dumbfuck*?"

He shrugs and his glare tightens. "No, your door was locked. They got in through the window."

"Did the thieves get anything of value?"

"Not that they had on them."

"Did the authorities—"

"Do you always talk like this?"

I pop a hand on my hip and even though picking a fight with a hot guy is very much not something Celia would do, I do it anyway. "What's wrong with the way I talk?"

"How many more questions do you have in that pretty head of yours?"

My mouth shuts, my mind goes blank.

He called me pretty.

I'm the twin who gets compliments on my eye color or my SAT scores. I'm the dedicated one, the one who would get a decent job, makes employee of the month, but I've never been called *pretty*. Celia and I are identical, but neither of us are spectacular looking. Our eyes are too big, our lips too full. But Celia has the expert-level makeup application skills to accentuate her everyday features and transform them to bombshell-worthy. Me? Other than the concealer to cover my freckles, I'm a blush and mascara girl. Blunt shoulder-length hair because it's easier to manage, and my best features get lost within my underachieving beauty regimen.

I open my mouth to say just that, but then remember he thinks I'm Celia and slam it shut again.

"That's better." He tosses his empty beer and it soars a good ten feet before landing in the trash. "Is there anything else I can help you with?"

"No," I whisper.

"Right, well, if you don't mind, me and my stinky unorganized ass are ready to throw some fish on the grill and get drunk."

What is it with this guy? Maybe showing up on his boat is some kind of maritime offense?

I follow him out and the sun has completely disappeared and left a sprinkling of stars in its place. I pass the hunched-over man with the weird eye and give a quick finger wave. "Nice meeting you."

"You be careful now." He attempts to get up and help me off the boat, but a stern look from Aden sits him back down with a *humph*.

"I'll walk you to the gate." Aden steps off the boat and onto the dock as if there isn't a foot of water separating the two. He offers me his hand, which is surprising after our heated interaction inside.

I take it and hold my breath while stepping off, making sure this time to steer clear of colliding with his big body. "Thanks, but I got it from here." I slip my shoes back on.

"I'm walking you to the gate," he growls, and again I wonder how I so easily piss this guy off.

I follow behind him trying hard not to check out the way his shoulder muscles bunch under the thin fabric of his tee, or the way his biceps stretch out the sleeve.

He hits a button on the gate, which releases the lock and swings it open. After I walk through I thank him but he remains in place.

"I'm good now. I have an Uber waiting."

It wasn't necessary to point out the car because when I peer back at Aden he's glaring right at it. "You came in that?"

"Yeah."

He blinks and seems to shake something off. "Be safe, Celia."

I flinch at his calling me my sister's name, then nod and scurry off before I say something else to upset him. Or worse, spill the truth.

I'm not Celia, and I need to pack and be on a plane to Phoenix before I slip up any more than I already have.

ADEN

"I'm tellin' ya, the thing had to be close to a thousand pounds. My line snapped so hard the recoil threw my pole forty feet!" Avery's booming voice drowns out the classic rock filtering from the jukebox speakers.

"Bullshit," I mumble into my whiskey glass while the washed-up sailor to the right of me continues on with his fish story.

Others chime in, making this another typical night at the Office. Too many dicks in one room make for a lot of shit talk.

The dive bar is right on the marina so I don't have to worry about getting a DUI added to my already growing record with the SDPD. I stare at the old black-and-white photos behind the bar, images taken back when the Portuguese dominated the tuna fishing industry here over a hundred years ago. This bar was built as a gathering spot for the men when they pulled into port. Not a damn thing has changed. I'd argue the place smells worse now than it did back then, but it does the job it's supposed to. No windows, no frilly features, just a wall of booze and a place to sit.

In the last few months I've become a regular and no matter when I show up—morning, noon, or night—my seat that backs up against the wall at the end of the bar is always empty and waiting like an old friend, which is exactly what I needed tonight.

"Colt, you remember when I caught that marlin!" Spit flies from Avery's slurring mouth. "Ask Colt, he was there."

I don't answer because it's all bullshit. That marlin was 240 pounds, but I'll let the asshole have his moment.

I find when I'm in this kind of mood I'm better off keeping my mouth shut.

After walking Celia to the gate I felt itchy, like sand crabs were burrowing under my skin. The mild confrontation with her sparked an edginess I can't shake. When I made it back to my boat I could still pick up the lingering scent of her perfume or whatever the hell that was I could smell on her skin and for some fucked up reason it made me restless. Nowhere near ready to hit the sheets, Jenkins and I decided to drop by the Office for a little sleep aid.

Nick, the bartender and owner, slides another glass of amber liquid in front of me and I nod my thanks.

"No way you caught no thousand-pound anything using that shit bait." Jenkins knocks back his drink and Avery glares at him.

"Shit bait? What the fuck are you talkin' 'bout, old man?"

They go back and forth and the argument turns to static as the liquor courses through my veins and numbs just about everything.

Feeling eyes on me I look across the bar and lock onto a familiar smile.

Sydney.

I lift my glass and she takes that as an invite over as she puts her tray down on the bar and heads my way.

I wish I could say that her presence made my pulse race like it used to. When I first met her I looked forward to her shift ending so I could take her back to my boat. Over time I've lost my taste for a lot of things and as much fun as she has been, I'm beginning to get bored with it all.

"Hey, Colt." She leans against the wall next to me.

I turn my head, but my elbows stay firmly planted on the bar. "Syd, how's it going?"

She shrugs, her eyes scanning the small bar. "Eh…it's been a slow night. I think Nick's gonna cut me soon."

Sydney's a good girl. I've learned she's led a rough life and at the age of thirty she's what I call a career waitress. She's beautiful, long dark hair that kisses her lower back and almond-shaped brown eyes that would make any man long for the bedroom.

She's the perfect diversion and I'm ashamed to say I've used her for that more times than I'm proud to admit.

"Is that right?" I turn more fully to her, my knees opened, and her eyes drop to my crotch. Yeah, I figured as much.

Thing is, as much as I've used Sydney, she's used me too. It's an unspoken agreement we have that's worked well.

"You feel like hanging out?" There's no expectation, no hopeful expression, it's always been easy between us, like asking someone if they want to go catch a movie.

Although, there will be no movie, no charming or need for seduction. Just sex.

When I don't answer her right away, she continues.

"Maybe when I'm off I could grab a couple drinks here and then we could head back to your boat."

"Make it fast." I nod to my drink. "Few more of these and I won't be much use to you."

She smiles and there's a tingling between my legs. Ah-ha, not totally numb...yet.

"No drinks, then." She scurries back to her station at the other side of the bar and has a word with Nick.

Jenkins mumbles something at my side.

"You got something to say?" I throw back a healthy mouthful of whiskey.

He stares at me with his good eye, then shakes his head. "You're a fool, Colt."

I toss back the rest of my drink and fish a few twenties from my wallet. "Tell me something I don't know, asshole."

I push up from my stool and cross to the door where Sydney's waiting. Throwing my arm over her shoulder I push through the door and lean into her ear. "You're too good to me."

Her arm wraps around my lower back. "You're not so shabby yourself, Colt."

What a joke.

If she only knew.

FOUR

SAWYER

It's too early to be awake.

Lying on Celia's couch staring out the window the ocean is barely visible through a thick layer of fog that rolled in sometime in the middle of the night. At least the sun is coming up, which means no more wrestling with sleep while organizing my to-do lists in my head.

After getting in the Uber at the marina last night I had the driver take me to a nearby grocery store to pick up a few things. It was dark when I got back to Celia's, and when I opened the door I was hit with the overly sweet and pungent stench of rotting food. The light switch wouldn't work so I fumbled around the kitchen using the flashlight from my phone and found some matches and candles. Perfect timing too, because shortly after I lit the final candle my phone died. Without electricity I managed to clear out the rotting disaster in the fridge and toss it in the dumpster out back.

The bedroom was even darker and was stuffy and hot from being locked up for months so I dragged my tired body to the living room.

Opening all the windows helped to air out the stagnant space, and even with the rhythmic crashing of waves filtering in through the screens, I wasn't able to do more than doze off a few times.

I kick the afghan from my legs and push to sit up, my back stiff from the thin cushion on the bamboo-framed couch. Stretching, I rub my eyes and blink until my vision clears. I peruse my surroundings as I'm finally able to see the room in the light.

It's a little over double the size of Aden's living space in his boat, but unlike Aden's place every square inch of Celia's home is covered in personal touches. The walls are painted in a pale coral and any artwork she has is clearly of the handmade variety—all of them abstract and colorful. There are a couple tall bookshelves, a small table with mismatched chairs that seats only two, and a handful of items that it looks like she picked up from her travels. A Native American rain stick, bongos, and a funky-looking vase that has to be four feet tall. It's a lot for the modest space, making me feel cramped and anxious. I need to get organized.

First things first, I need to scribble out my to-do list. My legs ache a bit when I stand and I feel like a ninety-year-old woman when I walk to the kitchen to find something to write on. A small pad of paper in the shape of a sunflower sits on the countertop and I pull a pen from my purse.

Making lists always manages to bring me back to center. To focus on the task at hand, the things I can control.

Electricity takes the number one spot. Maybe I can drive into town and find an electrician—

Movement from outside catches my eye. I squint through the thinning fog to see a well-built man, shirt off, hat on backward, jogging away from the cottages. I guess I can see why this place appealed to Celia; the view isn't just *good*, it's spectacular.

ADEN

The sky is finally light by the time I hit my stride on Sunset Cliffs. It's not my usual route, but it's longer than the jogging trail I take along the marina.

After waking up with the sound of small-round fire still popping in my head I needed to move and couldn't get far enough away from the guilt. That pain in the back of my throat and tightness in my chest wouldn't let up.

The soles of my running shoes grit along the sandstone while NOFX blasts in my ears. I focus on the words and the steady beat of my footsteps, my muscles warm and soft and on the verge of exhaustion. The occasional surfer or jogger snags my attention reminding me that the warmer summer weather will fill the beaches today. Best I get my shit moving and get back on the boat and out on the open sea.

Crowds make me anxious as fuck.

A chain-link fence looms up ahead, and I instinctively slow my pace not realizing how far I'd run. I haven't been to that spot since the day the city put up the protective barrier, never wanting to be reminded of what happened there or how low I'd sunk.

I turn my back on it and face north toward town, the sun beginning to shine on La Jolla's hilltops and burning off what's left of the marine layer. The ocean breeze cools my sweaty skin and I prop my hands on my hips to catch my breath.

Was it only months ago that I stood in this very same position in a very different location? I can still feel the weight of my IBA on my shoulders and my M4 in my hands. As if on cue a jet engine roars above my head, the first flight out of San Diego airport. I turn my music up to drown out the sound, but fuck, it's like I can feel the vibration beneath my feet.

My palms sweat and my pulse jerks inside my veins. No, it's too early for this shit. I shake off the urge to study my surroundings, to analyze the surfers standing watching the waves, or the single guy walking his purse dog.

Let it go, Aden.

I jog back to the cottages, keeping my focus trained to the ocean as a reminder to my brain and my body that I'm no longer surrounded by mountains and villages that camouflage the enemy. That I'm as far from war as I could possibly be, and more importantly, that no one is out to kill me.

Pushing my muscles to the extreme I hope to hit my heart hard so exertion will out-pump my fluttering fears. It works, and when the row of eight beach huts comes into view I'm gasping for air, but breathing a lot easier.

I take the concrete path that leads to Cal's old place and focus on my breathing so I don't pass out. Sensing a presence to my left, my eyes snap up. Celia's standing on her porch, one hand white-knuckling the rail, with those same expressive eyes aimed at me.

I pop my earbuds out and study her. There are dark circles beneath her eyes and all that thick hair is piled high in a mess on top of her head. Those freckles I saw last night are intensified in the light of day and while she nervously fumbles with the front of her oversized T-shirt, she pulls the wide neckline down low enough to see more of those freckles disappear between her cleavage.

"What are you doing here?"

I motion to Cal's place with a nod. "I work here."

"You're not wearing a shirt."

The corner of my mouth pulls up. "No, I went for a run." As if my sweat-soaked skin doesn't make that obvious. "You okay?"

She blinks and the shock bleeds from her expression. "Yes."

I take a few steps closer, not convinced. "Why do you look freaked out?"

She blinks again then visibly relaxes, but something about the way she does it seems forced, as if someone behind her presses her shoulders down from her ears. "I don't have electricity. I probably didn't pay the bill."

"Nah, electric is included." I'd expect her to know that. "Could be the breakers. I'll check it out."

I round the corner of her place to the back where the breaker box is. The soft thwacking of flip-flops echoes behind me, and she scurries to my side.

I pop open the rusty lid. "These boxes are old and the fuckin' salt air does them no favors."

"Should you have them replaced with new ones?" I can feel her heat at my side and with the endorphins filling my bloodstream her closeness is doing wicked things to my body. It's not that I'm a perv, I'm just always aware of my surroundings, occupational hazard, and something tells me the adorable Celia is without a bra and possibly panties.

Come on, Aden! Everything isn't a damn porno.

"Yeah. But it's expensive and Cal refuses to raise the rent." I palm the broken circuits and nod to her bright orange Volkswagen Thing that's parked by the dumpsters and in desperate need of a wash. "Did you check to see if it starts?"

"What?" She follows my line of sight and her lips curls in what seems like disgust. "That's…my car."

"Cal used to start it a few times a month, I guess." I rub the back of my neck, feeling like a bit of a fuckface. He asked me to do the same, but I never did. "The battery might be dead on it."

"Great." Her fingers tap almost impatiently against her bare thigh and I'm drawn to how stark white her skin is. I don't see a lot of pale skin here at the coast, never would've thought I'd even be attracted to the sickly-looking color, but I have an overwhelming urge to touch it and see if it feels as soft as it looks.

Her fingers ball into a fist and I realize it's probably because I'm staring right at them. I slide my gaze back to her eyes and sure enough they're resting uncomfortably on me. "I'll go get those new circuits, get you all set up."

Maybe grab a cold shower and a reality check while I'm at it.

SAWYER

I've never been the type of woman to swoon. I've always found it petty and reserved for women who don't think with their heads but rather their hormones. But being around a sweaty, shirtless Aden, I wouldn't be surprised if I had those cartoon hearts throbbing in my eyes. And I hate sweat. It always grosses me out, but leave it to Aden to make even perspiration sexy. Every time I manage the strength to act unaffected, he throws me off with that lopsided grin as if he can read my thoughts and finds them highly x-rated and totally doable.

Those shoulders that look as if they've spent a decent number of hours pumping iron, round balls of muscle that pulse under the smoothest-looking skin. And judging by his tan I'd say Aden spends a good deal of his day outside without a shirt, and why not? Hell, the city of San Diego probably pays the guy to walk around topless as an act of goodwill.

Luckily he can't see me gawking as he walks away, his back straight, chin held high like a man with confidence, accustomed to commanding whatever space he's in and doing so unapologetically. Which makes sense now that I've seen his tattoo. Scrolled from one shoulder blade to the other are the words *Death before Dishonor* and in the middle there's a dagger going through a skull wearing a military-style beret. So Aden is in the military. That explains a lot.

Does he still serve? Maybe he's home on leave?

I jerk when I realize I'm still standing in the same spot by the circuit box with my mouth gaping at where Aden disappeared around the corner. I wander back inside and grab my list and pretend that the round paper against my linear list isn't irritating the hell out of me. Paper should be rectangular, square maybe, but never a circle.

Forcing my mind on the things that need to get done, because thoughts of Aden Colt will get me nowhere, I run everything through my mind.

Starting at the top. I outline the word *electricity* and my stomach jumps at the idea of crossing it off once Aden gets the breakers replaced.

I add car battery to the list and frown just thinking about how I'm going to get that rusted piece of metal back to Phoenix. Maybe I can leave it here, it'll get towed eventually, Celia never has to know.

Last night I found the Yellow Pages under Celia's sink. It's a little water damaged but I managed to find a place in town that sells boxes. They don't open until nine so until then…I look around the room and as much as I love how the chaos of it all fits my sister's personality, the lack of uniformity makes me agitated.

A click sounds followed by the hum of power. Yes! I draw a line through my number one to-do and am instantly reenergized. Aden's head passes by the window as he rounds the porch. Oh crap, he's coming in.

I hop up from the table and straighten my shirt just in time before he pops his head in. "Hey."

I wave pathetically.

His dark eyes study me and narrow. "Can I come in?"

"Oh, um…" I look around as if the messy room will give me a reason to say no, but I find nothing helpful and resign to the inevitable. "Sure."

He steps inside, his eyebrows dropped low as if he's on a mission. He finds a lamp and clicks it on, then stands and props his hands on his hips in a way that draws my eyes to that spot where the muscles form a V and a light dusting of dark hair peeks up from his shorts. "You should check the bedroom."

"Good idea." I hop and whirl around as if his words sent an electric shock through my central nervous system. I give him my back so he doesn't see the furious blush coloring my face. With such pale skin I've never been able to hide my embarrassment. I scurry to the bedroom, clicking on the lights, and return hoping Aden will be outside because being in this tiny space with him is smothering.

No such luck. "They work."

"Did you check to see if anything had been taken?"

I wouldn't know so I just nod. "Yep, everything's here."

"Hmm, that's what I thought." He moves over to the bookshelf, his eye caught on something. "I was pretty sure I got to them before they managed to grab anything."

I'm stuck staring at his back as he studies the bookshelf so it takes a second to register what he'd said. "Wait...you *caught* the guys who broke in?"

He makes an affirmative grunt. "No big deal, heard something that didn't sound right for three-thirty in the morning, came to check it out and saw two guys rootin' around in there."

"I thought you lived on the boat?"

His eyes slide to mine but only for a second before he's back to studying a photo. "I do, but I used to stay here in Cal's old place."

I open my mouth to ask why he moved.

"You ran with the bulls in Pamplona?"

"Ha! Yeah right—"

He plucks a framed photo off the shelf and flips it to face me.

I bite my lip remembering I'm not me, I'm Celia. "You betcha'."

His mouth twists at my response and he turns back to the bookshelf. "Huh, you don't strike me as a risk taker."

My chin tucks back into my throat. "How would you know what

I am? You know nothing about me." Or maybe I need to try harder to not be *me*.

"African safari." He plucks another photo from the shelf. "Is that a lion you're petting?" He stares down at the frame.

"Uh-huh…" I think.

"How did you get close enough to pet a lion?"

Great question. "They have, like, a lion whisperer. He got the lion to let us pet him." Please, don't ask more.

"It's some kind of big cat sanctuary?" He's still studying the photo. Sanctuary, of course! "Mm-hm."

He pulls at another framed photo. "From Africa to…Vegas?"

"I like to travel."

"Who's the dude?"

"A friend." I think.

He narrows his eyes. "You're kissing him."

I cross to him and snatch the photo away. "He was a good friend." I put it back on the shelf, then groan when I see a handful more. This was a mistake, I can't explain all these.

He reaches over my shoulder and pulls another one down. "You're with a different guy in almost all these pictures."

"I have a lot of guy friends."

He frowns. "Huh…" He studies another photo. "Friends with benefits."

A flash of heat ignites behind my ribs and I rip the picture from his hand. "Why don't you mind your own business."

He steps back and holds his hands up in surrender. "Easy there, freckles. I was just making an observation."

"Well…" I flip a few photos facedown. "Your observation is wrong."

"I'm not judging. Nothing wrong with a woman who uses sex to get what she wants." He shrugs and hits me with that lazy grin that only works to further upset me.

"You think you can come into this house, see a few pictures, and think you know me? That you can throw your *observations* around like you're some pillar of virtue?"

He doesn't seem at all fazed, and tilts his head watching with interest as I completely lose my shit.

"So what, ya know? So what if I dated guys who could take me on these fabulous trips, huh? That doesn't make me a slut, it makes me a go-getter. It's not like both parties weren't enjoying themselves. Stop looking at me like that!"

"I don't know what you're talking about."

"You're looking at me like I'm pathetic all while implying that Celia is a slut."

His eyebrows pop high on his forehead and I freeze at the realization of what I've done.

I grab the first photo I see and shove it in his face. "This girl, Celia, me, is living life to the fullest."

He eyes the photo then chuckles. "*Yeah*, she is." He squints. "Those real?"

I flip the photo around and then smash it to my chest. "Pretend you didn't see that." God, Cece, Stephen Tyler signing your boobs?

My breath saws in and out of my lungs as I try desperately to regain my composure. "Listen…" I place the photo on the shelf, facedown. "I'm moving out. It'll take me a week or so to pack up and arrange for movers. Since I'm paid through to December I'm going to need to get a prorated refund for the months I won't be here."

He crosses his arms at his chest and I almost get distracted by how the position accentuates his biceps. "'Fraid I can't do that."

"Of course you can."

"No, you signed a one-year lease. If you leave before your lease is up, that's on you."

"You're joking."

"I'm not."

"That's not right."

He shrugs.

"It's unconstitutional!" My high-pitched shriek bounces off the walls.

"It's contractual."

"So that's it, you're not going to help me."

"I'm trying to help you, but you're asking for something I can't do. It's out of my hands, freckles."

My hands fist uncontrollably at my sides and damn him and his growing smirk.

"I expected more from a military man."

All the humor in his face dissolves. *Gotcha!*

"Isn't your motto to protect and serve?"

"I ain't a cop."

"No, you're not. A cop would have enough integrity to prorate my money back."

"Feel better?" It's casual but I don't miss the tick in his jaw.

"Guess the whole military respect thing is a foreign concept to you."

The light spark in his eyes dies and he stares at me blank-faced, completely emotionless.

I should stop, but Celia is dying and what kind of sister would I be if I just sit here and let him talk like she's some money-hungry whore. "I guess I shouldn't expect much from someone who *kills people* for money!"

"Fuck this." He turns and stomps to the door, slamming it behind him so hard the walls shake.

I expect him to take a hard left in the direction of his cottage, but instead he jogs toward the beach.

"Dammit." I huff out a breath, the anger in my blood calming with the growing distance he put between us.

Guilt washes in, but I push it back. I may have attacked his integrity, but he deserved it.

Okay, so he didn't exactly call Celia a slut, I suppose all he did was point out the obvious. But no one talks shit about my sister. No one. Not even good-looking military men who go out of their way to get my electricity back up.

I plug in my phone and once it's charged enough to turn on I dial my sister's number all while ignoring the weird heaviness in my chest.

"So?" She answers right away but sounds tired. "Tell me how much you love my life."

"Celia…this was such a stupid idea."

"I got your message last night. Stop sounding so miserable and talk to me."

I sigh and drop back to the couch as far as the phone charging cord will let me. "I think we should've talked a little more before I agreed to do this. Why didn't you tell me about Brice?"

"Is he still there?" She laughs. "Man…we had some fun times together."

"He kissed me!"

"Toe curling, right?" How can she sound so excited when I feel like I've been put through an emotional wood chipper?

"That's not the point."

"Of course it's the point. Tell me right now you didn't enjoy that kiss."

I did. I totally did. "It was awkward, Cece. I don't even know the guy!"

"So what? Haven't you ever kissed someone you don't know before?"

I roll my lips between my teeth.

"Your lack of response tells me all I need to know." She huffs out a breath. "Jeez, Sawyer, you needed this more than I thought."

"You should've told me."

"If I had you'd go in with too many expectations."

"Did you know your place had been broken into?"

"No."

"Mr. Hurtado's nephew runs the place now, he said he left a message."

"I don't listen to those." There's sadness in her voice. "I don't want to know about everything going on outside of my bedroom. It only reminds me of what I'm missing."

"Yeah." I guess I can understand that.

"So you have to have sex with Brice."

"Celia!"

"Shhh…" She laughs quietly. "You'll give us away."

"I have a lot to do, I just wanted to call and tell you I hate you for making me do this."

"You love me. And if you have sex with Brice you'll *really* love me."

"Oh my GAWD!"

She's still laughing! "I promise when you get back to Phoenix and your nine-to-five life you'll thank me for making you do this."

"Maybe." So far I've met a gorgeous man who kissed me until my head spun, and an even better-looking, albeit rougher man who managed to excite me as much as he drove me crazy. "How are you feeling?"

"Fantastic. I have a ton of energy, might even go run some errands with Mom today."

I grin to myself. "That's good news."

"All right, go pack up my stuff, and Sawyer?"

"Yeah."

"Don't be afraid to have a little fun. You've earned it."

"Love you."

"Yeah, you do."

"Bye."

What do I do now? A small voice in the back of my head says I need to find Aden and apologize, even though that's the last thing I want to do.

Digging into my pocket I pull out the single quarter Celia gave me and I close my eyes. "Tails I apologize, heads I get packing."

I toss the coin and when I hear it land on the hardwood floor with a thump, I squat down to learn my fate.

"Shit." This should be interesting.

FIVE

ADEN

I'm always amazed by how different the sun feels at the same temperature in different locales. How the same ball of flaming gas can feel like a blowtorch blasting against me when I'm belly down in the dirt staring through the scope of my rifle, and a warm blanket when I'm on the boat, hunched over an ice chest pulling out a cold beer.

Granted, no one's trying to kill me when I'm grabbing a beer, I suppose that could be a contributing factor.

"Where're you headin', Colt?" Jenkins's rusty cough caused by a lifetime of cheap cigars comes closer.

Somewhere far the fuck away from here. "San Clemente Island."

He smells like stale smoke, bait, and wood rot, like any old-timer fisherman should. "Yellowtail's bitin'."

I crack open the pop-top on my beer and help myself to that first refreshing swig that soothes a bit of the fury left over from my encounter with Celia this morning. "You putting in your dinner order?"

"Damn straight." He wobbles off, half hunched over from years of slinging fish. "I'll be at the Office."

His unsteady gate down the dock reminds me of what Celia looked like negotiating the planks in those ridiculous heels.

What the hell does Cal see in that woman? I mean, besides her being attractive, which she most definitely is, but not in an obvious way. I suppose my uncle being a dirty old man, he may have been able to look past her uptight attitude. Where's the girl from the picture? I didn't see even a hint of the carefree smile that screams of a well-loved life. And really, how can she be pissed at me for asking questions about photos she has proudly displayed in her place? Makes no fucking sense.

And her response, bagging on the military, the men who've become more family to me than my own blood, the men who died horrific deaths defending her freedom to be a bitch. She's got some fucking nerve.

I bring the beer to my lips and my hand shakes uncontrollably. Shit. I squeeze the can so hard it dents and drain what's left of the beer. And here I was doing so well.

I go about readying the boat for a day at sea, away from people who only manage to grate against my nerves just by breathing. There's something so calming about being on the ocean, as far away from the desert and valleys that constantly haunt me. When I've got a pole in my hands they don't shake, and my thoughts don't drift to all I did wrong and all I lost.

With the bait hold full of sardines I check my gas gauge, poles, and step on the dock to untie. It's when I'm untying the bow I hear a voice that makes my skin vibrate, whether it's with interest or irritation, I'm not sure.

"Aden!"

Fuck. How the hell did she get past the gate? Maybe if I pretend I don't see her she'll leave.

I toss the tie-up ropes into the boat and move to the other side, but she intercepts me. Persistent little thing. "What do you want, Celia?"

She opens those thick lips, closes them, licks them, and fuck, I can't take much more of that. Is it bad that I want to suck the mouth off a girl I can't stand? I sidestep her and move to untie the other side of the boat. She follows on my heels.

"Aden, please, I'm—"

I get right in her face. Damn if the way she stumbles over herself isn't cute as shit. "You're what."

She gasps and her wide green eyes move from my nose to my mouth to my chin and I curse under my breath because it feels like she's stroking me with them. "I'm sorry."

"Okay." I slide around her again and climb on board.

Her arms drop to her sides and she watches as if she expects me to say more, but the truth is, I've never been good at relationships, friendships, fuckships, all ships I pretty much fail at. Boats I know. Boats I'm good at.

I fire up the engine.

"Wait, Aden!" She scrambles around to the stern and grips the side.

What the fuck is she doing?

She throws a leg up over the rail—I dart to the edge and grab her to wrangle her flailing body on board. "Are you fucking crazy? You can't jump on a boat when the prop's on!"

She pushes her shoulder-length hair behind her ears, her face pale.

Staring up at me, there's something in her eyes, a vulnerability that calls to every male cell in my body to fix whatever it is inside her that's broken, which is fucking bullshit. I don't even know this girl.

I release her shoulders and stomp back to the cockpit to shut off the prop, then whirl on her. "Get off."

Her eyebrows pinch together and she tucks her chin in, something

I'm beginning to notice she does often. "You're kicking me off your boat?"

"I'm going fishing, so unless you feel like playing deckhand all day, yes. Get off."

She rolls those lips between her teeth and I have to look away to squelch the desire to kiss this obnoxious broad. She turns around suddenly and heads to the stern but freezes with her hand on the latched door. Then she pulls something from the waistband of her skirt, something small. She looks down at whatever it is, her shoulders slump, and she turns back toward me. "I'll stay."

"What?!" Is she insane?

She defies everything I thought I picked up from her and stomps to my side. "I'm staying."

"I think you're making a mistake."

She rolls a silver coin between her fingers before tucking it back into her waistband. "I think you're probably right."

Fuckin' hell, this woman! "Fine." I turn and throw open the floor storage to snag a faded orange life vest. It smells like mildew but it'll do the job. I hold it out to her. "Put this on. You wear it at all times."

The light breeze brings the scent right to her and she crinkles up her nose.

"Do you, um…I mean, is it possible to get a cleaner one?"

I thrust it toward her.

Using her fingers like pincers she takes it and slides her arms through the holes. Acting like she'll contract some fatal disease by touching it, she fumbles with the straps and clasps.

"Fuck, this'll take all damn day." I push her hands out of the way and fasten the straps, tightening them until I'm satisfied it won't come off.

Then I turn my back on her to fire up the engine and pull out of the slip. "I got two rules on my boat," I yell to her so she can hear me. "One, deckhands bait line. That's it."

She doesn't reply but as I negotiate steering the boat away from the dock I catch her slowly sliding into a seat.

"Two, all deckhands drink beer on my boat."

I peek down to see her arms wrap around her middle as the wind throws her hair around her face. Poor girl looks miserable. I grin to myself.

This might actually be fun.

I always did love a good torture session.

SAWYER

I'm on a boat. A real boat headed out into the middle of the ocean with a man I've known for twelve hours and managed to insult. Despite my apology, he's hardly looked me in the eye. If the firm set of his jaw is any indication, I'd say he's still pissed.

I don't have time to concentrate on that. Right now all I can worry about is the two possible outcomes brought to me by using Celia's stupid effing coin—I'm either going to throw up all over myself or die.

The farther away from land we go the more intense the ocean swells get, tossing the boat around with increasing aggression. Every muscle in my body is flexed to the point of pain, my hair is a massive crown of knots, and no matter how many times I try to slick it down, the wind manages to pull it back up. Not to mention I was not at all dressed for a day on a boat, not that I'd even know what's appropriate for that, but my guess is a long skirt, tank top, and flip-flops only works in Ralph Lauren ads.

Okay, so sue me for wanting to look nice when I apologized. I stared at my clothing options for an hour before I finally dug through Celia's closet looking for something halfway between sexy conservative and full-blown hooker. The skirt is long but sexy and tie-dyed in different shades of blue. I paired it with a navy blue spaghetti-strap tank that accentuates what little curves I have. The downside of the tank is my pasty skin is going to get fried out here in the sun. That's okay; a sunburn I can get over, but death is hard to come back from.

I attempt to soothe my nerves by coming up with a plan for every possible scenario. Aden's boat is equipped with shelter for a hurricane, a life ring if I go overboard, a bathroom for peeing or vomiting—whichever comes first. On cue my gut rolls in protest.

I feel full even though I haven't eaten anything but a muffin and a cup of coffee, and yet something tells me if I coughed hard enough I'd lose everything in my stomach including, possibly, the organ itself.

Stop being such a wimp, Sawyer. Celia would do this, there's no reason I can't do it too.

The internal pep talk continues for a while until land fades and there's nothing but water three hundred and sixty-five degrees around us. I don't know how long we've been going, but the sound of the roaring engine and slap of the waves against the boat start to lull me to an acceptance of my fate. I'm stuck on a boat at sea with nothing but a contagious flotation device to protect me. If the ocean doesn't kill me, whatever creeping fungus living in this thing around my neck will.

My eyes scan the water encompassing the vessel, keeping a lookout for a huge dorsal fin. The ominous *du-dum*, *du-dum*, *du-dum dudum* plays over and over in my head. This boat does kind of remind me of Quint's. My pulse speeds. I'm going to *die*. I curse Celia for putting this damn coin in my hand. This was a mistake, a huge mistake.

I'm breathing in through my nose and out through my mouth when the boat slows and the engine cuts. Aden's powerful legs come into view and I tilt my head back to peer up at him.

His light brown hair is streaked lighter in places from the sun, and though it's not long enough to be a mess from the wind, it's angled away from his forehead and strong brow line.

He pushes his sunglasses up. "You look like you're gonna puke."

Hearing the word calls the urge to do just that even closer to the surface. "It's a possibility."

He grunts, then turns and ducks into the belly of the boat. I stand up and sway with the rocking of the waves, which does nothing for my stomach. I grip the railing and look down into the water. It's dark blue and so deep there's no way I'd be able to see in time to react if a shark jumped up and pulled me under—*oh God*.

I stumble back at the thought and hit a solid wall of muscle. Steel bands come around my waist to steady me and I'm hit with the scent of soap, sunblock, and beer.

"Sit." He motions to a padded bench seat that runs along the side of the deck.

I start to ask if we're safe out here, but decide that's not something Celia would say, so instead I nod. He guides me there, then hands me a little white pill and a bottle of water.

"What is it?"

"It'll help with the motion sickness."

I try not to think too hard on the fact that there's no way he washed his hands before palming the tablet. "Oh, thank you." I stare at the pill and prepare to toss it to the back of my throat, but again...I don't know this guy. What if he's trying to drug me so he can push me off the boat and leave me out here to drown? I'm still staring at it when suddenly his nose appears just inches from mine. Bracing his hand on the railing at my back he glares at me with a fierceness that makes me cower.

"Regardless of what you *think* you know about my integrity, Celia Forrester, I would never...ever...hurt a woman, understand?"

His nearness combined with his rumbled demand has me frozen beneath his gaze.

"Tell me you understand that."

My eyelids flutter.

His expression turns sad. "Cece…"

I startle at his calling me by my sister's nickname.

"Cal adores you. You're practically family." He pushes an errant hair that got stuck between my lips off my face.

I lean forward, drawn to his tender touch.

"I'm sorry about the conclusions I drew from seeing your photos. And I'm sorry about being a dick earlier. Just…" God, his voice is so soft, so vulnerable. "Take the pill."

His command is firm and the sincerity I hear in his voice is impossible to deny.

"Here's to swimming with bow-legged women," I mumble, and toss the pill to the back of my throat, then wash it down with enough water to get the job done without overfilling my sensitive stomach.

"Was that a quote from *Jaws*?"

I smile and tug on the collar of my infectious life vest. Truth is, while Celia was out seeing the world, I was home experiencing the Hollywood version of it. "Yeah."

He stares at my lips until I shift uncomfortably.

"Right." He pushes up and puts some much needed space between us. "That should kick in pretty quick."

"Thank you."

He squints out into the ocean then tilts his chin. "See that?"

Gripping the rail firmly to make sure I don't topple over the edge, I follow his line of sight to see a cluster of birds diving into the water. "Are they—" I'm robbed of breath when I see my worst fear materialize in the distance. "Sharks!" I clutch my gut and drop back down to my seat, my pulse pounding in my neck. "Oh God, we're gonna die!"

"Porpoises." He moves around me with all the control and elegance of a man who is comfortable negotiating the unsteady footing of a boat out in open sea. "And they don't kill people."

It's a good thing he never met my sister because he'd know right away I'm not her. Hell, she'd already be swimming circles around the boat, probably naked, with a bag of old bread to feed the fish with. She sure as heck wouldn't be swallowed up by her fear, balled into a semi-fetal position on the verge of passing out.

"The porpoises and birds follow the schools of sardines." He grabs a fishing pole and messes with the thin line. "The yellowfin are below the sardines."

I blow out a long relieved breath. "Not sharks. Okay." I can do this. What would Celia do? "So how do we catch them?"

"*You* are a deckhand. You won't be catching anything."

"So…what will I be doing?"

My question seems to intrigue him. He smiles. It's slight, slow, and sends butterflies through my belly. "Stand up."

He leans the tall pole against a single chair sitting in the middle of the back of the boat. I stand and wobble a bit with the instability of the rocking waves. His warm callused hands grip my shoulders to steady me. "You good?"

"Yeah, I think so." I don't know what's making me dizzier, the ocean or his proximity.

He steps back and runs his eyes down my body in a clinical way and I'm surprised to feel disappointed in his lack of interest at what he sees. "This won't do." He drops to a squat at my feet and cups my calves over the cotton of my skirt.

I sway. My hand shoots out to brace myself against his shoulder. He runs those big hands up the back of my legs, taking the fabric with them and stopping behind my knees that are now practically knocking together with nerves.

"What're you—"

With a jerk to the material he bunches it between my thighs and ties it in a knot, front to back. Great, now I look like I'm wearing a saggy diaper. "Much better."

Reluctantly I drop my hand from his shoulder so he can stand.

"Not that I don't appreciate the effort, but a skirt isn't appropriate for deckhand work." He stares at me for another second, then turns to the doorway that leads into the cabin and snags something from inside. He shakes open a pair of dark sunglasses, classic black Ray-Bans, and slides them on my face. Then he pops an old faded green ball cap on my head. It smells like dead fish and has sweat rings circling the base. I'm tempted to throw it off and douse my hair in hand sanitizer, but what would Celia do?

I reach up and tug the hat farther down my forehead, hoping he doesn't notice my fingers tremble while the fear of lice and random skin diseases flitter through my mind.

"There. Now you're ready." He winks, then pulls the pole from its lean-to and motions for me to join him at the back corner of the boat.

I follow and he flips open a lid, then directs me to peek inside. I shuffle up to his side and peer into the container to see it's filled with water and little fish.

"Bait."

I swallow back a gag. "They're alive."

He chuckles. "These big fish ain't stupid." He reaches in and snags a sardine about half the size of his palm. It flips around in his grip, its mouth gaping. "You wanna hook it here, right behind the eye."

"What?" I step back. "I'm not doing that."

"Of course you are." He tilts his head and meets me with a glare that I wish was more intimidating than it was attractive because I'm really trying to be tough here, but when he looks at me like that it's impossible. "You jumped on my boat, I gave you a chance to get off, and you chose to stay. No one gets a free ride. You're here, you work." He holds up the fish, swiftly slides the hook into the thing's head, and smiles. "There." He heads to the opposite side of the boat and with a powerful flick of his arm he casts the line out toward the cluster of porpoises. He drops the pole into a metal tube attached to the backside rail, then grabs another rod.

My stomach drops.

"Your turn." He shoves it into my hands.

"You're crazy."

His eyes narrow on me again, but this time he's looking deeper, searching for something I'm glad he can't see behind the dark shades. "She eats raw oysters…runs with bulls, but she can't bait a hook."

I'm Celia.

Be Celia.

"Give me that!" I swipe the line from him.

"Careful, that hook will go right through your hand."

I bite back a snarky retort and hover over the small pool of little swimming fish. "So what, I just…" This is so gross. "Grab one?"

"That's right. The faster the better."

I lick my lips and feel his eyes on me, but I focus on the slimy scaled creatures that stand between me and my goal. I imagine the step-by-step instructions written out like a to-do list.

Number one, snag a fish.

My hand plunges into the tank. I miss. "Dammit."

"That's all right, try again. A little faster."

I nod and focus, then plunge again, faster. My fingers wrap around a slippery body but it wiggles free. "Crap!"

He pushes up behind me, the heat of his chest and abs through his thin tee warming the back of my arm. "Like this." His hand dives and snaps back with a fish. "Fast." He drops the victim back in. "Try again."

I belly right up to the tank. My pulse roars but with something different. Something I'm not used to feeling. It's unease, but it lacks the bite of fear. It feels like...excitement.

My hand darts into the water. Snaps back. And..."I did it!" I shove my fist into the air and whirl around to Aden. "I got one!"

His lips stretch into a full, wide grin and he laughs. "You did! Good job."

I feel energized by conquering something I feared that even the possibility of sharks just below my feet can't wipe the grin off my face. I mentally check off my number one. Moving to number two. "Now what?"

"Hook it." He points to a spot on the fish's head. "Right there."

I rake my teeth along my lower lip. He makes a funny sound in his throat.

"What?"

He clears his throat. "What?"

"You made a noise. Did I do something wrong?"

His eyes dart to my lips, then to the hook in my hand. "No, nothing. Go ahead."

I turn back to the second task on my mental list.

Hook the fish. I line the sharp point up with the silvery top of the creature's head. "I'm so sorry," I whisper. With a squeal and a retch I slide the hook through, surprised at how easily it goes in. "I did it."

"Like a pro."

A spot of red on my hand catches my eye. "Ugh!" I shake my hand like a wet dog, barely containing a full-blown freak-out.

He grabs my wrist midair and presses it to his firm belly. "Blood."

Panic seeps from my body with every swipe against his rippled abdomen as he cleans my palm on his shirt.

"All gone." He drops my hand and grabs a pole, leaving me to fight off an unmanageable blush. "All right, deckhand, it's time to pull in some fuckin' fish."

He demonstrates how to cast the line, but tells me casting isn't my job and directs me to a seat.

"You take the fighting chair." He helps me up into a seat that is fully equipped with padded armrests, drink holders, and even a place to put my feet. "Good, now open your legs." I almost expect there to be some kind of hidden innuendo in his request, but sadly he's all business. "The pole rests here between your thighs." He places the handle into a metal tube. "Beautiful."

I shift uncomfortably. "I thought you said I couldn't fish."

He leans against the side of the boat, his gaze cast out over the water. "You're not. You're watching that line for me and if you get a bite I'll take the chair."

"You don't trust me to reel it in myself?"

"These aren't lake trout, Celia. These fish could weigh hundreds of pounds. That chair is made for the hours-long fight it takes to reel them in." He stares at me and shakes his head. "Something's missing." He pops an ice-cold can of beer and slides it into my hand.

"Oh, no thanks. I don't really like beer."

"My boat. My rules." He takes a swig from his can, then nods to mine. "You drink."

It's hot. The beer's cold. It's something Celia would do. I tilt my head back and take a gulp. Huh...not bad. Why didn't I like beer?

The sun feels great on my bare shoulders and arms. I have a moment of anxiety where I think like Sawyer, think I don't need skin cancer, or a few thousand more freckles that will come and never go away after a day in the sun.

But rather than flip to decide what I should do, I go with the least responsible choice and close my eyes as I soak in the rays.

And damn, but maybe Celia wasn't totally wrong. In some situations, being carefree isn't half bad.

SIX

ADEN

This woman is a walking contradiction.

Nothing about her adds up.

Gorgeous face and body but no clue how to use them.

She's lived the life of an adrenaline junkie, but freaks out around live bait.

Even now, looking at her soft shoulders as the sun turns them a light shade of pink, I have to wonder when was the last time that beautiful skin had even seen the sun.

I'm on my third beer, the boat rocking gently, a fishing pole between my legs and Jimmy Buffett's "A Pirate Looks at 40" filtering through the speakers and I'm thinking thoughts that I should not be thinking about my uncle's favorite little tenant.

I crush my empty beer can and chuck it into the garbage.

Celia turns to me, startled by the sudden noise. "I think I lost my bait."

I grab a fresh beer from the cooler. "Reel it in, let's see."

She reels it in, her eyes on the line and her mouth pursed in concentration. "I felt a tug, but then nothing, and that was a long time ago."

I snag her line from the water and, sure enough, it's an empty hook. "Yep, you're fishing naked." I pass her the hook. "You know the drill."

I watch in fascination as she swings her leg over to slide off the fighting chair and moves to the bait tank. She doesn't ask for help, and after a few tries she snags a sardine and hooks it.

"I did it!" Her bright smile is almost blinding as she holds the baited hook up with pride.

"Good job."

"I'm the master!"

I shrug. "Eh…you have a great teacher."

She hands me the pole to cast. "Admit it, you didn't think I could do it."

"I had my doubts." It's too much to look right at her when she's dropped all the stuffy formal crap so I keep my eyes on the water. "You proved me wrong."

"So…you're saying I *am* the master."

"Fine." I settle back into my seat. "You're the master. Feel better?"

"I'm the master!" She yells it loud and out to no one.

"Baiter." I bite my lip to keep from laughing.

"I'm the master *baiter*!"

"Say it again, freckles." I can't stop laughing. "A little louder."

"Oh my gosh!" She's smiling so big and seeing it makes something uncoil in my chest. It's a weird feeling. I don't question it, but I'm grateful nonetheless.

"Oh, come on. Don't tell me girls don't do it, I know they do."

She brings her beer to her lips and mumbles, "Maybe the girls *you* date."

"I'll give you that." I turn away from her grinning face because looking at her smile makes me smile and then we're just smiling at each other, which makes me want to kiss her and I can't kiss her.

She clears her throat. "Where'd you learn to fish?"

"Grew up on the water."

"Here in San Diego?"

"North of Santa Barbara. My parents still live in the same house I was born in, my sister lives twenty minutes from there." I take a swig of my beer wondering why I'm giving away information she didn't ask for.

"You didn't want to stay close to your family?"

I tried. But being around my family only served as a reminder of how far I'd fallen. The pitying looks would only lead me to outbursts and I couldn't stand the way they'd look at me as if I were a stranger. I knew if I stayed I'd kill what little relationship we had left. "I'm only a four-hour drive away."

We stare ahead at the water as Jack Johnson's voice fills the space between us until I see her move out of the corner of my eye. She's pressing on the bright pink skin of her shoulder.

"Shit…you're burning." I shove off my chair and grab a bottle of sunscreen from inside the cabin.

She presses a delicate fingertip against her forearm. "I guess I am. It feels so nice, it kinda crept up on me."

I grunt and squirt a liberal amount of lotion into my palms, then push the thick life vest aside to expose the cap of her shoulder. She stiffens and I take advantage of the fact that she's locked in the fighting chair.

"I got it." I run my hands over her skin and—fuck me—it really is as soft as it looks. Warm, and like silk beneath my palms. Sliding my thumbs beneath the vest, I press into the tight muscles of her shoulder blades. Awfully tense for a woman who spends most of her life traveling. I could get lost in a moment like this, forget who she is, what she means to my uncle, and seduce the fuck out of her.

Get your head out of her pants!

I hurry to thoroughly cover her shoulders with sunscreen, then work my way to the tops of her arms.

She tenses again. "You don't have to do that. I can get my arms."

I'm sure she can, but I'm incapable of taking my hands off her.

"One of us needs our hands free in case we get a bite. Unless you want to trade—"

"No. I'm good."

I run my thumbs down the lean muscle of her forearm as the seconds tick by and she slowly relaxes under my hands. Her body falls limply forward as I move back up to her shoulders and massage there. *Walk away. Right fucking now.*

She hums low in her throat, a sweet and sultry signal to continue. If that's the noise she makes when she's being touched innocently, what kind of sounds would she make if I were touching her with purely sexual intentions? Who am I kidding? My thoughts regarding Celia are far from innocent.

Don't go there, Colt. I blame the beer, and the sun, and the quiet solitude of the sea. "What do you do for a living?" It's the first thing I think of as my hands refuse to release her.

"Accountant." Her spine goes upright as if she's holding her breath. "I mean…" She slips out from under my hands. "I think I'm good now. Thank you."

Hidden at her back, I adjust myself in my shorts before I move around to my chair. My dick may not care about social politeness, but I do. "So between your bucket list jaunts around the world, you're a number cruncher." I guess I could see that. Living the straight life in the city has to be boring as hell. I'd need to skydive on the weekends too just to remind myself I was still alive.

"Mm-hm." She peers over at me and not for the first time I regret giving her the sunglasses and wish I could see her eyes. "How about you? What branch of the military were you in?"

I hear nails on a chalkboard in the back of my brain, but I've learned how to talk about my military experience without giving everything away. "Army."

"Huh…" She turns to stare back out at the ocean. "Listen, I know I said it earlier but…" She seems to try to avoid looking at me. "I'm really sorry about what I said this morning. I'm sure you were a very honorable soldier."

If she only knew.

"I tend to…lash out when I feel threatened."

And doesn't that make me feel like an asshole. "You felt threatened by me?"

"Not you, but about what you were implying."

Now it's me who's avoiding her eyes. She's right, I practically called her a gold-digging slut to her face. "I'm sorry about that. I find I usually say the first thing that comes to mind without giving it much thought."

"It's okay." The boat rocks steadily. "You were mostly right about what you picked up from those pictures."

"Nah…I don't believe that." Because nothing about this girl screams money-hungry leech.

She laughs, but it lacks humor. "It's true. She…the girl in those pictures had a lot of growing up to do." There's sadness in her voice now.

"Or maybe she had life all figured out." I've known too many men who lost their lives too soon. Who lost their chance of living by their own rules and enlisted and risked it all to fight for the freedom of others. No chance of once in a lifetime opportunities because of one pivotal moment, one split-second decision, and their chance at *lifetime* was taken from them.

"Because life is beautiful and terrifying," she whispers. "And we deserve to feel it down to our bones."

"Yeah, maybe." I study the horizon, poring over her words and being calmed by the gentle swell of the ocean when the pole between her knees arches, suddenly followed by the whirr of the line. "Fish on!"

"What do I do?" She squeals and reaches for the pole with both hands.

I race up behind her and grip the reel, locking it down. "Hang on tight! We're gonna reel this bitch in together, got it?"

"Got it." Her hands are shaking.

The delicate scent of her skin mixed with coconut sunscreen assaults my senses. I lean in so that my lips nearly touch the shell of her ear. "Deep breath, Cece."

She gulps the air, then blows it out and I can't help the satisfied smile that pulls my lips.

It takes almost an hour before the fish tires and I'm able to reel it in. My muscles are soft from exertion and my shirt soaked with sweat.

"What is it?"

Pulling the tired fish to the side, I grab the line and peek over the railing. "'Bout an eighty-pound yellowfin."

She pushes up next to me. "No way! You caught that?" The excitement in her voice is contagious, there's just something euphoric about reeling in big fish.

"You baited, so…" I hook it by the gills and heave it up and on the boat. Blood spills onto the deck. "Guess we both did."

She covers her mouth with her hand. "Aren't we going to throw him back?"

"Throw him back, are you kidding? This is dinner, freckles."

Her jaw falls open, and those lips taunt me.

"Feel like lunch on the fly bridge?"

"The what?"

I point up top to my favorite spot on the boat.

Her gaze follows my line of site. "Sure. What's for lunch?"

I wipe the sweat off my forehead and grin. "Sushi."

SAWYER

Oh no, fuck no!

I thought he was kidding. I should've known better. Aden's intentions with me since I stupidly boarded this boat have been my torment for his enjoyment. He loved watching me squirm over the bait tank and when I proved I wouldn't shy away from a challenge, he pulled out the big guns. From his flirty smiles to his teasing touches, he's discovered my weaknesses and is exploiting them for his own entertainment.

Now this? Raw fish probably still warm from fighting for its life.

And now I'm God knows how many feet above water sitting on a two-seater bench held up by rusty ladders and staring down a piece of glistening pink meat.

"You have to eat it, it's a rite of passage." He offers the meat to my lips and I quickly turn my face away.

"I'm really not hungry." As if the idea isn't enough to turn my stomach, watching him clean the fish before sectioning off enough for lunch wasn't much of an appetite builder.

"Of course you are." He brings the piece to his own mouth and takes a bite, closing his eyes with a moan as he chews.

I feel a rush of bile hit my throat, or maybe it's beer, either way it's warm and it burns. "That's disgusting."

"You're telling me you don't like sushi?"

My eyes widen. Sawyer would say she's never had sushi. But Celia's a different story. She ate a live cricket in the eighth grade on a dare. She didn't even flinch. "I like sushi, just not directly from the...um...source."

"Doesn't get fresher than this." He takes another bite and I can't deny that his response to eating it does give it some appeal.

"I think I need soy sauce or that green stuff." What's it called?

"Just try it."

"I really don't want to."

"Oh come on." He smiles in that cute crooked way that makes my heart dip and dive. "Live a little."

I chew the inside of my mouth debating the cost/benefit of taking a bite of this fresh-out-of-the-ocean fish. On one hand, I'll impress Aden. That in and of itself is worth the ick factor. But what if I throw up all over his boat? Is the chance of impressing him worth totally humiliating myself? I groan when I realize what I'm doing, exactly what I swore I wouldn't do. I'm making an internal pros and cons list. I close my eyes and steel my resolve and my spine. Don't think, just decide. I pop open my eyes followed by my mouth.

"Yeah?" He stares at my parted lips.

I nod, hoping he'll hurry before I change my mind.

Lifting the rose-colored flesh forward, he places it between my teeth. It's a small bite so I close my lips around his fingers expecting him to pull away...but he doesn't. For a moment I'm suspended in his gaze, totally stuck while his hot fingers rest between my lips. This should be grossing me out; after all, I watched him gut this fish with his bare hands and to wash off all the blood he merely dipped them into the ocean. But all the thoughts of raw fish and a stranger's finger do nothing to stave off the warmth blooming in my belly. My tongue pulls the meat deeper into my mouth, brushing against the rough pad of his forefinger. He bites his lip but finally drops his hand.

He watches intently while I chew and swallow.

"How was it?" His voice is low and gruff.

Lost in the heated moment, I barely tasted it. "Good."

His hand cups the back of my head and he pulls me toward him, stopping just short of our lips touching. "I can't fucking take this anymore." His breath is sawing in and out, bursting against my mouth with impatience. "Let me." It's a demand, not a question.

A kiss. I don't need to channel Celia or flip a coin...I know what I want.

I lick my lips and close the slight distance between us.

The moment our mouths come together a fire like I've never felt before bursts through me. He presses against my neck, tilting my head and probing my lips open with his tongue. I gasp as the heat of his mouth invades mine and he takes full advantage. My eyes slide shut on a long moan as his attention pulls at something deep inside me. His other hand comes up to cup my jaw and the touch is so innocent yet conveys a feeling of being cherished. Protected. Like I'm something valuable and breakable.

He sips from my mouth while taking time to lavish each of my lips in sensations. Alternating between gentle tugs from his teeth and soothing suction as if my mouth is his favorite playground. My hips tingle, my thighs tremble, and I ache in places I never knew it possible to ache in. He slows the kiss, and I chase down his lips, not ready to give them up. He chuckles but indulges me, kissing me so deep my body seems to liquefy. This time when he pulls back and I go after him again, he presses his thumb against my chin and nips at the corner of my mouth.

"I'm sorry, Celia. I can't."

Hearing him call me by my sister's name does the work of a cold shower. Reality crashes down all around me and shame at what I've done fills my chest. How could I lose all control so easily?

I scoot as far back as I can on the love-seat-sized bench in the sky to reestablish a safe distance between us.

"Shit. Don't do that." He runs a rough hand through his hair and I turn to hide my quickly heating face.

"Do what?"

"Don't act like I'm rejecting you."

That gets my attention and I brave a peek only to find him staring at me looking as close to regretful as I've ever seen him. "But you are."

Stop it right now, Sawyer. Cut this off right here. Whatever I've been feeling since I met Aden is nothing more than the backlash of being Celia. This isn't me, it's nothing like me. I don't kiss men I hardly know.

His beautiful face twists in a grimace. "I guess it would seem that way, but it's not." He scoots closer to me so that our thighs are touching and when he leans in I'm grateful the sunglasses are blocking the shock my eyes would surely give away. "If you were any other woman…" He blows out a breath. "The things I would do to you."

My entire body warms and I resist the urge to rip the hat from my head and use it as a fan.

"But you're not. You're *Celia Forrester*."

His words douse the raging fire in my belly.

"Uncle Cal thinks the world of you." He laughs, but only barely. "Pretty sure he'd disapprove of me fuckin' his favorite girl."

Fucking.

Right, because we're virtual strangers.

No, he thinks I'm Celia Forrester, which means we're literal strangers.

My skin practically crawls when I realize how close I came to doing something I'd surely regret. A one-night stand with a handsome man I hardly know. "You're right. I'm not the type to sleep around—"

He lifts an accusing eyebrow, but it's more of a gentle tease than an accusation.

"Okay, maybe I was once the type, but I'm not anymore."

"No?" He readjusts to put some space between us. "You one of those born-again virgins?"

"Not exactly, but let's just say casual sex has lost its appeal."

He flashes me a playfully confused smile. "Is that English you're speakin'?"

I laugh and just like that we're back to comfortable conversation. "You wouldn't understand."

"Damn straight I wouldn't." That beautiful crooked grin shines in the sun. "We better get back to fishing. Here." He reaches into a small cooler I thought was only filled with beer and hands me a wrapped-up sub sandwich. "I'm assuming you're no longer a vegetarian?"

My cheeks warm beneath his gaze. "It would seem that way."

He chuckles. "I hope you like roast beef."

I take the sandwich from him, smiling. "You had this the whole time?"

"Of course." He pushes up to stand. "Man can't live on raw fish alone." He eyes me in a way that ignites my blood again, as if he could live off me if I were on the menu. Which he's made very clear I am not. And I agree. "Fishing."

"Yeah." It's agreement with a hint of disappointment, because I won't lie to myself. I want Aden, in more ways than my imagination can even conjure. And what's the harm really? People have summer flings all the time. In a week or so I'll be gone and he'll never know who I really am.

SEVEN

ADEN

The sun is setting by the time we get the boat back to the dock. It's a mostly quiet ride except for the times I point out something I think Celia might find interesting—the lighthouse on Point Loma, Navy ships docked on Coronado Island, and the clusters of sunbathing sea lions on buoys.

The seagulls soar over our heads, their eyes downcast in search of fish scraps they can scavenge as they squawk every sailor's welcoming song.

"Who's Nancy?"

Celia's no longer wearing the sunglasses, but the hat is still on, which is surprising with all that unruly hair fighting to get free from beneath it. "My aunt. Uncle Cal's wife, he never talked about her?"

"Of course he did." She adjusts the straps on her life vest. "I just...the boat is named after her, right?"

"Aunt Nancy is a good Catholic girl. She hated the name *Nauti Nancy*. They'd always fight about it."

Her lips tip up warmly. "I can see why."

"I'm surprised Cal didn't tell you that story." I head north toward the marina.

She dips her chin, but only slightly. "Yeah...maybe he did and I just didn't remember."

I steer the boat slowly through the inlet. "You mind throwing those bumpers over?" I motion to them and she hops up to play deckhand while I back into the slip and cut the engine. "Toss me the rope." I jump over the railing to the dock. She tosses me one tie-up rope and I secure it to the cleat before following through with the others.

Not gonna lie, having a deckhand was helpful. Usually it's Jenkins and he can't really do more than sit with a fishing pole in one hand and a drink in the other.

When I come back on board she's moving around the deck putting things away.

"Don't worry about that. I'll get it."

She ignores me and continues wiping everything down with a dirty rag. "No, it's fine."

I grab her forearm and her eyes come to mine. It must be because of the contrast against her sun-kissed cheeks, but her eyes appear even greener than they did this morning. "Stop. You're sunburned, you should go shower and put some aloe on. I got this."

She twists to see her shoulder. "Oh, yeah. That's a good idea."

Against my own will I release her and stand back to keep from pulling her in to my chest.

And what the hell is that all about, anyway?

A drunken kiss that leads to sex and an awkward goodbye is what I'm best at. But what happened today with Celia was totally unplanned. I knew going in for the kiss was risky, and I expected her to shoot me down. What I never expected was voracity. If she were anyone else I would've dragged her down to my cabin and taken her on every available surface. It took all my military training, every ounce of learned control and counter-interrogation strategies to peel myself off of her. And even though I know it was the right thing to do I've regretted it ever since.

She bends and fumbles to untie her skirt.

"I got it." *Anything to put my hands on you.* I drop to a squat and just like before I'm tempted to lift the skirt like some horny teenager hoping for a panty shot. I wonder if they're conservative white cotton, or if Celia has an inner sex goddess and they're red lace. Either one would be a fantasy in the making.

I force myself to be a gentleman and untie the fabric, watching it fall to cover what little of her skin she was showing. "There." I stand and her chin tilts to meet my eyes.

"Thanks." She flashes a bashful smile.

"I have to say...your deckhand skills were impressive." I lean back against the railing. "Didn't think you had it in you."

She pulls off the hat I gave her, tossing all that wild hair around her face, and hands it to me.

I take it from her and resist the urge to press it to my nose to see if it smells like her shampoo.

A few beats of silence stretch between us until she blows out a long breath and dips her chin. "Right, well...I better go."

She grabs her purse from inside the cabin and runs her fingers through her hair in an attempt to smooth it down as she heads to the back of the boat to disembark.

An impulse to call out to her pushes at my chest, an urgency to keep her close.

You use women as a distraction, a hobby to fill your mind so you don't have to think about what happened in the valley.

The shrink's words tumble through my head.

Celia is most definitely a distraction. I may have instigated the kiss and there's absolutely a desire for more, but I'm not chasing after her as a means to run away from my problems.

And Cal wouldn't appreciate me using his friend as amusement for my dick. No, that's not what this is. I actually enjoyed myself today. The view was a lot better with Celia around, and we had some good laughs, she didn't seem at all uncomfortable when the conversation died and we'd sit for long stretches of silence.

"Aden?" She's on the dock gazing up at me. "Thank you for today. That was a lot more fun than packing would've been."

That's right. She's moving. "You're welcome."

Well, fuck...any time I'm going to get to spend with her is going to have to happen before she leaves to...where is she moving?

"Is there a number I can reach you, ya know, if I have any questions?" She's rocking back and forth, shifting her weight from one foot to the other, and I notice she's rolling a silver coin between her fingers.

I hop over the railing and she jumps when I land just a few feet from her. I hold out my hand. "Phone."

She nods and fishes the device from her purse. I add my cell, my chest feeling warm at the idea of her using it.

"There." I hand it back and she shoves it in her bag.

"Great, so..." She looks up at me with those eyes and those fucking lips. "I guess I'll see you around."

Limited time.

Cal's gonna kill me.

Fuck it.

I hook her around the back of the neck and pull her to me. She stumbles and places both palms against my chest. Her touch feels amazing. "I want to kiss you again, you good with that?"

"But I thought—"

"Just a kiss." It's risky, but I have to try, because the alternative is nothing at all and I don't think I could stand knowing Celia is in the same town as me and I can't put my lips on hers.

Her breath hitches, and damn, the sound is an injection of pure lust. "Yes."

"Good." I brush my thumb along her jaw and my eyes are drawn to her tongue as it swipes her lower lip. I groan and every part of me wants to get closer. "And what about tomorrow?"

"You want to kiss me tomorrow?" Her pulse beats a rapid rhythm against my palm.

"If I did, would you let me?" I stare at her lips and prepare to suck them between mine when she nods.

Thank fuck!

Pulling up to bring her mouth close, she's forced to her tiptoes and I smile seconds before I press my lips to hers. Damn, but her mouth is like falling onto the softest pillows after a lifetime of resting on concrete. I lick my way inside and close my eyes when our tongues slide together. My body throbs for her. My fingers fork into her hair and it's so damn soft and smells like strawberries, I could literally eat this woman alive.

But I won't.

I have the willpower of a seasoned soldier; surely I can resist every urge to possess the woman in my arms.

It's just a kiss.

Even as my defense blares in my head so does the truth.

This is *not* keeping my distance.

* * *

I watch as the taillights to Celia's orange Thing round the corner of the lot and disappear. That car has to be fifty years old, I'm shocked it even started. My jaw clenches at the thought of her driving around a tin can—*dammit, Aden, she's not your problem.*

Shaking off my unwarranted worry, I contemplate heading to the

Office for a drink, but know if I do it'll be— My gaze darts to movement from the corner of my eye. A man with a full dark beard and heavy coat walks with his head down. Something about him seems off, way off, and way too familiar.

There's a whiff of smoke.

Gunpowder.

Not real. This is not real!

Alerts sound in my head and I glare at the fucker only to have him glare right back.

"You got a problem?" I keep my eyes on his.

He shakes his head and quickens his pace. "No."

"Little fuckin' warm for a trench coat." I call out after him and he stops and stares. Suspicious asshole. My pulse rockets through my veins and I move toward him. "You got something to say?"

"Do I know you?" the guy asks, and I could swear I picked up a slight accent.

American pig!

"What did you say?" I reach for the waistband of my shorts only to realize I don't have my gun.

Explosions light the backs of my eyes and mortar fire pounds in my ears.

"I d-didn't say anything," he stutters.

"You're a little far from home, *sadiq*." As I get closer he ducks into the fish market.

"What the hell are you doin'?"

I whirl around to the voice from my back. It's Jenkins with his hands up and his eyes tight.

"Fuck! You can't creep on my back like that, man!" I inhale a lungful of the warm briny air and try like hell to calm my racing pulse. I search my mind for the sights and sounds of war but what was so real seconds ago is gone.

"Need to get that shit in check, Colt," he mumbles for only my ears.

I push past him to head to the sanctuary of my boat. "You don't fucking think I know that?" I step onto the deck only to hear him lumber aboard right behind me. I fist my hands in my hair and then lock them behind my neck. *Breathe...Breathe.* "I'm trying."

He pulls a beer from the ice chest left over from fishing. "You want any chance with a woman like Celia..." He cracks the top and takes a swig. "You're gonna have to try harder."

"Who says I want a chance with her?"

"Saw you suckin' her face off." He shrugs one bony shoulder and sits down. "Figure you want a chance."

I blow out a long breath and drop to the padded bench along the railing. "It's getting better." It's not, but I'm avoiding triggers more, like crowds, my family, people in general. They all manage to infuriate me without even trying.

I moved home after my honorable discharge and I didn't last a week under my parents' roof. They don't get it. Fuck, I don't get it. Jenkins...he served in Vietnam. He gets it.

"Can't keep pushing it down, Colt. That shit you can't seem to shake? It'll fester inside you and kill everything you got in life until it's just you. That's the bitch of it, ya know? It kills everything...everything but you. You got a choice, you wanna live or you wanna die. You pick death, that's easy. You live...." He takes another gulp from the frosty beer can. "Well, that's worse than dying, so either way you're fucked."

I snag a beer and pop the top. "Anyone ever say you give shitty pep talks, Jenks?"

He grins, flashing black holes where teeth used to be. "I've heard that a time 'er two, yeah. Don't change the fact that you know I'm right."

"I'm workin' on it. VA wants to shove pills at me, but I can't function on 'em, can't think straight. They want me to talk to someone, but that means going back there in my head, and that shit feels too real."

"I gotcha', you don't have to explain it to me. It's a bitch. Difference 'tween us is I'm old and past my glory years, you starin' 'em right in the eye. Still hope for you. But you can't keep pickin' fights with anyone who reminds you of the enemy. You want a chance with a good woman, you're gonna have to try harder."

"Nah…she leaves in a couple weeks. We're just having fun."

"Mmmm." He stares out across the docks.

I shoot him a side glance, not at all comfortable with his silence. "What?"

"Hm? Nothing. Sounds like you got it all figured out, that's all."

"Yeah." I swig from my beer. "I do."

I can hold it together for a couple weeks to spend time with the woman whose photo I've been staring at since I moved here. Then I'll go back to being miserable, fucked up, and alone.

SAWYER

After fishing all day with Aden I hit a U-Haul for boxes and the local market for some food to stock the fridge. It wasn't until I got into the shower that my thoughts hit rewind on my day.

What was supposed to be a quick trip to the marina for an apology ended up a day at sea that included sushi and kissing. Lots of kissing.

The memory of Aden's powerful lips moving against mine force me to cold water to temper my sunburned skin as well as my lust-burned thoughts.

What did he mean when he said he'd want to kiss me tomorrow? The idea of seeing him again, that look in his eyes seconds before he kissed me has me bracing my weight against the tile wall to stay upright. Is it possible to fall for someone so quickly? I dated Mark for six months and never felt so…unstable at the thought of his mouth on mine.

Climbing out of the shower, I dry off and cover my tender skin with a healthy amount of lotion. It's finally dark out and my eyes are dry and heavy, but I can't go to sleep until I talk to my sister.

I dial her number while crawling beneath the covers. My cell phone practically tingles against my palm knowing Aden's number sits there just waiting to be used. Even pretending to be my fearless twin isn't enough to get me to push the right buttons. Calling him now would seem too eager. I'm afraid of what I'd say if he answered. Afraid he wouldn't answer. Terrified he came to his senses in the few hours of separation and reject me.

"Hey, I'm busy vaccinating orphans in India, so leave a message."

Before I open my lips to do just that a call beeps through on my other line. Celia's face and big smile take up the screen.

"I was just leaving you a message."

"I'm moving a little slower and my phone only gives me two rings before the fucking voicemail picks up. But enough of that, tell me how you're loving being me."

She sounds tired. I check the clock that's shaped like a pineapple. It's just after eight-thirty. "Did I wake you?"

"Sawyer, we can talk about my sleep patterns when you get home. Tell me about your day."

I curl up onto my side and can't fight the smile that's splitting my face. "Oh my God, Cece, you'll never believe what I did."

She laughs soft and low and I can tell she's probably curled up in the same position. "What's his name?"

"Aden Colt."

"Whoa…that is definitely a hot guy name."

I go on to explain everything from my insulting him to my attempt at an apology, how the coin flip kept me on the boat, and of course the kissing.

"See! I told you being me is awesome!"

Now it's me who's giggling and I'm not a giggler. "It really is, but it's also terrifying. I don't know how you do it." A long sigh falls from my lips. "I really like this guy, but he thinks I'm you. So what do I do now?"

"I once told a guy I hung out with in Miami that I was a South African princess named Tina. We had a good five days together and he never knew the truth. No harm, no foul."

"Tina doesn't sound like a South African name."

"Details."

"So you're saying I should…that I should just—"

"Don't bust a forehead vein, Sawyer. Yes, I think you should hang out with him. It's totally natural to have a quick summer fling with a hot guy at the beach."

I bite my lip, feeling conspiratorial and kind of loving it. "Shouldn't I at least tell him the truth? Tell him who I am?"

"Where's the fun in that?"

I wonder if I should list all the ways spending time with Aden in any kind of a sexual way would be very fun. God, what is wrong with me? That's so *not me*!

"Besides, if you tell him now you could piss him off. That would ruin everything. And Sawyer…"

"Yeah."

"I really don't want anyone over there to know I'm dying."

My heart squeezes painfully. "Don't say that—"

"I'm serious. If you tell him you're not me, they'll wonder where I am and you'll tell them and then my whole plan will be blown to shit." A few beats of silence stretch between us. "Please, Sawyer? You promised."

"Yeah, okay. It shouldn't take me long to get done what I need to do, I'll be out of here before anyone figures it out."

"Thank you." She yawns and it triggers a yawn of my own. "You sound exhausted."

"I was going to say the same to you." I snuggle deeper into the bed.

"I want daily updates."

Another yawn crawls from my throat. "I know, I'll call you every night."

"Love you."

"Love you too."

I fall asleep shortly after with the phone still clutched in my hand and visions of Aden sailing through my mind.

EIGHT

SAWYER

The sound of a garbage truck in the alley pulls me from sleep. I blink open to sun shining through the window and stinging my bright red forearm. The events of yesterday flood back and pull my lips into a wide grin.

As much as I could lie under the covers obsessively reliving Aden's kiss, my to-do list creeps in and pushes all thoughts of sexy sailors and summer flings aside.

After three cups of coffee to wake myself up and another liberal application of lotion to my crispy skin, I begin to sort Celia's things. I assumed the process wouldn't take more than a few hours, but I keep getting distracted. It'll be a box of keepsakes that sends me to the couch to sort through so that I can learn a little more about my sister's life, or a photo that makes my chest hurt so badly I have to go outside to get some fresh air.

Which is what I'm doing now.

The photo was of her blowing out birthday candles at what looked like some super-posh restaurant on the other side of the world. If she had any idea that this birthday was going to be one of her last—I suck in the salty air and focus on the crashing waves, trying to take a full breath.

My eyes scan the horizon, taking in the view. The seagulls that perch on the cliffs, some other kind of bird with a long, needle-like bill that digs in the sand by the water's edge. There's the cluster of surfers out past the breaking waves, and the occasional jogger that passes by. The wind is cool against my face and I consider going for a walk to try to clear my head, although being alone with my thoughts doesn't seem to make any of this easier.

I soothe my anxiety by pulling out my notepad, this one rectangular because the sunflower was driving me crazy, and I rewrite my list.

Sort and divide.
Separate valuables.
Infrequently used items first.
Label, label, label.

The thwack of a screen door has me whirling around to see a woman on her porch. It looks like she's trying to pull a garbage bag from inside but can't seem to manage it with her walker.

"Good morning." I make my way to her and her eyes narrow on mine through thick Coke-bottle glasses. I open my mouth to introduce myself, but decide I'll wait for her reaction to see if we've already met, or rather, her and Celia have already met.

"Oh…good morning." She's out of breath and there's a light sheen of sweat on her upper lip. "I think my garbage got too full is all." She's playing tug-of-war with the screen door and the bag.

I scurry to help her, freeing the overflowing bag and scooping up some of the trash that escaped. "I got it."

"Thank you." She leans her weight on the walker. "This didn't used to be so hard." She smiles and I return the sentiment.

"I'm happy to take this out for you."

"Oh no, I wouldn't ask for—"

"It's no big deal. Really."

"Thank you, um…oh…I'm sorry, I don't remember if we've met."

Perfect. "I'm Celia, I live in number four."

"Right, I know I've seen you around." She holds out one hand, fingers curled up with what I'm guessing to be arthritis. "Mrs. Jones, but you can call me Mary."

I shake her hand gently, not wanting to hurt her. "Nice to meet you, Mary. I'm running to the dumpster. Is there any other trash you need me to take?"

"No, but thank you."

I open the screen door to help her back inside. The smell of rotting garbage becomes overwhelming and I wonder how long it's been since she took out her trash. "Are you sure there's nothing else I can run out for you?"

"No, I don't think so." I shut her door for her as she walks deeper into the dark cottage.

Holding the bag as far from my body as possible I race to the alley and heave the stinking mass into the dumpster. Then, holding my hands away from my body, I head straight inside for a long hand wash followed by hand sanitizer because you can never be too safe. In my haste I practically knock over a tiny girl. "Oh crap! I'm so sorry."

Not a girl. A short woman.

"Celia, you're back."

I jerk my head up at the sound of her saying my sister's name and have a brief *oh shit* moment because I didn't have my Celia mask firmly in place. Standing just a foot away with a nose ring and a

blond pixie haircut, the petite woman smiles and I immediately recognize her from some of my sister's pictures.

"It would seem so, yeah." Wearing a pair of yoga pants and an
oversized tee I pulled from Celia's closet that reads "The Confession
Bar, New York, NY," I hope I'm convincing enough.

She wraps me in a hug. "It's great to see you."

I pat her awkwardly. "It's great to be seen."

Pulling back she grins wide. "How was your trip…" She purses
her lips. "Where were you again?"

"Ah…" Shit, what did I tell Brice? I clear my throat. "A little bit
of everywhere, and then Phoenix."

"Is everything okay? You took off without a word."

I stare beyond her shoulder, her inquisitive eyes seeming to see
right through me. "Fine, yeah. I'm good."

She tilts her head. "You seem…different."

"Me?" I allow my body to turn to Jell-O. "Oh, *psht*, no. I'm good,
just…hung over from being out *all night*, you know how it is." I trail
off with nothing more to add because I've never stayed up past midnight unless it's been to watch the ball drop on New Year's Eve from
the safety of my bed.

"Oh yeah, where'd you go?" Her eyes flash with interest and excitement. "I heard Blink 182 played a surprise show at the Casbah.
Were you there?"

"Uh…no, I was…at a bonfire party and everyone was night surfing and there was this ex-football player so we all played football on
the beach. It was dark but they used the headlights from their cars
and stuff."

Her eyes narrow and I try not to shift in my flip-flops. "Isn't that
a movie?"

"Hm?" Oh shit.

"*Point Break*. The movie, you just—"

"What? No. *Lame.*" I can't believe I actually thought I could pull this pretending to be Celia thing off! I paste on a big smile. "How've you been?"

"All right, I guess. You know me, never a dull moment in the life of Zöe. Hey, everyone's been asking about you down at the bar. Think you might be able to drop in tonight?"

"Tonight?" I dip my chin seeing the word *confession* on my shirt and wishing I could do just that, confess who I am and be done with this stupid charade. I crank my mind back to the photos I saw of this woman and hope they'll give some hint as to what bar she's talking about. "Maybe, it depends how much I get done here."

Her perfectly sculpted brows drop over crystal-blue eyes and she tilts to look through the window of my cottage. "Are you moving out?"

"Yeah, I'm going back to Phoenix."

She sticks out her lower lip. "What a buzzkill." The disappointment is short-lived and she grins. "All the more reason for you to come to the bar."

"I'll see what I can do."

"Great!" She leans in and wraps me in another hug. "You'll keep in touch from Phoenix, right? Maybe come out for a visit? Oh! Will you still be here on the Fourth? OB is one of the best places in the world to spend the holiday."

"Yeah, maybe. We'll see."

She pulls back and smiles. "Cool! So I'll see you tonight?"

"Mmm." I roll my lips between my teeth to avoid giving a definite answer.

She doesn't seem to mind and skips away with a finger wave.

I'll need to figure out what bar she's talking about. I'd ask Brice, but after that kiss he gave me the first night I'm afraid to bump into him again. God, I've been here two and a half days and kissed two different guys.

I didn't kiss Mark until our second date.

Suddenly feeling naked and exposed I turn and duck back into Celia's house. Oh my God. I'm a slut! And strangely the idea of seeing Aden again makes my pulse jump in my veins and butterflies race in my belly. He's the most masculine man I've ever known. Not as pretty as Brice, but he wears his male sensuality with the kind of confidence I rarely see on men.

My nerves tingle and stir.

Leave it to Celia to talk me into living as her, and leave it to me to enjoy it. At this rate I may never want to go back to being myself.

ADEN

I managed to stay away from the cottages most of the day. Having no good excuse to go there, I spend my time on the boat doing some minor repairs that I'd been putting off for weeks. I kept my phone in my pocket in case Celia called. And when it buzzed less than an hour ago I forced myself not to answer it on the first ring.

It's when I answered to the shaky voice of Mrs. Jones from cottage six that I was disappointed as well as charged up to have an excuse to drive to the cliffs. I took a quick shower and put on my cleanest T-shirt in the off chance I might run into Celia. I contemplated what I'd say on the drive over. If I bumped into her would I invite her to dinner? I haven't been on a real date since before I enlisted and that was at eighteen years old, almost ten years ago when I was still thinking mostly with my dick. From then on, knowing I was married to the military indefinitely, I didn't want to create any long-lasting attachments so my "dating" life was mostly the fly-by kind. In and out, not a chance of building any kind of connection longer than the physical.

When I pull up to the cottages I park in my property manager assigned spot and see Celia's Thing parked down by her place. Something that feels an awful lot like excitement stirs in my gut and calls me up short. What the fuck? It's been so long since I've felt excited about anything.

Soaking in this strange new feeling, I head over to Mrs. Jones's cottage, making sure to keep my eyes forward when I pass Celia's place. Last thing I need is to be caught looking in her damn window like some kind of stalker. But still, I can't help but wonder why she hasn't called me. It's been almost twenty-four hours since she left the boat with the possibility she'd be in touch, and in that time she's managed to turn me into a desperate jackass who's hoping for the second date that never happens.

"Oh, Aden…" Mrs. Jones must see me from her open door as I make my way up the steps. "I'm so sorry to bother you, honey."

"You're never a bother." I push in through the screen door and it slams closed behind me.

"I don't know if I believe all that." Her voice shakes with age and her eyes disappear behind her cheeks when she smiles.

I motion to her ancient television. "What's this one about?" Mrs. Jones is always sitting in front of some cheesy Hallmark movie.

"This man is in love with this woman that he thinks is a waitress, but she's really a very famous foreign actress in hiding."

Wow, that's stupid. "Sounds interesting."

"Oh it is." She places one frail hand covered in protruding purple veins to her chest. "She's leaving for her country and if she doesn't tell him soon he'll lose her forever."

I feign interest watching as some good-looking actor charms his way across the screen. "Hm." A few seconds pass and I turn away from the TV before my balls shrivel up and fall off from the estrogen-infused romantic overload. "Is it your kitchen or bathroom sink?"

She struggles to stand, her arms shaking with the effort of pushing herself up.

I lay a hand on her shoulder. "You sit still, just tell me which sink and I'll take care of it."

She blows out an exhausted breath and smiles up at me, accentuating the grooves around her lips, evidence of the long and happy life she's lived. "It's the bathroom, honey. Thank you."

I head to her bathroom and turn the water on, then drop to the pipes below to see a slow drip coming from the slip nut. I pull a monkey wrench from my tool belt and tighten the nut. I flick the water back on and watch for a leak.

Nothing.

After wiping up the puddle beneath her sink, I wash my hands, check the pipe one more time and, satisfied it's fixed, head back out to see her dabbing her eyes with a tissue.

"You're all set."

She sniffles and jerks around to grab something off her side table. "Thank you, Aden." She pulls a few dollars out of her wallet with knobby fingers.

"No." I hold up my hand.

"But—"

"I'm just doing my job, Mrs. Jones."

She blinks in confusion and then focuses back on me. "I have to wonder if today is my birthday." She laughs softly. "Everyone is being so nice to me."

"Is it your birthday?"

Her cheeks flush and she shakes her head. "I don't think so. But the sweet girl from next door helped me with my trash and then you rush over to—"

"What girl?"

Her gaze swings to the window and she dips her chin toward Celia's place. "Her. I can't make it to the dumpster as easily as I used to."

Celia did that? I feel my lips pull into a wide grin and follow her gaze out the window just as a flash of strawberry-blond hair catches my eye. My pulse kicks behind my ribs. "That's nice…listen, I better get going." I'm already moving to the door. "Enjoy the rest of your night." I slip out the front door to see Celia walking to the cliff's edge.

She's dressed in a pair of jeans that hug every curve of her round ass, giving away everything she was hiding under her skirt yesterday. A black silky top with only strings to hold it up brings attention to her sun-kissed freckled shoulders and light hair.

My muscles tense when she gets to the railing and braces her weight on it as if she's just run a mile and is trying to catch her breath. I come up behind her but not wanting to scare her I stop a good distance away.

"You okay, freckles?"

She whirls around and it's then I notice she's wearing makeup, not a lot but enough to cover the sprinkling of color on her nose and cheeks and accentuate her eyes. She either just got home or is headed out. The thought makes me agitated and curious. I rub the back of my neck as I tilt my head and continue to take her in.

Her eyes widen on me and she puts on a fake smile. "I didn't know you were here."

I study her from top to bottom and make sure to take my time so she can *feel* me doing it. It's only when she shoves her hands into her pockets self-consciously that I finally ask the question I'm dying to know the answer to. "Where you headed, Celia?" The menace in my voice makes my own skin prickle and the way her breath quakes before her eyes grow wide tells me my question has an effect on her.

"I—I don't know."

I run my teeth along my bottom lip and lift my brows at her high-heeled shoes. "All dressed up and you don't know where you're going?" Dammit to fuck, it's a date. She's going on a motherfucking date.

"No. I mean…" She holds back strands of hair the breeze tosses into her face. "Maybe."

"You going on a date, Cece?"

"Please." Her face scrunches up. "Don't call me that."

I step closer. "Why not? I had my tongue in your mouth just yesterday and now you're offended by a nickname?" I move even closer until our toes are practically touching. "Who's taking you out tonight?"

Her eyebrows pinch together. "I'm not going out with anyone, I just don't know where I'm going."

"Explain that."

She rakes the silky strands of her hair off her forehead. "This girl, Zöe, asked me to stop by a bar and I…" It's hard to focus on what she's saying with her lips covered in a pink gloss that makes them look like the sweetest candy. "It's a long story."

I cross my arms at my chest. She doesn't owe me shit, but I'm a selfish bastard and I want to know why going to a bar is making her so edgy. "I got time."

"Zöe asked me to meet her at a bar, but I don't know which bar she's talking about and I could ask Brice, but I'm afraid he'll think he can come with me and to be honest with you I'd rather not go with Brice, or I'd rather not go at all, but I told her I would and if I don't then…then…"

"Shh…You're gonna hyperventilate." I'm half teasing, but the way her hands are bunched at her sides makes me think it might not be far from the truth.

She blows out a long breath and shakes out her arms. "I know."

"Are you always this high strung?"

"Do you always feel it's important to point out my flaws?"

"Why do you care if I point out your flaws?"

"Why do you care about where I'm going?"

"I think we could go on for hours like this."

A tiny smirk hits her lips. "You're probably right."

"The bar she's talking about is probably Lenny's. She works there."

"Oh…" She chews her bottom lip and a jealous urge to rip that lip from her teeth and pull it between mine tugs at me. "Do you know where it is?"

I do, but if I tell her she'll go, and looking like that I'd rather she stay home, preferably with me.

"I mean, do you, would you want to, if you're not busy, can you come with me?"

"I don't think that's a good idea." Lenny, the owner, never officially told me I wasn't welcome in his bar again, but the look he gave me that night I was arrested outside of his place about ten seconds after he fired me made it pretty clear he never wanted to see my face again. Not that I blame him.

"Why isn't it a good idea?"

I shrug and try to act casual. "When I first moved here Zöe got me a job bouncing there on weekends."

Her eyes narrow. "You and Zöe, did you guys…?"

"No." Okay, almost once but I was too drunk to make that night fun for either of us. Not that Celia needs to know about that.

"So what happened? Why don't you work there now?"

"Nothing to tell, just didn't work out." *Lie, lie, lie.*

"Oh, well, I don't see why you can't come with me, then."

"Freckles—"

"Pleeeeaaase….?" She puffs out that fat bottom lip and my blood howls in my veins to drag her back to my boat caveman-style.

I step close to her so that we're almost touching. "Kiss me and I'll go." Yep, I said it, and I meant it. I'd face Lenny and all his bullshit if it means I get at those lips.

Her jaw drops open, and not at all in a bad way. "You can't be serious."

"I'm dead serious." I run my hands through her hair at her nape and my thumb along her jaw. "Thought about you all day."

"You did?" she whispers, and her breath ghosts across my lips in a brutal tease.

"Mmm." I pull her close until she reaches for me by pushing up on her toes. "You come the rest of the way, I'll go to Lenny's." I'm a lying dick, I'd go anyway just for a chance to spend some time with this woman who keeps managing to totally fuck with my head.

She licks her lips and I'm amped with the anticipation of tasting her tongue again. In what feels like slow motion she presses the softest close-mouthed kiss to my lips. I clasp her hip and pull her body flush with mine, her breasts mold to my chest, and being on her toes she stumbles into me, giving me her weight.

Fucking perfect.

My arms hold her tight as I tilt my head and coax open her mouth. She hums low in her throat while letting me in, the sweet flavor of her lips and gentle friction from her gloss have me growling in response. When was the last time I've been this turned on by something so benign? Maybe it's because I'm sober. Booze dulls everything and if this is what hooking up sober feels like, fuck, I've been missing out.

She relaxes into my grasp and the simple act makes me feel something I haven't felt in a long time. Strong. Powerful. As if there's nothing I can't conquer, and I haven't had that since the day I led my battalion on the last mission of our deployment. The one last op before we all got to come home.

But only half of us made it.

A flash of gunfire lights behind my closed lids and I jolt back, breaking our connection.

She's breathless, her eyes still closed, not affected by my brief freak-out. She slowly blinks up at me. "Do you kiss all women like that?"

My lips twitch. "Only know one way to kiss." But somehow kissing her feels different. Better in a way I can't put my finger on.

"So you'll go with me?"

"Yeah. I'll even take you to dinner first."

"A date?" Her smile is so big it stretches across her perfect face.

"A date."

"I'll just grab my purse." She steps back and stumbles over a patch of ice plant.

I put my arm around her waist hoping our kiss is the cause of her lack of balance. "I'll go with you." Judging by her blush I think it might be.

I guide her to her place and once inside my stomach hardens. The main living space is littered with boxes and stacks of her things, a reminder that she'll be moving soon.

"It's in the bedroom. I'll be right back." She's steadier on her feet as she goes to get her purse. I set down my tool belt and move around the room.

Stacks of books, tons of little junky figurines I'm guessing to be from all reaches of the world, are piled around along with packing paper. It doesn't seem like she's been working on any of this for very long, as all the boxes are still empty.

"I'm ready." She smiles with a fresh coat of lip gloss that I can't wait to wear all over my neck.

Down, boy! There will be plenty of time for making out later.

"I'm driving."

As we're walking to my Blazer I fight the urge to pull her hand into mine, because seriously, what the fuck is that all about? I'm not the hand-holding type, but with Celia I can't seem to get her close enough when we're together.

NINE

SAWYER

I was on the verge of an anxiety attack when I'd finished getting ready to go out tonight. I'd flipped that stupid coin like I promised my sister I would, and of course it determined I would go out to the bar tonight. After tossing around all the clothes I brought to San Diego searching for the right thing to wear, I succumbed to picking through Cece's closet.

Tight jeans, a loose-fitting and still insanely flattering tank, and I left my hair wavy the way Cece wore hers. I felt pretty good when I was swiping on makeup heavier than I usually wear, but it wasn't until I stepped in front of that mirror that I saw it.

It wasn't Sawyer staring back at me.

It was my sister.

I was Celia.

The clothes, the hair, all of it was my sister, but that wasn't what made the image before me so surreal; after all, those things are only skin-deep. It was the glow on my cheeks that even the most expensive makeup couldn't provide, the spark in my eye that was looking forward to doing something irresponsible. It was my posture, the confident bend in my knee and the strength in my shoulders that spoke of a woman not constantly bogged down by worrying about every single tiny detail of life.

What I saw in the mirror was a girl who, even if for only that brief second, had given in to what *could be* rather than having her hands wrapped up in manipulating her future into what it *needs* to be.

And as soon as I recognized it, I chased it away.

Suddenly the room was too small, the clothes were cutting off my circulation, my legs felt numb, and I raced outside for air…

Only to run into *him*.

Aden.

The way he looks at me dulls my pulse to a slow and desperate throb. With him, I'm not Celia or Sawyer, I'm some hybrid that he seems to find interesting enough to be around, to kiss, to date.

When he opens the passenger-side door to his truck he flashes a cocky smile that makes me think he can read my thoughts. That he knows the effect he has on me. And he likes it.

But when I smile back something happens. His grin falls and he's briefly knocked off his game as wonder dances behind his eyes.

A tense moment builds between us until he clears his throat.

"Buckle up." He dips his chin and runs a hand over his hair before shutting me in.

I pull my seat belt on and blindly buckle it as I watch him jog around the hood with all the grace and agility of a seasoned athlete.

He climbs inside and the engine roars to life. "You like Italian food?"

"Yeah."

He cranks the wheel around and takes us toward town. "I know a place. It's a hole in the wall, but they have the best baked rigatoni I've ever had."

"Sounds good." I struggle for something to talk about as he turns the dial on his radio to some alternative rock station. There's no CD player, but only an old tape deck. Although the thing must be vintage, its interior is clean and well taken care of. "This is a great truck."

"Thanks, it was Cal's. It's old but I like that I can pop the hood and fix shit if it breaks. No computers on these old Chevys."

I don't know anything about cars so I simply nod and grip my purse in my lap to hide my nervousness.

He makes a sharp right turn and something silver slides from beneath my seat to settle at my shoe. I reach down and scoop up a set of dog tags. They jingle as I pull them closer to inspect the name.

```
COLT
ADEN, R
A304823
O POS
CHRISTIAN
```

"Are you still in the Army?"

His eyes dart between the tags in my hand and the road ahead.

"No." He leans over, pops open the glove box, then swipes the tags and tosses them in.

"Were you in the Middle East for a long time?"

He works his jaw back and forth for a few seconds then nods. "Four deployments, longest was fifteen months."

"Fifteen months?" That's insane. "I thought you guys only go for a few months at a time." Over a year in a war-torn country sounds like hell. "You must've had a pretty important job."

His eyebrows drop low and he hits the brakes so hard that if I weren't wearing a seat belt I would've hit my head on the dashboard. He turns and smiles, but it seems forced. "We're here."

I look out the windshield to see a sign that has *Rizzario's Italian Ristorante* painted on a red brick building. It's quaint and has a romantic feel, which sends my stomach tumbling.

He hops out of the truck and circles the hood, but the way he's carrying his body is different. Stiff shoulders and slower, more controlled movements. He opens my door, avoiding my eyes, but gives me a hand to help me slide as gracefully as possible out of my seat.

To my disappointment he releases my hand and walks ahead of me and into the restaurant. Weird because he seemed to purposefully slow his pace to walk side by side when we left the cottages.

After a quick request for a table on the patio we're led to a small outdoor area that's sheltered by wisteria vines and twinkle lights. Aden pulls my chair out for me and despite the 180-flip in his mood I smile at the gentlemanly gesture.

"What?" He sits across from me, his gaze intent on mine.

"I've never had a chair pulled out for me before."

"No?" He raised an eyebrow. "None of your globetrotting boyfriends pulled out a chair for you, huh?" He shakes out his napkin and drapes it across one thigh. "All money. No class." He cringes but only slightly.

I try not to read too much into it or let his opinion of my sister's dating life make me angry; after all, he's probably right.

I pick up my menu and pretend to be looking at the options when I'm really trying to figure out where I went wrong. He's only been like this with me twice, and both times it was when I brought up the military.

"Can I get you something to drink?" A female voice sounds from our tableside and before I can open my mouth to order an iced tea, Aden's barking an order for two whiskeys.

I curl my lips between my teeth and wait for her to leave before leveling him with a stare. "I don't drink whiskey."

He leans back and drops his hands to his thighs. "Why am I not surprised?"

I keep my eyes fixed on his and hope he looks away first but he tilts his head and keeps his gaze locked with mine.

I lean in. "I'm sorry."

He blinks.

"I didn't know," I whisper. "Now I do, and it won't happen again."

"What're you talkin'—"

"Your military career."

He jerks like I socked him in the gut and his shoulders tense.

"It's a topic you're not comfortable with, I see that now. I didn't know that before, so please stop punishing me. I made a mistake, I apologize, so you can stop looking at me like I'm the enemy here."

His mouth opens to say something but the waitress comes with our drinks. She puts them on the table and turns to leave.

"Wait," he snaps at the poor girl. "She'd like to order something else."

I envision Celia in the seat instead of me and imagine how she'd respond.

The waitress looks at me and rather than order an iced tea I pick up the whiskey and nod. "This is fine. Thank you."

He narrows his eyes. "Really?"

I take a sip and fight the cringe that crawls up the back of my neck as the burning booze slides down my throat. "Delicious."

A hint of a grin curls his lips and he sips from his own drink staring at me like I'm some freaky side-show he's enjoying.

We keep the conversation relatively impersonal from that moment on. I ask him about fishing and he seems content talking about different fish, market prices, and San Diego history.

Turns out whiskey isn't all that bad and the baked rigatoni was as good as he promised. It isn't until our waitress asks if we'd like dessert that I remember why we're here and begin to get nervous about going to Lenny's.

Chances are there will be a lot of people who know my sister and will be asking me things and talking about situations I know nothing about. Luckily Aden will be with me. I figure, two whiskeys and I'm almost slurring, anyone who notices my lack of memory will just chalk it up to me being drunk.

I try to pay half of the bill but Aden stares at me in a way that says "Don't you fucking dare pull out your wallet."

Having not been on many *real* romantic dates, I'm not familiar with protocol, but I allow him to pay. He seems more at ease, and when we're walking out to his car and he hooks me around the waist I practically melt into his arms.

"Whoa, you drunk, freckles?" He chuckles at my ear, sending goose bumps down my arm.

"I told you I don't drink whiskey." I try to push off of him but his powerful arm holds me close.

"What I saw, I'd say you drink it just fine." There's humor in his voice as he steers me away from the parking lot to the sidewalk.

"Where are we going?"

"Lenny's. It's on the next block over." He peeks over at me. "How do you not know where Lenny's is?"

I pretend to window shop in the beachside boutiques so he can't see my face as I struggle for a believable answer. "I do, I just meant, why aren't we going to the car?"

"I figured it would be better for you to walk off some of that liquor."

"Hmm...probably smart."

It's a short walk and I'm having a hard time keeping one foot in front of the other with the way his thumb is tracing circles on my hip.

The neon Lenny's sign comes into view up ahead. It's on a corner, and reggae music filters from the retractable windows along the two street-facing walls. It is what I'd consider to be the typical beach bar but with a modern flair.

Just like earlier, Aden tenses and loses his good humor the second we walk through the door. He leads me to a high-top table in the corner right by an open window, but his eyes are fixed on an older man who is making drinks behind the bar.

That must be Lenny.

"You okay?"

"Yeah."

He's lying. "We don't have to stay."

Finally he moves his eyes from the man at the bar, but he doesn't look at me. Now his gaze is shifting from person to person, from one side of the room to the next, and then he pushes in beside me so that his back is to the wall and something about the new position seems to make him relax a little.

"You want me to go get us drinks?"

He lifts an eyebrow at me, but doesn't smile. "You sure you need one?"

Yep, grumpy Aden is back.

And suddenly I long to be back at Celia's wrapped in a cozy blanket with a good book.

"Celia!" Zöe comes up from behind me and wraps me in a hug. "You made it."

Her eyes land on my empty hands. "You need a drink."

"Oh…actually, I think I'm good."

The girl's eyebrows pinch together and she studies me for a moment before she bursts into laughter. "Good one, I'll grab you a drink." She spots Aden and does a double take. "Hey, Aden."

"Zöe." He doesn't even look at her, his eyes are still constantly scanning as if he's looking for a threat.

"Lenny know you're here?"

"Don't know, but I'll go say hi to make sure he does." He grins wickedly and whispers in my ear, "I'll be right back," followed up by a quick squeeze before moving through the crowd toward the bar.

Zöe watches him walk away, then turns back to me with huge saucer eyes. "You and Aden?"

"No, er....I don't—"

"I can't believe you're bumping uglies with Aden Colt!"

"Gross, I'm not bumping...*uglies*."

"Sure you're not. The guy is hot as hell and you're not screwing him. That's the funniest damn thing I've ever heard, Celia."

"I swear we're not doing anything."

She props her hands on her hips. "Who are you?"

If it weren't for the back of my barstool I would've fallen right off it. She sees right through me. No crap, Sawyer! No drink, denying a meaningless relationship, sitting with my legs crossed—I'm not even trying to act like Celia.

I give into the lingering pull of liquor in my blood and allow it to turn me into a noodle. "Okay, fine, you got me. We're dating."

"Dating?" She scoots in closer. "You and Aden Colt are *dating*?" Her expression would indicate that I'm still not a convincing Celia.

"Dating," I say, using air quotes. "You know what I mean, hooking up."

Silence stretches between us and she searches my eyes before she finally nods. "I knew it."

"It's just temporary, ya know, something to pass the time until I move." My stomach feels sick at how easily the words are falling from my lips. Casual sex isn't something I've ever supported or been party to, but Celia has mastered it.

She studies me for a moment, then nods. "Whatever you say." She shrugs. "Just be careful."

My ears perk up. "Why would you say that?"

I follow her gaze that's on Aden talking to who I assume to be Lenny behind the bar, neither of them looking all that excited to see the other.

"He's got a bit of a reputation." She scoots a stool closer to me and drops down to sit. "Brice and his friends call him Sergeant Psycho."

"Why?"

"The dude isn't stable." Her eyes widen. "But who cares, he's sexy."

"What makes everyone think he's psycho?" I'm reminded of his sudden mood swings, how he goes from being flirtatious to angry, he's easily irritable, and seems to have very little impulse control. What if he is psycho? My heart thuds dully in my chest thanks to the booze pumping through my veins.

"He used to be a bouncer here. I heard they fired him because he attacked a cab driver." Zöe's eyes are wide. "Totally unprovoked."

I have a hard time believing that. Aden's a tough guy, but to attack someone for no reason makes no sense. *Unless he's crazy.*

"Not too long ago he *had an accident* at the cliffs." Her thinly shaped eyebrows are high on her forehead. "He said he slipped while he was running, but rumor has it he jumped."

I turn to look at him, his maroon tee hugging his thick, tan biceps and his strong jaw locked as he listens to whatever that Lenny guy is saying. He seems so capable, I can't imagine him taking the coward's way out and trying to kill himself. I also saw him balance on one foot while leaning over the edge of his boat to bring in a fish and I can't see him *accidentally* slipping off anything.

"I'm sure he told you he put the guys who broke into your house in the hospital."

I blink, barely registering her words. "Hold on…he did what?"

"He used to live in Cal's cottage. He caught the guys who broke into your place and beat the shit out of them. After that he moved to Cal's boat."

I cover my mouth, shaking my head, and words fail to form.

"There were two of them, decent-sized dudes, but Aden bloodied them both."

"Whoa…" I knew he was a tough guy, ex-military, but I didn't know he was violent. My belly rumbles and threatens to spill.

She leans back nodding. "Aden is gorgeous, but there's something off about him."

I look back to find him watching me. When our eyes meet, the corner of his mouth lifts in a crooked smile that sends flutters throughout my body.

Sawyer would never give a guy with this kind of violent history a second of her time.

Leave it to Celia to fall for a guy who's nothing but trouble.

TEN

ADEN

"So we're good?" I toss cash on the bar for the two drinks Lenny just made for me.

He snatches the money and nods. "As long as you're a paying customer and you don't start shit in my bar we're good."

I try to ignore his condescending tone and move through the room, weaving around people and tables. The cramped space has paranoia clawing at my nerves. My gaze is steady on Celia and imagining peeling those clothes off her to see how far those freckles go distracts me from the delusions.

"Here."

Celia takes the drink from me and sniffs it. "What is it?"

"Ginger ale."

She seems relieved and takes a long pull from her straw.

"Whoa, ginger ale." Zöe's words drip with sarcasm. "You guys are going big tonight, huh? You better not be driving."

I take a swig and frown at the sugary sweetness. It's been years since I've had a soda that didn't have rum or whiskey in it, and the absence is an odd change. I have a limited number of days with Celia and if this date leads where I'm hoping, there's no way I'm going to be drunk for that. "I don't see you with a drink."

Zöe jumps off her stool. "Excellent point! I'll be right back."

Celia's stirring her soda with the straw and motions to the recently vacated stool. "Have a seat."

"Nah. I'm good." I lean back against the brick wall and the hardness buys me a little peace of mind. Thankfully the whiskey from dinner is still coursing through my veins, which takes the sting off being in a room with this many people. But even still, I can't give them my back. Not if I want to keep my promise to Lenny about not starting trouble.

She shifts around uncomfortably in her seat and fidgets with her straw. I zero in on her body language; one hand rubbing up and down her thigh obsessively, chin dipped to her chest, avoiding eye contact.

"Hey."

She peers up at me and her eyes dart around.

"What's going on?" I ask.

"What makes you think there's something going on?"

I place my drink down and lean in close, making sure to hold her violently green eyes with mine. "Don't answer a question with a question. You're not comfortable here. Why?"

Her eyes flare wide and then she blinks. "I guess…let's just say I came back here a different person and…" She takes a sip of her drink. "I don't want to run into people I used to know."

"Then why did we come here?"

She shakes her head and mumbles, "It's stupid."

I hook her chin and bring her eyes back to mine. "Tell me."

She searches my eyes, I assume trying to figure out what her chances are of me letting her off the hook. I lift a brow, hardening my gaze. She sighs and straightens one leg to dig into her pocket and pull out a quarter. Flipping it over in her hand she shows it to me. "Because of this."

I grab the coin from her and study it. Nothing special about it, looks like an average everyday quarter. "I don't get it."

"I tend to overthink things so when I'm forced with a decision I flip the coin."

"No shit?"

She smiles, but it's shy, almost embarrassed. "I told you it was stupid."

"What if it lands on something you don't want—"

"Hey, Celia!"

Her eyes flash with panic before she turns toward the voice of a woman who is shoving her way through the crowd toward us. It isn't until she emerges from the crowd that I recognize her.

She throws her arms around my date. "Zöe told me you were back!"

Celia's eyes dart to mine in a silent plea for rescue as she awkwardly pats the back of her unwanted guest. "Yeah, I am back."

"It hasn't been the same here without you!" She pulls away and looks at me as if she just realized I'm standing here. "Aden, hey…Lenny know you're here?"

"Polly." I grit my teeth. "He does."

She drops onto the stool closest to Celia. "So? Where were you this time? Bali? Portugal? Spain?"

Celia shifts on her seat, the discomfort she spoke about earlier clearly showing in her body language. She clears her throat and sips her soda. "Phoenix."

Polly wrinkles her nose. "Phoenix. Like Arizona?"

"Mm-hmm." Celia has her straw in her mouth guzzling down her drink and pretty soon it'll be gone and she'll have no excuse to avoid talking.

"Why Phoenix? Sounds…boring."

"Family stuff."

"Oh yeah? Like what? Everything okay?"

The bubbling slurp signaling the end of her drink sounds just before she sets the empty glass down. "Sure."

"Were you there to see your sister?"

Celia's chin jerks toward Polly. "Why would you think that?"

Polly frowns. "I know you worry about her."

"I do?" Her voice is almost a whisper and I have to wonder if she really spoke or I imagined it.

"Oh, I don't know, just from what you said about her having no life and having that thing where she's afraid to leave her house and stuff…what's that called…" She purses her lips.

"Agoraphobia." Celia's face looks paler than usual.

I put my hand on her shoulder and squeeze, hoping to signal to her that maybe it's time to go. Clearly whatever shit she's dealing with about seeing old friends is more serious than I thought.

"Yes!" Polly grins. "Was that why you went?" Her eyes widen. "Did your sister finally snap and lock herself in her house like you predicted?"

Celia's eyes come to mine and the terror I see flash in those emerald depths triggers something in my chest that has me helping her off her stool. "Come on, it's time to go."

"Hold on, Aden…" Polly stands too. "You guys just got here."

"I'm sorry." Celia stumbles to get through the cluster of barstools. "We have plans to, uh…"

I wrap my arm around her waist, surprised at how quickly she leans into me for support. "We're late for our movie."

"Movie…?" Polly mumbles.

"Yeah, we'll catch up later." Celia doesn't look at the woman, but allows me to guide her out of the bar.

"Okay, call me!" Polly yells to our backs as we push through the crowd.

Once we're outside I lead her down the sidewalk toward the beach, allowing the silence between us to stretch on until we reach a bench just shy of the sand. I motion for her to sit and she drops like dead weight, her eyes fixed on the black horizon, the only light coming from the moon and a flickering street lamp.

Too anxious to sit and trying to ignore the unwarranted paranoia, I pace with my fists propped on my hips. "Start talking."

She blinks, as if my voice called her from wherever she was. "Excuse me?"

I stop right in front of her. "Your face went ghost back there. I want to know why."

"It's nothing." Her gaze moves back to the horizon and I want to shake her to get her to look at me.

"You're lying." I hate how easily she can lie to me. "Answer me."

Her eyes snap to mine. "Stop barking orders at me."

"Where I come from someone's body language could mean the difference between life and death. One shifty fucking stare could mean you've got four seconds before someone strapped with C4 explodes in your face. The second Polly started talking to you it was like you wanted to jump the fuck out of your skin."

"I don't like talking about it and you can't make me. Just because you're used to bossing around men on the battlefield or wherever you *came from*. I'm not one of your men."

I run my hands over my head wishing my hair was longer so I could pull it from my fucking scalp. This woman is infuriating. What the hell is she hiding and why the fuck am I so damn desperate to figure it out?

"I'd like to go home now," she whispers.

"Celia—"

She cringes and squeezes her eyes closed. "Please, Aden…I don't want to do this anymore."

I stare at her, her usual stiff spine hunched over, her hands balled up in her lap. Whatever is hurting her is more serious than simply coming back from vacation a different person. I know what it's like to carry around shit inside that's not suitable for public consumption and I understand how it feels to have people beg for information you just can't give.

I know what it feels like to have something living inside that eats away at your sanity. They call it trauma, a deeply distressing experience, but God…it's so much more. It's alive and breathing, it eats and rarely sleeps, it's a monster that demands attention and never ever gives in. I understand hurting in a way that feels incurable, and no matter how many times people offer to hear it out, to take some of the burden, the idea that anyone would ever really understand the pain is laughable.

"All right." I hold out a hand and she takes it so I can help her to her feet.

We walk in silence back to the truck and even though she's not communicating with words she's giving off some serious back-off vibes.

I can't expect her to share with me.

But maybe we can help each other forget. If only for a little while.

SAWYER

Agoraphobic?

What a bunch of bullshit!

Why would Celia share those things about me? Just because I didn't have the social life she had and spent my weekends at home watching movies doesn't mean I'm a damn mental case. Sure there was a time where I didn't leave often but Celia was halfway across the world while I was suffering. And I worked through it eventually—thanks to therapy.

I'm so sick of feeling like just because I'm not as free and uncomplicated as Celia there's something wrong with me.

Did your sister finally snap and lock herself in her house like you predicted?

We hadn't spoken much at all before she came home and yet she's making predictions about my life. I rub the center of my chest hoping to push back the weight of betrayal.

This is what she thinks of me, and I'm giving up my vacation time, my pride, my freakin' identity to help her out! And I'm lying to someone who I'm starting to care about, all for my sister who spoke about me like I'm some Howard Hughes freak show.

No, I'm not doing this! I won't. It's not fair to me and it's not fair to Aden.

I'm telling him. Tonight. I'm going to confess and tell him who I really am.

He deserves to know. This charade has gone on long enough, and why I thought I would be able to pull this off, to live wild and unburdened for even a short amount of time was a joke.

This is the most burdened I've ever felt, and pushing against all my fears, smothering all my instincts is exhausting. I don't have it in me to lie. It's only been days and the guilt is smothering.

And Aden…he's been so good to me. Sure he's moody, but that hasn't bothered me much. I've been flat-out lying to his face since the day we met, and something tells me he's not the kind of guy who'll forgive that kind of thing easily.

He pulls his truck up to the cottages and figuring he was just going to drop me off, I'm surprised when he shuts off the engine.

"You don't have to walk me—"

He turns to me, the intensity of his eyes silencing me immediately. "I think we can help each other out."

"What does that mean?" My voice sounds breathy even in my own ears and I can't control the quickening rise and fall of my chest.

"That thing…whatever it is that you don't think I'll understand… I know what it feels like."

"How could you—"

"I have it too."

To anyone else what he said would sound ridiculous, but for me it's as if he's reading my soul and understands the words. "You do?"

There's no way a man like Aden could understand what it's like to struggle between who he is and who he's trying to be. That every day I spend as Celia only makes me more frustrated at being Sawyer. But I can't change who I am, no matter how much I want to. The guilt and the self-hatred is crippling and I'm so lost in who I am and who I wish I could be that somewhere along the way, I've lost my way.

His gaze turns tortured and pleading. "Let me help you."

"How?" I force myself to breathe, feeling light-headed at the way he's staring at me, as if I'm the key to something he's desperate to unlock.

I'm frozen, tangled and consumed by his penetrating presence. He leans in and as if we're magnetized I mirror his movement. His hand cups my jaw so gently, his fingers sift into my hair and I press into his palm, fitting into his hand as if I were made to be there.

"I know the struggle," he whispers, his gaze locked on mine in an unbreakable bond. "I can help you let it go." He slides the quarter I gave him earlier into my palm. "If you'll let me."

I want that, I want to release all the back and forth, throw my hands up and succumb to every desire I've managed to suppress.

I don't have to flip the coin to know I want to get lost in Aden's touch without a single thought to the consequences. That's what I want.

But there's something I need to do, he needs to know the truth. He deserves—

"Don't. Whatever you're thinking, stop." Our breath mingles as the way our eyes are locked together robs me of coherent thought. He flashes a tiny smile before he kisses me.

My eyes shut as the heat of his mouth invades mine. I'm caught in the power of his lips as they draw me in. Consumed, dominated, all the reasons why I should pull away dissolve with every slide of his tongue. My thoughts scramble and sink, leaving nothing but my desire for more. Every nip of his teeth and brush of his callused thumb against my sensitive skin is like a soothing balm to my overactive thoughts.

I loop my arms around his neck and he moans into my mouth as I crawl closer. My leg gets stuck on the stick shift and he chuckles low and deep, the vibration humming against my lips.

He uses both hands in my hair to pull my mouth from his and I'm panting, pathetically, and hating the space between us. "What?"

"You're eager." He licks his bottom lip as if savoring the taste of my mouth from his. "I wasn't expecting that." His crooked smile makes my belly flip-flop.

I should probably be embarrassed, but he's ignited something in me that refuses to take a backseat to anything else. "You started it."

"I did."

I push hard against his hold to get my lips back on his where I whisper, "Then finish it."

He groans and his hips flex into me. "Not here."

I kiss a trail down his jaw enjoying the bite of his stubble against my skin.

"Fuck, I'd kill anything that got between me and that mouth." He lifts his chin, directing my attention to the middle of his throat. "You feel too good." His fingers grip my head, pressing me lower. "Keep going." I tug at the neck of his shirt. His pecs contract with every brush of my lips.

I dart my tongue out to lick along his collarbone and my eyes slide closed at the spicy, salty taste of his skin. I lick at him again, then pull the firm flesh into my mouth hoping it'll leave a mark.

"Enough." He pops the handle of his door and slides out so quickly I almost fall forward after him. His hand stops me from face planting and he practically lifts me from the truck and sets me on my feet. "Inside. Now."

"You like ordering me around."

"Fuck yeah I do." He kicks the door closed behind me, then presses me back against it. He buries his face into my neck and nips at the sensitive skin. "And you like taking my orders."

I blink up at the stars while he peppers my neck with kisses. There is something nice about trusting someone enough to know I can do what I'm told and he'll take care of me. Then there are no lists, no overthinking, but rather a complete release of power. The idea is intoxicating. "Yes."

"I can tell." More kisses up my jaw. "On the boat, at the bar, and now…you relax when I take control."

I do? "I do?"

"Mm-hmm." He licks at my earlobe. "It's fucking beautiful."

I'm breathless in his arms.

"Your place or mine?"

"M-mine."

He grabs my hand and just like that he's tugging me down the paved pathway to Celia's cottage.

ELEVEN

ADEN

Stumbling through the door to Celia's place, I tell my body to calm the fuck down but my hands aren't receiving the message. I don't want to scare her away by pawing at her like a teenage boy. This isn't a drunken fumble-fuck where we both race to the finish line. I want to go slow, make her feel cherished. It's what a girl like Celia needs, and I can give her what she needs.

I want to erase the anguish I recognize in her eyes. That look is one I see in the mirror daily, and though she may not be happy about being my distraction, I'm fucking eager as shit to be hers.

She drops her keys on the coffee table and the sound serves as a big fat green light. I pounce.

She squeaks as I bury my hands in her hair and delve into a kiss that has my pulse pounding in my ears. Her mouth is warm and sweet and the whisper of perfume from her skin is a buffet for my senses.

Walking backward, I guide her through a maze of boxes and piles of things that need to be packed until we're at the doorway to her bedroom. I can't pull my lips from hers, so I pop open an eye and spot the bed. Pressing her back and down, she grips my biceps as I lower her to the mattress. I follow her down, making sure to hold up my weight to avoid crushing her.

"Where's the light?" I whisper between breaths. "I want to see you."

She motions to the bedside table and, reaching over her, I click on the lamp. It's dim, but it's enough that when I peer down at her she blushes. Actually fucking blushes. The last girl I was with who blushed was my high school girlfriend. I brush my thumb along her cheek. "What's this for?"

She shakes her head and turns away, her skin growing brighter, and fuck if her modesty isn't a damn aphrodisiac. "I'm not used to feeling like this."

"Embarrassed?"

"No." Her head turns back to me and she meets my eyes. "Out of control."

I nip at her lips, needing to feel them. "When was the last time you felt out of control?"

Her breath hitches as I kiss down her chin to her neck. "Th-the boat. Fishing."

I blink and pull back, studying her. "And the time before that?"

Another furious blush. "So long ago that I don't remember."

I can't help the slow grin that spreads across my face because it feels fucking fantastic to be the only person who's made her feel wild. "And I'm only getting started."

Her muscles tense and I don't miss the flash of panic in her eyes.

"We don't have to do anything you're not ready for. I'm content to kiss you all night if that's what you want." I push her hair off her face and kiss the tip of her nose. "When was the last time you had sex?"

Her nose crinkles up and she turns away from me only to have me gently maneuver her face back to mine. "Don't get shy now, freckles."

"I lived with my ex just days before I came to San Diego."

I try to hold back my surprise, but that was not the answer I was expecting.

"We were having problems long before we broke up so sex wasn't something—"

I press my thumb to her lips. "This isn't couples therapy, I don't need the details. Just a number." I release her mouth but run the pad of my thumb along her thick lower lip and resist the urge to bite it as punishment for giving herself to some dickwad douchebag who didn't appreciate what he had.

"A month."

"What the fuck is wrong with that guy? Having you under his roof, sleeping in his bed, he doesn't touch you for a *month*?"

"He wasn't the type—"

I cover her lips with mine and finally sink my teeth into her plump lip. She whimpers and her nails bite into my skin. "No more talk of that idiot."

"Okay." She breathes out hard and her entire body turns to jelly beneath me.

"I want you, but we'll take it at your pace." I lean in and kiss her until she's squirming beneath me. Her hands slide up my side, nails dragging along my ribs, and my hips jack forward of their own will.

I break the kiss just long enough to pull my shirt off over my head. Her gaze slides over my chest, down my abdomen, and widen at the bulge behind my pants. Hunger flares in her eyes and a slow smile curls my lips. Something tells me *her pace* will be faster than I thought.

We are a tangle of arms and legs, tongues and teeth, and before

I'm even aware of what's going on she's slipping her tank top over her head. I follow her freckles down to her breasts where they disappear behind the black fabric of her strapless bra. I fist my hands to keep from helping her as she reaches behind her back and unhooks the bra before letting it fall to the bed.

Oh God, those gorgeous specks of color are everywhere and I plan to taste every, fucking, one.

I pull her lips back to mine and absorb the feeling of her bare breasts pressed against me. My heart hammers against my ribs and I have a brief moment of insecurity wondering if she can feel how affected I am by her touch.

Even if we're using each other as a distraction, what a sweet fucking distraction this is.

I cup her ass, grinding against her and wanting so badly to feel her completely naked and bared to me. Her body is soft and round in all the right places and all my blood rushes between my legs until I'm painfully aroused.

She rolls her hips against me, the motion so erotic it makes me light-headed. A soft whimper vibrates up from her throat.

"You good, baby?" I whisper against her lips.

"No."

What? I pull back to see her face only to find her eyelids heavy and her mouth curved up into a seductive grin.

"I want more."

Sweetest words I've ever heard.

SAWYER

I can't believe how bold I'm being. But I can't help but feel like Aden's holding us back.

It's not that I don't appreciate him thinking I need to take things slowly, I do. And this is without a doubt the hottest make-out session I've ever had and probably, I'd venture to guess, in the history of the world, but it's starting to feel like the world's worst tease.

My skin is practically vibrating, my body aching, and my legs falling open just to get him closer to me.

I reach down and rub him over his jeans and groan when I feel just how much he wants me too. I pop the buttons of his fly and he must take that as an open invitation to do the same to mine. My jeans are tight, but he manages to slide his big hand between my legs just as I grip him over his boxers.

Our breath mingles as we pant in unison while stroking each other.

"I'm not the type of man who begs." He hisses through his teeth when I grip him tighter. "But I'm begging, please, let me fuck you."

His dirty mouth has me clenching down around his fingers. "Aden…"

"I can feel you want it as bad as I do, freckles. Tell me I'm wrong."

"I can't."

With a growl he flips us so he's holding himself over me. Pushing up to his knees, I lose his hand, but keep my grip on him. His abs contract with every pump of my fist as he watches me pleasure him.

Mark and I always made love in the dark under the sheets. After our faces were washed and our teeth were brushed, and after the evening news. It was like clockwork. Safe. Predictable. Everything I thought I needed. I've never been with someone like Aden, someone so overtly sexual and open about wanting to see everything that happens between us. It's the most arousing thing I've ever experienced.

"You like to watch."

His eyes slide from the vee of his open fly, up my bare torso, dance between my less than impressive breasts, my lips, then he stares me in the eyes. "I like watching with you."

"Why?"

He bites his bottom lip while toying with my nipples. "Mmm…'cause I don't ever want to forget a single detail. Don't even like closing my eyes when I kiss you."

"You're sweet."

"I'm not." He leans over me and flicks my breasts with his tongue, making me arch off the bed. "You're sweet. So fucking sweet."

He shifts off me to stand at the end of the bed. With a little help from me, he manages to peel my jeans off until I'm lying completely naked and exposed. His eyes devour me while he fishes in his back pocket and pulls out a condom. He drops his jeans and kicks them off, then hands me the foil packet. "I want to watch you roll it on. Nice and slow."

I scramble to my knees and do exactly what he asked, thinking I'd never found condoms the least bit sexy before, but somehow Aden makes protection placement feel like foreplay.

The room is quiet except for the sound of our eager breaths and the occasional moan as I slide the condom over him. Being this close I start to wonder what he'd taste like there and craving the salty—

I'm pushed back to the bed and he follows me down.

"You lickin' those lips while staring at my dick is going to make it impossible for me to go slow."

"I don't want to go slow."

He pulls back and now it's his turn to smile in a devilish way that has all my insides clenching. "You're a constant surprise, you know that?"

"Yeah." Because damn, I'm surprising myself!

With that one word he pushes between my legs and enters me with the care and consideration of a tender lover.

"You good?" He kisses me softly and rests his forehead against mine.

I nod frantically. "Are you?"

He laughs and starts to move, picking up his pace with every deep, consuming thrust. "Better than ever."

Our bodies move in unison, as if they were designed to work together for the simple act of bringing the other immeasurable pleasure. What I think will be rough and animalistic ends up being sensual. He worships me with touch and whispered words while we move together in perfect rhythm. Like some sexual shaman he manages to arouse not only my body but my mind and soul. Electrified with sensation he grips my hair tightly at the roots, awakening every nerve. "You're so beautiful."

"Aden...I don't...I can't hang on—"

"Shhh..." He licks at the seam of my lips. "Don't hang on. Let go."

I bite my lip to keep quiet as my back arches off the bed. My nails dig into Aden's shoulders as what feels like a thousand stars explode beneath my skin. He falls forward and groans into my neck. His body crushes mine in a delicious weight that keeps me grounded while the aftershocks of my release threaten to send me sailing.

After a few minutes of what seems like synchronized breathing he pushes up, presses a kiss to the tip of my nose, and peels himself off me to go to the bathroom.

I stare at the bamboo fan spinning above the bed, following one blade with my eye and hoping that doing so will manage to untangle my thoughts.

I just slept with a virtual stranger.

Someone I'm not in a serious relationship with.

Someone I know nothing about.

Why do I feel so good? My heart is still racing, my thigh muscles tingling with exertion, and this stupid grin on my face won't go away no matter how many times I try to force it.

"You look happy." His voice sounds just seconds before the bed dips and the heat of his body hits mine as he gathers me to his side.

"Happy is an understatement." My grin widens and I'm glad my cheek is pressed to Aden's chest so he can't see it.

"I hear that." He yawns and turns the light off.

My pulse quickens. Is he spending the night? I assumed he'd get dressed, grab his phone and make some excuse for having to leave like I've seen happen in the movies after a one-night stand. What I didn't expect was for him to hold me close, run his fingers through my hair, and...doze off?

I wonder how often he does this kind of thing. As handsome as he is, I'd guess he does this often. Thinking on that is another brutal reminder that I know zero about this guy. My naked body is pressed against his, and he could have a freakin' girlfriend for all I know.

I chew my lip as unease seeps into my chest, pushing away my good mood. Surely if he had a girlfriend I'd know. Right? What if he has a wife? Kids? What if he's a felon? What do I really know about this guy? How stupid could I—

"The fact that you're able to think so hard I can fucking *feel* it tells me I didn't do my job." There's humor in his voice, but I still stop breathing hoping to hide how right he is.

"Your job?"

He traces patterns on my hip. "To take your mind off things."

"You definitely took my mind off things." Pretty sure I had an out-of-body experience at one point. "Now I'm thinking about other things."

"Like?"

I swallow and pull up whatever's left of my courage, then tilt my chin up to look at him. "I've never slept with a stranger before."

He frowns, looking almost offended, and I'm reminded of how terrible I am at post-orgasm pillow talk. "I'm a stranger, am I?"

"I just don't know that much about you and I have my naked body wrapped around yours."

He clears his throat and looks up at the ceiling fan. I'm about to tell him it's a waste of time, that the damn thing has no answers, when he starts talking.

"I was born in Santa Barbara. Played football, was pretty decent at it, got a scholarship to play at Washington State, but my dad was Army, my granddad was Army, all my uncles were too, so I gave up football and enlisted one week after I graduated high school."

Giving up college for war? "Why would…I mean, you didn't fight your dad on that?"

"I didn't want to fight it. I wanted to go. I was raised to believe the most honorable thing a man could do was serve his country."

"But what about your education?"

"I got an education in the Army. What I learned in the military was more valuable than anything I'd learn going to college. I liked football, but there was no guarantee I'd go pro. Knowing our country needed men, that we were fighting to protect innocent people, to ensure freedom, football paled in comparison to all that."

I guess I understand. "You mentioned you have a sister, are you two close?"

"Not anymore." He clears his throat. "She's married, has two kids."

"I'm sure they love having you back."

His body stiffens at my side. "I, uh…I don't see them much."

"Why?"

"I came back and they all looked at me like they didn't know me. They wanted answers I wouldn't give and the more they pushed the more I shut down."

"Why not just answer their questions?" I'm not one hundred percent sure what we're talking about, but I fear we're breaching the subject of his military life and I promised him I'd stay away from it.

He's quiet for a few beats. "I refuse to bleed on the people I love."

I stare blindly at the wall in front of me, all too familiar with how difficult it is for family to see a loved one struggling with something and not being able to help them through it.

"What about you? Tonight, Polly mentioned you had a sister." He's trying to change the subject from him to me; it's what I would do in his shoes. But I can't tell him about Celia, about how hurt I am that she'd share my ugliest secrets with people she hardly knew.

"I do."

"What's wrong with her?"

"Nothing!"

He raises his eyebrows.

"I mean…" I rub my forehead. "She's not as bad as Polly made her seem. She's not agoraphobic."

I roll to my back and he pushes up on his elbow looking down at me. Silence stretches between us until it becomes suffocating.

"She thinks she may have killed our grandmother when we were kids."

"How does a child kill her grandmother?"

"She gave her the flu. Complications of that caused her death and I guess ever since she got weird about…stuff."

"Stuff like…?"

"She became much more aware of germs, that's all. More than what they considered normal. After high school she spiraled a little but she's better now." I pick at the edge of my fingernail. "She's mostly better now."

"Are you two close?"

I shut my eyes and bite back the swell of emotion building in my chest.

"Celia?"

I jerk in his hold hearing him call me by my sister's name.

He squeezes me closer, probably interpreting my reaction as meaning something different. "All right. Enough of this shit, you up for a little adventure?"

Yes, please. Enough. Wait, did he say *adventure*?

I peek up at him and he must sense the question in my stare.

He jumps from the bed bare-ass naked and heads to the bathroom. I prop myself up on my elbows to admire the view of his very firm backside and I frown when he returns with a towel wrapped around his waist and one in his hand. He tosses it to me. "Come on, get up and wrap that around you."

I sit up and the sheet falls down around my hips so I cover with the towel and scoot to the edge of the bed. "Why?"

"I have an idea." He holds out his hand and I take it.

I barely have the thing secured and tucked around me when he drags me through the cottage to the front door. "Whoa." I dig my heels into the shag rug. "I'm not going outside like this."

"Why not? It's dark, no one will know you don't have a bathing suit under there. Plus…" He swings open the door and guides me out. "No one's around anyway."

I lean back and really push my heels into the ground but it's pointless, he's too strong, and if I fight any harder I might lose my towel. "Aden," I hiss through clenched teeth. "Where are we going?"

He doesn't answer me with words, but soon we're at the top step of the staircase that leads down the cliffs to a small beach.

My mind scrambles as I stumble behind him down the stairs.

Naked.

Towels.

Beach.

He's not expecting me to swim, is he?

Panic flares in full force and I really put the brakes on this time by dropping down to sit my ass on the cold concrete step. If he expects me to get into that water he's going to have to pick me up and carry me.

He whirls around, studies my seated position, then shrugs before leaning in and putting his shoulder into my stomach. He scoops me off the step and hoists me up. "Aden, no, put me down!"

"Stop yelling or someone will call the cops."

He jogs down the remaining few steps and the cold ocean air hits my bare butt, making my entire body flash with the heat of a red-hot blush. "Good! We'll need the cops to pull what's left of our naked bodies from the ocean after a shark kills us!"

I squeal when he jerks to a stop and drops me back down to my feet. The movement takes my towel and I scramble to cover my body when Aden stills my hands. "Don't."

"Are you crazy?" I spit through clenched teeth.

The corner of his lips pull up into that lopsided smile I'm starting to like more than I should. "Would it scare you if I was?"

I look deep into his eyes, unsure of how to answer his question. His crazy scares me, there's no denying that. But it also makes me feel more alive than I ever have. "A little."

He rewards me with a slow soft kiss and just as I tilt my head to get more he pulls away and leaves me pouting. "Lose the towel."

"You first."

He steps back and drops the terrycloth. Every ridge of his muscles catches the moonlight, making it look as if he's cut from stone.

"Your turn."

His voice brings me away from his impressive thighs and I shake my head. "I can't...I don't know...Shit!"

"What is it?" This time there's no teasing in his voice, just pure concern.

"I'm not a great swimmer and I've seen one too many shark movies to feel comfortable in the ocean at all, let alone at night."

He pulls me to his chest, tilts my chin up so he can look me in the eye. "You think I'd ever let anything happen to you?"

"I don't think you have any power over whether or not something hurts me."

He flinches as if my words delivered a physical blow. "Ouch."

"Ya know how most people think things would never happen to them? I'm the other girl." I'm rambling, my nerves making my lips move faster than my brain can keep up with. "I'm the kind of girl these things always happen to. If there's danger out there it'll find me, trust that."

"This coming from the same girl who ran with bulls and pet a damn lion like it was a kitten."

Oh shit.

A wave of heat washes over me from the top of my skull to the backs of my legs with the realization of what I've done. I forgot. "I…" I close my mouth, my emotions scrambling to come up with a justifiable excuse.

"You'll be fine, now dig deep for that adventurous girl I know lives inside you." He winks and pries my hands off the towel to get it loose from my body and tosses it aside. In an attempt to hide from any and every one, I hug myself to him, pressing into his muscles and hoping to disappear. He wraps me in his arms and for a moment we stand there holding on to each other.

"See, isn't this nice. Wouldn't you rather just stay here like this?"

He nuzzles my ear. "Nice try."

Grabbing my hand, he leads me down the beach to the water's edge. The cool waves hit our feet and send me stepping back as far as I can while still holding his hand. He looks at me as if to gauge my fear, but remembering who I am, who I'm supposed to be, I just smile back.

"It's cold." My voice trembles with anxiety, but I can't deny the butterflies of anticipation that swarm in my chest at the thought of taking a risk, trying something new, and coming out on the other side alive. It would be a huge victory against the fear that shackles me. I allow him to lead me out into the breaking waves until we're about thigh level.

"You good?"

"I can't believe I'm doing this." The last word ends on a high-pitched squeal that surprises even me.

He chuckles and leads me farther out into the waves. Something brushes against my leg and I jump and cling to him. He holds me close and hums in his throat as his hands cup my backside. "Scared?"

I look up at him and get lost in the warmth of his gaze. "No. I feel safe with you."

"Yeah?" His lips part and his breath dances across my lips. "So I'm not a stranger anymore."

"No." I run my hands up the back of his neck into his hair and slide against his hard body. "You make me feel like I can do anything."

His eyebrows drop low and his jaw ticks. "And you make me forget."

"Forget what—"

His lips devour mine and all my concerns melt away until all that's left is Aden.

TWELVE

ADEN

It was the best night's rest I'd had in a while. Usually I can't sleep with the memories that haunt me. Maybe it was the exhausting swim with Celia, or the sand-covered heavy make-out session that followed, or maybe it was having her warm back pressed to my front, my arm slung over her and resting between her breasts, whatever it was had sleep pulling me under quicker than it typically does.

I didn't dream much because I was so afraid of having a night terror and scaring Celia I kept waking myself up. But even with those interruptions, I still slept better than I had in a long time.

The sun shines through her tie-dyed curtains and lights the small bedroom, making it look like an acid trip. I contemplate waking Celia up with my hands and mouth between her legs, but judging by the not so feminine way she's snoring I think she could use a little more sleep. After staring at the back of her head and breathing in the saltwater scent left on her hair my stomach rumbles and it forces me up to hunt down breakfast.

I slip on my jeans from last night and sneak into the kitchen, making sure I don't wake Celia. I swing open the fridge and prop an arm on top to lean in and peruse my options.

There's a jug full of green juice that looks like swamp water, a loaf of *sprouted* bread, whatever the fuck that means, and—I pull out a package and glare at it. "Tofu egg substitute." There's nothing edible in here.

There's a thump from the bedroom seconds before Celia comes racing out into the kitchen in a blur of bedsheet and blond hair. She slides on the hardwood, nearly falling over, and stares at me with wide puffy eyes and swollen lips.

I smile with pride knowing I'm responsible for her sexed-up disheveled look. "Mornin'."

Her eyes land on me and she blows a wavy strand of hair from her face. "You're still here."

I shut the fridge door and cross to her, completely aware of her eyes as they hungrily take in my naked torso. "I am. I was going to make us breakfast but there's no way I'm eating tofu or any other tree-huggin' food you got in there."

She licks her lips and a flash of irritation bubbles up in my chest at how easily she can distract me by doing something so simple. "You were going to make me breakfast?"

"I was, but…" I tilt my head and study her knuckles as they hold her sheet in a death grip. "If you'd rather I take off I can do that too."

Hurt crosses her features. "You want to leave?"

I stop and take a deep breath. I'm not good at this shit, this morning-after crap, but I really don't want to mess things up with Celia. She's more sensitive than most girls I'd use as a distraction, and it's clear she's also more than a distraction to me now. If she were, I'd have whispered pretty words into her ear and left her sated and sleeping shortly after her last orgasm. No, she's more, and I need to choose my next words wisely.

As much as I want to reach out and pull her to my chest, I don't. I tuck my hands under my arms and hold her eyes. "I want more time with you."

Her eyes dart from where they were dancing across my pecs and land on my lips. "Wait, what? Why?"

"I want more time with you because, well…you're the most entertaining girl I've met in a very long time."

A small smile curves her lips. "Really?"

"Yeah." I nod to all the boxes that litter the small space around us. "I know you're moving, I know you have shit to do, but before you go, for however long you'll be in San Diego, I want to spend that time with you."

Long thick lashes flutter over gorgeous eyes and she nods. "I'd like that."

"Come here."

She doesn't seem to even contemplate disobeying, and her feet bring her closer. Her fingers are no longer curled up tightly to the sheet and it falls a little to reveal the gentle swell of her breast. I hook her around the neck and pull her to me. Kissing her head and breathing in the gentle smell of the sea on her skin, I relax even more with her in my arms.

"Anyone ever tell you these freckles are really sexy?" I slide the tip of my finger along the dip of her collarbone.

"Never."

Fighting off the annoyance that not a single man she's been with has appreciated her incredibly beautiful skin, I drop a kiss to her shoulder. "I was dying to know how far down they go."

She sighs as I dance my lips up her neck to her ear.

"Now I know, they go all the way down." My hands grip her ass and I'm itching to drag her back to bed when she falls heavy against me.

"You hungry, freckles?"

"A little." She pulls back and grins. "I should grab a quick shower, though. I have sand in places I shouldn't."

I lift a brow. "Ya know, I happen to have extensive training in sand removal. Army trained."

"Is that right?"

"Mm-hm." I bury my nose in her neck and take her scent deep into my lungs, allowing it to wash over me.

"I think I could use some help, but first…" She pulls back and flashes a teasing grin. "You'll have to catch me."

She takes off running and I catch her just as she reaches the bathroom door. Pulling the sheet from her body I press her back to the wall and drop to my knees at her feet. "You might want to hold on to something."

* * *

It took everything I had to pull myself away, but I knew if I didn't I'd end up in the shower with Celia and we'd both eventually starve to death.

She's slumped on the floor of the bathroom, still against the wall, but now on her ass with a towel gathered to her torso.

"You good?"

Her lazy smile makes my chest swell with pride. "Oh yeah."

"Come on." I turn on the shower and hold out my hand. "We've both got things we have to get to today, but first, shower so I can feed you."

She grabs my hand and I pull her to her feet. "You don't have to do that, I have food—"

"Real food. Not fucking tofu eggs. And I thought you weren't a vegetarian."

"I'm not, I just don't like eating something that comes out of a chicken's butt."

Damn she's cute.

She pulls back to peer up at me. "Besides, they taste just like real eggs."

"I don't believe that for a second." I drop a kiss to her forehead. "I'll go to Cal's and get cleaned up. Can you be ready in thirty?"

"Yeah."

"Good." I smack her ass and she melts deeper into me. It takes all my control not to bend her over the sink, and I pull away. "I'll be back."

"*I'm a friend of Sarah Connor,*" she says in her best Schwarzenegger voice.

I shake my head, grinning at this new nerdy side of Celia.

"You have a great smile."

"Stop trying to seduce me." I give her a quick kiss because judging by the way she's looking at me like she's hungry as hell and not for breakfast combined with my already hardening dick, I need to get the hell out of here. Plus, I like the idea of leaving her wanting more, so I snag my shirt from her room and slide on my shoes.

There's a buzzing from a small desk in the corner of the room and when I look up I see it's Celia's phone. I pull it from the charger and take it out to her.

"Phone's ringing."

As I hand it to her I see the caller ID lit up with the word *Dad*.

"Thanks." She checks it and sends it to voicemail.

"You could've answered it." I have a sister and understand protective parents. Growing up in a strict military family, my dad hated it when my sister was old enough to date. If they spoke on the phone and he heard a man in the background, he'd send me to wherever she was to check it out. It's no surprise the girl got married at nineteen. "I'd have kept quiet."

She laughs, but it's awkward. Uncomfortable. "Oh, no, it's…not that, it's, I don't know—"

I press my thumb over her lips and dip down to replace it with my mouth. "Shh…it's cool. I get it." I drop a couple long, soft kisses to her lips until I know for a fact if I don't leave we'll end up back in bed. "Thirty minutes."

I rush out before I change my mind, walking awkwardly back to Cal's cottage with the mother of all hard-ons between my legs.

This woman…shit.

"Yo! Aden!" My jaw locks down at the sound of Brice calling after me, the slap of his flip-flops chasing me down. "Wait up!"

Thankfully the guy's voice does wonders to deflate my dick, so with a quick adjustment, I turn around just as he makes it to me. His wet hair hangs over his forehead and a towel is slung over his shoulder like he just came in from surfing.

"What's up?"

His eyes shift between me and Celia's front door. "You and Celia hooking up?"

Bored, I stare at the guy. "You're seriously asking me this shit?"

"No, I mean…" He shakes his head and chuckles. "It's just, before she left we were hanging out and I guess, I figure ya know, now that she's back…" He shrugs.

Celia and Brice? She mumbled something about him yesterday, something about not wanting to see him at Lenny's.

"I don't know what to say, man. She never mentioned that you two were together." And why the fuck not?

He stares longingly at her door and I flex my hand to keep from slapping him to face me instead. "Huh…"

"All right, well…good talk." I spin around. He snags me by my biceps from behind.

Red.

Sirens.

Panic.

I grip his wrist. Whirl around. Break his hold, and twist.

He cries out, his body turning to try to alleviate the pressure on his wrist.

"*Do not* fucking touch me or I will break your shit off, do you understand?"

"Yeah, man, fuck!"

My heart hammers behind my ribs as I tell myself this isn't real. I glare at him, assessing. He's not a threat. This isn't war. These feelings aren't real. I release him with a shove and a wave of shame and guilt washes over me.

"Shit, Brice. I'm sorry."

"Dude, you almost broke my friggin' arm!"

A woman walking her dog past the cottages turns to us, her eyebrows low in judgment.

"Don't ever come at me like that again, okay." It's as much as I'll give him and he bitches as I leave him behind and head to Cal's. I manage to keep my cool long enough to push inside and lean against the door. Sliding down to my ass, I cup my head and practice the breathing techniques the VA therapist taught me.

In through the nose. Out through the mouth.

One thing is for sure, I absolutely would've broken Brice's wrist.

Six months ago, if someone grabbed me from behind like that, the least of their worries would've been a fractured arm.

Back then...I would've killed 'em.

SAWYER

"Yeah, Dad, things are moving right along." I spin in a slow circle, counting all the boxes. All the *empty* boxes.

I've been there three days and have completed about three hours of work, if that.

All because of Aden.

When I walked out this morning to see him hunched into the fridge, shirtless, all that smooth skin just beckoning to be touched, I had to white-knuckle my sheet to keep it around my body when all my instincts demanded I tackle him to the floor.

And then he said he wants to spend time with me? I've never received an offer so tempting in my entire life. I almost lost my sheet altogether right then and there. What is happening to me? I'd never consider pushing off my responsibilities for…sex. That's gratification at its basest form. I had a moment where my insecurities flared, but when he kissed me so sweetly as if I was delicate and he didn't want me to crumble, my heart did just that. It shattered, but not in a bad way. It was more like shaking off a tough exterior. I felt exposed and protected all in the same moment, which would've confused Sawyer, but Celia would just roll with it and never look back.

So I did.

I showered as quickly as I could, threw on a breezy pair of pants and a tight tank top that shows a tiny strip of my stomach. It's risky but Aden said he loved my skin. The freckles were always something that made me self-conscious in the past, but with him they feel like a superpower. And by showing them off I'm hoping it'll serve as a gentle reminder to him of what we did.

I never understood what they meant in movies when they would say the sex was "earth-shattering," but oh boy do I get it now. Just thinking about it warms my skin and my body yearns to relive it again and again.

"Sawyer…did you hear me?"

I jerk at the sound of my dad's voice and rip my eyes from the view of the ocean. "I'm sorry, I got distracted. What did you say?"

"*Distracted?* Are you okay?"

"Yes, Dad, I'm fine. I was watching the waves and…" This is not something Sawyer would've done. I'd never get distracted by something as ridiculous as the view. So I lie. Something I'm apparently getting pretty good at. "I haven't been sleeping well so maybe that's it."

"I'm sure it is. Take your time, okay? Don't run yourself into the ground to get back here. And please, Sawyer, call if you need me."

"Thanks, Dad. I will."

We say goodbye and I drop onto Celia's couch hating the guilt trickling in. It's one thing to honor my sister's wishes but I've completely sidelined my responsibilities. I have about five minutes until Aden will be here so I'll check my e-mail and see if things at work are running smoothly in my absence, hoping it'll alleviate the self-directed disappointment.

I have two e-mails from Dana. She needs my signature on a document, but I don't have a printer or scanner. I add searching for FedEx Office to my list of responsibilities expanding the day's productivity and making me feel better in the process, when a knock on the door is followed by a click of the handle and Aden strolls in.

His tall body takes up the door frame and I try not to stare at how sexy he looks in a pair of board shorts and a simple brown tee.

I smile, but quickly frown with the intense way he's glaring at me. "Aden, is everything okay?"

He crosses to me, pulls my phone from my hand and drags me to my feet to press a kiss so slow and sensual on my lips I lose the ability to stand on my own. Thankfully, he holds me up. "Better now."

"Whoa." I blink. "What was that for?"

He smiles, but it's tight. "Tell me about you and Brice."

Dammit.

As hard as I try I cannot force myself to look him in the eye. "There's not much to tell."

"He seems to think you two are a thing, that true?"

No clue, Aden. Maybe you should ask my sister! "A thing?" I shake my head. "No."

"You done with him?"

"Mm-hm."

"And the ex from Arizona?"

God, I sound like ho! "Uh-huh."

He presses a kiss to my forehead and I resist the urge to flop my arms to cool off my sweaty armpits. I don't know what Aden did for the military but it must've been something dealing with interrogation because he's fantastic at it.

I'm still recovering from his questioning when he hands me my phone back. "Did I interrupt something?"

"Huh?" I follow his line of sight and coherent thought comes back online. "Yes, er…no, I mean, I was answering some e-mails while I waited."

"Everything okay?" He releases me and I miss him instantly.

"Yeah, although you wouldn't happen to know if there's a FedEx Office nearby would you? I need to find a printer and a scanner—"

"There are both at Cal's place. I'll let you in after breakfast and you can work there as long as you need to."

"Really?" I'm smiling so hard it hurts.

He chuckles and shakes his head. "Don't look at me like that, freckles."

My grin expands. "Why not?"

"Because. You're going to ruin my reputation of being a hardass dickhead." If I'm not mistaken, I'd swear his cheeks turned the slightest shade of pink as he ducks his head and turns to the door.

"We wouldn't want that."

"Come on, I'm starving."

"Yes, sir." I salute his back and happily follow him out the door.

Hardass dickhead?

Sergeant Psycho?

It's possible he's showing me sides he rarely shows anyone else.

* * *

"This is so cool!" I'm sitting up as tall as possible to see up over the railing of the pier from the rusted chair on the café patio. I broke into a cold sweat as I walked down the wooden planked structure with waves crashing under my feet, but with Aden's arm around me I melted into his safety. "I've never eaten on a pier before. I've never even been on a pier before."

Right when the words come out of my mouth I look over to see Aden's dark brows pinched together. "With all the traveling you've done how have you never been on a pier?"

Excellent question.

Dammit!

"I don't know." I sip from my orange juice and hope like hell he'll drop the subject.

He's leaning back in his seat, one ankle resting on his powerful thigh, and his arms propped on the armrests. He's the epitome of masculinity and with the sun baking his skin the scent of spice and cedar penetrate the ocean air. "Out of all the places you've been, where was your favorite?"

Where was Celia's favorite place to visit? No fucking clue.

"Probably home."

"Phoenix?"

"Yeah. I, uh…I miss my family."

"Do you talk to your sister much?"

I rip at the edges of my paper napkin. "Uh-huh." I know he's asking about Sawyer, me being Celia, but I answer honestly.

As soon as she turned eighteen she left home and our paths only crossed on the occasional Christmas if she just happened to be passing through town. We never really knew where she was at any time, and that made remaining close difficult.

Until she got sick.

Funny how it takes something like illness and death to bring people back together, and by then...it's too late.

"You said you don't really talk to your family anymore, does that include your sister?" I internally pat myself on the back for redirecting the conversation off of me like he did the other night.

His fingers drum against the chair. "Yeah, pretty much all of them."

"I bet they miss you."

He cringes. "I don't know about that."

"Why? I know this probably won't come as a surprise to you, but I personally think you're a pretty decent guy."

He studies me for a few seconds, then leans as if to avoid anyone overhearing what he's about to say. "They don't think I'm... safe...anymore."

"Why would they think that?"

"Because I told them I'm not."

I shake my head hoping the action will make whatever he's trying to tell me fall into place and make sense.

"I can be around them for limited periods of time, but my sister worries about me being around her kids..." He purses his lips. "Fuck, I really don't feel like talking about this."

Instinctively I reach out and grasp his hand. "You sure? I'm a pretty good listener."

He flips his hand around to hold mine, interweaving our fingers. "I know you are, but would it be all right if we stopped talking about this deep shit and moved on to something a little lighter, like say..."

He brings my hand to his lips and kisses my knuckles. "You spending tonight with me on the boat?"

My stomach flips over on itself. "Sleeping on a boat?"

He scrunches up his face in the most adorable way. "I can't promise the sleeping, but I will absolutely promise it'll be a night you'll never forget."

I'm nodding before my lips can even form the word. "Yes."

Because soon enough I'll be out of his life and I'll go back to being Sawyer, the kind of girl who would never turn the head of a guy like Aden, and I'll be able to go on living my sheltered safe life knowing what it's like to truly live.

That is, if I survive it.

THIRTEEN

ADEN

"Sorry about the mess." I shove away a stack of papers to clear a spot for Celia's laptop on Cal's old desk. The rusty chair creaks as I pull it out and I motion for her to sit.

She has her computer clutched to her chest and she nods and drops slowly to the seat. "When was the last time you actually stayed here?"

I run a hand over my scalp. "It's been awhile. I know it looks out of control, but I swear there's a logical method to all this madness."

Her eyes scan what must be close to a month's worth of unopened mail. "Does that *logical method* include actually opening the mail?" She plucks up an envelope, setting down her laptop before grasping another, and another. "Aden, these look important."

I rub the back of my neck feeling a little guilty and a lot stupid. Thing is, Cal comes down every couple months to take care of all…those, whatever they are. "Yeah, the bank has been on Cal about this property. My job is to keep them away, not get involved, and let Cal take care of it. It's not my business. I'm just here to fix shit that breaks and collect rent."

"Uh-huh." She doesn't seem to be listening to what I'm saying as she creates four small piles in front of her, sorting through the mail and placing each envelope in a different pile.

I slide a stack of *Sport Fishing* magazines off the dusty black machine. "Here's the printer." I lift the top to expose the scanning glass. "Here's where you…" She's not even looking my way. "Celia." Her shoulders pull back and her spine stiffens before she peers up at me. "Are you listening?"

She eyes the printer and nods. "I'll figure it out." She goes back to organizing.

"You have work to do and this ain't it."

"I don't mind." She's practically glowing as she organizes each piece of mail with a practiced ease. The expression on her face reminds me of my own when I bust open a new lure to play with.

"I can see that, but still." From the way my uncle spoke of Celia I know he trusts her so I don't think twice about her going through his mail and sorting it for him.

"Aden…" She slaps down another envelope in a pile. "Don't you have something to do, like fix shit and collect rent, ya know? Like you said."

I get the feeling she's trying to get rid of me so she can indulge in her freakish need to organize. She's right, though. I should go fish. I need the money and I'd like to catch something for us to have for dinner tonight. "I'm not leaving you in this place alone. I don't trust you to leave it trashed."

A tiny smile tilts her lips, but she doesn't stop with the stacking. "You're probably right, but I'll try."

"Hey."

Now I get her eyes, wide and as green as fresh grass.

"I'm serious. I'd insist you stop doing what you're doing but you look so fucking happy doin' it I don't have the heart to make you stop. Get your work done first, okay?"

"I will."

I grip her chin and lean in to bring her mouth to mine. She tastes like syrup and orange juice. Wanting to consume her, I nip at her full upper lip. "Meet me at the boat tonight at sunset?"

"Okay."

"Bring an appetite."

"Yeah…" Her voice is breathy and so damn sexy.

I pop open her laptop and point to it. "I'm serious, Cece. Your work first."

Her shoulders deflate and her eyes drop to my stomach. Shit, I'm fucking this up. I need to walk away before she changes her mind.

"See ya tonight." I drop one more kiss on her head and force my feet to move, leaving her alone in Cal's place.

I slide into my truck and fire up the engine, excited about getting out on the ocean and getting some distance between me and the girl who's quickly consuming my every conscious thought.

* * *

Fishing was more successful than I thought it would be. I was only out for an hour before my lines started tugging. One after another, the fish bit. It was after five when I pulled back into the slip. Just enough time to get the fish off to the market, and I was pleased to see they were in desperate need for halibut and albacore, so I made serious coin right off the bat. I had just enough time to clean the blood off the back of the boat, and shower to be ready for when Celia comes over.

I'm wiping down the counters and checking to make sure the white wine I bought from the market is chilled enough when I hear a knock on the back deck. Smiling, I turn...then frown when I see Jenkins grinning with his broken smile of missing teeth.

Shit. He's here for dinner. So much for my date night with Celia.

"You hungry, old man?" I pull a beer out of the fridge and notice Jenkins doesn't have a bottle in his hand so I grab him one too and meet him out back.

"You bet." He takes the offered beer and drinks about half in one gulp. "What're we eating tonight?"

"Halibut." I drop down to the padded bench and notice the sun is dipping below the line of boats in the marina. "We're having company tonight."

"Figured as much." He takes another long swig.

"How's that?"

"We've missed you at the Office." His eyes dart to me and it doesn't take a genius to figure out he's noticed I'm not hanging off Sydney.

I stare toward the parking lot, pushing back a flicker of guilt. "Been busy."

"Busy...right. Celia's gorgeous. You'd be stupid not to chase her tail."

"You must've been around her before, what do you know about her?"

"Can't say I know anything. I heard Cal talk about a Celia, but she never came down to the boat. I never talked to her until this last time." He turns his foggy eye on me. "Better question is, what do you know about her?"

I shrug and notice my eyes keep drifting to the gate to the dock, anxious to see her again. "She's smart, funny in a weird way. We have a good time together. She's leaving in a couple weeks so we decided we'd hang out until she goes."

He nods thoughtfully and stares out at the horizon.

"Don't go silent on me now, Jenks. You always got shit to say about everything."

"Find it interesting you don't got any friends and far's I know you don't date, but you know this girl a few days and she's your friend and your date."

Excellent point, I'm kind curious about that shit too. Ever since I was released from the army, most people annoy the crap out of me. Women complain about their favorite shows being canceled or the fact that they had to sit in traffic for thirty minutes on their way to work. Men complain about not getting laid enough or the battery in their latest smartphone dying halfway through the baseball game they were watching.

The petty complaints of people who have never lived for fifteen months in a shitty hut with a couple dozen men, sleeping with their M4s on their chests because at any moment the enemy could open fire on their asses. The average American sits on their cushioned couch with a beer in hand, a hot home-cooked meal in the oven, and bitching to their sixty-inch flat screen about how much the government sucks, about how the country is going to hell in a scrotum sack while me and my men are over there jumping in front of bullets to protect the innocent, fighting the terrorists that have ravaged not only Americans but people all over the world.

They don't know what it's like to have to dig through dirt to find all the body parts of a brother who gave his life to save theirs. Collecting fingers and toes and half-legs, matching them up to send back to their wives and children in a fucking box. People bitch about getting their kids into the right schools while over there parents are burying headless children. So yeah, maybe I'm a little fucking intolerant.

"Fuck." I grip my now empty bottle to my chest feeling that familiar static that'll lead to anxiety, which will end in paranoia. That's the shit that fucks me up. *Perfect for a date night.* "I don't know what I'm doing."

Jenkins nods. I can see he carries what happened in Nam around as clear as if I were staring at my own reflection. "She's just a woman."

Yeah, just a woman. She's not a threat to me. She doesn't know how fucked up I am and as far as I know she seems to enjoy being with me. Don't read too much into this, Aden.

Suddenly antsy, I hop up and light the charcoal on the grill, trying to stay busy; it's the best thing to do to keep my thoughts from taking my body back to Iraq.

The sweat.

Racing pulse.

Delusions.

Stabbing coals, my gaze is drawn back to the gate and this time they're not met with disappointment.

"She's here." I move to the dock and hop off the boat, hearing Jenkins's garbled chuckle as I make my way to the gate.

She's wearing cutoff shorts and a sweatshirt, her hair pulled back off her face in one of those headband things. Casual, and perfect. I have an overwhelming urge to take her straight to bed and hold her close. *What the fuck, Colt! Get it together!*

"You made it." I hit the button on the panel to release the lock and swing open the gate for her.

"You said sunset." She smiles and I'm gone.

I pull her to me and melt around her tiny body, liking the way her arms wrap around my waist as she fits herself to my chest. I'm grateful to see she has a bag slung over her shoulder. I was worried she might change her mind about staying the night.

I slip the bag from her and release her just enough to throw my arm around and walk her down the dock to the boat. "You're right on time."

She tilts her head and looks up at me. "Did you have a successful fishing day?"

"I did. We're having halibut." I kiss the top of her head and her hair smells like fucking heaven. "Don't worry, it's vegetarian halibut."

She giggles. "I told you, I eat meat."

"There's a dirty joke in there somewhere, but I'm staying away from it."

She slaps my chest. "Oh my God, you're disgusting."

"I'm a man, freckles. You say 'eat meat,' my head goes to the best possible translation. Don't blame me, blame my DNA."

I straddle the boat and dock and lend her a hand, making sure she gets on board okay. She struggles a little, but seems a lot more confident this time around.

"Jenkins, you remember Celia."

"I do, I'd stand to say hello but my knees are killin' me today, honey."

She smiles warmly at the old man. "No need. I'll just come to you." She leans in and wraps the crusty pirate in a hug.

His hand hovers over her ass and he waggles his eyebrows at me. "Sure wish I hadn't wasted all those erections in my youth."

"Jenks." Dirty old man.

"Oh wow." Celia pats him with a closed fist and pulls away. "Thank you…I think?"

"Don't mind him." I glare at the fucker as he coughs and laughs at his own joke. "Grab a seat. You like white wine?"

"Sure, sounds good."

With one more warning look at Jenkins to behave I head back and toss her bag on my bed, then pour her a glass of wine while grabbing me and Jenkins another beer. Moving through the cabin back out to the deck my gaze snags on the purple bag on my bed. It's surreal to think there will be a woman in my bed all night, not just for as long as it takes to get off. This isn't some drunken hookup. It actually feels like we're building something here.

Whatever it is will end in friendship. And why the fuck does that bother me?

Not wanting to ruin the night with overthinking, I head outside and I'm hit by the throaty sound of Celia laughing. I hand her the glass of wine. "What did I miss?"

"Nuthin'." Jenkins smiles into his fresh beer.

I lift a brow at Celia, who's now snorting back her laughter.

"Jenkins told me a story about you waking up on some strange boat off the coast of Mexico surrounded by a bunch of half-naked men?"

I tilt my head and stare the mouthy bastard down. "Did he?"

He grins, flashing his three front teeth. "I may have."

"Is it true?"

Fuckin' prick. "It's true."

Celia leans back grinning. "Oh, I have to hear this."

I shake my head, wanting to shot-put my elderly neighbor into the open sea. "I took the boat down to Ensenada, drank too much at the bar, got back on my boat to sleep it off, but didn't realize I was on the wrong fuckin' boat."

"He was on the Weenie Yankin' Yacht."

Celia bursts into laughter and Jenkins follows.

"No, I was not. It was a bachelor party or some shit. The boat must've come untied because when I woke up we were a good hundred yards from land. I could see the dock so I jumped off and swam back to find my boat."

"You swam?"

"Yes, and what's worse is I was hung over as hell."

Her smile falls and her pale eyebrows pinch together. "That's dangerous."

"Eh...I lived."

"But sharks—"

"I was on a two-day bender. Pretty sure the smell of booze coming from my body repelled any living thing within a five-yard radius."

Jenkins cackles. "Except the weenie yankers."

"Laugh it up, old man. Maybe we should tell her about the time you got pick-pocketed for seven hundred bucks by a transvestite prostitute the last time we were in Mexico together, huh? Talk about weenie yanking, that girl had her hands in *all* your pockets."

"Hey, I'm not complaining. Best hand job I ever had."

Now we're all laughing.

"Worth every dollar he took."

SAWYER

"I'd be happy to walk you back to your boat, if that's okay with you?" I'm helping Jenkins off Aden's boat after an amazing dinner and even better conversation.

He leans his frail body against me, his hand around my back and resting curiously close to my ass. "Oh yeah, I could use a little help, honey."

Aden makes a sound of disgust and he shakes his head, but he's smiling.

"Which one is yours?"

He smells like stale beer, sweat, and dead fish. Each smell separately would turn my stomach but when combined, if the smell had a face, it would be Captain Jack Sparrow. Limping at my side I have to wonder if he's doing that for my benefit or because his knees are bothering him. A loud thump sounds behind me and I don't have to look to know that Aden is following us.

"Right here." He motions to an old sailboat with chipped paint and a rusty anchor. "I could use your help gettin' to bed, gettin' my pants off and—"

"Drawing the line there, old man." There's humor in Aden's voice.

"Fine." He leans in to my ear. "I had to try." His wheezing laughter makes me laugh and Aden groan.

He pushes off from me and boards his boat without the slightest struggle and it's then I know for sure I'd been had.

Aden's arm comes over my shoulder and I melt into his side. "Good night, you old fart!"

"Yeah…you too, you lucky son of a bitch," Jenkins mumbles, making Aden chuckle.

"Sorry about that." He swings me around to head back to his boat.

"He's pretty funny. I can't believe he's sailed around Mexico."

He does what he did earlier, straddling the gap of water between the dock and his boat to help me on board. "Yeah, he's been around for awhile."

I grab a few empty beer bottles and paper plates, tossing them in the garbage. "You guys seem close."

He rinses out my empty glass and grabs a water bottle out of the fridge, handing it to me. "He's probably my only friend."

I take the offered bottle and cock a hip. "Your *only* friend?"

His hands slide around my waist and his eyes flare, the brown seeming to go from solid to molten. "Are *you* my friend?"

I gasp as he grips my ass. "I'd like to think so." My voice shakes and he stares at my mouth.

"You're more."

"I am?" The two whispered words fall from my parted lips.

He leans down, hunching his tall frame to bring his mouth close to mine. "So much more." Raining kisses along my jaw my knees wobble with the force it takes to remain standing.

I slide my hands up his arms, over the muscles at his shoulders, and lock them behind his neck. "I can't explain any of this."

"Don't even try." He nuzzles my throat. "Let's just go with it." He bends his knees and in one powerful swoop I'm cradled in his arms.

In a couple long strides he lays me down on the bed and slides a flimsy accordion door closed behind him.

"The walls of the boat are a lot thinner than your cottage." He's flashing a half smile while pulling his shirt off over his head.

"You worried I'll wake the neighbors?" I kick off my shoes and pull my sweatshirt off so I'm sitting in nothing but a plain white bra and cutoffs.

He crawls over me, forcing me to my back, then slides his knee between my thighs and parts them. "I'm counting on it."

ADEN

It's been said that there are two kinds of women.

The kind you fuck.

And the kind you marry.

I'm overly familiar with the first kind. Accustomed to the rushing-for-the-goal kind of sex that meets those basic needs and helps to redirect my thoughts to something more pleasurable.

But this…Fuck. This is most definitely not that.

I want to spend days in Celia's body. I want to slow things to a crawl and feel every single touch, every brush of her fingertips, slide of her tongue, all of it. I even stopped drinking hours ago to sober up for this and that shit is so far from my norm it's borderline scary.

And how in the ever-loving hell can she bring me to my knees in a white cotton bra and shorts? No clue, but the second she pulled her sweatshirt off I almost dropped right then and there.

"Why are you staring at me?" I blink up and am met with those green eyes, but they're clouded with insecurity. "I probably should've brought something sexier—"

"You fuckin' kidding me?" I cup her face and make sure she's locked there, unable to look away. "You're so hot, I can't stop looking at you."

Our lips come together in a kiss that I feel down my spine. There has to be some explanation as to why everything with Celia is so much more...intense. Maybe it's because I know she's leaving? The thought that I can't have her whenever I want her, which if she stayed would be always, is making me want her more.

Whatever it is, I like it. A lot.

Just like last night we strip each other naked and take time learning each other's bodies. She runs her lips across my chest, her tongue up my neck, and I'm helpless in her hands. Tasting every part of her I discover there isn't a spot on her that isn't sweet. She practically purrs when I lap at her breasts and every time she reaches for me I have to hold her off to keep up the unhurried pace.

When I finally get the condom out I haven't the willpower to watch her put it on without exploding. The desire to be inside her is too strong.

She lies still, her legs open to me in invitation, and I bite my lip as I fall into the cradle of her thighs. "You're holding back."

Fuck yeah, I am. "I want to take my time, but...damn, freckles, it's killin' me."

Her nails scrape up my sides, over my shoulders, and through my hair hard enough it's sure to leave marks. The sting is all the motivation I need. I flex my hips, sliding deep inside, and swallow her sigh of approval.

"Better, baby?"

She arches her back taking me deeper. "So much better. Now...move."

I take her on the bed, against the wall, on the floor, and finally when I can't take another second of the torture we both finish together in a heaving lump of sticky skin, panting breath, and pounding pulses.

"Did I hurt you?"

She's crushed beneath me on the floor, her arms and legs wrapped around me and holding me inside her. "Not at all."

I chuckle into her throat and breathe in her scent, which has changed to something more pungent and sexual. "You want to let me go so I don't crush you?"

"No." She convulses around me. "I kinda like you where you are."

"Mmm…" I thrust into her a few more times, nice and slow, easing myself away so I can trash this condom and get this woman who deserves to be made love to in a bed with fancy fucking sheets and goosedown rather than on the floor of an old boat. "Let me at least get you into the bed."

She sighs. "Fine."

I push up and lift her limp body up and into the bed, covering her with a thin sheet. "Be right back."

I move quickly, eager to get back to her, but when I do I find her sitting up and curled around something in her hand.

"Hey." I cross to the other side of the bed and with her hair falling forward I can't make out her expression. "What's…" I stare at the object in her hand.

An earring.

Sydney's earring.

Fuck!

"Celia…"

"I'm sorry, I wasn't snooping. I got up to get my panties and stepped on it—"

"Don't apologize. You didn't do anything wrong." I drop down on the bed next to her feeling like the hugest asshole in the world.

Her big green eyes come to mine and I force myself to look right at them even though the hurt I see there rips through my chest.

"There's this girl—"

"Oh God." She drops her chin to hide her face behind her hair.

"Please, just hear me out. I haven't touched her or talked to her since you and I started hanging out."

"But—"

"Listen to me." I hook her chin and tilt her face up. "I…" Fuck! This is uncomfortable as hell, but I don't want to lose her. "I've been single for a very long time and, shit, you're the first girl in as far as I can remember that I've wanted to spend time with. Not just a quick roll, but actually hang out with." The words keep pouring out before I can stop them. "You said it yourself, I'm not a pillar of virtue, but I can say that since our first kiss, I've never even thought of other women, let alone touched one because all I can think of is you."

She licks her lips and then hands me the earring. The piece of metal practically burns my palm so I chuck it across the room toward the kitchen.

"It's cool, Aden. I get it." She flashes a shaky smile.

"You know how it is, right? I mean, you didn't marry any of the men I saw you in those photos with, so you understand the concept of casual sex."

She seems to deflate from my words, but nods. "Yeah, I guess you could say that."

"Come here." I pull her to my chest and she falls into my arms. "I promise, freckles, you're the only woman in my life now."

She lays her hand over my stomach and holds me tighter as I run my fingers through her hair.

"You believe me, right?" I sound so fucking pathetic, but I need to know she does.

"I do." She yawns and as much as it pains me to let her sleep thinking she might still feel a little unsure about whatever this is between us, I kiss her head and whisper, "Go to sleep."

As soon as her breathing evens out I slip from under her and grab the earring and toss it into the bay still feeling like a dick. I lock up the boat and then sit on the edge of the bed to watch her sleep for a few minutes until I feel like a creepy dickhead and curl in behind her. She grumbles a little and I kiss her head and run my fingers along the soft planes of her belly. "Shh…it's okay."

A sense of purpose settles inside me. Something that tells me I'm right where I need to be and doing exactly what I was called to do. It's a feeling I've only gotten before when overseas on deployment. And I've certainly never felt it simply holding a woman.

God, Celia has my head all fucked up.

I close my eyes and begin to drift, thinking only of her as sleep pulls me under.

When I wake up, she's gone.

FOURTEEN

SAWYER

I've been sitting on Celia's porch watching the sun slowly light the Pacific Ocean, trying to decide if it's too early to call.

After finding that earring at Aden's and having Celia's sexual history thrown back in my face, I took the coward's way out and pretended to fall asleep. It was childish, but I couldn't stand the idea of Aden sleeping with a woman right where we had just made love. Sometime in the early morning I finally dozed off only to wake to sounds of fishing boats prepping for a day at sea. I hated sneaking out of Aden's bed but I was desperate to talk to my sister.

Two cups of coffee later, I check my phone. It's nearly seven in the morning, and there's a good chance she might be awake.

I hit her number, fully expecting another ridiculous voice message.

"Sawyer, hey…"

She sounds sleepy, and usually I'd feel like shit for waking her up, but I need to talk to her.

"How do you do it?" The words come out in a rush of breath as I'd been holding them in all morning.

There's the sound of rustling in the background and she clears her throat. "If you're asking how I pull off being awesome it's just a gift—"

"Cece," I whisper, just to ensure no one overhears. "I'm serious."

"I can see that. You're always serious, Sawyer, that's your problem. What happened?"

I tell her the story about Aden, how I'd slept with him and was staying at his boat, and then about the earring.

"I'm trying to be like you, but I need some help here. How do you share something as intimate as sex with someone without growing feelings for them? Finding that earring made me feel horrid. And it wasn't just feeling like another notch in his bedpost, I felt *disappointed* in him."

"You're passing judgment on the guy when you know nothing about the kind of relationship he had with that woman."

"I am not passing judgment—"

"You're doing the exact same thing he did when he saw those photos in my place. You're drawing conclusions that may or may not be accurate." She sighs. "Sawyer, this is one of the reasons why you needed this so badly. You broke up with a guy for tucking his T-shirts into his underwear."

"I did not!" Mark didn't do that, thank God, because that's just weird.

"Everyone has faults. And I know this might come as a surprise, but you're not exactly perfect."

My pulse pounds in my neck and I'm reminded of what Polly said to me at the bar the other night. "Oh yes, and thank you for reminding me. I heard from a woman I've never seen in my life that I'm some kind of agoraphobic freak. Thanks for that. It's nice to know how you see me."

I'm met with silence and the hurt from that night combined with the knowledge that Aden was fucking some other girl in his bed just days before all comes crashing down over me.

"That's what this is about anyway, isn't it? You trying to fix everything you think is wrong with me before you leave me forever?" My eyes heat with tears. "Well, guess what? Maybe I don't want to be the kind of girl who whores herself off just to chase a good orgasm. Maybe I like the idea that I could share something special with one man, one who values me enough to keep me around for longer than it takes to come, huh? Maybe you should spend some time being me for a bit, see what it's like to work a real job and date like a normal person!" I'm practically hysterical now, tears streaming down my face and my muscles twitching with adrenaline.

"Feel better?"

No, I do not feel better. I feel like a giant piece of shit.

I'm out of control and I hate it.

"I'm sorry, I gotta go."

"Don't you want me to answer the question you called to ask?"

When I don't respond, she continues.

"How do I do it? It's easy not to get attached when you don't put these ridiculous expectations on people."

"Ridiculous? So monogamy is a *ridiculous* expectation, is that what you're saying?"

"All I'm saying is not everything has to have significance or lasting consequences. Some people have sex because it's fun or they're bored and when it's over they move on."

"I'm not like that. I can't separate sex from feelings."

"I think you can, just not with Aden."

"What does that mean?"

"You didn't seem to have a problem moving on after Mark."

Stunned, I drop back and stare motionless at the yawning sea.

She clears her throat. "Maybe you and I aren't all that different after all."

"What do I do now?" The words come from my lips but sound

as if they're coming from someone else. Is it possible my feelings for Aden, a man I hardly know, are stronger than what I felt for a man I *lived with* for months?

"I say just go with it." There's the sound of rustling sheets. "Have as much fun as you can with the time you have left."

If this is "fun," why does it hurt.

"I better go. Love you."

The line goes dead.

I push up from my seat and go back into the cottage, my thoughts mulling over Celia's words. Unable to make sense of any of it, I stay busy by rinsing out my coffee mug and get back to packing.

I don't know how much time has passed, but I'm covering the last knickknack on a bookshelf with bubble wrap when a knock sounds at the door.

My heart leaps, thinking it might be Aden and fearing what I'd say to him, but the shadowed outline through the curtains proves my visitor is way too small to be him.

"Come in!"

Zoë comes bouncing through the door in a pair of spandex capris and a sports bra, her skin glistening with sweat. Does anyone in this town wear a shirt when they jog? "Hey, whatcha' doing?"

My eyes dart from side to side thinking maybe Zoë isn't the brightest seashell on the beach. I'd think it was pretty obvious. "Packing."

"Cool!" She drops down on a stool. "So what happened to you guys the other night? Polly said Aden got weird and dragged you out of Lenny's." Her eyebrows pop high on her forehead.

"What? No, that's not what happened." I continue to tape up the bubble wrap, keeping my eyes down. "We were late for a movie."

"Oh yeah, what movie did you see?"

Shit!

I shrug one shoulder, wondering what Celia would do, or say, in this situation. My mind completely blanking, I can't think of a single movie that's even out, so I do what I'm beginning to do best. I lie. "No clue. We were too busy making out, all I saw were the ending credits."

"You little skank!" The way she says it is like she's giving a compliment and I'm reminded how different from Celia I really am. "So where's Sergeant Psycho now?"

"He's not Psycho." I rein in my urge to defend him and smile, but it's all teeth. "Probably fishing."

I have no idea where he is. I'm sure he was surprised when he woke up to see me gone, I know I would've been if the roles were reversed, but then again he's accustomed to casual sex so...maybe my leaving before the sun came up won't even register on his radar.

"Do you need any help?" Zoë scans the room, her eyes landing on the pot of coffee. She hops off her stool and helps herself to a cup, then heads over to flop on the couch next to me. "I can keep you company while you pack."

"Sure, sounds good." I scream internally and throw on my best Celia mask.

This is going to be a long day.

ADEN

"I'll be damned, Colt. You hit the mother lode." Paul who does the buying for the fish market looks down at my day's bounty. "Yellowtail, barracuda, halibut, there's over two hundred pounds of fish here."

Yeah, well, that's what happens when you fish for twelve hours straight. "You interested?" My question is clipped, but I'm fucking exhausted and edgy as shit.

"Let me grab the checkbook." Paul disappears into one of the offices and comes back with a couple men who he instructs to weigh each type of fish and report numbers.

I slide down the wall and to my ass, holding my head in my hands. It's been throbbing like a motherfucker for the last few hours. I'd like to say it's from the sun but the overwhelming urge to down a bottle of whiskey tells me it's probably from my modest drinking day.

It's not that I didn't want to get fucked up, and Lord knows I had plenty of shit on my mind I would've liked to numb, but I was a machine today. I headed out to my secret spot and was pulling fish in one after the other, I barely had time to throw back a few beers let alone eat.

Or think about Celia.

It was what I wanted, to overwork my body so I wouldn't focus on my thoughts. Being out at sea meant I couldn't give in to my urges to call her, to ask her why the fuck she snuck out on me.

And to ask myself why I even care.

The sound of a check being ripped from its book calls my eyes to Paul. He hands me my payment that is just over three thousand dollars. Not bad.

I'd smile and pat myself on the back if I wasn't so pissed for fucking everything up with Celia last night.

I go back and forth between wanting to kick my own ass for not seeing that damn earring earlier, and wanting to shake her for being so sensitive about it. She had to expect I'd been with other women before her, I know she'd been with Brice and I'm not over here pouting about that.

Pushing up, my muscles protest as I head back to the dock to shower and hopefully fall into a dreamless sleep. Music comes filtering out of the Office as I pass and, just my fucking luck, Syd is heading into work from the parking lot.

"Aden, hey."

With my eyes to the ground I consider just ignoring her, but I'm not that much of a dick. I stop and meet her eyes. "Syd, what's up?"

"Eh…same ole shit." Her hair is down, silky dark waves falling over her shoulders, and looking at them only makes me crave Celia. Syd tilts her head to study me. "You just in from fishing?"

I grunt and nod.

"Why don't you come in for a drink?"

My mouth waters at the prospect of getting drunk, something that never really bothered me before, but now makes me feel like a lush. "Not tonight."

She frowns. "You haven't been around lately."

"Just been busy."

"Oh, okay…maybe later."

I shake my head. "I don't think so, Syd."

Her lips purse and she nods, then studies the ground between her feet. "It's cool, I get it. I better go. I'm gonna be late."

I don't say a word, just stand there in my own fuckedupedness as she scurries through the door.

Here I assumed we'd been hooking up to meet a need, but it seems maybe Sydney's feelings run deeper. Why did I never consider that?

I'm a selfish prick.

My muscles feel tight and although I'm tired there's a pent-up energy brewing dangerously behind my ribs, calling me to my trusted coping skills.

I want to drink and get in a fight and then fuck until I pass out.

Celia's smile flashes behind my eyes and I punch in the code to the gate with more force than needed.

I can't believe she blew me off.

I head straight for my boat when I pass a group of guys huddled around talking.

"…shot down with an RPG."

I freeze mid-step.

"Did they say how many were killed?"

My pulse slows to a dull thud.

"No one survived—"

"What happened?" The barking tone of my question sends all eyes to me.

They're grim-faced, but Rick whose boat is docked two slips down from mine is the one who answers. "US transport helicopter got shot down over Syria."

"Transport…?" That means the fucker was loaded to the hilt with US troops. "Death count?"

"They're saying thirty-seven, but no official confirmation yet—Colt, where're you going?"

I jump on my boat and go straight for the liquor cabinet. Grabbing a fresh bottle of whiskey, I take it with me to the shower. Hitting on the cold water I pour gulp after gulp of the booze down my throat, not feeling the burn but rather the sweet relief.

Men are dying and I'm stuck here doing fucking nothing about it.

Worthless.

Drunk.

A fucking disgrace to the uniform I'm no longer allowed to wear.

FIFTEEN

SAWYER

I've run out of things to do.

I packed until I had no more boxes, took a long hot shower, even blow-dried my hair and brushed on some light makeup hoping Aden would show up unexpectedly, but it's almost seven o'clock at night and I've heard nothing.

To say I regret sneaking out of his bed in the wee hours of the morning is an understatement. I should've at least let him know I was leaving and promised to call him later. Because I didn't, now everything feels weird.

I wonder if he's sitting on his boat staring at his phone waiting for me to call.

Just like I've been waiting for him.

As if a man like Aden would ever pine after a woman like me. How long would he wait before he invited a new woman into his bed?

Some people have sex because it's fun or they're bored and when it's over they move on.

Could I be that girl? The kind that takes what she wants when she wants it?

A flash of silver on the coffee table catches my eye.

The coin.

I snag it and roll it around between my fingers.

It's what Celia would do.

Heads, I call him.

Closing my eyes I flip the coin and hear it thump to the ground. Scrambling over it I squint and—tails. Huh. I fall back onto the couch and although I hoped to feel some relief at leaving this decision up to fate, I'm let down by the result.

I flip the coin again.

Tails, I call him.

I bend over the quarter after it hits the ground and—heads.

"You've gotta be kidding me."

Pacing back and forth in the room, staring at the quarter on the ground, I chew my lip—"Best three out of five."

I close my eyes and toss the coin once more. Peeking with one eye—"Don't call him."

I stare across the room at my phone. "Screw it."

Still pacing, I hit his name on my contacts and press the phone to my ear before I can change my mind.

It rings and with each one my pulse pounds harder behind my ribs.

"Colt's phone."

My feet still. "Jenkins? It's Celia."

"Know that, it's why I answered the phone."

"Right, um…Is Aden around?"

"He is…and he isn't."

I open my mouth to respond, but then shut it, not sure exactly what to say.

"You coming over?" He asks almost like I'm late to an expected arrival.

"I...should I?"

"Yep."

"Um...so, Aden is there, with you, correct?"

"He's here."

"Okay, I'm on my way."

Weird.

I grab my keys and purse and after a short five-minute drive to the marina I'm greeted by Jenkins who's sitting on the bench by the parking lot staring at the water. When he sees me coming he stands and the movement looks painful, although his face doesn't register it.

"You didn't have to meet me out here, Jenkins."

He shifts on his feet and the handful of gray hairs he still has on the top of his head blow in the mild offshore breeze. "Came to let you in the gate." He stiffly turns toward it and we both move in that direction. "And warn you."

My stomach turns a little at the seriousness in his voice.

"Colt's three sheets to the wind."

"Is he okay?"

He shrugs one bony shoulder. "I don't know. Wouldn't have invited you over but he seems upset. You seem to be able to calm him."

Sergeant Psycho.

"Upset. Is he violent?"

"No, no, nothing like that." He punches a code into the keypad and I push the unlocked gate open. "Colt's a complex son of a bitch."

I stare at his boat while we walk down the dock. It takes some restraint to keep pace with Jenkins when part of me wants to sprint to see if Aden is okay. "I'm not sure what you think I can do. We hardly know each other."

"Funny. That's what he said."

I turn to look at the old man just as we make it to the back of the *Nauti Nancy*. It's dark except for a dim light hardly noticeable from outside.

"Good luck." Jenkins continues down the dock toward his boat.

"Whoa, wait. You're not coming with me?"

"Nah…you got this."

I can't believe he'd leave me alone with a drunk and upset ex-army sergeant who may or may not be furious with me. Not that Jenkins would be much help if Aden really is Sergeant Psycho.

The big step onto the boat is easier than it used to be and when I get to the back door of the open cabin I knock. "Hello?"

No answer.

I go inside and my eyes are immediately drawn to the hulking man on the couch, his knees spread wide, arms propped on the back cushions, and a mostly empty bottle of booze hanging from his hand. His head lolls to the side, his lazy eyes fixed on me.

"Aden, what happened?"

The corner of his mouth lifts on one side. "You tell me, freckles." He's slurring, and as often as I've seen him drinking, I've never heard him slur.

I nod to the bottle in his hand. "This a party for one?"

He swings his arm out toward me. "Always room for one more."

I take the bottle from him and place it on the counter and spot a bag of coffee next to the coffee maker. Aden remains quiet while I get a pot started, but I don't miss that his eyes track every move I make. I hit power, praying for a quick brew, and move toward him, then sit on the couch close enough that our knees touch.

"I shouldn't have snuck out on you this morning."

His eyes narrow and he seems almost shocked. "Was that only this morning?"

"It was. I couldn't sleep, I was thinking about…everything, and then I went home and thought about you all day wishing I'd stayed."

The corner of his mouth lifts in an almost boyish way. "You mess me up, you know that?"

"Is that why…I mean, you didn't call."

His smile falls and he leans in close. "Neither did you."

"I wanted to, I thought you'd be mad."

He cups my jaw and the heat of his palm sends goose bumps down my neck. "I was, but it all went away when you walked in here. I look at you and I forget."

"What do you forget?"

He leans in and brushes his lips so softly against mine. "Everything."

I hold his hand against my cheek and close my eyes. "Aden, why are you so drunk?"

He nuzzles my neck, kissing a path from my collarbone to my ear. "Shh…I just want you to make it go away." The whiskey from his breath is overpowering.

I pull back and stare into his hazy eyes. "I won't sleep with you if there's a chance you won't remember."

"No way I won't remember." He rests his forehead against mine and whispers, "You're branded inside me."

Wow…he must be drunker than I thought. I pat his hand and pull back a little. "How'd you like to join me in a cup of coffee…or seven."

He scrunches up his face adorably. "Then you'll let me kiss you?"

"Yeah, then I'll let you kiss me."

"Deal."

ADEN

Hours have passed since Celia showed up and between the cups of coffee and full glasses of water I'm finally starting to feel somewhat sober.

"Omelet, extra cheese." She places a plate in front of me with steaming eggs and a piece of buttered toast. "Eat up, it'll make you feel better."

As if I didn't already feel pathetic enough, now she's babying me. I'd tell her she doesn't have to, but I fear if I do she'll find no other reason to stay.

"This looks amazing. I didn't know you could cook real eggs."

She props her hands on her hips and shakes her head. "Just eat…smartass."

I shovel a bite into my mouth and moan. "This is great." How long has it been since I've eaten?

"So finish your story, the one about LaRoy." With two hands wrapped around her coffee mug she stares intently at me.

With the booze loosening my lips I've been blurting old war stories, nothing too graphic, just things that happened between me and the men I served with for what seems like the better part of my life.

"Right, so me and the other guys had Private Schmitt in the body bag. He was lying so still, ya know, I'm still shocked he pulled it off." I smile to myself thinking back to how hard it was for him not to laugh and blow the prank. "Me and three of my guys had on rubber gloves, we made it look like we were mourning, hats pulled down low, shaking our heads. Asked LaRoy to come help us identify the body, that it was someone from our base camp." I chuckle at the memory. "Probably seems like a shitty thing to do, but death was such a normal part of our day-to-day…" I trail off as I consider all the death we dealt with and how desensitized we became to it. I blink that away and stall by taking another bite before I continue. "LaRoy knelt down, he unzipped that bag and we were all fucking acting like we were tearing up, sniffing, soon as he got it down to Schmitt's waist the fucker jumped out and scared the piss out of LaRoy. He flung himself back so hard he cracked his head on a rock and cut it open."

"That's awful!" Celia's laughing, but yeah, she's right, it was fucked up, but also funny as hell.

"We never let him live that shit down." I fork another bite into my mouth.

"I bet he'll never forgive you. Do you still talk to LaRoy?"

My fork screeches against my plate and the all too familiar ache flares in my chest. "No. He didn't make it back."

She places her mug down. "I'm sorry, I shouldn't have—"

"Hey." I grab her hand and bring it to my lips, kissing the inside of her wrist. "It's okay. Thank you for coming over tonight."

"Of course." She seems to sag a little and then pulls her hand from mine to get up and start rinsing dishes into the sink.

I go around to her and push up behind her, resting my chin on her shoulder and wrapping my arms around her waist. "Stay with me."

"Aden, I—"

"Please. I missed you this morning. I've been missing you all day. That earring…"

She turns to me, but I stay pressed to her. "You don't have to explain. I just, this thing between us, it's happening so fast and it's not fair to put demands on you, but…" Her chin juts out as if she's forcing a strength she's not feeling. "I don't want to sleep with anyone else while we're together, and I'd like to know you don't either."

"I already told you, since our first kiss, it's only you."

She breathes out as if in relief and smiles. "Good." Her eyebrows pinch together. "Aden, why did you get so drunk tonight? Was it because of me?"

Now I step back, putting space between us because I don't want her to know I'm a fucked-up mess who doesn't deserve to breathe the same air she does. "Nah…it was a lapse in judgment. It won't happen again."

Her expression says she doesn't seem convinced, and I can't stand to see the questions in her eyes. I hit the light on the wall, plunging us into darkness.

Gripping her by her hips, I spin her around, lift her to sit on the counter, and step between her knees. "Now…about that kissing you promised." I slide my fingers into her hair and tug at her bottom lip with my teeth. The earthy scent of coffee on her breath swirls around me washing away the tension of the day.

Her breathing speeds and she scoots to the edge of the counter, pressing the heat between her legs against me I grasp her thigh and moan at the friction against my hardening dick. "A deal is a deal."

Our mouths mold together and we make out like teenagers in the kitchen. In a frenzy of hands and tongues and teeth, I carry her to my bed and sink deep into her body, losing myself again to the spell she casts over me.

SAWYER

My eyes dart open. It's dark. My pulse races as I try to place myself.

I'm on Aden's boat—a stabbing pain shoots through my thigh. I reach for it. There's a cry of anguish, but it's not mine.

I rub my leg and kick the other to move away from— Heat slices my shoulder blade.

I cry out and attempt to scurry off the bed. Powerful hands grip at me so tight I whimper.

"Let me go!" I kick and he releases me so hard I'm thrown off the bed. My back slams into the wall.

Another guttural whimper comes from the bed and everything comes rushing back.

"Aden?" What is he doing?

He thrashes violently and I back up to avoid getting caught up in it.

Tears burn my eyes as he mumbles something incoherent and buries his fists into the bed.

"Stop it!"

"…killed them…you…" another cry of agony. "…they're dead…" He pushes up and punches the mattress.

Tears fall, streaming down my cheeks as I watch the big powerful man I've come to know dissolve from a feral animal to a broken and fragile man.

He's on his knees, his body hunched over, fists dug into the bed. His tattoo gleams in the dim moonlight with sweat-soaked skin. The rise and fall of his shoulders slows.

I approach him cautiously. My hand shakes as I reach up and lay it on his back—

He moves so fast that when my back hits the bed I don't know how I got there except for the fire burning in the eyes that bore into mine. His grip on my arms is so tight I cry out in pain. "You're hurting me."

He snarls. "I trusted you. You fucking…" He chokes on a sob. "…killed them."

"Aden, no. It's me. Sawyer…I mean." Fuck! "Wake up." I stumble over my words and he blinks. His grip lets up. "Wake up, you're dreaming. Ow, Aden…please." The tears are falling faster now. "You're hurting me."

I watch in shock as his eyes go from unfocused to clear, his jaw from rock hard to slack. He pushes himself off me and scrambles to the end of the bed, his eyes tracking around the small space.

I push up and put one foot on the ground, not sure if I want to run or stay. What the fuck just happened?

"Aden…?"

"Are—" His voice cracks. "Are you okay?"

I'm sore, and scared, but I'm not hurt. "You were dreaming."

He runs two hands over his head and rocks back and forth. "Fuck. I'm so fucking sorry. I'm so sorry."

I crawl to him and reach around his big body, pushing up on my knees to hug him close. I expect him to pull away, to push me off, but instead he clings to me as if I'm a life ring in a hurricane. He buries his nose against my neck and the moisture of his sweat and tears cools my skin. "Don't leave me."

My heart beats frantically and nausea builds in my gut, but he's crumbling in my arms and there's no way I could walk away from him like this. "I won't."

"I want to forget." His lips run from my earlobe down to my collarbone and I shiver in his unrelenting hold. "Make me forget."

"How?"

He lays me down on the sweat-soaked sheets as if I'm made of the most fragile china. "Let me inside." He crawls between my legs and presses his bare chest to mine.

"Your heart, it's…" It's thunderous behind his ribs. "Aden…" I run my hands up and down his back in soothing stokes. "Breathe."

He takes a deep but shaky breath. "I need you." An animal-like sound claws up his throat when I widen my legs and flex my hips.

I have so many questions, but this isn't the time. For now, he needs me. This powerful soldier needs me to save him from the nightmares in his head.

"You have me."

He holds his weight up to reach over me and grab a condom off the nightstand. Ripping it with his teeth, he rolls it on and enters me slowly.

He gives me his weight then, and we lie there connected until his pulse slows and he kisses me like a man desperate for a kind of healing only I can provide.

And then, he starts to move.

Pushing up he pulls my hands above my head, pressing them down into the pillow. He holds them there, towering above me, and when he'd usually keep his gaze fully focused on mine, now his eyes are closed. His brows pinch together as if he's in pain and he grunts with every forceful thrust.

His jaw ticks and the sound of his teeth gnashing together mixes with his panting breath. My heart throbs as I watch him wrestle with his own mind, as if he's pushing out the negative thoughts with every push inside my body.

Tears spring to my eyes as I find it impossible to look away from the anguish he wears so plainly on his face.

I flex my hands, wanting to free them from his unyielding grip. "Aden…" It's as if there's a wall between us as he refuses to even acknowledge my voice, and my chest seizes at the thought. "Please, let me touch you." I give another tug of my hands only to have him clasp them tighter.

"I don't deserve your comfort." His hips jack forward. "I don't deserve your hands on me."

His movement becomes uncoordinated and he whimpers as he fights to purge the memories.

Sickness turns in my gut coupled by a pleasure that I've come to associate with Aden. This shouldn't feel good, this isn't for me, and yet I'm powerless against the moan that tumbles from my lips.

He stills and looks down at me, his expression softening. It's then I realize that my cheeks are streaked in tears.

He releases my hands and presses his chest to mine, burying his face in my neck, he moves with more deliberate strokes.

"I'm sorry, baby." He bathes my throat in wet kisses. "It's okay. Please, don't cry."

I wrap my arms around him and hold on, hoping it'll keep him with me, that I won't lose him again to the darkness I managed to help chase away.

SIXTEEN

ADEN

I fucked up.

Watching the sun rise from the back of the boat I've gone over what happened a million times in my head and one thing is clear.

Whatever chance I had with Celia I blew last night.

After I scared the shit out of her she selflessly let me inside her, allowed me to do exactly what the therapists say I should never do.

I used her as a diversion—a warm body to help wash away the images of all the dead ones that haunt the backs of my eyelids.

I haven't had a night terror that bad in a long time. I don't know what brought it on. The downed helicopter I obsessed about yesterday was the farthest thing from my mind when I finally fell asleep last night. Maybe that was the problem, that I'd let myself relax more than I should have. Who fucking knows, but it doesn't change the fact that I woke up beating the shit out of my bed with Celia beneath me.

I clench my fists. I was stupid to think I'd be able to be with her for even a few days without her knowing what a fuckup I am. Wrecked beyond repair. Not fit for civilian life.

My skin crawls as I hear her feet padding through the boat's cabin, knowing I'm going to have to face what went down, drag the ugly into the light. Her footsteps get closer until she's outside and I can practically feel her breathing against my shoulder. Fuck, but I can't even look at her I'm so damn ashamed.

"Good morning," she whispers.

I lick my lips, and as much as I wish I could avoid her, I can't. She deserves to know what happened last night. I peer up at her and she's wearing shorts and the tank top she put on after I selfishly used her last night. Another thing I hated, having to watch her cover her body before crawling back into bed with me, putting a barrier between us. Not that I didn't deserve it. "Hey."

Her eyebrows are dropped low as if she's worried. She turns to pull a chair close and the sight of her back has me grit my teeth so hard I see fucking stars.

"Aw shit, Celia." Unable to stomach the evidence of what I'd done I turn away. "*Fuck.*"

"What?" There's concern in her voice.

"Your back." I spit the words to the bay, avoiding the purple bruise that mars her shoulder blade.

"Don't, listen, I have fair skin. I bruise really easily. It wasn't that bad I—"

I stand up so fast she stumbles backward. "Don't make excuses for me."

She swallows hard and stares up at me with eyes wide as saucers. "You were dreaming."

"It doesn't matter, my God, look at your…" I tilt my head when something on her arm catches my eye. "That me too?" I nod to her arm, then see another mark on her other biceps. "I beat the shit out of you."

She shakes her head and steps close, but I hold up a hand and move back. "No, you didn't."

"And there?" I point to the discoloring on her thigh.

"Aden, just tell me what happened, okay? I know you'd never hurt me."

"How can you say that? Look at you!"

She doesn't look, but she doesn't say a word either. *Looking* is probably unnecessary as I'm sure she can feel the damage.

"I'm so fucking sorry. You shouldn't have been here for that."

"Been here for what? A nightmare? How could you have known that was coming?" She comes at me again but this time I don't have the self-restraint to stop her. I want to fall into her arms and never come up for air, absorbing the sweet medication of her touch.

I look around to see a few people on the docks watching us a little too closely. "Let's go inside."

She seems surprised by my request, obviously unaware of the suffocating threat creeping in on us. No one ever sees it. I know it's a figment of my imagination but I can't help feeling the need to be on guard all the fucking time.

I head in and she follows. I motion for her to sit on the couch. She lowers herself without taking her eyes off mine as they beg for me to explain. I lean against the small kitchen island and cross my arms over my chest as if I can hold myself together when I'm this close to losing what little control I have left.

Her body language is far from relaxed, and it might have something to do with the fact that I can't stop glaring at the dark marks I put on her body.

"What is it?"

I lick my lips and clear my throat, struggling to get those first few words out of my mouth. "My job in the Special Forces was to train Iraqi and Kurdish soldiers to protect their country against the ISIL."

"Go on."

I hadn't realized I'd stopped talking as my head throws me back, slamming me into the past.

"I can't give you everything, I can't…" *Talk about it.* "I don't like going back there."

"I understand," she whispers.

"I trusted the wrong person and because of that I sent my men to the ground."

She grimaces in what I'm sure is disgust, the reason I know is because I'm just as disgusted with myself. "Oh, Aden…"

"They had wives, kids, one of them was engaged to be married the month after our tour was up." I shake my head as the weight of it all comes back to hang heavy on my neck. I can't do this, not now, not with her. She'll hate me if she knows. I hate my-fucking-self!

"You dream about them."

"No." It takes all the strength I have to look up at her. "I dream about killing the rat who betrayed me."

Her jaw falls loose on its hinges.

"I dream about crushing his skull with my bare hands." My fists clench as the adrenaline reignites my hate. "That corrupt fucker got away and I buried my men all because he *lied* and I didn't see through his bullshit."

"Aden—"

"It was my job to protect my men!" I pound my fist into my chest. "Mine! And I failed them. Widows and fatherless children are out there because of me!"

Her face drains of color.

I rub my eyes with both hands and try to cool my temper. "He lied and I'd give up everything I have to make him pay."

Her throat bobs with a heavy swallow.

"Fool me once. I will never be deceived again." I blink in an attempt to clear the fog of fury from my vision. I slow my breathing, calm my ass down because I'm clearly scaring the shit out of Celia. "I'm sorry, I don't mean to scare you."

She shakes her head and studies the floor, unable to look at me. "It's…no, it's fine, I just…that had to be horrible for you."

Once my pulse slows to a reasonable rate I cross to her and drop to a squat at her feet. Her eyes come to mine, but they're cautious. Tentative.

"I don't expect you to be okay with this. I was hoping to keep my shit together for however long we'd be hanging out, but you saw for yourself, I have no control over it."

"They call you Sergeant Psycho." She immediately covers her mouth as if she didn't mean to say that out loud.

My lips pull up at the sides on their own accord. "*They're* probably right."

"The guys who broke into the cottage, you beat them up."

Not a question, clearly she's been talking to others about me. "I did." I shrug. "I can't say I regret it."

She rubs her neck. "And the cab driver?"

Fuckin' hell. My jaw locks down and I push back up to standing and cross to the opposite side of the small cabin.

"Aden—"

"What do you want me to say?"

"The truth."

I whirl around. "He called me *sadiq*."

Her expression twists in confusion.

"It means *friend* in Arabic."

"So you attacked him?"

"Yes." She wanted the fucking truth, well, there it is.

"I don't understand."

"No, I suppose, you wouldn't." I'd only been back on US soil for a month and that fucker was speaking in Arabic not thinking I could understand. I was already on edge, the crowded bar and the drunks, but when that word came from his lips directed at me it was a portal to the past. I felt everything—the fear, defeat, the fucking shame. All of it hit at once and I was far from prepared.

God, I am such a fuckup.

She licks her quivering lips.

"This was a bad idea." I've chased off everyone I care about, my own parents look at me like I'm a stranger; why did I think I could maintain any kind of relationship with a woman, especially one as sweet and unaffected as Celia. "You should probably go."

"Don't push me away." Her bare feet pad against the hollow-sounding floor and I spin around, hating the feeling of someone approaching my back. She seems shocked and stills for a second, taking me in, possibly gauging if I'm safe enough to get close to. Shit, I did a number on this girl without even trying. Feeling like a total dick and wishing I could express how fucking sorry I am, I do the only thing I can think of and open my arms.

She doesn't hesitate and rushes into them, gripping me tight around my waist.

"I'm so sorry."

"I know you are, and I'm so sorry for what you've been through. But Aden…I don't want to leave."

I drop a kiss to the top of her head, breathing in the sweet scent of her hair. "No?"

She shakes her head, her cheek pressing deeper into my chest.

"God, look at your skin, baby." I squeeze her tighter to me but am mindful of her bruises. "How can you stand to have me touch you again?"

"You were sleeping, you didn't do it on purpose. In the time we've been hanging out I've never once been afraid you'd hurt me.

Maybe…" She peers up at me. "If it'll make you feel better, maybe we don't sleep over anymore."

I'm not jazzed on the thought of not having her in my arms at night, but she's right. She's safer in the cottage.

"If that's what it takes." Her body presses to mine, her hands splayed against my lower back as she clings to me, it all feels too good, too safe, and impossible to let go of. And for the first time I wonder how I'm going to say goodbye when she moves back to Phoenix, how I'll ever be able to get through a day without the promise of seeing her at the end of it. "You know, at this rate, I may never let you go."

Her breath hitches and I cringe, thinking if my night terrors don't scare her away my brutal honesty might.

"Let's go do something fun today."

I push her strawberry-blond hair off her forehead. "I gotta fish today, freckles."

She melts back into me. "I could go with you. I've been told I'm a pretty good deckhand, and a master baiter."

Squeezing her tighter I chuckle and bury my nose in her hair. I close my eyes, thankful as hell that after all she knows she's still willing to spend time with me. "Are you sure?"

"Mm-hm."

I'm not one hundred percent sure about what the hell we're doing or where this is going, but I'm greedy enough to not push away whatever part of her she's offering.

"Did you bring a swimsuit?"

SAWYER

"Are you insane? I'm not getting in that thing!"

Aden's grinning in that stupidly sexy way, his dark Ray-Bans covering those chocolate-brown eyes that I know are dancing with humor. "Oh come on, ya big baby." He knocks on the faded yellow plastic. "It's solid. Nothing can hurt you in here."

My eyes dart from him to the cluster of small islands behind him as we bob and sway with the swell of the tide. Aden called them the Coronado Islands and explained we're about eight miles off the coast of Baja. They're majestic the way they sit out in the ocean, waves crashing against their rugged shorelines, and sea lions sun bathing on the rocks, but that was before I was asked to get off the safety of Aden's boat. Now they look like the enormous teeth of a sea monster inviting me in to be eaten alive!

"Jenkins, back me up here." I sidestep and hide behind the old man who is leaning back with a cigar between his teeth. He invited himself to come along, and though I could tell Aden was disappointed that we wouldn't be on the boat alone, after what happened last night I think he felt I'd feel safer with a chaperone. "A shark could bite right through that…that…what is that?"

"It's a kayak, princess." Jenkins laughs but it sounds more like a cough. "Stop being a pussy and get your ass over there."

"A *pussy*?" I don't think I've ever been called that in my entire life. Aden's shoulders are jumping in silent laughter.

"You heard me." He jerks his chin up. "I want to take a nap and I can't do it with you here squawking."

"You asked for something fun." Aden holds up an oar. "Now come on, freckles, get in the fucking kayak."

My gut tumbles and clenches at the sound of him calling me freckles, but nerves have my knees practically knocking together. I did say I wanted to do something fun, something that would help us forget, but that was to redirect the conversation, an attempt to erase the battle that waged in his eyes as he spoke of his military past. And yeah, it was also a way to move away from the sickness I felt at his telling me of his betrayal. How he'd been deceived.

It was a way to change the subject, to ease my own guilt about lying to him. I almost confessed. My mouth was forming the words when I realized...

He can never find out.

Ever.

If he did he'd feel duped, manipulated.

I'd be no different from the snake who deceived him.

It was in that moment I decided I'd keep my secret. When my time here is up I'll move back to Phoenix, and never talk to Aden again.

It's such a bummer because there's a little part of me that wondered what would happen if we stayed in touch, how long things would last between us if I were Sawyer, but after hearing about how he was lied to it was clear that there could never be anything more between us.

All we have is now. And however long it takes to pack up Celia's place, which at this point shouldn't take much longer. The promise I made to my sister is now also a promise I've made to myself.

For now...I am Celia.

Staring out at the vast open ocean I can't believe I'm actually considering putting nothing between me and Jaws but an old faded piece of plastic.

"Woman!" Jenkins tosses one wrinkled hand toward Aden. "Get out there!"

"I'm not ready! I—Aden, what are you doing?" I stare in horror as he slowly prowls toward me.

"You wanted an adventure." His long strides are calculated because every adjust I make he counters with one of his own until I'm backed into a corner. "I'm giving it to you." His eyes track to my chest that's rising and falling way too fast. Even though he insisted I wear a T-shirt over one of Celia's bikinis it's the burn-out kind, tight with a v-neck and covers little more than the bruises on my upper arms and back.

"I'm scared."

He closes in. "Don't be."

"I don't know how to *not* be scared."

His big hand covers my hip. "I'd die before I let anything get to you."

I blink up at him, shocked by his words. "Don't say that."

"I'm serious." He leans in and his breath is hot against my neck. "Dying to protect the life of a beautiful woman is an honorable way to go."

I press my forehead to his shoulder, hiding the pink I know is rushing to my cheeks and whisper, "You think I'm beautiful."

His other hand clutches my hip. "You know I do."

Now I'm practically panting and even though I can't see anything around Aden's big body I know Jenkins isn't more than a few feet away. "Well…" I swallow hard, trying to regain my wits. "What are the chances of you having to sacrifice your life for mine?"

He smiles against my skin. "You want a calculated risk assessment?"

"Please…" My breathing is so loud I should be embarrassed. "Yes, please."

He shrugs one big, tan shoulder. "Less than one percent."

"Less than?"

He steps closer, brushing his hard chest against mine. "Despite what happened last night—"

"Aden—"

"You're safe with me." He presses his lips against my temple. "I'm sorry." His voice cracks, but he quickly clears his throat.

"I know you are."

He nods and backs up, giving me back a little oxygen. "So…you comin'?" That friggin' crooked smile flashes, turning me into a brainwashed minion.

"Yeah."

He grabs my hand and leads me to the back of the boat, where he heaves the kayak over and into the water. He easily slips into the back seat of the two-seated vessel, then holds his hand out to me. "Nice and easy, I'll do my best to keep it level."

My lips knit together as I concentrate on stabilizing myself on the bobbing banana-looking thing, and with him lending me his strength I manage to drop my ass into the front seat.

"Atta girl, freckles."

"I did it!"

He chuckles. "See, that wasn't too bad, huh?"

It really wasn't, but now that I'm floating over God knows how many things that could kill me, my victory is short-lived.

"Jenks, don't go anywhere!" Aden yells out as he thrusts one side of the oar into the water, propelling us toward the islands.

The man grumbles something back that I can't make out over the splash of the water around me and the roar of my pulse in my ears. "Where's my oar?" I search the small space, but there's nothing.

"Relax. Leave the paddling to me." His powerful strokes push us through the dark water and I try hard to do what he said. I practice deep breathing, blowing out through my mouth, focusing on the land ahead rather than contemplating the wildlife that dwells below.

The wind blows my hair around my face and the sun warms my skin. This time Aden insisted I slather myself in SPF 50, so while the heat touches my skin it doesn't burn. I imagine what he must look like behind me, the muscles in his back and shoulders contracting with every push through the water, a fine sheen of sweat making his bare torso sparkle in the light. Unable to resist a peek, I turn around and the tiny boat rocks to the side, sending water spilling in around my butt.

"Gah! That's cold!"

He chuckles. "Eyes forward, ya perv."

I gasp and my face flames. "Perv? I was just trying to see how far away from the boat we'd come."

"Sure you were."

I open my mouth to defend myself but figure he's got me figured out already so I'll quit while I'm ahead.

It takes longer than I thought it would, judging by the distance from Aden's boat to the islands, but he finally slows his rowing in a small inlet where the cliffs shelter the water from the wind to make it still and glassy.

"You okay?" I hear him fumbling around with something behind me, but I don't dare look now that I know it'll throw us off balance and keep my eyes on the rocks.

"Aden, this is amazing." I tilt my head way back to see to the tops of the rocks towering above us.

"It's called Lobster Shack Cove. We'll anchor here."

There's a splash to my right and a rope that dangles off the side of the kayak.

"Anchor?" There's a good twenty yards between us and a small strip of beach. "Are we getting off?"

He hands me something over my shoulder. "Put this on."

"A mask?" I turn around, this time more carefully to avoid rocking the tiny boat.

He's slipping a mask over his head, wearing it like a headband with the snorkel dangling. "Yeah. Here." He snags the mask from me and slips it over my hair, popping it over my eyes and making a few adjustments to the strap. "Put this in your mouth." He guides the snorkel to my lips with a devilish grin on his face.

"Who's the perv now?" I mumble as he puts the damn thing in my mouth, sealing my fate.

I'm going to have to get in the water.

Looking over the edge of the kayak I can see the ocean floor. There's a few fish, but nothing big and toothy waiting for me at the bottom.

"Remember what I said about keeping you safe?" He pulls the mask over his eyes, then grabs my hand.

Unable to speak with the snorkel in my mouth, I nod and squeeze his hand.

"If you let go of the fear you might actually enjoy yourself." He brings my knuckles to his lips and then lets go and dives off the kayak.

The abrupt motion rocks the boat and I scream through the snorkel tube and try to steady it. Aden pops up just a few feet away.

"Come on, freckles."

Yes, I can do this. I try sliding one foot into the water, but my weight tilts the kayak.

"Just jump!"

"Shut up!" It's what I say, but what comes out is a jumbled mess of gibberish through the filter of the snorkel.

I push up to a squat and look over the edge. You can do this, Sawyer. Celia would do it. She would push me off the side of this boat and laugh hysterically when I came up gasping for air.

But these are things I'll never get to do with my sister, and as much as I want to believe she'll recover, the odds are unfairly against her. She'd give anything to be where I am, to be standing on the edge of something amazing and all I have to do to enjoy it is let go of my fear.

With renewed strength I push to stand. I do it with so much force that it sends the kayak out from under me. I stumble backward and land ass first and gracelessly into the water.

I kick and spew the sea from my mouth when two strong arms come around me.

"That's one way to do it." He pushes my hair off the front of my mask and puts my snorkel in his mouth, blowing out all the water that shot into it. "Here." He offers it back to me and I take it, making sure I can breathe through it before I nod. He pops his back in his mouth and waves for me to follow.

My entire body revolts against this, my muscles protesting movement, but if I don't duck my head under and follow, I'm stuck here treading water in the middle of the ocean. My heart races behind my ribs and I take a huge breath and submerge my face.

It takes a second for my eyes to adjust to what I'm seeing. The ocean floor is all rock with cracks and gaps teeming with living things. Coral, seaweed, small colorful fish...it's nothing like I thought. Not a vast forest of deep ravines and hidden caves where all sorts of God knows what can live. This isn't like I've seen in any nature channel documentaries.

If ocean spots had levels, like school, this would be snorkeling preschool. My chest warms when I think Aden chose to take me here because he knew I'd be nervous. That night when we swam off the cliffs I made my views about the deep blue sea pretty clear. Maybe because of that he brought me here.

I meet up with him at a spot where he motions to a school of small silvery fish. He grabs my hand and together we kick around the calm cove. He points out things as we stumble upon them, all of it fascinating, and quickly I get lost in this undersea world. It's quiet except for the kicking of our feet, and with the sun warming our backs and his hand warming my heart a contentedness washes over me. I'm not focused on lists, on all the reasons why spending any amount of time with someone I'll never see again is a complete waste. All my worries and fears fall away until all that's left is Aden and the view before me.

He points out a cluster of lobster, a big silver fish with a yellow tail like the one we caught together. I'm happy to go along with the tour, nodding and discovering some of my own finds, which include a jellyfish that nearly scared the piss out of me. Aden calmed me and we floated along, watching as it drifted past us.

He gives me a thumbs-up and pops his head above the water and I follow. "What do you think?"

I don't risk losing my snorkel and just yell through the tube, "This is amazing."

He pulls me close and presses a kiss to my jaw. "Knew you'd like it." Popping his snorkel back in, he pulls me along with him and we explore a few reefs.

I'm happily kicking along when I feel him stop swimming beside me. I search beneath him, expecting to see him point at the reason he's stopped, a fish or maybe a sea turtle.

He doesn't. Tension fills the space between us and I'm about to pull my head out of the water and ask what's going on when he shoves his finger down to point to a dark spot directly below us. I drop my head and—*holy fuck!*

Leaving all my pride and strength behind, I scream.

Loud and blaringly clear, I holler through my snorkel until I'm coughing and forced to spit it out.

"Shark!" I spot the kayak in the distance and swim. No snorkel and my mask fogging up with the fear emanating from my body. I rip it off. No clue if Aden's behind me, I kick and throw my arms forward, Michael Phelpsing myself through the water.

I hear Aden call my name, but I'm helpless against the terror that drives me to safety. He could be getting ripped apart by the apex predator, and I'll have to explain to his family that I wasn't brave enough to save him, but oh well.

Racing against death, I throw myself at the yellow banana, hurling one leg over and a piercing pain rips across my inner thigh.

I scream again. I'd been bit and was going to die on this stupid fucking kayak. Scrambling into the vessel I'm breathing hard. My heart hammers behind my ribs. I'm gonna pass out. I grab my thigh. Look down at my legs.

No blood.

But I thought…?

Then I hear his laughter.

He's laughing at me!

"You'd pass the SERE course in a heartbeat with that evasion and escape."

He's still laughing.

I'm still trying to breathe. "I…almost *died*." God, my heart feels like it will pound out of my chest.

He hoists himself into the kayak with ease, and I cry out when the thing rocks a little because suddenly the faded old plastic feels like a steel plate standing between me and certain death. "It was only a leopard shark."

"Keyword being *shark*."

"It was two feet long, Cece. Hardly a threat."

"Shark. Teeth." Still trying to breathe. "Threat."

"Right." There's humor in his voice. "You should've seen how *threatening* he was when you took off for the kayak like a drowning elephant. Scared the shit out of the poor fish."

"I did?"

"You think you were more scared of him than he was of you? You screamed like a demon straight out of hell and thrashed all the way to the boat." He's really laughing now. "I think you cleared out the entire ocean floor."

"For your information…" I'm still catching my breath. "I hurt my thigh."

His big warm hands cup my thigh, fingers tempting me between my legs while his thumbs rub circles on the sore muscle. "You may've strained it throwing this leg into the kayak."

It's a little sensitive, but not too bad, and the way his eyes dance up and down my bare leg is enough to make me forget.

"Ever think of giving up your day job to become a trick rider in the rodeo?"

Laughter bubbles up in my chest. It sounds a little maniacal in my own ears, but I think relief at surviving a near-death experience will do that to a person.

"You good now?"

"Yeah."

He pats my leg, then pulls up the anchor and I right myself from the wounded victim position. "I owe you a mask and snorkel."

"Nah, I have plenty. Besides, I like the fact that you're leaving your mark here. Every time I come to spear fish and pass by your abandoned mask and snorkel laying down there I'll remember the girl who got away."

My spine stiffens. *The girl who got away.* I know what he means, away from the shark. Or does he mean something more? I suppose it doesn't matter. I'll never really know.

ADEN

Damn, I haven't laughed that hard in a long time. I almost couldn't make it back to the kayak chasing after Celia as she pummeled the surface of the water. I've jumped from a B-12 into the ocean and it was a breeze compared to trying to chase after Celia *while* laughing my ass off.

My muscles warm and relax with the exertion of rowing. It's as if all those years in the army, training constantly, staying in peak physical condition, gave my body a taste of the good life and now that I'm not using it to its fullest potential on a daily basis it begs for a good workout.

And fuck, but I feel good. Really good.

When we're together like this, she makes me feel like a hero again, like a soldier with a mission. Staring at her back through the thin fabric of her shirt, I can make out the clasp of her bikini top that's come slightly undone probably due to her frantic fight for survival. One flick of my fingers and the top would drop right off her perfect breasts. If Jenkins, that cockblocking bastard, didn't force his way onto my boat, I'd strip Celia bare the second we set foot back on deck.

She's silent, but I notice more relaxed and content than she was when I brought her out here. I'm sure the adrenaline fall combined with the sun and all the swimming is making her tired. What I wouldn't give to have her curled up to my side, sleeping peacefully while we're rocked to sleep by the ocean swells.

But sleeping together is out of the question now.

"Old man!" I maneuver the kayak right up to the back and steady it as best I can. "Go ahead and step out."

She rises up on shaky legs and I am the perv she accused me of being because I stare at her ass the entire time she hefts her tight little body onto the boat. My dick responds to her immediately so I force myself to think of Jenkins waiting up there, that foggy eye sure to be staring at me while he puffs his cigar and drinks all my damn beer.

Thankfully, those thoughts do the job and curb the swelling in my short—

"Aden!" Celia's frantic calling of my name brings me to high alert.

I scramble off the kayak, tie it to the boat, and race into the cabin where Celia is kneeling on the floor next to Jenkins. His face is pale…too pale.

"Shit." I drop down to my knees and check for a pulse. "Jenks, man, wake up." He's breathing, but it's shallow.

"Oh God, is he okay?" Her voice shakes with something bigger than fear.

I wave her over. "Sit here. I'll go radio the Coast Guard and get us moving."

Her eyebrows pinch together and tears gloss over her eyes, but she nods and pulls Jenks's hand into her lap. "Okay."

"Stay low. This could get bumpy." I race to the cockpit and fire up the prop while grabbing the radio. "Coast Guard, this is the *Nauti Nancy* off the Coronado Islands." I flip the anchor windlass and take off before it's fully up. "We've got a man unconscious, possible heart attack. He's breathing, but he doesn't look good. Coming in to south Islandia Marina. We need an ambulance. Over."

I look back to see the kayak floating in the distance, having become loose due to my quick takeoff. "Celia! Talk to me!"

"He's still out! He's…breathing, but he won't wake up!"

"Okay, baby, you keep talking to him! Let him hear your voice!" The roar of the engine and waves makes it hard for me to hear what she says but the sweet murmur of her voice is constant over the time it takes us to pull into San Diego Bay.

Ignoring the NO WAKE buoys, I race to the marina, picking up a small harbor patrol boat flashing its lights for me to slow down. Too bad. He can give me a ticket once I'm finally back and Jenkins is on his way to the hospital.

I'm forced to finally slow, but still skid like a downhill skier into the closest dock, shutting off the engine and tying it off. Waving down the paramedics that are pushing in through the gate I go in to see Celia's put a pillow under his head and is still holding his hand in hers.

Tears stream down her cheeks as she peers up at me. "He's gonna be okay, right, Aden?"

"Yeah." I check his pulse again. It's barely there. "He'll be fine."

The stomping of feet enter into the cabin as the paramedics file onto the boat. "Go get dressed."

She seems stunned by my sending her away, but whatever happens next I don't want her to be witness to. I've seen men fight for their lives on the battlefield while a medic goes to every possible length to save him. She doesn't need to carry those images around with her for the rest of her life.

Plus, the boat's cabin is only big enough for a handful of people. They'll need all the space they can get.

"Can you tell us what happened?" one paramedic asks as he drops down to check Jenkins's vitals.

I face Celia, and she jerks at whatever she sees in my expression. "Go."

Quickly she darts to the bathroom and once she's safe inside I explain to the paramedics how we found Jenkins. "No clue how long he was out for."

They fire off questions while working on getting him strapped to a stretcher. "We're taking him to Scripps. If you could inform his family."

Family. As far as I know he doesn't talk to his kids anymore. I'll have to call Cal and see if he knows who to contact. "Will do."

They take him away and I snag my phone to make a quick call for two cabs before heading back to the bathroom to get Celia.

I knock once. "He's okay, they're taking him to the hospital."

The click and then slide of the pocket door and she peers out. She's removed her wet shirt and is standing in nothing but her bikini. My eyes zero in on the bruises of her upper arms and I cringe and drop my gaze to the floor. "I'm gonna leave the boat here and head down to the hospital."

"I'll go with you."

"No." I shove a couple twenty-dollar bills into her hand. "A cab is on the way. I'll call if there's any news." I don't wait for her to respond because I didn't ask a question. Jenkins could be breathing his last breath and what I don't need is a woman keeping me from him.

"Are you sure you don't want company?" Her timid voice comes from my back and I clench my fists to keep from grabbing her and shaking her.

"If I did, I'd ask."

"Oh…" Her voice is so soft the pain is audible. "Okay."

I grab some clothes and stomp off to the bathroom to rinse off the salt water and dress. By the time I'm done I walk out and find Celia gone. All her things are gone as if I'd only imagined her being here.

I pretend not to care; after all, she did what I asked. Storming through the kitchen, my eyes snag on a small piece of paper with girlie handwriting.

Aden,

I'm sorry about Jenkins. Call me if you need me.

I'll be here. Waiting.

xx

My fist closes around the paper to ball it up and toss it in the trash, but in the end I shove it in my pocket, meet my cab, and head to the hospital.

Distractions are good when they're pulling you from where you don't want to be, not so good when they're taking you from where you need to be most.

SEVENTEEN

SAWYER

It's been over twenty-four hours since the paramedics took Jenkins off Aden's boat. As the sun sinks into the Pacific Ocean so does a little of the hope that I'll ever hear from Aden again.

I thought for sure he'd call last night. That he'd apologize for being so cold. That he'd blame it on his concern for Jenkins and then follow that up with an update to let me know the old man was doing better. That he'd suffered from some benign medical thing and would make a full recovery.

I've waited for that call.

It never came.

The good news is I got a lot of work done at Celia's place. I wrapped and packed fragile items and took a box to the local Goodwill. I'm still amazed at how little she held on to her past. I couldn't find a single photo of anyone in our family, not even a keepsake like the first-place prize she won at the pie-eating contest when we were twelve. Everyone in town was amazed someone so small could eat so much. It was a crowning moment for Celia. I was proud to watch it all from the sidelines.

Clearly our memories mean more to me than they do to her.

I wrap the Mexican-style blanket tighter around my shoulders.

Realistically I've got a few more days of packing and then I'll be done.

That's all Aden has to do is ignore me for that little amount of time and sooner than he even realizes I'll disappear from his life forever.

A door to one of the cottages slams shut and it gets my attention. I turn and blanch when I see Brice headed my way. Trying my hardest to smile through the pain in my chest, I manage to slide my Celia mask into place.

The fact that it's getting easier and easier should worry me more than it does.

"Hey, I saw you standing out here alone and thought I'd come keep you company." His grin is a little shaky and he seems to lack the confidence he had the first night we met.

"Yeah, I'm just soaking up the last few sunsets before I head back." I'm a little surprised he's keeping a good foot of space between us, maybe the inner Sawyer is showing through more than I thought and he's decided Celia's not his type.

He stares ahead at the waves, then peeks over at me from the corner of his eye. "You and Sergeant Psycho, huh?"

I jerk my gaze to his.

"It's no secret. I saw him leaving your place early in the morning."

"Oh…" I go back to staring out at the ocean, trying desperately to figure out how Celia would respond in this situation. It doesn't take a genius to see that Brice isn't unfazed by my…er.…Celia being with Aden, so what does that mean?

"It's cool, I mean, it's not cool, but I understand. What we had wasn't exclusive." He sniffs, not like he's sad, but more like he's trying to act more unaffected than he is. "Just…be careful, okay?"

"I don't know what you mean. Aden and I are just fooling around." I want to bite back the words as soon as they leave my mouth. Fooling around? What we have is so much more than that, or at least, it is to me.

He shrugs, not looking completely convinced, but goes back to studying the ocean as silence stretches between us. After a couple of minutes, he blows out a breath. "If you're here on the Fourth, we'll all be down at the Breakers Bar celebrating. You bring Aden and maybe he'll let me buy you a going-away drink." His eyebrows are raised in a boyish way I think Celia would've fallen for instantly.

"I'd like that, thank you."

He leans in and I tense, fearing he's going to wipe all memories of Aden clean with one of his brain-scrambling kisses, but presses a soft kiss to my cheek instead. "I'll see ya around."

"Yeah, see ya."

He shoves his hands in his pockets and walks away and my heart aches a little at what Celia's lost. Maybe Brice would've one day been my brother-in-law. He and my sister really would have the cutest babies. I'm strangled in sadness at the thought of Cece losing her chance to be a mother, a wife, a grandmother—life is so fucking unfair.

Afraid I'm going to start crying, I turn to head back to Celia's cottage when I see Mrs. Jones staring over at Aden's uncle's place.

For a split second I panic thinking she's staring over there because Aden is there, but from a quick glance I see the place is still dark and looks just as abandoned as it did before. "Everything okay?"

She eyes Cal's cottage, her arms shaking with the effort. "Oh, yes, hi there, I've been trying to call Aden, there's something wrong with my television."

"I haven't seen him."

She frowns, the wrinkles around her mouth intensifying. "Oh, dear. He's not answering my calls."

I try to ignore the sinking in my chest at the reason Aden wouldn't be answering his phone and cross the few yards that separate our front steps. "Maybe I can help?"

Her white hair is curled to perfection around her face, but when she turns to look at the cottage again I see the back is completely flat, probably the result of sitting in a high-back chair. Her hand is curled around the banister, her thin skin showcasing blue protruding veins as she braces her weight as best she can. "I don't want to be a bother."

"It's not a bother at all. As a matter of fact, I could use something to do." Anything that'll take my mind off worrying about Jenkins and obsessing over Aden's brushoff.

She grins and struggles to get herself turned around so I hop up and loop my arm under hers for support. "Thank you."

I push open the door with my free hand and guide the woman into the living space of the small cottage. It doesn't look any different than the others except for the décor that speaks of a long life lived in the tiny house.

"I don't know what happened, it just stopped working." She pats my hand and I release her to sit in an oversized chair that's just feet in front of an old television.

"I'm sure it's something I can figure out." The screen on her TV has the green, red, and blue bars on it. I pick up the remote on the food tray to the side of her chair.

She grunts as she adjusts in the well-used and sagging seat. Her eyes almost disappear under her paper-like skin. "How's everything going over there?"

Other than the fact that I'm living my sister's life and screwing everything up by falling for a guy who doesn't know who I really am? "Pretty good."

"I don't mean to pry." She waves me off. "Mind your own business, Mary."

"It's all right. I don't mind." I try not to stare, but can smell the sickly-sweet stench of rotting food from her messy kitchen. "Mary?" I kneel down to look her in the eye. "I'm trying to kill some time and I'd be happy to clean up a little around here if you'd be okay with that?"

Her blue eyes twinkle as if my offer is making her emotional, but there's a hint of embarrassment there too. "That's not necessary. You have more important things to do than tidy up after an old woman."

"I really don't. What I do have is a killer sense for organization and cleaning is my drug of choice." I turn toward the TV and click through the channels manually, getting snow and static on every one. "You'd be doing me a huge favor."

"That's sweet, but you— Oh! You fixed it!" She grasps the remote and hits the buttons with a bony finger.

"I think you must've accidentally changed the channel on the television rather than the cable box." I push up and pat her on the shoulder. "I do it all the time."

I move into her kitchen, noting that she didn't really give me permission to tidy up but I'll go ahead and start and see how far I get before she tells me to stop. As it turns out, Mary has a family member that drops in once a week with groceries and clearly hasn't realized just how bad off she is because there's a ton of food to make anything from lasagna to tacos, but the only proof that she's even eating is a trash can full of frozen dinner boxes.

After I finish the dishes, disinfect the counters and sink, and mop the floor, we've watched the evening news and an episode of *Dick Van Dyke* on some vintage rewind channel. Mary seems to have forgotten I'm even here as she dozes off and on in front of the TV. I throw together lasagna and while it cooks I sit in a metal folding chair watching *Leave It to Beaver* to the tune of Mary snoring.

I check my phone obsessively for missed calls, but outside of a few texts from my assistant back home there's nothing. When the buzzer sounds that the lasagna is done, I pull it out and head to Celia's for small Tupperware so I can divide the dish into single serving pieces and pop them in the fridge. It's just after eight o'clock when I run out of things to occupy me at Mary's. I place a slice of lasagna on her table along with a fresh glass of water and gently wake her.

She blinks and after a moment her eyes take focus on me. "Celia, I'm so sorry. Did I miss the end of *Dick Van Dyke?*"

I grin at the worry I hear in her voice. "You did, but it didn't come as a surprise that they weren't actually married so they decided to go get married that night but couldn't because they didn't have a babysitter."

"Oh, dear…" She giggles.

"I'm sure they'll rerun it."

She spots the food. "You cooked?"

"I hope that's okay. I put the rest in your fridge. You should have enough for a few more dinners and some lunches."

"Smells delicious." Her shaky hand grabs the fork to dive in. "Won't you join me?"

"I can't. It's getting late and I have to finish up at my sis…" I clear my throat. "Have some things to finish up at home."

She takes one small bite and exhales out her nose. "This is good."

"I'm glad you like it." I cross to the door. "Thanks for helping me kill some time."

"Thank you, honey." She doesn't even look at me, but continues to stuff her fork with lasagna. "Such a treat."

"If you need anything I'll be right next door, Mary."

I head out into the night and because there isn't a cloud in the sky, the moon paints a path of light over the ocean so solid it almost looks as if it could be walked on.

As I'm heading up the stairs to Celia's place my phone buzzes in my pocket. My heart leaps in my chest when I see it's from my mom. Not Aden.

"Hey, Mom."

"What happened, you sound exhausted?"

I slump onto the bed and blow out a long breath. "Nothing. I'm just about finished here. I think I'll be able to get home in the next couple days as long as the movers can pick this stuff up."

"Not a day too soon."

I squint at the weird tone of my mom's voice. "What do you mean?"

She huffs out a breath in a way that makes me think she's trying to choose her words wisely. My pulse instantly pounds. "Celia's vision is getting worse. I don't know, I'm just worried."

"I talked to her the other day. She said she was fine, that she felt better than she has in months." Leave it to my mom to overreact and see things that aren't there.

"She puts on a show for you—"

"Mom." I sit up. "Celia doesn't fake it for anyone, least of all me. She's fine."

"Sawyer—"

"Can I talk to her?" She'll prove my mom wrong, and once I tell her Mom's freaking out she'll say something to make us all laugh and set Mom's mind at ease.

"She's sleeping."

"Oh, well, I'll call her tomorrow and check in, but I'm sure you're blowing this out of proportion. You said the meds make her tired, and she's probably bored out of her mind being stuck in bed all day." There's a throbbing in my neck that matches my beating heart. "Have you thought about getting her out of the house? Maybe if everyone stopped treating her like she was already dead she'd start feeling like she had more to live for." I'm practically seething now, the combination of worry for Jenkins, Aden's rejection, my mom's overprotective doting, and I can't hear Cece's voice to see if she's okay and it has me wanting to punch something. And I'm not a violent person.

Ever.

"Sawyer, just finish up soon and get home, okay?"

I grip the phone so tightly I'm afraid it'll crack. "That's the plan."

We say goodbye and I lie there for a few minutes wondering what the hell just happened. I'm spinning out of control and can't seem to find a level head.

I want to talk to Aden. He's been through so much, experienced loss, he'd know exactly what to say to help me deal with this, if only I could tell him the truth and lean on his strength. But I know if he knew the truth he'd hate me.

Still, just being around him would be enough. He makes me forget all I'm not and all I'm pretending to be. With him I'm someone different, not Celia or Sawyer, but just…me.

I've never missed a man this much.

Why won't he just call!

I toss the phone to the rickety bedside table followed by the sound of something small hitting the hardwood floor. I push up on my elbow and right there staring up at me like an omen from my sister is that damn quarter.

Heads up.

Call him.

"I can't call him," I whisper to no one. "I'll seem desperate."

You are.

Am not!

For him, you most certainly are!

I sit up and stare at the coin. I chew my lip and grab my phone. If I call him he could just ignore it. Even Mary mentioned he's not answering his phone.

I could just show up at the marina.

Jenkins was my friend too.

It wouldn't seem weird for me to check in on him to see if he's okay.

I swipe the coin and with a deep breath I toss it in the air.

It hits the ground with a loud thump behind me as I head out the door to confront Aden.

EIGHTEEN

SAWYER

The marina is dark except for a few lights shining on the dock and a handful of boats that are occupied and lit by their inhabitants. The gate is locked, as always, but it doesn't keep me from gripping the cold steel and squinting to see if I can catch movement on the *Nauti Nancy*. A soft light in the back is on, but other than that the windows are dark. I dart my eyes to Jenkins's sailboat and it is completely black with no sign of life. I pray that's not an indication of its owner, and hope that he's just in the hospital recovering.

The not knowing his condition is what's making me crazy. How could Aden not let me know how he's doing? I was the one who found him passed out for fuck's sakes. The madder I get, the tighter my grip is on the gate. I deserve to know what's going on! And fuck him for thinking I'd just walk away when he's done with me.

I shove off from my snooping and plop on a bench that's shrouded in shadows to wait for someone to open the gate. I'll storm in and demand answers if that's what I have to do.

My muscles quake, and even though it's chillier tonight than the last few nights, I don't think it's from the cold. Jenkins could be dead. His last hour on this earth could've been spent in my arms and Aden didn't even give me the courtesy of a phone call!

Time passes and as the temperature drops the heat of my anger increases. I cross my arms over my chest, my foot tapping frantically against the concrete. Every time someone passes matching Aden's description I glare until my temples throb, sending even the manliest men to the far side of the sidewalk. Couples hand in hand, people walking their dogs, the occasional jogger, all of them pass and still no Aden.

It's after one in the morning, my butt is numb from sitting, and I'm contemplating the possibility that he may not show up tonight. Where else could he be? I shove away thoughts of him with another woman when the door to a nearby bar swings open. Music pours out along with a man and a woman. She's talking fast but I'm too far away to hear exactly what she's saying. A drunken lover's quarrel? Hidden in the dark I watch as she pleads with the man for something and when he finally gives in she ducks under his arm and they head toward me.

As they get closer there's something familiar about the man, the way he holds his shoulders and his gait that stiffens my spine.

Then I hear him mumbling. It's deep and dark, a voice I've come to know all too well.

"I told you I'm fine, Syd." He releases the girl and she seems disappointed. "I'll take it from here."

"Colt, wait."

He stills and drops his chin.

"If you need to talk—"

"No." He shakes his head and I'm immobile watching this all unfold before me and hoping to God I don't end up seeing something I can't unsee. "I already told you—"

"I know. Just…I'm here if you need me." The woman, Syd, turns and disappears back into the bar.

He nods and passes right by me as he stumbles up to the gate.

But seeing him brings all my nerves to life.

Feelings explode behind my ribs—anger, hurt, sympathy, as well as something deeper that I wish I understood.

He punches in a code and his big body sways like his boat on the open sea. I stand silently, holding my breath and ready to catch the gate once he passes through it.

He freezes.

His shoulders square.

Spine straight.

It's as if every bit of booze he'd ingested has dissolved instantly. He doesn't move a muscle and neither do I. "I know you're there."

My eyes dart around us, trying to figure out whether or not he's talking to me or some drunken figment of his imagination.

"I can *smell* you."

I warm as his words roll over my skin like a sweet seduction. God, what is wrong with me?

He drops his chin to his chest. "Why are you here, Celia?" He still doesn't turn to look at me, so I approach slowly. "Stop!"

My feet grind to a halt. "Aden—"

"Leave. I don't want you here."

His words slice through my chest. What he's saying might be true, but I can't overcome the urge to comfort him. I move with my hand out to soothe him with a touch.

He spins on me faster than I'd think possible for someone in his state. "Never come at me from behind, understand?! Especially when I'm drunk." He's growling he's so angry.

"Okay, I'm sorry."

With his face under the light it looks like he hasn't shaved or showered since yesterday. His eyes are masked under the shadow of his strong brow so I can't tell how he feels at seeing me. With a slight tilt of his head I feel his eyes run the length of my body and I wrap my arms around my waist. "How long have you been out here?"

"Not long." *Lie.*

"It's the middle of the fucking night, Celia." He runs a frustrated hand over his hair. "What do you want?"

I lick my lips, nerves pricking my skin, but I move a step or two closer until he jerks his head for me to stop. "You never called."

His gaze tangles with mine and now I can see the war that wages behind his eyes.

"You told me you'd call. I've been worried about Jenkins and wondering if—"

"He's dead."

I gasp and stumble back a step. Dead. "No…when?"

"On the way to the hospital. They couldn't revive him. He had a massive embolism."

My jaw is so tight it hurts. "Why didn't you tell me?"

He doesn't answer, but only stares with a blank expression that makes him look inhuman.

"He died and you didn't tell me! Why?" My voice cracks with the force of my anger and sadness that I lost a…well, a friend.

"Go home, Celia." He turns to head through the gate.

Panicked, I grab his bicep.

He whirls, grips my forearm. "What did I fucking say about that, huh? I don't want to hurt you…" *Anymore* is unspoken but communicated through the regret that shines in his eyes.

My chest rises and falls faster and faster. My head gets light with the hold Aden has on me along with his hot whiskey breath panting against my neck and the news that Jenkins's last hour on this earth was spent in my hands.

"If you hadn't…" I choke on emotion as it bubbles up in my chest. "Made me go on that kayak."

"Do you think I don't know that?" He pulls me close enough to get my full attention. As if he didn't already have it. "You think I don't blame myself?"

I let out a cry and he must think it's from his grip on me because he releases me and puts distance between us. My knees fail to hold me up and I drop, cradling my head in my hands. God, what is happening to me? Why does it feel like my chest is being ripped in two? Tears burn my eyes and my throat tightens with emotion. I just don't know why. The logical side of me tries to convince me that Jenkins was old, that he'd lived his life, that this kind of death sneaks in when it's least expected and no amount of medical intervention could've saved him.

But none of that helps.

Because it's not so much Jenkins's death that hurts.

It's the thought that Aden is hurting and he's thrown up some kind of impenetrable wall between us.

I've been nothing more than some plaything that he can cast aside without concern when he's become so much more to me.

"This wasn't supposed to happen." The mumbled words fall from my lips. I wasn't supposed to become attached. I wasn't supposed to get close enough to get hurt.

ADEN

This is exactly why I didn't tell Celia that Jenkins died.

By the time I'd gotten to the hospital it was too late to even say goodbye. I waited as they pumped his chest, shocked him with enough volts of electricity to light the whole city, but he never responded.

So I did what I do best.

I drank until the pain went away.

Then I came back to my boat and passed out only to wake up sober enough to get it back to my slip at the marina and head to the bar to pick up where I left off.

The thought of calling Celia passed through my head once or twice, but when it did I chalked it up to being too sober and took three shots to drown out reason. Worked too. Until I stumbled home to find her fucking waiting for me with those big coaxing eyes and those damn lips that even the sanest man would sell his soul to taste, I fucking lost it.

And now she's on her knees looking up at me as if I have the power to fix this. As if I'm the hero she's been waiting for rather than the coward who's perfected the art of hiding in the bottom of a bottle.

"Fuck." I hold my hand out to help her up. This woman doesn't deserve to feel the cold hard ground beneath her perfect skin, let alone sit out here in the dark alone waiting for an asshole like me. "Come on. I'll walk you to your car."

She takes my hand and once her warm palm hits mine I can't help but tug her in and crush her to my chest. Her arms come around my waist and her body shakes with a silent sob as she leans on me for comfort.

"I'm not a good guy." It kills me to say it, but she needs to know.

"You lost a friend, Aden." Her fists grip the back of my tee and her breath skates along my skin. "You're hurting. Don't shut me out."

I pull back knowing if I keep her close for a second longer I'll take her to my boat and beg to get lost in her body. "You shouldn't have come here."

The soft mounds of her breasts press against my ribcage and I hiss as blood roars through my veins. "I tried to stay away."

"I should let you go." My fingers dig into the soft flesh of her hips going against the words that tumble from my lips.

"Or maybe you should hold on."

I fork my hands into her hair and lift her lips to mine. The second they touch I know I'm not walking to her car. No force of will or military trained obedience can get me to release her.

I'm drowning in her.

In her touch, her effect, the way she looks at me as if she sees past the darkness in my soul to the man I was meant to be. The honorable man I was before. God, how I want to be that man again.

When I rip my mouth from hers, I punch in the five-digit code and grab her hand, leading her through the gate and down the dock to the boat.

She doesn't speak or try to get away, but succumbs to my control as I help her aboard and usher her through the back door. I hold her hips from behind and steer her to my bed, the sheets balled up from a restless night's sleep. Her thighs hit the mattress and I skate my hands up her sides, pulling her shirt up. She lifts her arms so I can tug it off and toss it to the ground. The moonlight casts her pale skin in an ethereal glow that makes her look otherworldly—an angel sent just for me.

I kiss a path from her shoulder to her earlobe, melting against the comforting warmth of her skin. "If you want to leave at any time, I won't stop you."

"I'm staying. As long as you'll have me."

I groan as her words soak through the drunken haze. "Always," I whisper, and hook my thumbs into the waistband of her shorts to push them to the floor. "It hurts." The weakness in my voice is humiliating, but I can't help it. Being around Celia is disabling in the best way.

Nuzzling her neck, she tilts her head to allow me full access to the velvety skin of her throat. "I know."

After I cover every inch with brushes of my lips I move to the other side. Goose bumps race across her skin and she goes weak in my hold.

Needing to feel her against me, I pull my tee off before wrapping a forearm around her chest and pressing her back to my front. "You feel so good." With a hand in her hair I tug her head aside to get back to her neck, playing with her breasts until she's arching and rubbing her round ass against me. Every stroke is like hitting a new button that lights her up even more.

Who needs booze when I have this responsive woman writhing with want in my arms?

I press between her shoulder blades, bending her over my bed. Following her down, I stretch her arms up over her head. "Stay like this. Don't move."

She sighs as I kiss a path down her spine, her skin like the sweetest silk on my lips. I move to her side and nip at the creamy mound of her breast that's pressed to the bed. She arches her back, her ass teasing me until I'm painfully hard. All it would take is one slide of her panties to be buried deep inside, but I want to explore every inch of her body and bring her to the brink until she's begging me to finish it. I want to be the man she thinks I am, strong and heroic, and hers.

With a frustrated grunt I flex my hips into her backside in a not so subtle request for her to be still. She whimpers and fists at the sheets as I move to her other side, nipping and licking until I'm bathed in the guttural sounds of her desire.

"You want this?" Another flex of my hips and she's pushing back into me.

Beautiful.

"Never felt anything like this…Aden, it…" She sighs when I rotate my hips against her. "Aches."

"Mmm…" I hum against her skin and kiss her lower back before sliding her panties down to her knees. My breath catches in my throat at the view of her before me and run my tongue up the backs of her thighs until her legs almost give out. "I want to take my time—"

"Please, don't." She rocks back into me. "I can't take any more."

"Shhh…" I cover her in worshipful swipes of my lips and tongue, making sure to linger on the spots that make her crazy. I remember telling myself one day I'd kiss every freckle and I intend to do just that.

I fantasized about feasting on her for hours and that's exactly what I do until I can't take another second of not being inside her.

I reach into a drawer at the side of my bed and pull out a condom, rolling it on quickly. I then push her panties to her ankles. "Keep these here." She nods and I move her to her back before I nudge my way through the gap in her panty-restrained legs. Her thighs cradle my hips and she gasps at the feel of my hard-on resting between us. Her legs surround me like the warmest blanket and with her ankles locked behind my knees we're fused together. "Want to feel you wrapped around me the entire time."

Her hands lock behind my neck and she pulls me to her lips and kisses me softly once, twice, then slides her tongue along mine in a tentative stroke. I pull back as far as I can with her shackled ankles, and as I slide my tongue into her mouth I inch my way inside her body.

She rips her mouth from mine to groan in pleasure just as a long hiss escapes my lips.

"You're so sweet, freckles. Every part of you, so fucking sweet."

Her nails dig into my back and I thrust forward in response. Her neck arches and opens enough for me to bury my face as I rock in and out of her in a slow and deliberate rhythm. Entranced by every sound she makes I lean to one elbow to watch as her body writhes and rolls with every stroke.

Hungry for more, I reach behind her knee with one arm and her back with the other rolling us so that she's on top, her ankles still locked behind my legs. Cocking my knees, she pushes up and—"*Fuuuck*, you're gonna wreck me."

She bites her lip and with her body towering over mine she grinds her hips against me. I slide my hands up to cup her breasts and toy with them until she throws her head back with a breathless gasp. Her pace quickens.

"Yeah, baby. Don't stop."

She doesn't.

"Gorgeous." My teeth grind together to hold back my impending orgasm.

"Aden." Her voice hitches on a quick breath and I know she's close.

"Right here." I grip her hips and hold her down while rolling in time with her, and that's it.

Her fingers dig into my pecs and she cries out my name.

"Dammit, fuck." I spit through my teeth as an orgasm bigger and more intense than I've ever felt shreds through me. My toes curl, my thighs constrict and bolts of pleasure shoot up my spine. My head gets light and I continue to move with her as every touch seems to extend the ecstasy.

She drops down on top of me, giving me all her weight, and I wrap her in my arms and try to get my head out of the clouds and back on stable ground.

"I've...that's never happened to me before."

I run my fingers up and down her back, her skin sticky from exertion and her sweet scent settles my soul. "It was new for me too."

A long and drawn-out sigh falls from her lips and she wiggles to free her ankles from her panties before pushing off of me and dropping to my side.

I trash the condom, then pull her to me, thinking it's been years since I've felt this sated, this totally and completely satisfied. Not just sexually, but down to my bones. She tames the monster inside.

She traces a pattern on my abdomen. "Aden?"

"Hm."

"That woman, the one who was with you…"

I pinch my eyes closed.

"Was she the owner of the earring?"

"Yes."

Her tiny frame seems to get even smaller at my side. I roll her over and position myself between her thighs, pinning her hips with mine. Cupping her face between my hands I lock eyes with hers. "One thing I will *never* do is lie to you, freckles."

Her gaze drops to my chin.

"Look at me."

Reluctantly, she does.

"Sydney is a waitress at the Office. Yes, it was her earring and yes, in the past, she and I have hooked up, but I haven't even entertained the idea of Syd since you."

"But tonight, she—"

"She knew Jenkins, hell, everyone in that bar knew him. We were all hurting, she brought up the idea of coming back to the boat but I told her no." I drop a kiss to the tip of her nose. "I told her about you, fuck…I couldn't shut up about you."

Her expression turns sour. "You didn't hurt her feelings, did you?"

The corner of my mouth ticks up. "I don't know many women who would genuinely be concerned about another woman's feelings."

She shrugs. "Well…that's because until now, you never knew me."

I groan and bury my nose into her neck. "Fuck, you're something else."

"Thank you for not sending me home."

Afraid I'm crushing her, I drop to my back and pull her to my side. "Sorry for bein' a dick."

"You were drunk and grieving."

"Still am."

She tilts her head up to look at me. "Which one? Drunk or grieving?"

I search my feelings for a split second, not wanting to lie. "Maybe a little-a-both."

Snuggling back into me, she kisses my chest. "Understandable. You feel like talking about it?"

Sex then talk?

I've never confided in a woman I've slept with.

But everything about this is different. Everything about Celia is different.

What that all means, I have no fucking clue.

NINETEEN

SAWYER

We stayed naked and twisted together for the next day.

I waited for him to tell me I should leave, expected at any minute he'd remind me that we swore we wouldn't spend the night together. He never did. Instead, he held me to him tighter than he ever has without even the whisper of a night terror. I suppose that might be because we seldom slept for any substantial period of time.

Between dozing off to rest we ate and showered, but everything would lead us back to the bed. I checked my phone to make sure my family wasn't trying to reach me and Aden would peek at his every now and then, but everything else we ignored.

In those glorious hours we focused on nothing but each other.

There were quiet times where we'd talk about Jenkins. Aden would tell me stories that would have me laughing hard enough to draw tears, and he shared with me that the old man had a fractured relationship with his family. He hadn't spoken to his children in a long time and didn't expect to be missed once he passed on.

When our conversation would become too much Aden would get

quiet and I would do my best to distract him, which was always easy seeing as we wore little to no clothes.

I had moments in the dark of night when his breathing would even out that I thought to tell him about Celia, but lost my nerve knowing the truth would burst the delicate bubble we'd created. I'm here because Aden needs me, but acting as some kind of salve to his pain is a double-edged sword because every second that passes with him is one more that I fall deeper in love.

I've made my mental lists. All the reasons we won't work, the obvious being that he doesn't even know who I really am. There's the geography, we live in two different states. I'd never expect him to give up the boat and his fishing to be with me. But when I start to convince myself to get up and walk away he'll smile at me, or touch me in a way that erases all rational thought.

I may not need him.

He may be the worst possible person for me.

But I want him in a way I can't even begin to understand.

And it goes well beyond what he can do with my body that makes everything outside of us seem insignificant. It's the way he makes me feel like I'm the only woman in the world. He responds to every word I say, every sound that slips unabashed from my lips, as if I'm giving him a secret he's been desperate to discover. When we're together it's as if I'm the air and he's begging for his next breath.

I've played second string to my twin sister my entire life. She was the funny one, the talented one, popular, artistic, smart, and sexy. I was average, awkward, ordinary, and even though I got decent grades that's where my credentials ended.

But Aden erases all that. To him I'm everything I'm not and so much more.

Especially now, in these moments, when he's looking down at me, his big hands framing my face as he moves inside me, his eyebrows dropped low in concentration like I'm speaking to him in a special language only he can understand. Whatever he hears makes the corner of his mouth tick up.

I wrap my legs around his hips and kiss him so deeply he moans and—barks?

"What was that?" The concern in my voice dissolves with my breathlessness.

He drops his forehead to my shoulder. "Ignore it."

Another bark, then another followed by a thump on the backside of the boat. "It sounds like a seal?"

He sighs long and hard, then pulls back to look down at me. "It's Morpheus."

My eyes pop wide. "What is Morpheus?"

He drops a kiss to the tip of my nose. "I'll show you, but we're coming back to this afterwards." He rolls off me just as another bark comes from the back of the boat. "I hear you! Shut the fuck up now!"

I scramble to throw on one of Aden's T-shirts and he tosses me a pair of boxers that I have to roll up a few times to keep them from falling down my legs. He puts on a pair of swim trunks and with a little maneuvering and effort, laces them up over his erection. I pat my heated cheeks, hoping they'll die down and that the effect of seeing Aden aroused after a day of sex would wear off. We move through the small cabin and out to the back of the boat.

"It's a little early for a wake-up call, man."

I peek around Aden's big back to see a dark gray sea lion the size of a small couch perched on the back deck. "Oh my gosh, Aden...he's huge," I whisper to keep from spooking the animal. He has to weigh five hundred pounds and his teeth are as long as my fingers.

"Huge pain in the ass." He pops open the live bait box and reaches in to grab a handful of sardines, then tosses them to the animal. "There. Happy?"

Morpheus swallows them whole and barks for more, which makes Aden chuckle.

"This isn't SeaWorld." He tosses him a few more. "And you're being rude." Aden nods toward me. "Can't you see I have company?"

It's almost as if the sea lion understands him because his big black eyes track to me.

"Here." Aden hands me a live sardine and I hold it tight to keep it from slipping from my fingers. "Toss it in the air. He'll catch it."

I do and sure enough he catches it on the fly. "Wow, he's good."

"Last one." Aden hands it to me and I do the same, watching how quickly the animal moves to get the fish. "Now go!"

Morpheus grunts and barks one more time before lumbering his big body down the dock where he stops at Jenkins's boat. He barks.

"Oh no…Aden." The animal barks again and again and I feel each one like a blow to the chest. "That's so sad."

He turns to head back inside the cabin and I meet him in the kitchen where he's washing his hands. "He'll get over it." He dries his hands on a towel and moves aside so I can wash mine. "In time, everyone will."

I tilt my head to peek up at him. His jaw is hard and his gaze is cast out toward the bay. "Including you?"

"Yeah." He squints out the small window. "Jenkins wasn't a young man, he—" Aden clears his throat. "There are worse ways to go."

"I'm sure there are." I move to a stool across from him feeling his need for space.

"Thanks for being here."

The seriousness of his voice calls my eyes to his. He doesn't look away and I watch as genuine appreciation shines back at me.

His lips tick with a tiny grin that has my belly fluttering. "If we don't get outside and in public I'll end up holding you hostage in my bed."

My belly flips at the promise behind his words. "What do you suggest?"

"Let's take the boat across the bay for breakfast."

"All I have is what I had on last night. I don't even have a hairbrush." I tug on the T-shirt I'm wearing self-consciously.

He comes around the counter and turns my stool before pushing his thick thigh between my knees and cupping my face. His dark eyes trace the line of my jaw, my eyes, then slide down to my lips. "Flushed cheeks, eyes always bright but they're shining now, thick dark pink lips from being sucked and bitten, freckles…never seen a woman wear the morning-after look as well as you." He licks his lower lip and I'm practically panting. "Matter of fact, lookin' at you now…" He slides his hand up my thigh to my ass and pulls my leg up so I'm forced to lean back against the bar. "I changed my mind about leaving."

"I thought, you said…" I squirm in my seat as he kisses my neck all while grinding between my legs. "Public."

"Yeah, we need to get in public fast."

"I'll get dressed." My thighs ache to clamp down around his waist as he pulls from between his legs, flashing me a smile that almost knocks me off my seat.

"Good idea."

He steps back and when I move he slaps me on the ass and groans.

So maybe I don't have the wardrobe of a fashionista on hand, but the way Aden looks at me in his T-shirt and boxers makes me feel like I'm wearing designer clothes. I keep Aden's shirt on, loving the way it smells like his cologne, but put on my shorts. I use Aden's toothbrush, wash my face, and pull my hair back in a ponytail. The boat's engine fires to life as I'm coming out of the bathroom and decide to quickly make Aden's bed before joining him at the wheel.

"Aden!"

The sound of an unfamiliar voice calling Aden's name pulls me to the window.

Aden jerks his head around to the dock with a surprised "No fuckin' way!"

A man with white hair climbs aboard and gives Aden a back-thumping hug. I can't see his face with Aden's big body blocking the view.

"What the hell are you doing here?"

I step outside, not wanting to be rude, and wait to be introduced. Aden must feel me close because he turns to me just as the man says, "After you told me about Jenkins I came right down. Here to pay my respects." The man startles when he sees me and narrows his eyes.

Aden runs a hand over his hair. "Fuck, man...I don't remember calling. Sorry 'bout that."

My stomach plummets when it hits me who this guy is.

"You were pretty fucked up. Thought maybe you'd accidentally drowned."

"Nah...I'm good."

Blood drains from my face.

The sky spins.

I dig my feet into the deck to keep from falling over.

"Uncle Cal, you remember Celia?"

This is happening. This is really happening.

Passing myself off as Celia to everyone else seemed easy enough, but judging by the way Cal's staring at me through tight slits I doubt Aden's uncle will be as easy to fool.

"Yeah, I remember Celia." He makes no move to come closer, to give me a hug or even shake my hand, but instead stands there thickening the air between us until I choke on it.

I cough to clear my throat. "It's nice to see you again."

His eyes move from mine to study me in Aden's shirt. His lip curls in disgust.

"Cal. Don't look at her like that." Aden throws an arm over my shoulder, pulling me in close. "Whatever you think this looks like…" There's a smile in his voice, but I can't see it because my eyes are glued to the floor as my cheeks ignite. "You're probably right."

"Jesus, Aden." Cal grumbles under his breath.

"We're all adults here." He kisses the side of my head and releases me to dip into the ice chest. "You want a beer?"

When I peer up and Cal's still staring at me, I shift inside and find a seat as far away from the men as possible, fearing a closer look will give me away.

"Sure." Cal follows me in and sits on a stool, propping his elbows on the small island countertop. "So, you hanging in there?"

Aden pops the top on the bottle and places it down for his uncle while I check all the available exits and scramble for an excuse to leave. "Better now, thanks to Celia."

I jerk my eyes to his to find both men looking right at me. My hands knot in the hem of the shirt and I try my hardest for a convincing smile.

"Is that right?" Cal's scrutiny continues, and a flash of sadness crosses his expression.

"No clue how long it would've taken before I finally sobered up," Aden mumbles, and holds up a bottle of water, accentuating his point. "Cece helped me to pull my shit together."

"*Cece*. Interesting." His words are muffled into the brown bottle as he swigs from it.

"Just happened so quick, ya know, Jenkins." Aden's talking softly. "Reminded me of before. Here one second. Gone the next."

"Understandable."

I watch as the two men talk using short phrases I don't totally understand but gather they're speaking about lingering effects of Aden's time served in the military. I make myself part of the décor, pressing back against the seat, hoping to blend into the walls, to become invisible until the opportunity to leave presents itself.

"The bank been up your ass?"

"I avoid them when I can, but yeah. They're not gonna be ignored forever, Cal."

Aden's uncle leans back and drums his fingers on the counter. "Might have to just sell the place. Hate it, but those back taxes are killin' me."

"Celia took a peek at the books. She pointed out some areas we could cut, told me how much we'd have to pay monthly. Made sense. You never told me she was an accountant."

"Didn't I?" Cal's eyes slide to mine and the steeliness I see there confirms my worst fear.

He knows.

My legs move faster than my thoughts and before I'm even aware, I'm up and moving toward the bedroom.

There's mumbling behind me followed by the thump of heavy footsteps and the slide of the flimsy door. Grabbing my things I turn and collide with Aden's chest.

He grips me by my biceps. "Hey, what's going on?"

"I…" I can't look at him so I busy my eyes searching for something I may have missed. "Forgot I promised Mrs. Jones I'd check in on her today."

"I'm sure she'll understand if you don't."

Gently removing myself from his hold, I turn my back on him and slip off his shirt to put on my bra. I move quickly because being naked in front of Aden feels wrong now. "I made her a promise. I can't break it."

Hands shaking, I scramble with the straps when his warm hands slide up my sides only to grip the elastic and fasten the clasps for me. "You're a good person, Celia."

The air in my lungs rushes out in one burst as his words increase my guilt. I bite my tongue to avoid saying that I'm far from a good person. I am the worst kind of person. I'm a liar and a fake and he really doesn't know me at all.

He helps me with my T-shirt and when I turn he's standing in my way so I can't escape. His arms are crossed over his chest and he's looking at me with an emotion I've never seen from him before. A soft, almost lazy smile, his deep brown eyes communicating warmth that I can actually feel expanding in my chest.

"I don't want you to go."

I lick my lips, hoping I'm capable of words because the way his soul seems to be drinking from mine leaves me feeling weak and needy. "I made a promise—"

"That's not what I meant." He takes a step forward, but his arms stay tucked away and he doesn't touch me.

This is good, because one touch would send the truth from my lips and my body to my knees to beg his forgiveness.

"I want to date you."

"Why?" I whisper, and then immediately regret giving my innermost doubts a voice.

His grin widens, but only slightly. "Because I like you."

"I'm moving back to Phoenix."

"I'm going to ask that you don't."

Oh my God, *what*? He wants me to stay—not me. It's Celia he's fallen for.

Fool me once. I'll never be deceived again.

His words from the other night flood my mind.

Oh, Aden, if you only knew, you'd never look at me like that again.

"I have to go." I push past him and he makes no attempt to stop me.

"Think about it, Cece."

The nickname sends my shoulders to my ears. Without a response I slide open the door, snag my purse from the couch, and with a wave to Cal I race from Aden's boat, knowing one thing with almost absolute certainty.

Cal's going to tell Aden who I really am and the truth is going to crush him.

TWENTY

ADEN

"Everything okay?"

When I'm finally able to pull my eyes away from Celia's retreating back after I made sure she got off the boat okay, I turn to find Cal's staring down the dock too.

"Yeah, she forgot she had somewhere to be." Even I know she's lying about that. Something spooked her, I just can't for the life of me figure out what it was.

"How long you two been hanging out?"

"Little more than a week. I can see why you talked about her so much. She's..." Visions of her smile, her laughter, her body moving above mine, all flood my vision. I blow out a hard breath. "She's amazing."

He frowns. "Mm-hm. Celia was something special." There's sadness in his voice that gets my attention.

"You implying now that she's been sleeping with me she's no longer special, Cal?" My pulse starts to thrum in my veins.

My uncle's never been the type to judge anyone, but he loves Celia, and he knows I'm fucked up. I can see why he'd be disappointed, hell, even I know Cece's too good for me. But I'm his fucking flesh and blood.

"You've known her a week."

"She's more than just a fuck buddy, if that's what you're implying."

"Aden, think about it." He props his elbows on the counter. "You're only replacing one addiction for another."

"That's bullshit, Cal."

"You said it yourself, she cleaned you up, took your mind off losing Jenks."

"Yeah, but…" I fist my hands, my mouth watering for a beer, but I push back the urge. "That doesn't mean I'm using her for sex."

"Really?" He shrugs and leans forward on his forearms. Challenging. "Tell me what you know about her."

"She's smart, compassionate, patient, and although she's scared of almost everything she'll walk through her fears with me."

His frown deepens.

"I'm serious, Cal. This woman, when I'm showing her something new and helping her through whatever she's afraid of, the way she lights up…When she comes alive like that it makes me feel useful again."

"You care about her or you just like the way she makes you feel?"

"I care about her because of the way she makes me feel."

"And you think that's fair to her?"

"I don't fucking know." Feeling cornered by his questioning my pulse kicks behind my ribs. "We've been together for a week, how the fuck should I know?"

"Look…" He rubs his eyes. "I've been driving all morning. I'm gonna head over to my place and crash before I start dealing with all this bullshit bank stuff." He stands and tosses his beer into the garbage.

"I'll get cleaned up and meet you over there in a few hours."

He smiles, but again the expression communicates more sadness than anything. "Sounds good."

He passes through the back door and I stare at nothing, the whole time my mind turning over Cal's words.

I asked her to consider staying because I love the way I feel when we're together. But what do I have to offer a woman like Celia? In one week I've managed to unleash all my demons on her. And yet…she keeps coming back. I'm being selfish and when the time comes I should just let her go.

The problem is, I don't think I can.

SAWYER

I've made more progress on boxing Celia's things in the last two hours than I have the entire time I've been in San Diego. With the threat of Cal telling Aden about who I really am I've never been in a bigger hurry to get this done and get back to Phoenix and far away from Aden Colt.

My chest aches at the idea of not having him in my life, which is ridiculous. I'm not some lovesick girl with inflated ideas about life and relationships. If my twenty-four years have taught me anything it's that shit happens frequently and I have a bull's-eye on my back.

Time's up, Sawyer.

Come clean and confess, or get the hell out as soon as possible.

God, what was I thinking!

I grit my teeth remembering the promises I made my sister. That damn quarter, taking chances, but all I've managed to do is create a web of lies I can't get out of without hurting someone I care deeply for.

After moving all the boxes to the front of the cottage I pull out the small yellow pages and dial the number for the shipping company who is responsible for getting all Celia's things back to my parents.

"Crosscountry Express, how can I help you?"

"Hi, I'm…" I look around to make sure no one's standing outside the open windows. "Sawyer Forrester. I arranged for you guys to ship some boxes back to Phoenix for me?"

"Yeah, I see it here. Pickup in Ocean Beach. We have it down for the fifth?"

"Yeah, but they're ready now. Is there any way they can be taken sooner?"

"Ohh, no can do. Tomorrow's the Fourth."

"So?"

She huffs in my ear. "We'll be closed for the holiday."

I rub my forehead, feeling completely dense. "Fourth of July, right. I'm sorry. I wasn't thinking."

"If you'd called yesterday I could've had the guys pick up the boxes today, but they're booked for the afternoon. I'm sorry."

"I understand. We'll stick with the fifth."

"It's better this way. No one in their right mind would willingly leave town before the Fourth of July."

"I wouldn't know," I say absently while trying to figure out how I'll be able to avoid Aden for another day.

"The fireworks go off on the pier and everyone paddles out on surfboards to watch. It's incredible."

"In the ocean? At night?"

She laughs. "You're funny."

Yeah, and she's crazy if she thinks I'd sit on a surfboard with my feet dangling like an earthworm appetizer into the dark waters at night. "I'll have everything ready on the fifth, then."

"Sure thing. We'll be there early."

I hit END and toss my phone on the couch. Looking around the room there's nothing but boxes, bare walls, and barren furniture. And I'm stuck for two more days.

There's no way I'll be able to avoid Aden for that long.

I chew my lip, my palms sweating and my pulse racing. A hotel. I'll go to a hotel.

A knock on the door nearly sends me through the roof as my nerves seem to crack and fizzle beneath my skin.

I don't want to see anyone. Can't bear opening the door to see the questions in Aden's eyes, or worse, the anger of betrayal.

"I know you're in there."

My stomach threatens to heave at the sound of Cal's stern voice as he calls me out. If only I could turn to liquid and melt off the couch and into the floor—

Another knock.

Shit!

"I have a key. Don't make me use it."

My shoulders slump and I push off the couch. This is happening. May as well get it over with. Tears spring to my eyes when I think how something that started out so innocent is about to blow up in my face. There's no way I'll be able to walk away from this without emotional shrapnel.

I unlock and crack open the door only to be met by his scolding stare. "Hey."

He doesn't take his cold dark eyes off mine. "Mind if I come in?"

I step back, bringing the door with me, hiding behind it as if the wood can protect me from his chastisement.

Steady steps carry him in and across the tight space, his eyes scanning the boxes and the walls. He's not a small man and even in a Hawaiian print shirt, shorts, and flip-flops he's intimidating. He doesn't seem angry, his body language not giving off irritation as much as grief.

I say nothing. There's just nothing to say. He must think the absolute worst of me and no matter how many ways I flip the story around in my head it all leads to the same conclusion. I lied to and deceived someone he loves.

"She didn't make it?"

My eyes dart to his. "I'm…what?"

"Your sister. Celia. She's…" He swallows and the lump in his throat bobs. "Dead."

"No, she's not." *Dead*. I can't bring myself to say the word.

He tilts his head and studies me. "Then…" He swings an arm around, motioning to the boxes. "Why are you here packing up her stuff?"

I run my fingers across my lips and wonder how honest I should be. Cal and Celia were close, and she assured me no one knew she was sick.

"You know?"

He looks down at me and the stern set of his jaw reminds me of Aden. "She confided in me shortly before she left. Made me promise I wouldn't say a word."

I motion for him to sit and then hesitantly move to the opposite end of the couch to sit on the edge. "She told me no one knew. She asked me to come pack up her stuff and…" As I line up my excuse in my head it sounds ridiculous, but it's the truth so I share, "Pretend I was her."

"And how's that working out for ya?" There's no humor in his voice, but rather a parental reprimand that has me curling in on myself.

I knew this was a bad idea, but I couldn't say no to my sick sister!

"It's working well, no one seems to know I'm not her."

"Including Aden."

"Yes." Shame soaks me in regret. "Including him."

He nods and leans forward to rest his elbows on his knees. "You need to tell him."

"I can't. He'll hate me."

He eyes me. "He cares about you."

"I didn't mean for that to happen—"

"Too bad. It did, and he deserves to know who you really are, Sawyer."

I startle at his use of my name. "She talked about me?"

He chuckles and nods. "She spoke of you a few times."

My chest expands with warmth that quickly cools when I consider what she told him about me. Does he think I'm crazy? Some kind of hermit like the girl at the bar did?

"If I tell him he'll feel deceived. I can't do that. But I can leave and he'll never have to know who I really am."

"You actually think that'll work? That you'll walk away and he'll let you go?"

I shrug. "Yes. I do. He might miss me for a day or two but some willing female will take my place." My stomach wrenches as my words bring forth a nausea I can't fight.

"Or...you tell him who you really are, explain—"

"The truth isn't an option now. He told me a little about his night-mares, about how he was let down by someone he trusted. If he knew I lied about who I am it would only hurt him."

"Shit..." He cups his head into his hands, rubbing circles on his temples. "That's true."

"I allowed myself to get off track with Aden and that was a mis-take. All I'm here to do is pack up my sister's stuff, get a glimpse into her world, and then leave here with everyone thinking she's liv-ing her life to the fullest to die a happy old woman rather than being robbed of her life." Tears spring to my eyes. "She asked me for a fa-vor, I couldn't say no."

His stern expression softens with sympathy. "This was not her brightest idea."

"Tell me about it." I search my brain for the umpteenth time trying to figure a way out of this that doesn't include hurting Aden and come up with nothing.

"I'd think it were harmless if my nephew's feelings weren't involved, but they are and I can't sit by while you toy with him."

"I'm not toying with him. I…" I care about him. "I don't know what to do."

"Finish what you came to do." He pushes to stand and stares down at me. The weight of his judgment has me studying the floor. "Then leave and I promise, as fucked up as this is, I'll keep your secret. I'll do that for Celia and for Aden."

"Cal—"

"But you can't ever come back here, understand? Once you leave, you make a clean cut and let Aden move on with his life."

His words stab me in the heart.

"Promise me, Sawyer."

"Okay, I'll disappear."

"And when Celia's…condition…finally takes her…" He clears his throat and I look up to find emotion shining in his eyes. "I'll let Aden know and that'll be the end of you two."

I nod, unable to form words because everything he's saying slices through my chest, but I know he's right. Aden will mourn her loss, and it'll be like none of this ever happened. He'll go on with his life thinking I was nothing more than a summer fling that ended before it even got started.

A single tear slides down my cheek.

"I'm sorry it has to be this way, but I think you're right, his mind may be too fragile to handle the truth and this is the only way it can be."

"Either way, I lose him forever."

His gaze swings out to the ocean, gray clouds beginning to form on the horizon. "Enjoy the rest of your stay."

"Cal, wait." I stand and cross to him, brushing away my tears. "How did you know I wasn't Celia?"

He smiles sadly. "I saw the fear in your eyes the second I walked on that boat. Your sister? She's never been afraid of anything. Not even death."

And with that, he's gone.

I stay rooted in place as one by one tears slide down my cheeks.

He's right. I'm a pathetic replacement for Celia. Whatever Aden feels for me isn't actually because of who I am but rather who he thinks I am. Someone who swims naked in the ocean at night and dives off a kayak to swim with sharks, the person I'm pushing myself to be. If I were able to truly be myself, he'd lose interest in a heartbeat.

Celia and Aden make a fantastic couple, they're cut from the same Technicolor cloth.

Sawyer and Aden don't make any sense. He'd get frustrated with my obsessions and I'd get irritated by his casualness toward just about everything.

Whatever future I could map out for us in my head is nothing but a fantasy, and a charade I could never keep up.

I dry my tears and straighten my shoulders as I digest Cal's words.

I have only a couple days left with Aden, so I'll take them and make every second count.

TWENTY-ONE

ADEN

The minutes that I'm not with Celia pass at an irritating pace. I hold back from dropping all my responsibilities and not breaking the speed limit to get to the cottages. I even considered not taking a shower, which is messed up.

When in the hell did this woman manage to crawl under my skin? I forget who I am when we're together, and as fucked as that is I feel better than I've felt in a really long time. I can't even think about her without grinning. Maybe it was spending so much time together, my body got used to having her within reach. Or maybe it was the awkward way she left, chased away by Cal's disapproving stare. Whatever it is, being without her leaves me twitchy and uneasy. I've spent hours in a ditch staring down the scope of my rifle and that wasn't as maddening as the distance between us.

Which is why I'm hauling ass through the cabin of the boat, grabbing my keys and sunglasses to get to the cottages to see her. It's only when I'm jumping from the back of the boat to the dock that I catch movement from Jenkins's sailboat.

My good mood dissolves instantly. The old man's only been gone four days and the vultures have already descended. Not on my watch. With light steps I creep to the boat and manage to slide aboard without being noticed. There's a shuffling inside the cabin.

I stand in the doorway and brace. "Drop whatever you have and come out with your hands up, asshole." My muscles jump and prep for a fight.

A slender body pushes out from the shadows. A woman, her eyes wide.

I try to relax my stance to keep from scaring her any more than I already have. "Who are you?"

"I'm Becky Muller, Billy's daughter."

"Oh shit." I step back. "I'm sorry, I didn't know."

"Who are you?"

I reach out my hand. "Aden Colt. I was friends with your dad."

"You must be the man the hospital said he was with." I nod and she shakes my hand. "It's nice to meet you."

"I'm sorry about your dad. If it makes you feel better, he talked about you all the time."

She blows out a breath and frowns. "I wish I could say that helps, but I haven't spoken to my dad in over ten years. My brother said I should just let all this stuff go, but I had to come."

I knew his relationship with his kids was strained. He was a washed-up sailor with a drinking problem, a bad temper, and a boatload of regrets, and after losing the love of his life he gave up trying. It didn't take a genius to realize that his stories about his children were always those from their childhood.

"Do you need some help?" I nod to a small box that has a few of his things in it. A watch, an old photo of his wife, and a couple records.

She picks up the box and clutches it to her stomach. "No, I got it."

She turns back to study the humble living quarters of the man who loved her but didn't have the balls to get his shit together and missed out on half her life. "Actually…I don't know what to do with his boat. Could you help me sell it?"

Sell his boat? This thing meant more to him than anything, which might be the reason Becky looks like it'll bite. The resentment makes sense, but damn, it's fucking sad. "Sure."

"Oh, and his ashes. He didn't have a will, but I think he'd want to be spread out over his favorite fishing spot? I don't know where that is, and I have to get back to my family in Denver."

"I'll take care of it."

She smiles sadly. "Thank you."

"Please, let me take that." I scoop the box from her arms.

"You don't have—"

"I know, but your dad would've given me shit for not being a gentleman to his little girl."

She frowns, and ducks back inside to grab a few more things. His Padres hat, his antique copper maritime telescope, and his tackle box that's faded and covered in close to fifty years of dirt, grime, and fish blood.

When she's finally ready to go, the box is almost overflowing with things. Staring at it, all I can think is that life is too short to live with these kinds of regrets.

She hands me Jenkins's fishing pole. "Here, I was going to give this to my son, but I can't fly with it. I think you should have it."

"No, I can't take that." I grab the pole and take in the torn grip and rusted reel. "It was his favorite. Your son should have it."

"It's too much trouble."

"I'll send it to you. Really, it's no big deal. Jenkins would haunt me forever if he knew I was using his lucky pole."

She smiles, but it's shaky. "Thank you."

About an hour later I'm loading the back of a rental car with two small boxes of Jenkins's stuff. That's it. All he'll have to be passed along to those who never got the chance to know what kind of man he was. Two boxes. And as much as the items they contain will shed light on the subtle things about Jenkins, they'll never tell stories of his love for his wife, his love of country, and the demons that held him back from being the kind of father and grandfather I know he could've been.

Just like the children of the men I buried.

Watching their wives at the graveside, clutching a folded flag to their chest as their sons and daughters clung to them. So young, and they'll never know the kind of men their fathers were. That they sacrificed their lives for someone so undeserving, someone who is right on track to make the same mistakes Jenkins did.

I've pushed away my family.

Alienated myself from the world.

I hole up in my boat just like Jenks did.

At this rate I'll die alone like he did too.

The sound of Becky's car door pulls me from my thoughts.

She hands me a business card with her name on it. "I'll call the morgue and have them contact you when his ashes are ready." Her eyes give away a hint of sadness, the truth that she's struggling more with her father's death than she's letting on. "If you could text me your number."

"Sure." I pull out my phone and hit the text icon when I notice I have a new text from Celia.

I'm all packed up and missing you.

My pulse quickens and I quickly fire off a text to Becky.

Her phone pings. "Thanks."

I nod and step back. "I'll let you know what the ship brokers say about selling his boat."

"I appreciate that."

After a few silent seconds she nods and gets in her car and I turn to my truck.

Life can change so quickly and in such abrupt ways that we never get a chance to see it until it's over.

I've let one too many suns set on my feelings for Celia without telling her what she means to me, how she calms the war in my soul and silences the screams.

I can tell she's hesitant to rush into something.

But I live with enough regret as it is.

Last thing I want is to regret never trying.

SAWYER

It's been almost an hour since I sent Aden the text about missing him and because he hasn't texted back I'm second-guessing the logic behind sending such an honest message. I should've thrown some kind of sexual joke in there to lighten the seriousness, maybe? My worst fear is that he's staring at his phone wondering how to respond appropriately.

This whole thing between us went from casual to something so much more really quickly. Too quickly.

Statistics have proven that the best relationships develop out of great friendships. That patience in getting to know one another is more lasting. Does that mean this urgency and intensity I'm feeling is nothing more than misplaced lust?

Mark and I were friends first. We took things slow. And I never felt even a fraction of what I feel when I'm with Aden, hell, I don't even have to be around him to feel the pull toward him.

What does it all mean?

I dial my sister's phone number for what seems like the hundredth time today and after two rings it goes to voicemail.

"…volcano diving in Hawaii and it's too hot for—"

I hit END and dial my mom's cell.

"Hey, Sawyer." She sounds tired.

"Mom, I've been trying Cece's cell all day but it goes straight to voicemail."

My mom sighs.

"Is everything okay?"

"Yeah, sorry. We had a doctor's appointment." There's the sound of a door shutting in the background and I imagine my mom tucking away somewhere so she won't be overheard. "It's her vision. The tumor is growing rapidly; she's only able to see shadows."

I swallow hard and fight the urge to cry; after all, this isn't something I didn't know on some level was coming, but to think she can no longer see makes everything so…real.

"What…" I clear my throat. "What does that mean?"

"It means that the pressure on her brain stem is increasing. They can't tell us how long she has because there's no telling what the pressure could affect."

"Is she in pain?"

"No, honey, she's lost a little of her spunk, but that's about it." She sniffs followed by the sound of something rubbing against the phone, as if she's dabbing a tissue on her cheeks. "When will you be home?"

"The movers come day after tomorrow, first thing. My flight leaves at seven o'clock in the morning." Everything behind my ribs hurts.

"Okay, that'll be good."

"Can I talk to her?"

"Sure. Hang on." There's more shuffling in the background and the opening and closing of doors. "Cece, honey, Sawyer's on the phone."

More muffled sounds like sheets rustling. "Mom, could you grab me a glass of water? Hello?"

"Hey, Cece."

"Finally a little privacy. Mom's been hovering."

I chuckle at the irritation in her voice. "Mom told me about your vision."

"It's not that bad. I can still watch TV. How about you? Have you ruined my reputation over there yet?"

I smother the urge to cry at my sister's blatant diversion and slip down onto the couch. "Not yet. Oh, I met Cal."

Silence, and then, "Oh shit."

"You told him you were sick. He knew I wasn't you."

"Eh, he's a cool guy, I knew he'd play along. If I told you Cal knew you'd never have agreed to go."

Play along, sure, but this isn't a game anymore. I chew my bottom lip and fight off the urge to cry. Again.

"Sawyer, what is it?"

"I think, I mean, I don't know because I've never really felt anything like this, but I think I'm in love with Aden."

There's not a hint of sound coming through the other end.

Not even breathing.

"Celia, did I lose you?"

"What did you just say?"

"I've fallen in love with Aden, but he thinks I'm you and—"

"Tell him the truth, Sawyer, tell him it was my idea and—"

"I can't."

"Why not?"

I stare out at the ocean thinking it wasn't too long ago that I was terrified of the massive sea and now I'm going to miss seeing it every day. "He was lied to about something, he hasn't totally confided in me, but something tells me this kind of deception would be unforgivable."

"But how do you know unless you try?"

"Cal made me promise I'd never tell. He knows Aden better than I do." And even though there's truth in those words they taste sour in my mouth.

"Tell him, Sawyer. Tell him it's my fault, that I put you up to it. If he hears the reasons why he'll understand. And if he doesn't then he must not feel the same and you're better off knowing that now."

"There's more."

"What?"

"Jenkins died."

"What? How?"

I tell her about how we were out on the boat and everything that happened after, making sure to gloss over the sex marathon.

"Aden's been through so much I can't bring myself to be the cause of more pain. Besides, it's not me he cares about anyway. It's you."

"Sawyer—"

"It's true. If he knew me...he wouldn't like the *real* me."

"Shit, I'm sorry. I thought this would be fun for you, that you'd let loose a little and live it up. Leave it to you to find some heavy emotional crap to deal with."

That makes me laugh. "Right?"

"So what're you going to do?"

"I'll enjoy my last couple days here and then come home and get back to the real world."

"Back to boring, huh?"

"You call it boring, I call it predictable." Even though going home just means walking from one broken heart to another.

"Do what you need to, but Sawyer?"

"Hm?"

"Remember what this feels like, okay? Don't forget what it's like to fall hard for someone and never settle for anything less than this feeling."

I don't think it's possible to ever feel this way about anyone again. "I won't."

"Good."

"Now, no more changing the subject, tell me about your doctor's appointment."

She goes on to tell me that all the doctors are kooks trying to scare her into dying when she feels great. I smile at her ability to shrug off the warnings and keep up hope that she'll fight death as long as her body will allow.

Death sentence be damned, if anyone could be the exception it'd be her.

I catch movement from outside the window. "Oh my God, Cece," I whisper. "He's here."

"Shit! Okay, go. Have fun. Tell him who you are!"

His heavy feet hit the steps.

"I gotta go!"

She laughs hard. "Make him wear a condom—"

I hit END with the irrational fear that Aden could hear her from the other side of the door, just as it swings open without him knocking.

I shoot to my feet fearing he's angry because he somehow found out the truth, but when I see the look in his eyes, I know it's a different emotion that's driving him.

He takes me in from head to toe and I step back at the primal hunger that shines in his eyes. "Where are you going?"

In the small space there's nothing behind me but the bedroom. He must read my thoughts and a slow grin pulls his lips.

He shuts the door and stalks toward me. "Got your text."

"You didn't text back."

"You miss me?"

"Yeah." The word falls out on a breath.

"How much?" He's right up to me now, his breath hot against my lips.

I tilt my head back to meet his eyes and when we're like this there is no Celia, it's only me and him and every single thing we make each other feel buzzing between us. "More than I should."

His hand sifts through my hair and I lean into his touch. There's never been a man who's communicated such stability and safety with a single caress like Aden does. "We're not in public."

"I know." And so does my body as it reacts instantly to the promise in his words.

"I want you wrapped around me." He leans down and presses the softest kiss against my lips. "I want to feel your heart racing against my chest and know that it's because of me." He nips at my bottom lip. "Hearing you moan my name chases away everything, freckles." He walks me back a step. "Nothing exists but you."

Once we're in the bedroom I pull away and he watches me shrug off my clothes. His eyes widen when my bra drops to the floor followed by my panties. "I don't want to forget you."

He pulls his shirt off over his head, his wide muscular chest on display and tensing with anticipation. "I'll make sure you never will." He pushes down his shorts and closes in until the warmth of his bare skin presses against mine. "I'll mark your fucking soul."

I force myself to stay present, to not think about having to say goodbye, and more importantly to not dwell on things I can't change. For now, I have this powerful, caring, deserving man in my arms, and that's where I choose to stay.

His lips touch the shell of my ear and he whispers, "The way you've marked mine."

TWENTY-TWO

ADEN

I woke that next morning to the gentle sounds of Celia breathing against my chest.

Not the panic of gunfire.

Or the visions of blood and death.

Just the warmth of the woman who has managed to bring a semblance of peace to my life like nothing else ever has.

Not booze.

Pills.

Or therapy.

Even now with her hair tangled and splayed out over my arm, her leg thrown over mine, her naked body works like an anchor in a sea of madness. I wonder if that's all this is, because like Cal pointed out I don't know much about her, except I know how she likes to be touched, what makes her breath hitch, and her body shake. I've memorized the hypnotic sounds she makes when I lavish every dip and flare of her frame.

I have to acknowledge that it's the sex that's making me feel things

I'm not used to feeling. It's as if I'm falling, but know the landing will be the softest I've ever felt. Something shifted, and no matter how hard I try I can't put my finger on exactly what it is. All I know is that someone I want to spend my days with is not under my control. The thought is as terrifying as it is comforting because coupled with the fear is the excitement that I've never had these feelings for anyone before.

This is why I shouldn't think. I should just act. Roll with it and see where things go. If Celia feels even a fraction of what I feel for her she'll consider staying in San Diego, or at the very least trying the long-distance thing. It's not ideal, but it's better than nothing.

As soon as the words tumble through my head my focus moves to the boxes stacked around her bedroom. She's clearly set on moving home.

I have twenty-four hours to convince her to stay.

And if she does, if she sticks around for me, when all these warm gushy feelings wear off, where will that leave us?

I groan and rub my eyes. Stop overthinking this shit!

Her legs shift, rubbing against me with the soft skin of her inner thigh. I bite back a hum of pleasure. "You up?"

She smiles and palms the length between my legs while pushing in close. "No, but you are."

"You can feel that, huh?"

She laughs and the sound is throaty and lust-heavy. What is wrong with us? If we didn't have jobs to do we'd both stay in bed and probably die of malnutrition.

Speaking of… "We skipped dinner last night. Since you're all packed up I'm assuming you don't have food in the house."

"I have a little, but probably nothing you'd like. I'm starving."

"Okay, so let me feed you."

"Mmmm…" She nuzzles my neck and shifts so that her body is half on top of mine.

I grip her hips to hold her to me. "You're gonna kill me, woman."

"Go on." Her lips brush against the sensitive skin below my ear. "Tell me more about you feeding me."

"I ah...what..." My words fade into a groan when she straddles my hips. "Food. Sex. And I thought we could—oh my—" I bite my lip as she kisses down my stomach and hovers over my hard-on.

She looks up at me with those big eyes and fat fucking lips and I'm lost. "You thought we could what?" Her tongue darts out, licking me until my hips jack off the bed.

"Town. In town...it's..." I fist the sheets to keep from gripping her hair and pushing myself down her throat. "Fourth of July."

She props her elbow on my quad and I blink down to see her grinning. "You want to spend the Fourth with me?"

I nod frantically. "Yes. So much, yes." *Now get your lips back on me.*

"Sounds like fun."

My stomach knots with anticipation as she settles back between my legs.

And after she feeds on me, I feed on her.

Then I take her to breakfast.

* * *

Don't be a fucking pussy.

The sun is setting over the water by the time we finally make it to town. It took hours for us to get ready and between the stripping, showering, and many attempts at dressing it was impossible to keep my hands off Celia.

I had no idea watching a woman blow-dry her hair could be so erotic.

Or doing her makeup.

Sliding jeans up those velvety thighs.

All of it was like a shot of adrenaline straight to my libido.

The only reason I finally left her alone is because I promised her we'd go out and see if a Fourth in OB lives up to the hype.

I haven't been since I was a kid, but it's exactly how I remember it, except maybe a little more crowded.

Which is why I've been giving myself a pep talk for the last forty-five minutes.

I told myself I wouldn't drink, that I'd be strong for Celia, but after fifteen minutes of being surrounded by hundreds of strangers I snapped at Celia for not walking fast enough.

The hurt on her face was enough to make me want to kick my own ass. I grabbed a beer from the rooftop bar, watching the sunset, hoping to mute the raging paranoia in my head.

I *feel* everyone's eyes like a prick against my skin, warning me to be alert. The only thing grounding me against the mounting panic is the melodic cadence of Celia's voice as she goes on about God knows what. I struggle just to pay attention.

Her gorgeous face is cast in the orange glow of sunset, making her already reddish-blond hair seem almost pink. Her eyes are on the ocean and I make myself take deep calming breaths to remain here with her rather than consumed by the memories of war.

"…I swear, sometimes I think I'm cursed." She turns to face me with a shy smile, and a small fraction of security returns to my chest.

"What do you mean?"

Stay focused on Celia. Let her be the only person in the room. And maybe I'll get through tonight without showing my ass.

SAWYER

I can't put my finger on when it happened, but sometime between the cottage and the bar Aden shut down on me. He probably doesn't even think I noticed, and I don't think pointing it out will do any good, but he's been looking everywhere but at me since we got here. I've filled the awkwardness with idle talk about things I know he's not listening to, hoping it would help him to relax. In the short time we've known each other I've found a few things that seem to put him at ease. Sex. Fishing. And taking all focus off of him.

So I'm babbling on about myself until something I say catches his attention. Finally.

"I've always felt, I don't know, I think the best way to describe it would be doomed." His lips twitch with a restrained smile, and God the view is such a relief the knot loosens in my chest. "It's not funny!"

He forces a frown. "I'm not laughing. Go on."

I sip my margarita and notice from a side glance that he's watching and waiting for my next words. I turn to face him head on. "It started when I was eight."

His eyes pop wide and another shadow of a smile begins to pull his lips. "How does an eight-year-old girl get cursed?"

"You don't believe me."

He gulps from his beer and flags the waitress for another. "It's hard to believe. Explain."

"I had a week where every day something bad happened— Stop laughing!"

"Bad, like, your dog ate your Barbie?"

"No, bad like I got in trouble at school for kicking a teacher, and before you go thinking the worst of me it was an accident."

"I believe you."

Picking apart my napkin I relive the week my life seemed to go wrong. "Then I got sick and…" I killed my grandmother. "Let's just say things just went downhill from there."

"Nothing you've said so far would lead me to believe you're cursed, freckles."

"Well, it gets worse."

He swallows back a healthy swig of beer, releasing his lips with a pop. "Go on, I have to know."

"When I was ten I got in a huge argument with my best friend, Amy Noelle. She told this boy at school that I liked him when she promised me she wouldn't breathe a word to anyone. Anyway, the boy ended up telling the entire school and they made fun of me for two months straight until summer came. I was so humiliated. I told Amy I hated her and wished she'd move to Korea."

"Why Korea?"

I shrug. "I don't know, maybe because at the time it seemed like the farthest away place there was. Anyway, two days after I wished that, she told me her dad got a promotion at work and they'd be moving to Florida. Still to this day I haven't heard from her."

His expression morphs into a skeptical scowl.

"It was all my fault."

"Something tells me there's more."

"At twelve I caused a car accident outside my house, fifteen I backed the car over our dog, fifteen and a half I made muffins for my class and gave everyone food poisoning, sixteen I got suspended for a poem I wrote about suicide that was really the lyrics to a song written by some metal band. I thought it was deep and thought-provoking. Do you want me to continue or do you get the idea?"

His jaw hangs open on its hinges and I take that as my cue to continue.

"Seventeen I broke my PE teacher's arm, nineteen I gave money to a homeless guy in my neighborhood who used it to buy drugs and OD'd, twenty—"

"Hold on, you've got something for almost every year of your life from the time you were eight?"

"Eventually I figured out there was something wrong with me, so…" I locked myself in my room for over a year. "College kept me indoors." Online classes. "I was relatively safe if I avoided people." I bite my lip, fearing I've exposed too much Sawyer to be Celia.

"And how old are you now?"

"Twenty-four."

"You realize this is ridiculous, right? Wait." His jaw gets hard. "The photos."

"The what—" *Oh God.*

I fucked up!

"You're so afraid to fuck something up, yet you take risks most people wouldn't, how?"

My mind scrambles to come up with an answer. If you don't know what to do, flip the coin. My sister's words come washing in and I blurt, "The coin."

His mouth remains tight, but his shoulders relax a fraction. "So you flip the coin to help you make choices you're afraid of."

I guess that's close enough to the truth. "Once it's taken out of my hands…" I can't even look at him while lying. I don't know what happened. I completely forgot to pretend. "Fate takes over."

"And you allowed these freak accidents to dictate what's safe and what's not."

"I didn't allow it, Aden. It just did."

"And what about now? Do you still feel cursed?"

A couple of weeks ago I would've said yes, but after this last week? "Not as much, no."

"Good." He leans back with a huff. "Because it's a horrible way to live."

"I just…I feel like I have blood on my hands."

He jerks his gaze to mine, and they flash with irritation. "You didn't kill anyone, Celia. Okay, maybe the dog, but you don't know what it's like to kill until you do it on purpose with intent."

I jump at the way his words are barked at me and remember he has a history of death and violence that I know very little about. His eyes are back to being cold and guarded and I want to kick myself for losing him again so easily.

"You're right, I'm just…" *Trying to get you back.*

Things between us are so easy when we are alone, but anywhere else everything with Aden becomes complicated.

He returns to scanning our surroundings and defeat punches me in the chest. "I'm going to go to the ladies' room."

He nods and has to back up so I can push my seat back as he'd had me pinned between a wall, the table, and him.

Before I walk away I gently touch his forearm. He startles and his eyes come to mine and immediately soften in apology.

"I'm sorry. I should've known better. I didn't mean to upset you."

He smiles shyly and takes my hand to bring it to his lips when—*pop!*

His big body slams into mine. I'm crushed between him and the unforgiving block wall at my back. He smothers me. My lungs pant for air.

I pat his lower back. "Aden, you're crushing me."

His muscles are tense and shaking. "What the fuck was that?"

"It was a firework."

Slowly he pulls away, his eyes looking wild and unfocused and—*pop!* Another fires. His shoulders tense, but he manages to hold back his response.

I reach up and cup his jaw only to have him jerk away from my touch. "We need to go."

"Okay."

His eyes scan the bar and I follow his gaze, expecting to see whatever threat he sees. People dressed in various arrangements of red, white, and blue, laughing, drinking, and harmlessly celebrating. "Aden?"

His face is pale and the muscle in his jaw ticks. He throws a wad of cash on the table and hooks me around the shoulders. "We can watch the fireworks from the cottages." He roughly guides me through the crowd. "The view, we can see the pier and it'll be more—" He glares at a group of men who stumble in front of us, blocking the exit. "Get the fuck out the way."

They turn toward us and Aden shoves me behind his back.

"You got a problem, asshole," the bigger one of the group says while his friends laugh.

Aden steps close and has at least three inches on the guy. I don't know what the dude sees in his eyes, but he backs off, shaking his head. "Damn, chill out."

They move and Aden grabs my arm and ushers me out the door, down the steps, and directly to his truck.

"Are you okay—"

"Of course." He swings the door open, not looking at me, and then throws it closed the second my feet are safe inside.

Another pop and Aden flinches while jogging around the hood.

What in the hell is going on?

It's a short and quiet ride back to the cottages, and other than the obsessive way his wild eyes check the rearview mirrors he seems to have calmed. He throws the truck into park and I hesitate to say anything, fearing that it'll trigger his anger.

"I'm sorry." He's stares blindly out the front windshield. "It's the crowds." He turns toward me and in the dark his eyes look black. "They remind me of a time when everyone was a threat."

I nod slowly. "Okay, I understand."

"It's bad enough when I'm alone, but with you it's…" He blows out a breath and the action seems to loosen his muscles a little more. "Worse. If anyone hurt you…" He shakes his head as if the thought is too deplorable to imagine and my whole body warms.

"Can I touch you?" Earlier my touch seemed to upset him and I want to make sure I don't cross some invisible boundary.

He takes my hand and presses it to his chest. The rapid beat of his pulse feels like hummingbird wings against my palm.

"Oh my God, Aden…your heart is racing."

He laughs humorlessly. "I know."

What happened to him?

"Do you want to talk about it?"

He drops my hand and stares directly into my eyes. "No."

I lean across the center console and he doesn't push me away so I press my lips to his. At first they're firm and unyielding but after a few gentle swipes of my tongue he hooks me around the back of the neck and devours my mouth. The kiss is desperate, angry, and he nips at my lower lip with an impatience I've come to expect from Aden when he needs me to help him forget.

I gasp as I come up for air. "Let's go inside."

He grins, and a sliver of my Aden comes back. "You go ahead, I'll meet you there in a few." With a long, lingering wet kiss I jump from the truck and head back to Celia's cottage with the lead weight of a plane ticket back to Phoenix weighing down my purse and my thoughts.

TWENTY-THREE

SAWYER

I'm back at the cottage waiting for Aden. I hit the bathroom, checked my hair and makeup, and traded in my skinny jeans for a pair of baggy drawstring pants. They're not the sexiest things in my suitcase, but I notice when I tie them loose and allow them to hang low on my hips they accentuate my backside, a part of my body that Aden seems to appreciate.

When I'm done touching up, I'm surprised to see he's still not here. I scurry outside to make sure he didn't dupe me and end up going back to the boat. I notice his truck is still there so I plop down on the deck assuming he's at Cal's catching up with his uncle.

Now that the sun has fully set, the ocean is nothing more than an endless inky pool of darkness. But in the distance there's a sea of glowing dots, and just as the girl from the moving company said, hundreds of people have paddled out past the pier with what has to be thousands of glow sticks.

"Hey." Aden's word is clipped as he takes the seat next to me with a bottle of whiskey in his hand.

Other than the few beers he had tonight, I haven't seen Aden touch liquor in days.

I eye the bottle, then him. "Everything okay with Cal?"

He grabs my hand and pulls it into his lap. "Cal? Yeah, he's good. He's really good."

I squeeze to get his eyes and they're a little wild again like earlier, but when he studies me for a few seconds he seems to calm. The pounding of music comes from all different directions, parties at neighboring homes, and there's a group of people around Brice's place with red Solo cups in hand, all watching the swarm of glowing surfers get bigger and bigger.

"Want to go inside?"

He leans in and presses a hurried kiss to my cheek. "No. I want you to see the show."

"Celia!" Zoë comes skipping toward us wearing a pair of cutoff shorts and a red, white, and blue bikini top. "We were just getting ready to paddle out." Her eyes track to Aden, who has become stiff at my side. "Hey, Aden."

He ignores her, which immediately strikes me as rude, but when I turn toward him it's as if he doesn't even see her.

"Oh, ya know, I'm not a very strong swimmer so I'll just—"

The sound of Zoë's laughter cuts me off. "Not a strong swimmer?" She cocks a hip. "You out-paddled Brice when we went surfing at Bird Rock."

Aden slowly turns toward me, his eyes morphing into slits of doubt.

"Yeah, well..." I squeeze his hand but keep my eyes on her. "That was a long time ago; besides, I want to stay dry."

I want to stay dry? What a lame excuse.

"All right, but you're missing out." She turns to see a few people around Brice's place with their surfboards making their way down to the beach. "It's almost time!" She jogs off, calling over her shoulder, "Enjoy the show!"

My muscles ache with tension and I expect Aden to launch into questions about my surfing, but after a few minutes pass, he seems more interested in emptying that bottle than anything else.

As much as I want to talk I get the distinct feeling he's not interested in sharing. So I remain silent, hoping my presence is enough to calm whatever battle is waging within him.

He continues to swig in rapid succession. My knee bounces with the energy it takes to keep from snagging the bottle from him and demanding answers. My phone vibrates in my pocket. With my free hand I pull it out and see it's from my mom.

It's almost nine o'clock at night.

I hit ACCEPT and press the phone to my ear.

"Mom?"

"Sawyer." She sounds breathless.

Aden's hand squeezes mine and I smile reassuringly.

"Mom, hold on." I press the phone to my chest. "I'm going to take this inside."

He nods and his eyes go back to scanning the horizon.

Once in the safety of the cottage, I put the phone back to my ear.

"Mom, what's going on?"

"Honey, it's Cece."

I freeze mid-step. "What happened?"

"She couldn't breathe, we…Honey, we had to get her help. She's at Good Sam."

"I'll be home tomorrow first thing. Will I be too late?" My voice cracks as the reality of what she's telling me constricts my throat.

"No, the doctors assured us we have some time, but Sawyer, we don't have much."

"No, Mom." My eyes heat with tears.

"I know, honey."

I push back my tears and focus on my last conversation with Celia, holding on to the health I heard in her voice. "How is she handling all this? Is she okay?"

"She hasn't lost her spunk. When I left to call you she was shoving away all the doctors and even called one of them a...*cockbag*." I smile and hear the first pop of fireworks from outside. "Your father was mortified."

"Tell me the truth, Mom. What does your gut tell you?"

A few beats of loaded silence swell between us. "It's time, baby. My gut tells me..." Her voice cracks. "It's time."

"I'll come straight to the hospital."

"Okay."

"Tell her I love her."

"I will."

I hit END and slump into the couch. What is supposed to be the greatest fireworks show in California goes off right outside my window but I can't even bear to look with knowledge that my sister will never see another firework again.

And something about that makes me straighten my spine. Saps the sorrow from my bones, leaving life and energy and gratitude in its place as the spirit of my sister fills me with appreciation.

This may be the last time in my life that I ever truly feel alive. Celia wouldn't want me to waste it.

"Aden, maybe we should paddle out!" I push myself up and force my feet to the door when I hear the angry rumble of a male voice.

"Stand down, Cal, or I'll put a fucking bullet in your head."

ADEN

They found me.

I knew they would.

I've felt their eyes. Always spying.

The ocean has never been safe. It's been their way to get at me.

No one is safe.

Mortar explosions are on repeat as incoming bombs hit too close. Close to everything I care about.

Close to her.

Too close to her.

I point my handgun into the face of the enemy.

His hands are raised. "I'm standing down. I'm not here to hurt you."

My hand shakes but I'm a good shot. Shaking or not, I'll blow his brains out with one bullet. "Me? You think I could give a fuck about me!"

"Aden, listen to me. You're in San Diego—"

"Back the fuck off, you fucking liar!"

Something brushes my back.

I can't see the threat.

Can't move fast enough.

Gun raised, I whirl around. Muzzle of my gun shoved into the face of—

"Aden, no!"

"Aden?" Her terrified eyes are big and so...so green...and *crying*?

"No, no." I lower my weapon. "Don't cry. I won't let anyone hurt you." I turn back to the man at the steps, my uncle, but now, my enemy.

Another mortar explodes.

"Get down!"

I crouch and back up until she's forced inside where I lock the door and stand guard.

"I'll die before I'll let anyone take her from me."

TWENTY-FOUR

SAWYER

He has a gun!

How did he get a gun?

Aden's pressed against the wall, his eyes darting to the window where fireworks explode out over the ocean. Every pop and bang manages to coil him tighter, closer to snapping.

"What are you doing?"

"Shh. Be quiet!"

"Aden…"

His gaze remains firmly set to the window.

"You're scaring me."

He blinks and slowly his eyes find mine. I gasp at the torture, the war I see raging behind his glare. "I won't let them get to you. You have my word."

I swing my gaze from him to the window and back. "Who? Aden, there's no one out there."

He huffs out a breath and seems to calm a fraction before another round of fireworks goes off in a string of explosions.

He jerks away from the wall and grabs me by my biceps, dragging me to the bedroom. "Stay down." He pushes me back on the bed.

There's movement from the corner of my eye and I watch as Cal creeps in through the door. He puts a finger to his lips and I grip Aden's hand before he turns around. "Wait."

His eyebrows drop low over his eyes as he stares down at me. The Aden I've come to know is gone and been replaced by a soldier in a fight for his life.

"Don't leave me alone back here." It's all I can think to keep him from catching Cal and accidentally shooting him.

Aden searches my face frantically. His lips are pale and there are beads of sweat on his skin. Whatever is happening inside his head his body is responding to as if it's real. He has a moment of clarity and the look of agony slices through his face. "Celia."

That one name carries so much pain. He has no idea, but what I wouldn't give to hear my name on his lips. My sister's name will always be the wall that divides us.

"I'm so sorry." He steps between my knees and hooks me around the neck to pull me to his stomach, the gun hanging to his side.

"What's going on, Aden?" I lean around to see Cal moving through the bedroom door.

Aden's body locks and the muscles of his abs tense.

He whirls around, pushing me behind him as he raises his gun. It happens so fast and next thing I know Cal is on the ground and Aden's standing over him with the weapon pointed at his uncle's chest.

I hop off the bed and wrap myself around Aden from behind. "Stop it!"

"Son…" Cal's voice is shaking. "Put the gun down. I'm not here to hurt you."

"Aden, listen to him." I try to pull him back but he shrugs me off with a powerful shove of his shoulder.

Cal holds a hand up. "Stand back, Sawyer."

My eyes meet his and he cringes when he realizes what he's done.

Thankfully Aden seems too caught up in his head to notice.

The fireworks continue to explode in a series of bursts that sound way too close.

My heart pounds in my chest.

"I just want it to stop." Aden's voice cracks. "The screaming, the blood, it never goes away!"

Cal pushes himself up slowly, not taking his eyes off Aden. "I know, son. I know."

"You don't!" He steps back, freeing Cal from his overbearing stance. "I can't get away from it!" He brings the gun to his head and taps his temple with the barrel. "It's in here, it'll never go away, it's in here! I want to die!"

A whimper slides from my lips.

He whirls around and stares at me as if seeing me for the first time. "Except when I'm with you…"

Locked in his eyes I take a step forward. "I can help you forget."

His eyes flare with hunger as his wild gaze traces my face to land like they always do on my lips. "You're scared."

"Yes."

I see Cal stand to his full height behind Aden and he fishes a bottle of pills from his pocket. "Aden."

The stern sound of his name locks his progress to me and he dips his chin.

"I'm not leaving you alone with Celia with a gun."

"I would never hurt her. I…" The strong soldier before me stares down at his hand and blinks at the weapon. He nods once, clicks something on the side of it, and holds it out for Cal to take.

Cal shakes out a couple pills and places them in Aden's empty palm then mumbles something close to his ear.

Aden nods and throws back the pills, swallowing them without water.

Cal meets my eyes. "You okay?"

"Yeah."

"You sure?"

The fireworks have stopped and that seems to relax him a little. "What did you give him?"

"Prescription from the VA to mellow him out." He looks at Aden then to me. "Do you want me to stay?"

I study Aden, who now resembles a broken boy. "No, I'll be okay."

"You sure?"

Aden cringes.

"I'm sure."

You know where I am if you need me is the unspoken message I see in his eyes.

With that, he turns and leaves me alone with the man who pointed a gun in my face.

And I can't bear to abandon him when he needs me most.

ADEN

It's not real.

None of it.

Fuck if my head knows that.

I thought I could handle the fireworks, that if I stayed grounded, stayed with Celia, that I wouldn't forget where I was. That my mind wouldn't have the power to take me back there.

I was wrong.

And I could've hurt the only person who has ever been able to calm the storm in my mind.

"Can I touch you?" Her soft voice calls my eyes and she holds her hands out to me.

I rush to her and wrap my arms around her waist making sure to not squeeze too hard even though all I want to do is crush her with my apology. "I'm so sorry, freckles. I'm so fucking sorry."

"I am too." There are tears in her voice. "I had no idea it was that bad."

"It's bad. It's so bad. But with you..." I pull away and catch her quivering lips with mine. She tastes of tears and disappointment. My chest aches to fix what I've broken. "I've never felt better, more whole, than I do when I'm with you. I thought you'd cured me."

She steps back and drops to the bed, taking me with her. I curl up to her side and throw my leg over her thighs as she runs a hand through my hair. "Tell me."

"I can't talk about it. I'm sorry, I just...I can't."

"Is this the worst?" The methodical scrape of her nails against my scalp has me relaxing even deeper into her hold.

"No."

She sighs hard and squeezes me tighter to her. "Tell me?"

"I moved down here thinking getting away from the people I love would keep them from seeing what I've become. I can't handle my anger, the paranoia. It never lets up."

"You said...you want to die?"

"It's true. I wish I'd died with my brothers. The way it should've been."

My voice is sluggish and my eyelids grow heavy.

"You can't die." Her arms close tightly around me as if she could keep me here, keep me stable, by sheer force of will.

"No, I don't think I can." I'm so fucking tired. I push back the urge to sleep, to slip away and out of Celia's arms. "Tried. Failed."

"Is that what happened at the cliffs? Did you jump?"

"Mm-hm. Waves saved me. Brothers saved me. Can't die no matter how much I want to."

"I'm glad you didn't die, Aden."

"Mmm." My body feels weightless and darkness closes in.

"Knowing you is the best thing that's ever happened to me." I want to soothe the sadness I hear in her voice and reassure her that I'll erase the ugly memories I gave her. "I'll miss you."

"Miss you…" I can't fight it anymore and sleep pulls me under.

From the depths of unconsciousness I dream of the sound of her tears and her whispered "*I love you*."

SAWYER

I wake from a deep sleep to find Cal standing at the edge of my bed.

"I hope it's okay I let myself in. I didn't want to wake you but," he whispers. He nods to Aden who is sleeping in my arms. "I wanted to check on him."

"It's okay." I slide out from under him and scoot off the bed and into the living room. Cal follows behind me and I quietly close the door to the bedroom. "Do you have a second?"

He grunts and leans against a stack of boxes while I drop to the couch, tucking my legs up under me.

"You have to tell me what happened to him, Cal."

He doesn't need me to explain it, the look in his eyes tells me he knows what I'm asking for. "That's not my story to tell—"

"Please. Aden says he can't tell me, not that he doesn't want me to know, but it's like he can't bring himself to relive it."

His jaw is hard and unyielding.

"I'm leaving in six hours, Cal. I'll never see Aden again, but I have to know what made him like this. He says he's 'wrecked.' I just want to understand why."

He huffs out a breath, turns to check on the closed door to the bedroom, then drops down on the couch next to me. He runs a hand down his face, looking as tired as I feel. "Aden was the commander of his battalion. He called the shots, his men were obligated to follow. And he was good. I'd say the best."

This doesn't surprise me. Aden has that natural born leader thing going on. I find it nearly impossible not to listen when he barks orders at me and I'm not a trained soldier.

"On his last deployment his Special Forces team was there to train the local Iraqi soldiers to defend themselves. They had a lot of success and when they were given an op to infiltrate a compound where ISIS members were hiding, Aden was looking forward to backing up the newly trained men."

"He said he trusted the wrong people? What does that mean?"

Cal nods. "One of the Iraqi soldiers under his training had pissed off some of Aden's men. They were concerned he was playing both sides. You can imagine how dangerous that could be, if there was a rat in Aden's team who was filtering information to the enemy, well…"

He doesn't have to finish the sentence. I can only imagine what that would mean for Aden and his team.

"Aden felt his guys were being unfair. He trusted this man with his life and the life of his men."

Oh no…

I dream about crushing his skull with my bare hands.

A chill slides down my spine. "He was wrong."

Cal turns his cold, hard eyes on mine. "He was wrong."

I stare at the floor trying to imagine how difficult that must've been for Aden, to know that his soldiers trusted him, had faith that he would lead them into battle with only the best men at their back, only to realize he—

"They were ambushed. Enemy knew their every step and attacked before they could even make a move. When they came, they came after Aden. His men, the same ones who warned him about the mole, threw themselves in front of enemy fire to save their commander. Aden lost all but two of his US soldiers and they died so he could live."

"Oh my God." His men knew better and died to protect him anyway. "I can't imagine the guilt…" Even hearing it as a third party is suffocating me in shame.

"Aden came home and he wasn't the same. He was dead on the inside. He couldn't get a job, felt useless. The guilt ate him up so bad he couldn't bring himself to do anything but drink. He lashed out at his parents, his sister, they begged him to get treatment and he tried, but those demons run so deep. I knew if I didn't get Aden away from his family he'd destroy their love for him and he'd have nothing left."

"So you invited him here?"

He turns to me and tilts his head. "The only thing that keeps a wild animal from destroying everything around him is to keep him busy, give him a job. I left Aden in charge of my boat, figured if he was fishing he couldn't piss anyone off. He tried to live in my cottage here, but after he beat those boys who broke into this place he knew he needed more distance from people."

"He's isolating himself."

He makes a noise of agreement. "It's the only thing that keeps him sane. The only thing that keeps him from hurting people."

I knot my fingers in my lap. "He told me tonight he tried to kill himself."

"Yeah, guess the booze wasn't working so he tried, hate to say it but my guess is that wasn't the first time."

I lean forward and with my head in my hands I try to stop the whirling as my thoughts spin out of control.

"I didn't know how deep he was in with you, but after tonight…" He stares at the ground. "It's imperative he not find out who you are, Sawyer."

"I know."

"I don't think it was your intention to deceive him, but if he finds out you've been lying to him this whole time, pretending to be someone you're not, this might break him completely."

Silent tears fall from my eyes. I don't wipe them away because I want to feel the sorrow of lying to a man who doesn't deserve so much dishonesty and betrayal.

"Wish it could've been different, boy do I. Never seen Aden fall for a woman like he's fallen for you. Shame to see something that could've been great never happen."

I drag in a fortifying breath and face Cal knowing what I'm about to say is going to kill, but needing the break to be clean. "I think it would be best if we moved Aden to your place. The movers will be here early and I'll be leaving for the airport at sunup."

He narrows his eyes. "You're not going to tell him goodbye?"

"If I do, I'll never be able to leave."

Understanding washes over his features and he pushes to stand. "Right. I'll grab him."

I don't follow Cal back into the bedroom, but instead open the front door and wait when Cal staggers out of the room with a half-sleeping Aden leaning against him.

I look down at my feet as Cal passes me, through the door, and carefully down the stairs. Walking quickly I get in front of him so I'm able to open the front door of Cal's cottage as he lumbers, breathing heavily, to the couch to drop his nephew there.

With a grunt and a moan Aden flops to his back and the gentle sounds of his snoring fill the space. I resist the urge to go to him, to press my lips to his one last time even if he doesn't remember it because it'll take herculean strength to hold me back from falling into him and hanging on for dear life.

"Do me a favor?" Cal's standing in the doorway, his expression grim. "Give Celia a hug for me. Tell her my life is better having known her."

"I will."

I back out of the cottage and turn toward Celia's.

"Sawyer."

I stop and turn. "Yeah."

"Give me a call when she…when Celia…" His lips curl between his teeth.

I nod and head back to get ready to leave. As soon as the movers show up I want to be in the first cab to the airport to be with my sister.

I only hope Aden can forgive me.

TWENTY-FIVE

ADEN

I'm shaking.

But I'm not in a dream, I'm actually shaking.

My eyelids feel like they're made of concrete and peeling them open takes serious effort. My head is foggy and when I'm finally able to focus I see my uncle staring down at me.

"Wake up." He slaps my face a couple times, making me groan.

The throbbing in my head won't let up and my body is heavy as I push myself up from...wait. "Why am I on your couch?" I squint against the sun that pours in through the window. "What time is it?"

"Almost noon." He grabs a mug off the table and hands it to me. "Coffee. Should help knock away the last of the pills."

I take the mug and the memories of last night come flooding back. I pinch my eyes closed and shake my head as shame rips away the lingering effects of the drugs. "How'd I get here?" Last I remember I was wrapped in Celia's arms.

Celia.

Will she ever forgive me for what I've done?

"I moved you over here early this morning."

I peer up at him, squinting. "I walked?"

"With some assistance, yeah."

I push to stand and set down the coffee. "I need to talk to Celia." To beg her forgiveness, to swear I'll do better, and hope that she understands.

As I reach for the door, Cal's voice stops me. "She's gone, son."

I turn around to stare at my uncle, swearing this is some kind of joke. "She left?"

He shoves his hands into his pockets and nods.

But...no, not like this. Not without saying goodbye. I'd planned to beg her to consider staying at least for a few more days. She can't be gone.

I swing open the door and stumble-jog down the steps and into the crisp ocean air, grateful for the swift hit from the sun that wakens me a little more. I don't knock, but throw open the door and find...nothing.

All the boxes are gone.

I race to the bedroom and as if last night were just a dream I find it empty. No bed. Nothing.

The kitchen counter is also void of anything that would give away that someone lived here just a handful of hours ago. The only thing that still lingers is the sweet scent of her skin that hangs in the air. I grasp onto that to stay sane because I know she was real and that the last ten days weren't a hallucination.

I hear Cal's footsteps cross the threshold and with my back to him I ask, "Did she leave anything for me?" *A note? A goodbye? Anything?*

"No."

I sigh heavily and nod. "Right." Because I'm a fucking nutcase. Ruined beyond repair. And so unworthy of her it's not even fucking funny. I could tell her these things one thousand times and she'd never believe me, but last night I proved it.

"I'm going fishing." I storm past Cal grateful to feel my keys in my pocket. Sooner I get out to sea the sooner I'll be able to shake this disgusting feeling that's tumbling around my gut.

"Aden, I'll come with you—"

"I need to be alone." I freeze and look up to Cal standing on the top step of Celia's porch. "I'm really sorry about last night. Thank you for…" I swallow my pride and the lump forming in my throat. "Intervening."

He nods, and I see the worry flashing in his eyes. "Don't do anything stupid, ya hear?"

I turn and storm off and head right for the boat.

What he really means is don't die.

He doesn't get that I've tried, but this fucked-up life won't give me up.

SAWYER

Walking down the cold hallway of the hospital sends chills through me as I drag my rolling suitcase to my sister's room. My flip-flops slap against the linoleum to the beat of my heart.

It was nearly impossible to walk away from the cottages this morning without seeing Aden one last time. All the lights in Cal's place were off and I hoped that Aden was sleeping well and dreaming of something other than war. I hoped he was dreaming of me.

"Sawyer!" The sound of my mom's voice comes from a small waiting room outside a cluster of hospital rooms.

I let go of my bag just in time for her to crash into my arms.

"Thank God you're here." She pulls back and I can see these last few days have taken a toll on her. The dark circles around her eyes and frazzled hair show the signs of little sleep and a lot of worry.

"Where's Dad?"

"He's with Cece." She takes my hand and I grab my bag as she leads me back to a room.

The lights are off but the hallway lights shine in enough for me to see her there. Machines beep softly and the unsteady rise and fall of her chest also has me fighting to take a full breath.

My dad peeks up from his position at her bedside and although he smiles it's grim.

"How is she?" I move to her and she has an oxygen mask on and wires coming from her chest.

"It's not good, honey," my mom whispers.

I nod, expecting the heat of tears or the slice of pain, but feel nothing. Numb. As if none of this is real.

"Can she hear us?"

My dad nods and gives up his seat, motioning for me to sit with her. "She's in and out. When she's here it's short, but she seems to understand."

I drop into the seat and stare at my sister, unable to take my eyes off her for a second out of fear that I'll miss a twitch that clues me in that she's still with us.

"Amazing…" my mom whispers.

"It's remarkable," my dad's rumbled voice says next.

I look up at them. "What?"

My mom is tucked under my dad's arm and even though we're surrounding my sister in what could be her final moments of life they're both smiling softly at me. "You look so much like Celia right now."

"I've always been able to tell you two apart, ever since you were babies, but right now…" My mom's lip shakes. "If I didn't know better I'd think you were her."

"Thank you." I don't know why but it feels like the best compliment I've ever received.

For the next few hours I sit in silence with my sister. My parents head home to grab a shower and some food and I share with Celia about my time in San Diego. I tell her about Brice and Zoë, about my brush with a shark, and the kind words Cal had for her. But mostly, I talk about Aden. His smile, his jokes, how he could be obnoxious and how much I'll miss him. I expect reliving the memories to make me sad but as I talk I find myself smiling as warmth fills my chest.

The doctors and specialists come in to check her vitals and with somber expressions they explain it's only a matter of time. The word hospice is tossed around and because I'm unable to comprehend what it all means I simply nod.

My parents come back and tell me to go eat, but walking through the hospital cafeteria, the food lacks appeal. And it's then that my thoughts drift to Aden.

I've checked my phone and despite the fact that he hasn't attempted to contact me I fight the urge to call him. But I can't, because stringing this out will only hurt worse in the end. I decide on a glass of orange juice and drop to a table with my phone in my hand. Going into my contacts, I hit Aden's info and my finger hovers over the button.

"Do it," I tell myself. "Then it'll be over."

I close my eyes and touch the one button that'll help me to move on from Aden. Not so much for my own good, but for his.

Block number.

Delete contact.

A wave of sadness crashes over me. I'd give anything to have him back. To call him up and spill everything I'm feeling. He'd comfort me. Call me freckles.

Or Cece.

How can I be so in love with someone who doesn't even know who I am?

My phone vibrates in my hand and I startle and hope that by some miraculous chance he was thinking of me and decided to call.

My hopes crash when I see my mom on my caller ID.

"Mom, is everything okay?"

"She's up. Hurry."

I race from the cafeteria to the elevators, grateful to see the doors slide open just as I skate to a stop. Hurrying in I hit the button for the third floor and squeeze out the slit in the door before it's fully open. Panting, I rush into the room and the movement causes my sister to turn to me. Her eyes aren't as bright as they used to be and they slide back and forth as if she's searching to find me. I cross to the bed and her gaze settles at my shoulders. "Sawyer," she says weakly. The oxygen mask is at her neck so when she smiles I can see the full extension of her lips.

"Hey." I cross to the bed and drop down by her hip, pulling her hand into mine.

"You're back." She draws in a ragged breath.

"We'll give you two some privacy." My dad ushers my mom out the door and closes it but I see them standing right outside through the window.

"How are you feeling?"

"Sucks being in the hospital…" She hesitates, trying to catch her breath. "But I'm not in pain or anything."

"Good." I reach over and pull the oxygen mask back up to cover her nose and mouth.

She takes a full breath and I realize then my mom was right. Celia tries to act tough around me, but she's been much sicker than she let on.

A few pregnant seconds pass between us.

"Are you tan?"

She really can't see me. Grief threatens to send me to my knees, but I push it back. "I am. Turns out being you requires more sun exposure than I'm used to."

Her smile falls. "I'm gonna miss that."

My nose burns and my throat swells but I refuse to cry. "I know you will."

"Did you take my advice...tell Aden who you were?"

I shake my head, unable to speak the words.

She must take my silence as a no and frowns. "Oh, Sawyer..."

"I'm fine. It was a summer fling, I'm happy it's over so I can be home and spend time with you."

Her lips quiver. "I don't have...much time left."

"Of course you do."

"You sound sad." She squeezes my hand but it's weak.

"I am." Tears burn my eyes. "I'm not ready."

"I know, but I am." She pats the bed next to her and I curl up beside her. She turns her body as best she can so we can face each other and our hands clasp together between us, just like we always do when we're in bed together. Her eyes search my face and settle on my chin. "Tell me, tell me you got...a taste of what it's like to not...get caught up in your head. Tell me..." She takes a few deep breaths, or tries. "You loved it and you're going to live the rest of your life...every opportunity even if...they don't make sense."

"I did. I will."

Her eyes slide shut and open so slowly. "Good. That's all...I ever wanted for you."

"Cal wanted me to tell you hi and give you a hug."

"Does...anyone else know?"

"No."

"You still have the...coin?"

"It's in my bag."

She takes a shaky breath. "Promise...you'll use it."

"I promise, Cece." I sniff back tears. "But you have to make me a promise too. Hang on a little longer. Fight for more time. Promise me."

She smiles. "Okay, for you…I will."

* * *

Celia kept her promise.

Five days later she slipped into a coma, but she refused to let go.

The doctors were baffled. They threw around words like *miracle* and *medically impossible*, but I knew better. Celia was stubborn and would die on her terms.

Thirteen days after I returned from San Diego, Celia took her last breath.

Cradled to our mother's chest to the soundtrack of our tears she was rocked softly into the afterlife.

Even though I swore to Cal that I'd contact him once Celia passed, I wasn't able to. I couldn't bring myself to reopen the communication between us and figured it would be better this way.

He'd never have to know that just four days before her twenty-fifth birthday she finally let go, and maybe he'd even believe she beat death back and went on to travel the world.

That's how she would've wanted it.

So that's how I'll keep her memory alive.

TWENTY-SIX

ADEN

"You sure I can trust you with this?" My uncle's giving me *the look*. I've seen it so often over these last however fucking long it's been that it's almost losing its punch. *Almost.*

It's the look that says, "Don't fuck this up" and "Is this really who you want to be?" It's testing and challenging and I'm sure it's meant to make me feel something that'll push me to action, but I'd have to give a shit to care and, well...I don't.

I haven't heard from Celia since the night she held me in her arms and calmed my inner raging seas. I don't know how long it's been but it feels like a lifetime since I've felt alive.

Cal has been a constant pain in my ass refusing to leave and taking over all my duties at the cottages when I couldn't pull myself out of a bar long enough to do them.

But he's put up with my crap, he's given me a purpose and hasn't intervened too badly when I've traveled down self-destruction lane. I owe him the effort.

"Of course." I don't blame him for being leery about leaving this up to me. The day after she left he donated her car and I lost it. I blacked out for an entire day. After that I made him promise to keep Celia's old place empty until I was ready to let it go. If it were my call I'd say we burn it down and put a fucking graveyard in its place, but it's not, so fuck it. Life goes on, I guess.

He shoves some of his things into a duffel bag and I'm grateful he's moved his attention off me so he can't see the battle brewing in my mind.

"Her name is Kate Something-field. She's coming by on her lunch break, so she won't have much time."

"I'll open the place up and be waiting. It'll be quick." It'll have to be. Because I haven't set foot in Celia's place since the morning after I held a gun to her head.

Just the thought makes me want to punch myself in the chest to push away the ache. Talk about showing my ass. She couldn't get away from me fast enough.

Cal swings his bag over his shoulder and grabs his keys. "All right. I want to hit the road before traffic gets bad. I'll try to get back down before the holidays."

I grunt and nod.

First Jenkins.

Then Celia.

Now Cal.

I always thought being alone was what I wanted, but the thought of being truly alone is fucking depressing.

He squeezes my shoulder, then pushes past me to the door of his cottage. "The key to number four is on the desk."

The screen door shuts behind him and I stare at the brass key remembering the way Celia's fingers closed around it the first time I gave it to her. God, was that only a month ago? Feels like a different lifetime.

There's a bottle of Jack Daniels under the seat in my car and as much as my throat longs for the heat of booze that'll take away the sting of my thoughts I can't show up at Celia's—number four—with a buzz and the stank of liquor on my breath. I also can't step foot into that cottage with an audience.

A quick walk-through should help to desensitize myself to the place.

I snag the key and move from Cal's cottage out into the bright sun. Such a perfect day to fish—my stomach aches with the loss of Jenkins. Never thought I'd miss that crabby old man giving me shit about nothing.

When my feet hit the porch I'd swear I could smell Celia's perfume in the breeze. Internally shaming myself for being a jackass, I distance my mind from my emotions and unlock the door.

At first glance, the space looks no different than any of the other cottages, but as my eyes track around the room I can see her everywhere. On the couch with her legs folded up beneath her, in the kitchen sorting through her ridiculous food, by the bookshelf defending herself in those photos as I implied the worst.

I assumed when I came through the door that it would smell of her. But the only thing that permeates my senses is the over-pungent scent of wood polish and Clorox.

A glutton for punishment, I allow my feet to carry me back to the bedroom. I stare at the spot where her bed used to be and thinking on that brings back all the memories of what we did on that bed. The room seems to shrink a little and I open the window for some fresh air. Standing with my back against the wall I'm hit with all that happened the night before she left and the shame and humiliation is suffocating.

I owe her an apology.

That's the least she deserves.

That, and an explanation.

But if I called would she even want to hear from me?

Should I give her more time— A loose floorboard creaks beneath my foot.

Figuring I have time to grab my nail gun and fix it before the prospective tenant gets here, I bend over and grab the loose plank to see how much work will be involved in repairing it only to see the piece comes all the way off and easily.

Below the wood is an empty space, roughly the size of a laundry basket. And in that space lies a shoebox.

I pull it from the hole. It smells a little like mildew from being kept beneath the floorboards but looks untouched by any kind of water damage.

Popping off the top I peer inside to see what looks like some kind of memory box. Keepsakes, journals, and letters—both opened and unopened—litter the small space. There's a generic trophy, a blue ribbon and—"Hello?"

I swing my gaze to the open doorway to see a woman cautiously peering inside. "Yeah, come on in."

Putting the top back on I slide it to the side of the room and am placing the floorboard back on when the woman I'm assuming is Kate steps into the room.

"You must be Kate." I offer her my hand.

She smiles up at me, her bright blue eyes twinkling and her cheeks turning the slightest shade of pink. "Yes, and you must be Aden."

"Nice to meet you." I shake her hand and when she doesn't take her eyes off me I redirect her attention to the room. "It's not much, but…" Some of my best memories were made here. "Can't beat the location."

She finally studies the room and walks over to the window to peer out to what I know is a sliver of ocean view that if the bed is placed just right can be seen from the comfort of pillows. Her foot hits the loose floorboard, making it squeak.

"I'll fix the loose board today."

Her high heels click against the wood as she moves into the kitchen and then out into the living room. "And you're the property manager of the place?"

I follow her out and lean against the wall. "I am."

She turns sending her long dark hair to cascade over her shoulder and grins in a way that's so openly flirtatious I almost roll my eyes.

Trust me, woman, you don't want none of this. I'm fucked up beyond repair.

"So? What do you think?"

She runs her finger along the countertop with long manicured nails. "I'll take it."

* * *

There's a storm coming. I've watched the clouds build over the last hour as I sit anchored somewhere off the coast of Mexico. With a bottle of tequila in one hand and an envelope in the other I feel connected to the turbulent sky as it matches the feeling in my soul.

Finding that box in Celia's floor was like opening a parallel universe. Everything I thought I knew...I didn't.

At first its contents seemed to be nothing more than a catchall for old memories. Concert ticket stubs, old faded photos of a younger Celia, school report cards, and a photo of an older couple, her mom and dad, I assume.

There were handwritten letters to Celia signed "Love, Mom and Dad" that talked about their missing her and asking about all her adventures. And cards, so many cards for just about every holiday, all from her parents and someone named Sawyer who must be her sister.

But those weren't the things that surprised me the most. Those weren't the items that sent me pointing my boat out to the open sea.

Who knew a box could cause my already crumbling world to completely dissolve.

It was the stack of letters from different medical institutions all bundled up in a rubber band.

Celia was sick.

She had been for a long time.

According to multiple neurologists she'd been diagnosed with a brain tumor that has a life expectancy of eighteen months. I did some research only to find out that the location of the tumor would affect things like her balance, eyesight, breathing, and in retrospect I can't say I paid attention enough to notice any of that.

Why didn't she tell me?

There I was having fits about my past and the entire time she was dealing with a life-threatening illness.

Terminal cancer.

I tilt the bottle to my lips and relish the burn of booze as it slides down my throat. Celia, baby…what secrets you keep.

Because I'm a glutton for punishment I open the letter with the most recent date and read it again.

Dear Miss Forrester,

There are no words to express our sincerest condolences for your recent brainstem glioma diagnosis. It is extremely rare in adults and as of now there is no cure.

We've attempted to contact you many times throughout the last few months to encourage you to join the group therapy we provide for people with your diagnosis. Knowing you're not the only one and joining with others might help to cope with the future you face.

We would love to assist you in any way possible.

Please contact us and know there are resources to guide you through what you're feeling.

A bolt of lightning streaks across the sky and I stare at it, welcoming it to take me, begging for it to release me from this torture.

I let go of the only woman I ever really cared for.

And she's out there, suffering, living out whatever time she has left without ever knowing how much I love her.

TWENTY-SEVEN

SAWYER

"The Monroe file is on your desk," Dana calls as I pass by her and into my office.

I snag the file and drop into an overstuffed chair. I'd always thought the thing was for decoration and wouldn't fathom doing work on it at the risk of it being unprofessional, but that was pre-Aden. The post-Aden me says fuck it. Kicking off my heels I tuck my feet up under me and crack open the folder.

It's been months since we buried my sister and though I don't think anything will ever feel "normal" again, my life is back on track. They say that staying busy helps with mourning. I can't say I agree, but it has to be better than sitting at home staring at the wall.

Dana pops her head in through the door. "The property manager from Paseo called and wanted to know if you're ready to put down a security deposit?"

I worry my lip. I've been living with my parents and as much as I know it'll hurt them for me to leave, I think it's time we all move on.

Lord knows I'm ready for my own space. "Sure, go ahead and give it to them."

Dana smiles sadly but nods. "Will do. Oh, and Mark is on his way up."

"Okay." I go back to my file and force the thoughts of Aden from my mind as everything, even the idea of renting a new apartment, makes me think of him.

His name alone makes me miss him with a fierceness I didn't think I was capable of. I'd hoped that over time his memory would fade into wistful thoughts rather than intensify, but no such luck. I only hope he's doing well, that he's managed to beat back what tortures him rather than end up alone and angry.

He deserves so much more.

My eyes drift to the photo on my coffee table. Celia and me at a holiday get-together a few years before she died. Her nose is pierced and she's wearing a headband around her forehead like she's straight out of Haight-Ashbury while I'm flashing a closed-lipped smile looking suffocated in my turtleneck. Her hair is falling all around her face and mine is pulled back in an extreme bun. If it weren't for our totally opposite styles no one would ever know the difference between us.

I've often wondered if she and Aden would've made the perfect couple. If she never would've gotten sick and come home would they have met and ended up together, married, babies. God, how could I sit by and watch without having a crush on my own brother-in-law.

I couldn't. I'd have loved him.

I love him.

"Knock knock?" Mark's voice calls my eyes to him as he walks through the door and drops down on the chair opposite me.

"Hey." I close the folder in my hands, genuinely happy to see him.

After Celia died, he's been a great friend. I know he's hoping for more but I can't give my heart to anyone as long as it's with Aden.

He tilts his head. "How're you doing?"

"Good." I frown. "Why?"

A shy smile pulls his lips. "Just checking in on you, ya know, with the date and all."

"Yeah…" It's the eighteenth. "I can't believe she's been gone for two months."

"How're your parents?"

I shrug one shoulder. "They're a little better every day."

"Good." He scoots to the end of his seat and sets his eyes on me and I see nothing but sympathy there. "If you ever need anything, I'm here for you, Sawyer."

I reach forward and grab his hand, squeezing it in mine. "I know you are and I appreciate that, but I'm okay."

His gaze moves from my hair to my chin, then back to my eyes. "You're different."

"Am I?" I lean back to put some distance between us. As much as I do appreciate Mark's attentiveness, I don't want to lead him on.

"Since you came back from your break you're more…" He shrugs and blows out a long breath. "I don't know."

"Well…" I smile at him. "Thank you. I'll take that as a compliment."

His expression grows serious, and as handsome as he is he doesn't light me on fire the way a certain someone does.

"Do." His cheeks flush a little and he stands to leave, but turns before passing through the doorway. "Listen, do you want to grab a bite after work?"

"Oh, um—"

"As friends. I swear, no funny business."

Friends.

It seems I finally have some, thanks to Celia.

My lips pull into a grin. "I've been dying for sushi."

"Sushi?" He looks confused but nods. "Okay, I'll be back to get you around six?"

My eyes land on the photo of me and Cece. "Actually, I wanted to swing by the graveyard first, drop off some flowers."

"I can go with you." There's a hopefulness in his expression.

"That's sweet, but...I need to do this alone. Why don't you go grab us a table at Stingray and I'll be there around six-thirty?"

"Sure." He grins and it really does seem sincere, then he passes through the door to leave me alone with my thoughts.

I'm going to have to move on eventually.

The problem is...I don't know if I can.

ADEN

CELIA MARIE FORRESTER
BELOVED DAUGHTER AND SISTER.
MAY YOUR ADVENTURES CONTINUE ON INTO
ETERNITY.

I stare at the tombstone waiting for a clarity that never comes.

She's gone.

According to the date etched into the stone she died two weeks after she left.

That must've been why she took off with no contact. She knew she had only a limited amount of time and I was her final hurrah. But she seemed so healthy, and staring at the proof with my own two eyes doesn't make it any easier to accept.

The wind kicks up, but even though it feels like a blowtorch of hundred-degree air it cools my sweat-sticky skin.

It's hard to trace my steps back to what brought me here. I was staring between empty bottles of booze and a full one in my hand and it hit me. Drinking myself to death wasn't going to solve a single fucking thing. It wouldn't bring Celia back to my boat, wouldn't put her back in my arms, wouldn't bring her lips back to mine when all I've ever dreamed of was to kiss her one last time.

Or even more, just to tell her I love her.

I loved her.

I gave in and I tried to call, even texted, but everything was a dead end. I pulled out her old rental agreement and dialed the number on there, but it had been disconnected.

Desperate to hunt her down, I logged on to the Internet and Googled her name and that's when I saw the obituary.

Celia is dead.

I lost my chance to tell her how much she means to me.

I had to come here, to prove to myself she was really gone, and to admit out loud, even if to only her tombstone, that I loved her.

I crouch down and place a bouquet of violets at the base of her tombstone, my mind reeling with all I should've said.

I've attended burials for more people than I can count and always felt cheated. Life taken too soon has become an ongoing theme, but the one woman I loved, the one woman I could've spent the rest of my life with is gone and I never got to say goodbye.

"Aw, freckles…" I bite back the pain that claws at my throat at the thought of her beautiful skin six feet below me in a dark coffin. With a heavy heart I drop back to my ass and stare at the fresh grass. "I should've told you before, but I'm a coward. I love you. I know, it sounds crazy, but I do. I wish I'd known how sick you were, I would've been able to tell you…" I drop my head forward feeling the rush of emotion that I'm so used to being able to drown out with liquor. I haven't touched a drop in weeks, forcing myself to feel for the first time in a long time. "I should've been there for you."

I sit in the quiet cemetery hearing nothing but the wind through the trees and the cars passing by on the nearby street. It's in that stillness that I sense movement at my back.

Paranoia pricks at my nerves and I jerk my head around to see—I go light-headed as the blood drains from my face.

"Celia?" I hop to my feet so fast she squeaks in surprise. My mouth opens and closes, but no words come out because—I'll be damned—but Celia, the woman I've fallen in love with, the woman whose grave I'm currently standing on, is staring at me with eyes so wide I'd swear she's just as shocked to see me as I am to see her, which is saying something since she's supposed to be dead!

"You're here." Two words spoken so softly as if they were whispered into the breeze.

"I don't…" My eyes skate between her and the gravestone. "What is this?"

Her eyes dart to the bouquet of flowers and I'd swear the corner of her mouth tilts up a little. "Violets."

I swallow and take a step closer, half thinking she'll disappear into thin air. "They were her favorite."

She licks her lips, those perfect thick lips, and I rub the center of my chest as something works fiercely behind my ribs.

With our eyes locked she steps closer and holds out her hand. "You must be Aden."

"Yes. And…" I blink and fight the faintness in my head. "You're Celia."

"No." Her smile falls. "I'm her sister, Sawyer."

"Sawyer." Of course. Her sister, but they're identical. I had no idea Celia's sister was her twin. "You…wow."

I shove my hands in my pockets to keep from reaching out to her and study the gorgeous woman before me. Dress slacks that hug every curve of her legs, white button-up shirt ironed to perfection, her clothes a complete contradiction to her hair that falls around her face and dances in the wind.

"You look just like her."

"We were identical twins."

I look down at the headstone hoping to sever the connection I feel to the stranger in front of me. "She never told me she had a twin."

"I know."

My gaze darts to hers only to find her eyes are firmly fixed on the tombstone. "How do you know that?"

She squares her shoulders and looks up at me with all the assurance of a woman who won't be intimidated. "Because *I* never told you, Aden."

"I'm sorry?" It's as if her words knocked the wind from my lungs. "When would you—"

"I lied to you." She takes a step closer and I'm too frozen to back away, because what she's saying can't possibly be true. "My name is Sawyer Forrester. I came to San Diego to pack up my twin sister Celia's house and..." She pauses. "I pretended to be her."

I take a step back, my stomach curling with revulsion. Could it be that she lied to me this entire time making me believe she's someone she's not? Who does that? "You're...Celia?"

She nods. "I'm Celia to you. But no, I'm Sawyer."

She's Celia, *my* Celia. And she's a fucking liar. "How...why would you do that?"

Her face grows serious. "Because she asked me to, and when you love someone and they have a dying wish you do whatever it takes to make it come true even if it breaks your own heart in the process."

I stare up at the sky and try to make sense of what I'm hearing. "I don't believe you. The woman I knew would never do something like that, the woman I loved was loyal and—"

"Loved?"

For a moment I wish I could draw back the words, but then realize that yeah, this is what I wanted, to tell Celia I love her so I nod. "Yes. I loved her. But *you* are not her."

She advances. "Aden, it's me—"

"Prove it."

Her big green eyes fix on mine. "You drink too much."

"It doesn't take a genius to figure that—"

"You have nightmares."

I freeze.

She takes a step closer. "You eat raw fish straight off the line. You named a sea lion Morpheus." Another step closer. "You don't like crowds," she whispers.

I open my mouth to defend myself, but she cuts me off.

"You blame yourself for the deaths of your men who died so you could live. You try to hide the fact that you're hurting."

She closes the last foot between us and it hits me. Her scent. The sweet smell of her hair mixed with the natural scent of her skin that I've dreamt about since the last time I held her. "Cece…"

"Sawyer." Her eyes brim with tears.

I cup her jaw and watch a single tear trace down her cheek. "It's you."

"Yes."

"You're alive?"

"I am."

Before I can barely think it, my lips find hers and her hands are wrapped around my neck and slipping into my hair. I nip at her mouth and when she opens to me I slide my tongue against hers. Her sweet flavor combined with her body pressed against mine is all the confirmation I need.

This is her.

The woman I fell in love with.

God, but having her back in my arms, it's like she never left. Everything about her feels like coming home.

"Why didn't you tell me?" Our foreheads pressed together, we breathe each other in.

"At first I didn't think it was a big deal, but then you told me about your past and after that..." She closes her eyes. "I knew telling you would hurt you, and I couldn't bring myself to do that."

"So you left thinking I'd forget you and move on."

"Yes. Then I'd always be the girl you had fun with one summer."

I tuck a lock of her shining hair behind her ear. "Only one problem with that, freckles."

She blinks up at me.

"I could never forget you."

Her lips quiver with emotion so I kiss her until I feel her fall limp into my arms.

Looking back, I should've known, if I'd paid more attention to the differences between how she acted and those photos of her...and the photo of her and Cal. I think on some level I knew something didn't add up but didn't want to accept it.

"Did Cal know?"

"Immediately." She shrugs and her eyes move to stare at nothing over my shoulder. "When it comes to Celia, I'm a lousy substitute."

I step back and stare down at the grave of the woman I thought I loved. "I wish I'd gotten the chance to know her."

"In a way..." She peers up at me. "You did."

"If you were pretending to be Celia, then..." I want to hold her to me, to force her to be the woman I came to know, but if I want a real chance with *Sawyer* I'm going to have to fall in love with someone I know very little about. "Who are you?"

"Sawyer Elizabeth Forrester." Her spine stiffens as if she's waiting for my rejection.

"Tell me more."

"I'm afraid of just about everything including the ocean. I killed my grandmother by giving her the flu and since then a lot of things have gone bad for me." Her eyes fill with tears. "But in the last few months I've experienced the best possible feeling in the world coupled by the absolute worst. I pretended to be my twin sister Celia so that she could die with the knowledge that in the eyes of her friends she lived on, but in doing so I fell in love with a man who brought out a side of me I didn't know existed. He helped me face what scares me, brought me to the edge of my comfort zone, and taught me that real living only happens when I walk through my fears. But he has a bad history of being lied to and there was no way I could break him with the truth so I gave him up, signing myself up for a lifetime of regret, and I'd do it again if I had to because in those two weeks I'd never felt more alive."

My thoughts scramble to understand what she's saying. A jolt of hope swells within me and I hold still in expectation.

"You changed me, Aden. I see it now, the whole point of all this. It was Celia's last gift to me. And because of you she was able to deliver it in a way that has forever altered who I am."

I'm mesmerized by what she's telling me. That she could see me as a person who could make her better when all this time I've been convinced it was only her who was helping me. How is it possible for her to view me as some kind of hero after everything I've put her through? And God, but up until five minutes ago she was dead and now she's standing before me confessing her heart and making me believe that there's a future for us.

"I can bait a hook. Swim in the ocean at night. Make out with a stranger."

I hold back a growl.

"But more than that, I'm not afraid to fall in love. I'm not afraid of getting hurt because you and Celia have taught me that two weeks of love are worth a lifetime of pain."

"No."

She jerks in my hold. "No?"

I sift my fingers through her hair and love how her breath hitches when I bring her lips close. "No. Not a lifetime of pain. Because I'm a man who has felt what it is to be loved by a beautifully loyal woman, one who would sacrifice her own happiness to grant a wish to her dying sister. I'm a man who knows what it's like to be selfish and lose the only person who brought peace into my life. One thing I am not, Sawyer Forrester…"

She whimpers at the calling of her name.

"Is a stupid man. I thought the woman I loved was dead, but she's here, standing before me, in my hands, warm and breathing, and there is no way in hell I'm letting her walk away again. Understand?"

"So…you're saying—"

"I'm saying…I love you. I'm saying I don't want to wake up another morning without you at my side. I'm saying I'm willing to give up whatever it is I need to give up in order to be with you."

"But Celia—"

"Is just a name. You're the woman I fell in love with, the one I've been thinking about every second of every day since the last time I fell asleep in your arms."

"You want me? Even now, after I lied to you?"

"More than I could ever say." I press a kiss to her lips.

"But…when you get to know me, the real me, not the one pretending to be someone else, you might not like what you see."

"You willing to swim with me at night? Go snorkeling with me out at some remote island? More importantly, you done making out with strangers?"

"Yes, yes, and..." She chews her lip and I'm about to give her a punishing kiss for her delay. "Absolutely."

"What do you say, Sawyer?"

She reaches into her pocket and pulls out a silver coin. I release her and she steps back. As if in slow motion, she flips the quarter, but as it's spinning through the air, her eyes come to mine and she rushes into my arms.

We kiss with all the passion of two people who lost each other forever only to find each other again. After long minutes pass and we're tugging at each other's clothes I pull away and whisper, "You didn't wait for it to land."

"That's because when I flipped it I already knew what my answer would be."

"Freckles..." My hands caress her delicate cheeks. "Sawyer."

Her eyelids close as she seems to bathe in the sound of her name. "You have no idea how long I've wanted to hear you call me that."

"I'll say it every day for the rest of our lives if you'll have me."

She blinks up at me. "Really?"

"Nothing will take you away from me again."

"Actually..." She checks her watch and those thick lips quirk so adorably I fall deeper in love instantly. "Right now, I do have to go."

I kiss her neck, soaking in her touch and scent that I've missed so much. "Where?"

"I'm having dinner with a friend." Her breathing speeds up with every brush of my lips.

"Yeah? And who is this friend?"

"His name is Mark."

My lips freeze on her neck and I pull back. "Mark."

"Yeah."

"A man?"

Her hands caress my cheeks and damn but her touch moves me

on a soul-deep level. I'd do anything she asked, grant her whatever she wanted. "He's a man, yes."

"Any chance you'd be willing to cancel with *Mark*?"

"No." She kisses me. "But...if you haven't eaten, how'd you feel about going out for sushi?"

I tug her to my side. "Didn't know you liked sushi."

We stroll to the parking lot. "A gorgeous guy introduced me to it awhile back."

"Oh yeah?" I stop and turn her to me. "And who is this guy?"

Her expression grows serious. "He was in love with my sister, but I convinced him I'm a good second."

Now it's me who gets serious. "You will never be second to me, Sawyer." The name feels as natural as if I've said it a million times, moaned it, whispered it. "You're my freckles. My love, and now...my life."

TWENTY-EIGHT

SAWYER

"Well…that was only mildly awkward." I fish my keys from my purse just as Aden's arm drapes my shoulders.

"I don't know what you're talking about. I thought it was great."

I stop walking and stare up at his handsome face as he tries to hold back his smile. God, I still can't believe he's here. "Aden."

He grins. "I'm serious."

"You told Mark you were Special Forces and then asked him how fast he could run!"

He pulls me close and guides me to the parking lot. "He looked like a sprinter. I was just making conversation."

"You implied you were carrying a gun."

"No, I asked him if he was aware that in the state of Arizona it's legal to conceal carry without a permit."

"Then told him about your gun."

He shrugs. "Yeah. But that was only after he told me you two lived together. I remember what you told me about the ex-boyfriend so—"

I cringe. "I never loved him."

"I know." He looks down at me and winks in a way that curls my toes.

I can't be mad at Aden. He was a perfect gentleman tonight, even picked up the tab when it came, but I couldn't help but notice how all his attempts at conversation made Mark's face drain of color.

I stop at my car, uneasy about what happens next. About where we go from here. He seems to read my uncertainty, and if I'm not mistaken I'd say he's feeling it too.

Shoving his hands in his pockets he leans against my car and for the millionth time in the last couple hours it hits me that he's here. Aden is here. In my life. And I no longer have to pretend to be some-one I'm not. Insecurity rushes to the surface.

"I'm boring."

His eyes jerk to mine. "No. You're not."

"I drive a Volvo."

He slides his gaze from me to my car and then back. "It's a safe car."

"Mark was safe."

He shakes his head and drops his chin to his chest. "And I'm not."

"No, Aden, that's not what I meant, I just…" I'm messing this up. "I'm in unfamiliar territory. I don't know where we go from here. I live in Phoenix, I have a job, I just paid a down payment and signed a lease on an apartment, I mean, nothing about us makes sense."

He tilts his head to meet my eyes.

"Nothing about us makes sense except for what I feel when I'm with you."

A chuckle rumbles from his chest and he pulls me to him, opening his legs to drag me in close. I throw my arms around his neck and he nuzzles my ear.

"I told you I'm not walking away from us, and I meant it."

"But how? How will we make this work when we live so far apart?" I pull back and stare into his eyes, searching for the answer. "Where do we go from here?"

"The first thing we're going to do is head back to my hotel so that I can make love to you until you pass out in my arms."

A full-body shiver takes over and that sexy, lazy grin pulls at his lips.

"I'm heading back to San Diego tomorrow, have a few meetings with investors and then—"

"Investors? For what?"

"I'm starting a commercial fishing company, got a couple boats lined up, some men who want in. Seems you weren't the only person changed by Celia's gift."

"That's wonderful!" I throw my arms around him and he follows suit by wrapping his tightly around my waist. "I'm so proud of you."

"After I sobered up and tossed all the booze, seems I started thinking more clearly, want my life to stand for something more than being a drunk. If I throw my life away it'd be like spitting in the face of everyone who died so I could live."

Tears spring to my eyes at his bold honesty. He's never been so candid about what happened. I swallow my emotions, refusing to allow sadness to rob me of the joy of this moment.

"So, what's your plan?"

He lifts an eyebrow but doesn't loosen his tight grip. "Ahh, so this must be a Sawyer thing, huh?"

Self-conscious, I struggle for a way to backpedal, to push Sawyer away and bring out the fun-loving girl he fell in love with. "No, no, I uh…I—"

His lips press mine in a closemouthed kiss so tender it seems even more erotic than the hungrier kisses we've shared. "I love you, Sawyer."

Those four words leave me breathless.

"And I could use someone to help me with a plan. Someone organized, good with numbers, someone to help me run the business side so I can run the boats."

"Are you offering me a job?"

He sifts his hand through my hair, cupping my nape. "I'm offering you more than a job, freckles. I'm offering you my life."

"But—"

"We'll figure it out."

"I don't—"

"One day at a time."

I slump into his body and release all the worries and what-ifs, giving into Aden's confidence.

"I'm gonna take that as a yes."

I nod, a freakish giggle bubbling up from my chest. "Sounds like a plan."

ADEN

Walking hand in hand with Sawyer through the hotel lobby and to the elevator it feels like no time has passed between us. Those months of living in a drunken fog, and then thinking she was dead have dissolved to nothing more than what seems like a pebble in our path, something easy to step over and leave behind.

"This is a nice hotel." She looks up at me, those green eyes and big lips that I thought I'd never see again, enticing me to engage. "My parents' house is just a couple miles from here."

I know. I found a listing for Tom and Darlene Forrester after reading their names in the obituary, which is why I chose this hotel. I'd planned on dropping by to give them the box I'd found in her cottage, and to introduce myself and see if I could get some information about Celia's last few weeks.

I was desperate to know if she thought of me.

If she cared for me as deeply as I had her.

"That reminds me." I guide her into the elevator, bummed when two people follow us in because that means I can't take advantage of the privacy. "I have something for you up in my room."

She turns to me with wide eyes and a smile.

I grin back. "Sawyer...so you're the little perv."

"Hey, you said it!"

The women in the elevator with us make a weak attempt to hide their laughter.

I cross my arms at my chest and watch Sawyer squirm with the discomfort, her cheeks flushed. Fuck, is it possible Sawyer is even more beautiful than she was as Celia? "It's not *that*." I shrug. "But after I show you what it is, I'll wanna give you that too."

The girls explode with snorting laughter and Sawyer covers her flaming red cheeks.

The door opens on the third floor and I grab my girl's hand. "Good night, ladies."

They reply in unison and Sawyer shakes her head. "You're so bad."

"You started it." I get to my door and slide in the card key, opening the door and ushering her in. "I really do have something for you."

I click on the table lamp and she sits on the couch while I go into the bedroom and pull the box from my duffel bag. When I head back in she studies the box with skeptical eyes. I place it on the table in front of her, then sit close.

"What is it?"

"It was Celia's."

She snaps her eyes to mine.

"I found it under a floorboard in the cottage."

Reaching over, she slides the box into her lap.

"It's how I knew that she was sick."

She pulls the lid off and her fingers shake as she fishes through the shoebox.

I watch intently as each item brings forth a different emotion on her face. Some things make her smile, others make her frown, and when she flips through the countless letters and cards she gets a lost look in her eyes that feels so fucking familiar, the look of loss. Of being robbed.

Minutes pass in silence as she goes through her sister's prized possessions, pulling them out and setting them to the side, until she gets to the letter. The one I'd read countless times.

She sinks into the couch and I watch as her eyes devour every line. When she finishes, she presses it to her chest.

She peers up at me. "Thank you."

"Don't thank me. I didn't do anything but drop off something you left behind."

"This is so much more." She folds up the letter and puts it back in the box. "I thought she'd forgotten us, ya know? Packing up her place there was nothing about us lying around. No photos, no keepsakes. I assumed she'd rather forget her past, that we weren't really worth holding on to."

I motion to the box. "Seems to me…she kept you all safe, in a place where her memories of your love would never be lost or tainted by her life."

She places the lid back on the box and turns fully to me. "You're a wonderful man, Aden Colt."

I tug her hips and bring her to straddle me on the couch, then look up at her. "I'm not, but because of you…I'm getting there."

She leans forward and kisses me, her tongue sliding against mine in a sultry rhythm. The hunger left neglected since she took off ignites with a furious demand. Her hips grind against mine, the heat between her legs teases me until I'm aching to strip her bare.

To feel her skin against mine, her pulse pounding behind her chest, all evidence that she's alive. Pushing off the couch to my knees, I place her ass on the coffee table.

The rise and fall of her chest, swollen lips parted to accommodate her rapid breathing, it all works to further arouse both my body and mind.

"Thought I'd never have you again." I unbutton her shirt, brushing my knuckles against the swell of her breasts encased in white lace. "But here you are." I slide my hand down the softness of her belly to pop the button on her pants. "I'm going to be the best kind of man for you, Sawyer."

She sighs at the sound of her name.

Dipping my fingers into her panties, she tilts her hips to give me better access. "Whatever it takes."

She lifts her hips and I help her out of her clothes, then she slides her shirt off so that she's in nothing but her bra, her legs open wide with me on my knees between them. There's something so dirty about her position, so vulnerable and exposed and trusting.

Painfully hard, I reach down and free myself from the confines of my jeans. She watches and scoots to the edge of the table, her eyes firmly fixed on mine. "Have you been with anyone since me?"

I wince, but not for the reason she'd think. My weakness is written all over my face. "I couldn't think of another woman but you, let alone touch one."

She slides onto my lap and I hiss as her bareness presses against mine. "I'm on the pill." She rocks her hips against me. "And I want to feel you, Aden."

With a groan I bury my nose into her neck, breathing her in.

She pushes up and slowly takes me into her body. My fingers bite into the flesh of her ass and she fucking purrs into my ear.

"Sawyer, baby…" I'm hypnotized by the way she rolls her hips in waves. "I'm fucking wrecked without you."

Bringing my lips to hers she whispers, "I'm sorry I lied to you."

For a moment I wonder if I should've been more upset about her pretending to be someone she's not, but the way her eyes flicker with apology, and having felt the heartbreak of losing her once, I cup her cheeks. "Don't."

"I'm scared, Aden." She melts around me, leaning on me for strength, and fuck, but it feels so good to be needed.

"It'll be okay, I promise." I kiss along her jaw to her ear, and knowing instinctually I can squash her concerns in a few simple words, I whisper them against her skin.

"It's always been you, freckles. Always."

EPILOGUE

Seven years later...

SAWYER

It's funny how a place can bring back a feeling.

How the whip of wind through my hair and the smell of diesel fuel and dead fish can bring me instant joy. There's a calmness that comes with the splash of a boat's wake through the bay. The seagulls squawking for a scavenged meal combined with the low murmur of fishermen as they commune before or after a day at sea make for a peaceful symphony.

It's why we chose this house, just a half mile from the marina right on the bay. From the front yard I watch Aden's fleet of fishing boats leave before dawn and return at sunset.

Calvin Jenkins Commercial Fishing.

It was a name he settled on immediately after Cal sold the Sunset Cliffs property and invested in Aden's idea.

All Aden needed was a job and someone to believe in him.

The first he had.

The second he had in two, but that number was growing rapidly.

"Listen, Pop! If yur goin' to be a deckhand on my boat I got two rules."

My dad salutes the pint-sized boat captain slash drill sergeant. "Ready for my orders, Captain!"

"Deckhands bait hook and drink beer. You don't fish!"

I mouth an apology to my dad. "C.J., your grandpa can fish if he wants."

Aden flashes me a proud smile and digs into the ice chest, pulling out three bottles of root beer before crossing to his daughter. "Nope, she's right." He hands her two bottles. "Those are the rules." His eyes slide to me. "They were good enough for you." He winks and butterflies tumble through my belly and not for the first time I wonder if his effect on me will ever die down.

"Yes, sir!" My dad salutes C.J. again.

She hands him the cold root beer. "It's ma'am, Pop! I'm a girl!"

He laughs and pulls her to him for a big hug. "I know you are, pumpkin. But you're a strong, tough little girl."

"Celia Jane, are you ordering around your pop?" My mom sidles up next to Aden and he pulls her in for a side hug.

"Granny!" C.J. rushes to my mom in a flurry of deep auburn hair. I don't know how she did it but she managed to get the darkness of Aden's hair with the red from mine.

Her skin isn't pale either, she tans like a sailor and hero worships her dad, swearing she'll become the best fishing captain when she grows up.

"We better get going if we're gonna make it out there before sunset." Aden crosses to me and holds out his hand to pull me up from my seat and to his chest. He runs his nose along my jaw, breathing in deep. "Have I told you lately that you're the hottest mom in Southern California?"

I cup his strong jaw and purse my lips. "Only Southern California?"

"I was going to say the world but thought it sounded too cliché."

I smile. "How was your appointment?"

Since I moved to San Diego shortly after I found Aden at my sister's grave, he's been attending a group for soldiers with PTSD. What started out as therapy turned into something so much greater as now he takes those who're willing and teaches them how to fish. The majority of his staff of fishermen are ex-military who suffer from the long-term effects of war. He says helping others makes him feel less guilty for the ones who paid the ultimate price for his life.

"It was good, just got a new guy who's starting next week after your folks leave."

I push up on my toes and kiss his soft lips. "Have I told you lately that I think you're the most wonderful human being I've ever met?"

His face grows serious. "Yeah. You tell me all the time."

"Well…" I push his shaggy hair behind his ear. "I mean it."

"I know you do." He kisses me again, this time deeper than before.

"Break it up, guys." C.J. wiggles between us, pushing us apart. "We gotta get to sea."

"Later," Aden whispers in my ear before scooping our daughter up and onto his shoulders and then heads for the dock.

ADEN

"Which one's gonna be mine, Daddy?"

With C.J.'s tiny legs draped over my shoulders and her hands gripping tight to my hair, all is right in the world. The sound of my wife's voice, light and carefree as she laughs with her parents, sends a warmth through my body that is indescribable.

It's better than any high.

"You're five, baby. Let's revisit this conversation in twenty years, 'kay?"

"But…you said I could be a fishing captain too and we need to have a plan!"

A plan. It's safe to say that little Celia Jane ended up the perfect combination of me and her gorgeous mother.

"I tell you what." I punch the code into the keypad to buzz us into the marina that now holds eight boats that I own. Six strictly for fishing, and two for personal use. We pass by Jenks's old boat, the *Amelia Lynn*, now updated with new hardware, sails, and paint and I look up, hoping he can see me now, praying he knows how much I cared for him and how his memory was a huge influence when it came time for me to get my shit together. "I'll get you a little sailboat and we'll start there. Deal?"

"Deal!"

"Colt, you got a second?" Ryan, an ex-marine I hired three years ago, jogs to me with a clipboard in his hand.

"Sure, man."

"Ryan! I'm gonna have a sailboat and sail around Messico like Jenks did!"

He looks up at her, making sure to overexaggerate his surprise. "Oh yeah? You leaving now?"

She giggles. "No, maybe tomorrow."

I take the clipboard from him, making sure to keep one hand wrapped tightly around the leg of the other half of my life.

"Just need you to give those numbers a skim and sign the bottom."

"I can do it." Sawyer scoots up next to me and I hand her the clipboard. "He's got his hands full."

I lean down and kiss my wife on her jaw, some of her long silky hair blowing into my face. "Thank you, freckles."

With a chin lift to Ryan I climb aboard my boat, the *Second Chance*.

When the company had its highest grossing year I decided it was time for an upgrade and bought the latest and greatest in yachts. It's not huge, only two bedrooms, but it has all the bells and whistles, including a full-functioning gourmet kitchen and full-sized bathroom with tub.

It's become our home away from home and Sawyer doesn't know I've arranged for her parents to take C.J. back to the house later so I can have my wife to myself tonight.

I gently take my daughter from my shoulders, bringing her around to blow a raspberry on her stomach before placing her on her feet. "Go get your life vest on."

"Daddy!"

"Don't argue with your dad, honey," Darlene says as she places a few items into the fridge. "Go get it on."

"Fine." She stomps off and I watch her until I'm sure she's safe in her life jacket.

"She is so much like her, ya know." Darlene shakes her head with a wistful look in her eye.

"So, my wife was this much of a pill when she was young."

Her expression softens. "Not Sawyer. Celia."

I look on as Sawyer scoops our daughter into her arms and holds her on her hip while pointing at something off on the horizon. "I love them so much. I can't imagine what it would be like to lose either of them." I turn to her, seeing the loss of her daughter is still so fresh in her tearing eyes. "I can't imagine what you must've gone through."

She smiles sadly. "You'll never have to."

I pull her in for a quick hug. "Now...how 'bout a root beer. We are subject to Captain C.J. Colt's orders."

"I'd love one—" Music comes from her pocket followed by the words of Akon singing, "I Just Had Sex." "What in the....?" She scrambles for her cell, but it's stuck in the fabric of her sweatshirt as the song goes on. "What is he saying about his penis?!" Her face is bright red as she finally gets the device released and pushes something to make it stop. "My gosh." She shoots daggers at my wife, who is laughing hysterically on the deck outside. "Sawyer Colt, you're gonna get it!" She presses the phone to her ear. "Kathy, I'm sorry, are you there, honey?"

I burst out laughing when I realize who's on the other line, earning a scowl from Darlene.

"Your son and daughter-in-law are driving me batty."

I lean in to the phone. "Hi, Mom!"

Darlene nods. "Your mom says hi and to stop tormenting me."

"Yes, ma'am." I pull out root beers and pop the tops, handing one to my mother-in-law.

"Of course, there's plenty of room for you and Paul and the kids. Is Stephanie coming? Great! We're so excited you could make it down while we're here."

I sip from my soda as Sawyer heads inside, looking like Morpheus does after he raids the bait tank when I'm not looking. She presses into my side.

"That was some funny shit, freckles." I kiss the side of her head.

She smiles up at me. "When will she learn to stop leaving her cell-phone unattended."

I motion to the woman responsible for the life of my gorgeous wife. "She's talking to my mom about tomorrow. The whole crew is coming out, my sister, the kids, I was thinking maybe we should take everyone to the zoo?"

Pulling the root beer from my hand, she tosses back a gulp. "I think that's a great idea."

I scan my surroundings, C.J. on the deck with Sawyer's dad, my mother-in-law laughing with my mom, and the most amazing woman on earth in my arms, and I can't imagine life being any sweeter.

* * *

Long after sunset when all the boats are rocking softly in their docks, I'm sitting on a lounge chair with my fucking sexy as hell wife between my legs. It has to be close to midnight, and after a long and very heated sex-fest we had to come outside to cool off.

Silently we sit and stare at the stars with nothing to interrupt or deter from each other. This is my happy place. The one place where the screams don't touch and the memories die.

It's not that I never have those moments. Since having C.J. my life has become more valuable to me, and the lives of my girls are my top priority. Because of that the paranoia still hits in crowded places, and we make sure to spend the Fourth anchored out at sea to keep away from the fireworks. But the nightmares are few and far between, my sobriety and therapy have helped me to cope with the trauma that I continue to learn how to live with.

Sawyer and C.J. make it bearable.

"Aden, if Celia hadn't been sick, if it was her who came back to the cottages, do you think you would've fallen in love with her?"

"Where's this coming from, freckles?"

Almost seven years of marriage and she's never once asked me this, though I've wondered the same thing and come to my own conclusions that I've yet to share with her.

She burrows in deeper to my chest, her silky robe the only barrier between me and her naked body. "She was so much fun, and, I don't know, I guess I wonder if you two would've been a better match."

"Hold up." With a little maneuvering, I manage to sit her upright so we're facing each other. "You and I are the perfect match."

She tucks a long strand of her hair behind her ear and dips her chin. "I know, but—"

"You balance me like no one ever could. You are beautiful, don't get me wrong, but what I fell in love with had so much more to do with who you are than who you look like." I grab her hand and kiss the underside of her wrist. "You're the most patient woman I've ever met. You're smart, so fucking forgiving. God, Sawyer, don't you see? You're every single thing I'm not, which is why I find you so fascinating. Why I *need* you. Just because Celia was more like me doesn't mean I would've fallen for her. Fuck, I can barely stand myself most days."

She blinks up at me with shining eyes and a soft smile.

"I would've thought Celia was very pretty, but I don't think we would've gotten along well."

Her body falls back between my legs, but her arms wrap around my waist. "No, I guess you're right."

"I know I'm right." I drop a kiss to the top of her head.

She sighs and a few seconds of silence pass between us. "We're gonna need a bigger boat."

My lips tip up on the ends at her *Jaws* quote. "*What are you, some kind of half-assed astronaut?*" I say in my best Quint voice.

Her shoulders shake with silent giggles. "That was good, but…" Her arms hug me tighter. "I was serious."

My smile falls instantly as my insides dare to hope she's saying what I think she's saying.

"This boat only has two bedrooms."

My pulse rockets through my veins, making me light-headed. "Um…are you?" It seems so unimaginable! We've been trying to get pregnant for the last couple years with no luck.

Pushing up my body she presses a kiss to my lips. "Congratulations, Captain Colt. You impregnated your wife…" She runs her lips up the side of my neck to my ear where she whispers, "With twins."

In the span of a heartbeat my joy doubles and right there in the arms of the woman I love, I pray to thank the men who died protecting me so that I could live and experience just how sweet life can be.

ABOUT THE AUTHOR

New York Times bestselling author JB Salsbury spends her days lost in a world of budding romance and impossible obstacles. Her love of good storytelling led her to earn a degree in Media Communications. Since 2013 she has published seven bestselling novels. Salsbury lives with her husband and two kids in Phoenix, Arizona.

Learn more at:

JBSalsbury.com

Twitter, @JBSalsbury

Facebook.com/JBSalsburyBooks

What do you do when you wake up with no
memory of what you did last night?

Don't miss JB Salsbury's thrilling novel that will
leave you guessing until the very end…

SPLIT

AVAILABLE NOW